# RING AROUND

# THE MOON

*Also by Mary Burnett Smith*

MISS OPHELIA

# RING AROUND THE MOON

---

A NOVEL

*Mary Burnett Smith*

*William Morrow and Company, Inc.*

NEW YORK

Library of Congress Cataloging-in-Publication Data

Smith, Mary Burnett, 1931–
Ring around the moon : a novel / Mary Burnett Smith.—1st ed.
p.  cm.
ISBN 0-688-15987-7 (acid-free paper)
1. Afro-Americans—Pennsylvania—Fiction.  I. Title.
PS3569.M537738R56  1998
813'.54—dc21                                         98-23520
                                                         CIP

Printed in the United States of America

First Edition

1  2  3  4  5  6  7  8  9  10

BOOK DESIGN BY VICTORIA HARTMAN

www.williammorrow.com

*Thanks to Ann Treistman,*
*my editor,*
*for her ever-ready ear*
*and for keeping me on track.*
*And again to Ray Lincoln,*
*my agent,*
*for her judicious insight.*

Words cause more trouble than weapons of war.

—*African proverb*

# RING AROUND
# THE MOON

# ONE

I saw my father today. I was coming from the garden store in Hillsboro where I had picked up a plant for my back porch. Some kind of broad-leafed thing that was too tall for the trunk of my car so it was resting on the floor in the back. I'd reached the top of Highland Avenue when I spotted him on the corner sitting on a bench outside of Orson's Drugs, so drunk he was falling sideways.

My heart sank at the sight of that old black man sitting drunk on a corner in a town where he's lived most of his life. If he had been able to step outside of his body and get a view of himself he would've kicked his own ass just as I wanted to stop my car and jump out and kick it myself.

But I didn't. I was in the wrong lane. I made my turn onto the road that would take me home. I looked into my rearview mirror to see if he'd fallen off the bench, but I couldn't see past the leaves of that stupid plant. I suppose I could've turned a corner and gone around and picked him up and taken him home. After all, he doesn't live too far from me. But no, anger made me drive on and I came home and went to set the plant in the entrance hall, all the time trying to push him out of my mind. But I couldn't, and just thinking of that old man all alone sitting on that bench made me begin to feel sorry for him.

Then I came into my kitchen and saw the mugs on the shelf beside my sink, only two left of the dozen or so that James and I got from Miss Ruby Davis that day so long ago. I lifted one up. It was heavy, all right. Heavy enough to cause a lot of damage to a tender head. And the pity I was beginning to feel for my father disappeared as I stared at that mug and thought about Mama and Lonnie and James and me and the troubles we had that first year we lived in Hillsboro.

☙

MY MOTHER WAS a country girl. She was born in 1908 in Mason County, Virginia, near Potter's Grove, far back from the main roads, back where the houses squatted among the tall pines. She used to laugh and tell us that she was raised so far back in the woods that not even a dirt road ran near her house; the only signs of human activity were the deep-rutted wagon tracks that led up to their barn. The nearest neighbors were at least two miles away in any direction; church was five; town was ten. She was named Arleatha, after the midwife who delivered her.

Arleatha's mother, Callie Winslow, was one of an illegitimate brood of children sired by Thomas Scanlon, a red-headed Irishman who ran the flour mill. Callie's mother, Alberta Winslow, was one of five daughters of a freed slave who owned a farm near the mill. One Saturday he let Alberta accompany her brother to the mill to pick up his flour and Tom Scanlon saw her and was smitten. It was illegal for blacks and whites to marry; Tom hired her as his housekeeper and they lived on a place in the woods and had seven children.

Callie was their middle child. She was a plump, fair-skinned girl who looked more white than colored, with red hair and an infectious laugh. At the age of eighteen she was spirited away from Alberta's side by the winning smile and quiet manner of a young black man, a tenant farmer named Ruther Eldridge. Callie and Ruther had ten children and lived a chaotic domestic life.

Ruther drank.

My mother, Arleatha, was the youngest of those ten children: last to be born, last to leave home. She, too, was a fair-skinned girl who looked more white than colored, with red hair, dimples, and a stubborn streak as wide as the Missouri. "A hard head makes a soft behind" were words she must have heard a hundred times a week. Just after her nineteenth birthday Arleatha followed her oldest sister Louise up North to Hillsboro, Pennsylvania, a small town just outside of Philadelphia. A few weeks after her arrival she met my father, John Beale, at a party. Within two months time she was happily telling Louise that she and John wanted to get married.

To hear Aunt Louise tell it, she and my mother were in her (Louise's) kitchen and she was ironing and Mama was shelling peas and they were discussing this and that when out of the blue Mama brought up the subject of John Beale and how he wanted to marry her and would kill himself if he didn't.

Aunt Louise was so outdone she almost burned a hole in her best silk blouse. "Then let the nigger kill hisself. Mumma let a black fool drive her to the grave; don't let one put you there."

"You don't like him just because he's black," snapped my mother.

Carefully Aunt Louise set the iron on its heel and turned to face her. "Black ain't got nothin to do with it, although John Beale must not like black hisself since he don't run after nothin but yallah women plus stay in the street and gamble up his money or drink it up and piss it out like a black fool. And with the kind of papa you have, you oughta have enough of black fools. Plus he got a temper worse'n that old blueballed bull Papa used to keep in the field behind the house."

Up jumped Mama, into the sink flew the colander and the peas, and with her nose to the ceiling she flounced from the kitchen and she (Louise) hollered after her that she (Arleatha) had a brass ass and a head to match. "You never do listen to anybody tryin to put some sense in you."

YES, MY FATHER DRANK, but he didn't think he had a problem. A few years ago I lured him to my house by pretending to need some advice on pruning a dogwood tree and while we were sitting on my back porch taking a break, I tried to get him to tell me a little of his life story. He was seventy years old at the time and puffing a smelly cigar and sipping a glass of Wild Turkey from a bottle I had placed at his elbow.

*"I was drinkin the day I met your mother. I was nineteen years old. My sister Leona was givin a Christmas party. Louise and Amelia, the sister you was named after, were there. Amelia had told me about Arleatha and how she was my age and how she was comin up around the holiday. At the party I was clownin around and drinking and I asked Amelia where this sister of hers was and she pointed across the room and said that was her in the chair near the steps. And I looked over there and saw this pretty girl sittin in Mama's chair fannin and rockin. She wasn't dressed too good, I noticed. I went over and said hello and she looked up at me like she thought I was a prince. I was still wearin my new coat, this fur coat with a fur collar. I was always in style. Always had a lot of girlfriends (and no messin up, neither). So she was rockin and fannin and eatin my candy that I gave to Leona for Christmas and I said, 'You better watch out eatin that candy or you'll get fat.' Well, she smiled and she had a big dimple and she like, blushed and put the candy down, and I said I was only foolin and she said that was okay, or somethin like that, and we went on like that, talkin and teasin . . . She was a poor girl, your mother. She didn't have many clothes."*

His eyes misted over when he said that. That would have bothered my father, the young dandy, that my mother didn't have many clothes, and it still disturbed him more than fifty years later. Not the fact that he had been drinking, but that my mother had been poorly dressed.

AUNT LEONA was probably even more strongly opposed to this marriage than Aunt Louise. She was five years older than my father and considered herself his guardian; their father had died when he was three years old, their mother when he was sixteen. Aunt Leona was seditty and airish with aspirations more middle class than the people she worked for. She was quick to tell her friends that my mother was too ignorant and countrified to be married to John and that her sister Louise was low class and ignorant. "The first word out of Louise Eldridge's mouth is 'black' and the last word is 'nigger.'" And to John,

"That Arleatha will bring you nothin but trouble. Her *and* Louise both."

But my mother and father were the babies of their families and had been spoiled rotten. They sulked and threw tantrums until Aunt Leona and Aunt Louise relented. They were married a few months later in Aunt Leona's living room while the two sisters stood around scowling and snorting like children being forced to swallow an extra-large dose of castor oil.

A sepia picture of my mother at that time rests on my bookshelf: an oval face, serenely beautiful, with a curving smile and wavy hair piled on her head. I have no pictures of my father at nineteen. He could not have been too different from the dark-skinned young man in his early thirties that I do remember, a man with big white teeth, a ready smile, a hearty laugh.

So my mother and father were married in the springtide of life, and as the years passed my father remained popular with the ladies, a fact I discovered when I was ten years old. By that time he and my mother had been married thirteen years and were the parents of three children: The youngest child, James, was six; the oldest, Lonnie, twelve. I was the middle child, Amelia.

IN THE SUMMER OF 1940 we were living about five miles from Hillsboro in a place called Westville, a tight little group of weatherworn houses and dirt roads that turned to mud when it rained. Westville. Whiskey town. Where weekends were wild—crap games, fistfights, and stabbings. Once in a while a police car came wailing in and the cops jumped out and, blackjacks twirling like batons, cracked a few heads and slung a few bodies into the back of the car; the ruckus would stop, then start again as soon as they took off in a cloud of dust.

By this time my father was a bootlegger as well as a gambler, and Westville was his kind of town. Within a few weeks after he had moved in, everyone for miles around knew there was a good time to be had at his house every Saturday night. His easygoing, hand-on-the-shoulder personality drew the fast crowd like a magnet draws pins. Before those days he'd always been called John. In Westville they began calling him "Blackjack" because of his prowess at that game; "John" now seemed too proper for a man of such talent. Before long they shortened it to "Jack."

At first my mother enjoyed the parties, and she especially liked to dance, even though once in a while a man might hold her too close or expel his whiskey breath in her face. As for my father, he was glad to see her dancing and mixing in. He didn't want his friends to think his light-skinned wife thought she was too good for them. But he was a jealous man, and when he saw how men enjoyed talking to her, he became morose and sullen after the parties, and more than once he slapped her over some imagined flirtation. Then, suddenly, when Blackjack Beale was thirty-four years old, four years after he'd moved to Westville and found the good life, the good life slipped from his hands.

ONE STEAMY SATURDAY night in July my father was having a rent party (a sedate sort of honky-tonk popular at the time as a way of raising quick cash) where folks came to gamble, drink, and eat in congenial company. I was lying on my stomach under the big dining room table that had been pushed against the wall to make room for dancing. A white tablecloth hung almost to the floor and I had hitched up a corner so I could get some air and an occasional view of the room. Just as I began to count the coins in the narrow triangle of light, someone pushed a chair under the table and sat down. Two legs appeared. A woman's. I drew back against the wall.

The woman's feet were bare and I reached out to pinch her leg because I thought she was my mother who was always walking around in her bare feet. I snatched my hand back. These feet had red toenails; my mother never painted hers.

Then a pair of black pointy-toed shoes and black trousers appeared next to the woman's legs and there were whispers and smothered laughs. The woman raised her foot and rubbed it up and down the man's pant leg. Then a hand was on her knee and disappeared behind the white cloth and I heard a muffled shriek. I squeezed my eyes shut and held my breath as if I were under water. Sweat was dripping down my face and just when I thought I could hold my breath no longer I heard the chairs scraping against the floor. I peeked through my fingers. They were gone.

I gasped for air and wiped my face with the hem of my dress. Then I stretched out again and lifted an edge of the tablecloth and looked out. Lonnie and James were sitting on the floor in the hall with their backs against the steps. Men and women were eating, laughing, talking, drinking, playing cards, ribbons of smoke swirling lazily up and drifting along over their heads. And music: throbbing, jumping, bluesy, intermingled with ice clinking in glasses and the soprano voices of laughing ladies.

I looked at their feet. No bare feet. But plenty of black shoes. It seemed that every man in the room was wearing black shoes. Unnoticed, I slipped out from under the table and made my way over to my brothers and sat beside them. We showed each other our money. James had found two quarters and Lonnie a whole fifty-cent piece, but I was satisfied. I'd found ten dimes and seven nickels.

I sat back against the staircase and looked around. I recognized everyone in the room. The same people always came to the parties. Mr. Jim and Miss Julia and Miss Harriet and Mr. Ralph. Could one of them have been at the table? I knew my father would be angry if I told him what happened. Especially after what he'd said that very afternoon.

We were in the kitchen. He was standing at the sink, a stocking cap on his head to press his hair (with Dixie Peach and water) as he washed whiskey glasses; I was drying them. He was wearing a sleeveless undershirt and his skin was smooth and dark and shiny at the shoulders where it was stretched tight like the skin on an eggplant. He looked so tall standing there at the sink, turning to look down at me.

"You're gettin to be a big girl, Amy." He rinsed a shot glass and handed it to me. "Almost as tall as your mother."

"I am as tall as Mama," I said, wondering what was coming next. My father never engaged in idle chatter with his children. A conversation with him would have been more properly labeled a conference.

There was only the clink of the glasses in the water while he rinsed them. Then he cleared his throat, handed one to me and said,

"Now, tonight, Amy..." He stopped as if searching for the right words to say.

I was becoming curious. My father was usually direct, never hesitant about saying anything.

"Well," he said at last, "if any man says anything fresh to you or touches you, you come and tell Daddy. Understand?" His dark eyes bored into mine.

I controlled a nervous urge to giggle, looked quickly away, down at the floor. I nodded. I was puzzled and uneasy. *Man. Fresh. Touch.* I kept staring at the floor.

My father cleared his throat again. "All you have to do is point at the man. He don't have to see you, understand?"

I didn't like this new tone of voice, earnestly touching upon subjects I didn't want to hear about. I nodded again, solemnly, as I dried the same glass again.

"I don't want to scare you. But . . . sometimes men do things when they get a few drinks in them that they wouldn't do otherwise. Do you understand?"

Still looking away from him, I shrugged and nodded.

"Look at people when they're talking to you, Amy. I said, do you understand?" His voice was impatient, almost angry.

I looked at him and nodded, not understanding, but not wanting to upset him further. And now I knew if he'd said that, he'd get real mad if I told him what that man was doing to that lady with his hand under that table at the party. Especially with me watching them, even if I didn't have any business there.

Mama was waving at me from across the room. I smiled and waved back. She was standing by the kitchen door, smiling and talking to Miss Edie Burrell, a lady who lived next door to us and watched us sometimes when Mama was at work. They were similar in looks. Both were light-skinned but Mama was not as tall as Miss Edie, and they were both slim, almost bony. Miss Edie had a soft voice and a laugh that started high and fell like a waterfall. Mama's laugh was louder, stronger. Whatever Miss Edie was saying to her was very funny because she threw back her head and laughed and showed her big dimple.

At that moment the kitchen door swung open and my father appeared. His hair was smoothed back in shining crimps and his eyes were squinted from the smoke of the cigar clamped between his teeth. A striped dish towel was tucked into his belt and he was carrying a plate piled high with food. Just then a lively song came on and he went over to my mother and Miss Edie. He handed the cigar and the plate to Miss Edie, then took Mama's arm and swung her around with his arm around her waist and they started dancing. She smiled up at him and he pressed his cheek against hers and started singing to the music. Suddenly I felt a rush of happiness; I wanted to run over and dance with them, then again as suddenly, I felt so sad that my eyes filled with tears. Daddy swung Mama around in a big whirl, and it was over.

Daddy took the plate of food from Miss Edie and kissed Mama on the cheek and said something in her ear and she started toward us. As Miss Edie handed Daddy his cigar she said something that made him laugh and he slapped her hand. I smiled. It was good to see them laughing and being good friends. Daddy went over to a table and set the plate of food in front of Mr. Linwood Rollins, who was playing cards. Mr. Linwood was one of my father's best friends, and Miss Edie's too.

Mr. Linwood reached over to a pile of bills in the middle of the table and took one and gave it to my father and they joked with each other for a minute and my father went back into the kitchen and Mr. Linwood switched his cards to his left hand and scooped collard greens into his mouth. Collard greens and potato salad and pig feet. Yuck. That's what they had at every party. A dollar a meal with a roll and butter. Drinks were extra. And that crowd drank a lot of whiskey. Lots and lots of whiskey.

My mother was leaning over us. "Time to go to bed." She lifted James who was leaning on Lonnie and cradled him in her arms. "This boy gettin heavier every day." She and Lonnie started up the steps, then stopped to look back and see why I wasn't following her. "Your daddy said it's time for you all to go to bed."

"I got to go to the bathroom," I said. I didn't look at Lonnie. He would cut me with his cat's eyes when Mama told him to go with me.

She did and he pushed past me in disgust. "Girl, you better stop bein afraid of the dark, because I ain't gonna keep on goin to the bathroom with you."

I didn't answer, just followed him through the kitchen, sliding through the crowd. Lonnie pushed the door open, I on his heels. We stepped into the pitch-black night. A bulb over the outhouse shone weakly.

Lonnie stood on the top step and folded his arms. "Go ahead. Ain't nothin gonna get you."

"It's dark!"

"Just go slow. And head for the light!"

I stepped onto the grass, damp and cool beneath my bare feet, and inched forward, guided by the bare bulb hanging over the door. As I drew nearer it seemed I heard voices. I stopped and waited, listening. I started forward again. I was halfway there when I saw a dark figure emerge from the shadows of the outhouse and step up under the light hanging over the entrance. A woman. A man came up behind her. Right on her heels. They were laughing. I held my breath, then dropped to the grass, sure that they could see me as clearly as I could see them. They went inside. I rose and turned to run and bumped into Lonnie.

I couldn't see his face, but I knew that he had seen as well as I who they were. Daddy and Miss Edie. "Ooohhh," I breathed.

Lonnie's hand went over my mouth. "Shhhhh!"

Now why was Daddy going in there with Miss Edie? "Why—" I started.

"I said be quiet!" Lonnie whispered fiercely. He jerked me toward the house and I hit my toe on a rock.

"What's the matter with you?" I was hopping around holding my foot in one hand. "You made me hurt my foot!"

"That's what you get for goin around without your shoes! Just come on back in the house, that's all."

"I gotta pee!"

"Go on over there in the grass then!"

I followed his orders and a few moments later I met him by the steps. "Why did Daddy go in the outhouse with Miss Edie?" I whispered. "There's only one hole in there!"

"Shut up, dummy. And when we get into the house, don't you say nothin to nobody." He grabbed my arm.

I jerked my arm away. "You better stop pullin me and makin me hurt myself. I'm'a tell Mama, too."

Lonnie's lips touched my ear. His breath was hot. "You got a mouth like a bell clapper. If you tell Mama anything about what we saw out here tonight, I'm gonna do more than pull your arm. Now come on back in this house."

After I got in bed I stared into the dark for a long time, thinking and wondering. Why had Lonnie been so mad at me? And why did Daddy and Miss Edie go in the outhouse together? I thought and thought but for the life of me I couldn't think of a logical answer.

SOMEONE WAS CRYING. I tried to wake up, but the heat drew me down into sleep again, and I slept as if drugged, I don't know for how long. Suddenly my eyes flew open. I felt the warm body of James, who had sneaked into my bed and was curled up next to me. I lay on my back staring into the dark, my heart thumping, thumping. I held my breath, listened. Nothing. Just the sound of Lonnie breathing in his bed across from me. I hugged James and closed my eyes.

Then, the sound again. Crying, like a cat mewling. I sat up in the bed. Mama. I could hear a man's voice, low and murmuring, then Mama crying again. I eased out of the bed and went over to Lonnie and reached out and touched him. He didn't stir. Usually he was the one who woke first, the one who pushed me back on the bed if I tried to go with him, the one who would go investigate the sounds. He never told me what happened, or what he saw. Go to sleep, girl. That's what he always said. Just go to sleep, girl.

I stood with my ears turned to the hall.

Nothing, then the voices again.

I felt my way out of the room, down the dark hallway to the top of the stairs. A dim light was coming from the living room where the voices were coming from. The stairway was dark. I eased down them and sat on the bottom one. I held my breath so I could hear the voices over the thumping in my chest.

"... sick of this nigger's shit." Mama's voice, moaning.

"I know, Arleatha, I know." The man's voice, low.

"His drinkin's bad enough, but when he got to have his woman right here in my *face*—"

"Arleatha, you know Jack loves you—" That sounded like Mr. Linwood.

"Love!" Mama choked. "Jack Beale loves hisself, do you hear me? His *self*! Out in the outhouse screwin and makin me the butt of his jokes in front of all his friends—and mine. . . . I never should'a married that no good nigger with all his fancy clothes and empty promises. . . . 'Marry me and I'll take care of you' . . . and every other woman around tooooooo . . ." Then she cried so hard that I began crying with her.

"Arleatha," said Mr. Linwood, "most men do something they're sorry for the rest of their lives . . . I know I have. But that don't mean I don't love my wife and children. Why not give him another chance?"

"I have! I done give him chance after chance! I been married to that man for thirteen years and he been screwin other women for ten and drinkin like a fool for six. I done lost a *baby* because of that man . . . do you hear me? And now you sit here and tell me to give him another chance. Hunh. Jack Beale better start talkin to God. That's who that man needs. God." Then Mama began wailing, loud, like a child being whipped.

She went on a long time.

When she quieted down, Mr. Linwood said, "Arleatha, Jack *needs* you. He needs his children. He needs his *family*. He ain't a *mean* man. He wants to be a good father to his children. He always tells me how he wants to be like the father he never had . . ."

"Drinkin don't help you be a better father." Mama sounded as if she were strangling. "And his drinkin's gettin worse. Look what he done tonight . . . eehhh eeehhhh . . . oh, God."

Silence, then Mr. Linwood, almost inaudible. "The children need their father and you need your husband."

"Not if he's gonna bring his women into my house. Nooooo. Before

God I don't need that." There was a long pause, then Mama again. Calm now. "He just got to stop, that's all."

Mr. Linwood, cautious like a stalking cat. "Like what?"

Mama again. "Drinkin, runnin around. That's what. Get a job. That's the only way I stay this time. The *only* way."

"Maybe he can stop, Arleatha. Tell him what you want. But think about givin him another chance. For your children if nothin else."

Mama didn't speak for a long time. Then she said, as if it hurt her to say it, "All right. I'll give him a chance. For our children. I'll give him another chance. I'm a fool. I'm a fool. But I'll give him time. A year. That's all."

Mr. Linwood said with a hard edge to his voice, "If Jack *don't* shape up he's the damnedest fool I've ever run across." Then his tone was softer. "He's out in the kitchen. Sober. He wants to talk to you. I'll send him in here, all right?"

No answer from Mama. I heard footsteps going away, then after a moment, more footsteps coming into the dining room. They stopped. Then I heard my father's voice.

"Leatha."

No answer.

"Leatha . . . I know I made you promises. I know . . ." His voice was low, shaking. "I swear to God I don't know what makes me do some of the things I do."

"Whiskey." The word was hard, sharp as the point of a tack.

"Tell me what to do, Leatha. Leatha . . . tell me what to do, and I'll do it."

Mama's voice was muffled. "No you won't, no you won't."

"Just tell me what to do, Leatha. Just—"

"I don't know what to tell you to do! I don't know!"

I heard a bump and a clattering sound, like a chair falling over, and I moved backward up a couple of steps. Footsteps were hurrying my way. I turned and jumped up the rest of the steps and flew down the hall and hopped into bed. I could hear my heart pounding. I lay there stiff, listening. Then footsteps, Mama's, going into her bedroom. I heard the bed creak.

Then nothing but the sound of Lonnie and James snoring and the sound of Mama crying softly.

I lay there thinking a long while about Daddy and Mama and whiskey and Miss Edie and wondered if I'd have to stop liking her. I stared into the dark a little longer then slid out of bed onto my knees and prayed. "Please God don't let Mama and Daddy get separated. Please help us be a family. If you keep us together and make us a family I'll never, never do anything bad in my life ever. Please, God. Amen."

# T W O

Sunday was my mother's only full day off and she always started it off with a wonderful breakfast. My brothers and I looked forward to that day; during the week breakfast was a bowl of cold cereal that we ate quickly and quietly in order not to wake my father who was usually hung over and grouchy before ten o'clock in the morning.

I awakened later than usual. As soon as I opened my eyes I remembered what happened the night before, and I lay still and listened for the noises that would signal my mother's presence in the kitchen. Yes, there were the sounds of clinking dishes and frying bacon and the smell of boiling coffee. My stomach gurgled.

I threw water on my face and tiptoed apprehensively down into the kitchen. My mother was at the stove singing softly as she scooped up blobs of dough (made the night before) from a large crock and shaped them into rolls for a pan sitting on the table. She smiled at me as I came in. "Mornin, Missy."

She was in a good mood; the tension left me. Almost shyly I said good morning so I wouldn't disturb the peaceful atmosphere. I squeezed into a chair at the table and rested my chin on my arm, watching her.

" 'What a friend we have in Jesus . . .' " She placed the last roll in the pan and dabbed each one with butter. " 'All our sins . . .' " She put the pan on a shelf near the stove so the rolls could rise, picked up another ready for the oven. " 'And grief to bear.' " She closed the oven door. "James and Lonnie still asleep?"

I nodded.

"This heat done knocked them out." She disappeared into the shed and returned with a pink-veined cow's brain. It was one of the delicacies she had every week. Shad roe or salted mackerel or brains and scrambled eggs. She laid it on a plate next to me as I grimaced. She padded around the kitchen in her flip-flops calmly conducting her Sunday morning ritual, frying bacon and apples, beating eggs for scrambling, occasionally throwing me a smile or a request. "Feel like settin the table for Mama?"

Could last night have been a dream? As I walked around the table, laying the dishes and silverware in place, I kept looking at my mother's face for puffy eyes or other traces of the outraged emotion I'd overheard the night before, but I only saw the face of the smiling, contented mother I saw every Sunday morning. There was a thump overhead, then another one, and in a few moments Lonnie and James were at the table and Mama quickly filled their plates.

"Can I have some of that?" said James as Mama spooned the brains and eggs mixture onto her dish.

"You wouldn't like it, honey."

Lonnie smirked. "He might not like it, but he could use it."

"So could you," I said flippantly. I was still peeved at the way he'd treated me the night before. He raised his fist at me and I said calmly, "I'm'a scream and wake Daddy up," and I turned my head to avoid his glare.

"Hah, hah. He's not upstairs. I looked," said Lonnie.

"Your daddy had to go down to Hillsboro with Mr. Linwood to see somebody. He'll be back soon."

I didn't know whether to be happy or apprehensive. I didn't want my father at the table, but I wanted him in the house so that his presence would check Lonnie, who always assumed the position of authority whenever he was away.

James's eyes were still on Mama's plate. "Can I taste it?"

"Better not," said Lonnie, grinning widely. "You too little for that stuff Mama's eatin."

James stuck out his tongue so Mama could put a bit of the mysterious concoction on it. He rolled it around on his tongue. "What is it?"

"Brains!" Lonnie burst out laughing. "Brains and eggs! Ain't it gooood?" He licked his lips. "Yummm yummm."

"Ugh!" James dropped his jaw.

"That's what you get when your eyes are bigger than your stomach, greedy gut." Lonnie stood and leaned over him, scowling in the manner our father took with us. "Swallow it! Swallow it down!"

"Stop teasin him, Lonnie," said Mama. "Eat before your breakfast gets cold."

James leaned forward. The mixture fell from his mouth.

Why is the memory of breakfast that morning lodged so deeply in my mind that I can recall it at will? Of all the times we ate Sunday breakfast together I can recall none of the details so vividly as I can of that particular morning. I see, I hear, I taste, I smell everything as if I'm watching from a corner of the room. The kitchen is bright as it is only on sunny mornings and the door is open and the cooking smoke drifts through the screen. Music from the Wings Over Jordan Choir is on the radio and Mama turns it up louder so it fills the room and sings along with them. "Let us break bread together on our knees. . . . Let us break bread together on our knees. . . ." We are not as reverent. We grin across the table at each other, swinging our feet, talking happily and loudly without our father there to cast a shadow across the scene. Our conversation is full of laughter and teasing. My mother tells us another story of her school days in the country; we tell her about our adventures at home and away, escapades we'd never mention in front of our father.

Now the stories are all told and Mama wipes her mouth and looks at each one of us, and smiling, asks the same question she asks every Sunday morning. "Get the dream book for me, Amy." And I bring it back to the table. "Now. Who had a dream?" And the kitchen is full of gabbling as we tell Mama our dreams.

My mother's interest in our dreams had its roots in a pastime engaged in by nearly every adult we knew: playing the numbers. Yes, numbers were as much a part of our world as the air we breathed.

They were the focal point of every conversation in Westville after three P.M. every day but Sunday. "Old Jim Thompson died today. What time you say? Three-thirty! Now that number just come out last week. Naw. Three oh three. Well, ain't that what I said? Now what is 'Death'? Seven sixty-nine. Gonna put a dime on that. In the box. Heard Lucy Parsons broke her arm last night. Arm, hunh? Ain't that two-fifteen? What was it today? Two-fifteen! I played that damn number all last week and just because I didn't play it today, out it come!" Ah, those fickle numbers. The poor man's investment. Three digits on which a man pinned his wishes and dreams every day of the week but Sunday.

Now these numbers were associated with a purple and orange paper booklet that Mama kept on a shelf over the sink. MADAM ZORA'S INTERPRETATION OF DREAMS was printed on the cover in bold black letters. DREAM NUMBERS based on the Ancient Science of Numerology. Those connected with this Ancient Science seemed to have "luck with love." One bold advertisement on the inside cover of the booklet touted the potency of ORIENTAL INCENSE AND MAGNET OIL. If you rubbed it on your body your lover would YIELD to your charms. Another just below declared that SOLOMON'S SEAL had LUCK APPEAL and would give you MIRACULOUS POWERS. Lonnie said he was going to send for Solomon's Seal, but he never did. It cost fifty cents.

This book also gave advice about luck as well as dreams. Going up was good luck. Going down was bad. Flying high, good. Flying low, bad. And whatever you dreamed really meant the opposite. If you dreamed someone was going to murder you, you'd really be safe. Time was essential, too. If you didn't dream between three and seven in the morning, your dreams weren't any good. After a page of this information, there were listed, in this miraculous book, in alphabetical order, the subjects of other events that might occur. Race riots. Love. Death. War. Hatred. Disease. Starvation. Next to each entry was a three digit number. Angels, 112. Argue, 511. Eyelashes, 390. After the subjects were listed names: Enid, Alberta, Ronald, George—any name you could think of. Lonnie and I had perused every page of that booklet and as far as we were concerned, it was all a lot of junk, but Mama ran her life by it, and every Sunday she picked our brains cleaner than one of the salted mackerels she loved.

That morning she sighed and took a sip of her strong black coffee and said, "Well, what did you dream last night, Amy?"

"Nothin," I said truthfully.

"I had a dream about a boat," said Lonnie.

"Boat," said Mama, flipping through her dream book. "Was it a sailboat or a motorboat?"

Lonnie shrugged. "Can't remember."

"Well, where was it?"

"I think I was on a lake . . ."

"Ah . . . to be on a lake is to be 'secure.'" Mama bit into her roll. "That's four thirteen. Your father played that for two months . . . didn't hit yet."

"Mama, what does it mean when you dream you're gonna get caught?" I asked. "One night I dreamed I was runnin and runnin from somebody and they were so close I could feel their breath on my neck and I was gettin tireder and tireder and my legs were gettin heavier and heavier and I could hardly pick them up. Then I was runnin up these steps and they kept foldin up and I kept slidin back and then just when I thought they were gonna catch me, I woke up. Whew! I was sweatin!"

"I dream that dream," said James. "I get real scared."

Mama flipped through the book. "Caught. Don't see it. That's probably because you was havin a nightmare because you were scared. And the dream book don't tell about nightmares."

"Mama, what does it mean when you're fallin?" said Lonnie. "Is that a nightmare, too? I dreamed that last night, too. But I always wake up just when I think I'm gonna hit the bottom."

"Aw, I dream that lots," said James.

Lonnie scowled at him. "How come you're always dreamin somebody else's dreams?"

"Now, Lonnie," said Mama. She smiled at James. "I used to dream that when I was a child, and my mama said if you hit bottom, you don't ever wake up."

"What does fallin *mean,* Mama?" said Lonnie.

"Fallin . . ." said Mama. "Fallin . . . here it is. 'If you ain't hurt you will overcome your troubles.' That's seven fifty-six."

Now was my time to get Lonnie for teasing James. "Mama," I held my foot up. "I hurt my toe. And it's swolled up."

Mama looked at my foot. "It is a little. After breakfast we'll soak it in some warm water. When did you do that?"

I could feel the heat from Lonnie's glare. "Last night when I went to the bathroom."

"Well, honey, you have to put your shoes on when you go outside." She frowned. "That's probably a good number. Here it is. 'Stump your toe.' That's nine twenty-one. I think I'll put a dime on that tomorrow. Straight."

A whole dime! My mother was a penny player. Occasionally she'd play a nickel. My father was the real gambler. He squandered dimes and quarters and sometimes even a whole dollar.

"And Lonnie," said Mama, "please don't get to playin tomorrow and forget to take it. I have a strong hunch about this one."

Just then the screen door opened and my father stepped into the kitchen and it was as if a cloud passed over the sun. James jumped up from the table and ran to him, eager to tell him about his dream; Daddy half smiled and leaned over and patted his head and then looked up and mumbled a greeting and we mumbled one in return. I was staring at him in wonder. He was sober. It had been a long time since my father had been home sober on a Sunday morning. I looked at Mama. The smile had left her face and her lips tightened. She closed the dream book and stood up and I knew that last night had been real after all. I sneaked a look over at Lonnie, but he was concentrating on his plate. With a sigh, Mama put the dream book back on the shelf, then went over to the stove. "Well, I guess I'll make some fresh coffee."

I escaped to the porch. A few minutes later Lonnie followed and we went down into the yard.

"You see Daddy?" I said. "He's sober!"

Lonnie pulled a bag of marbles from his pocket. "So what?" He dropped to his knees and drew a circle in the dirt. "You think you're smart, don't you. Tellin Mama about your toe. I bet if I wasn't there you'd'a told her everything. Blabbermouth. Tell everything you know."

"No I don't." My voice wobbled. I'd been ready to tell him about what I'd overheard the night before, but water stung my eyes, and I turned to go up on the porch.

"Girl, you want to play marbles or not."

The grumbled invitation was his way of apologizing. I came back and dropped to my knees. "Maybe now things will be different. Maybe Daddy's gonna change."

"Change how?"

Maybe now I could tell Lonnie about last night. "Well, last night when Daddy was drunk—"

"Forget about last night, I told you!"

He was so fierce that I almost threw my marbles down, but I was afraid to upset him further. I played three games and lost all of them.

VERY EARLY the next morning, just before dawn, I heard someone rise and go downstairs. Mama? Too early for her to get ready for work. I sat up. A few moments later more sounds of someone going downstairs. I went to my door again and listened. Talking. Pans clanking. Silverware and dishes clinking. I settled down and waited, listening to my own breathing. Finally I heard my father murmuring, the screen door clapping shut, then Mama softly coming back up the steps.

A while later, still very early, I heard Mama go back down to the kitchen. This time I followed her down. These were the moments I always had with her, before the men of the house got up. She poured me a cup of coffee and diluted it with milk and the back door was open and we sat quietly and enjoyed the cool morning air. At seven o'clock, just before the time came for her to go to work, she told me to go upstairs and wake Lonnie.

I didn't want to disturb my peace and quiet, which usually lasted until well past nine o'clock. "What for?" Lonnie was hard to arouse, and he was a surly devil when he didn't get a complete night's rest.

"Just go get him, Amy," said Mama.

Surprisingly, Lonnie awakened as soon as I called to him from the safety of the upstairs hallway, and a few moments later he and James were leaning on the kitchen table yawning as they waited for my mother to disclose her reasons for disturbing their sleep.

"Lonnie," she began, "you and Amy have to take care of James from now on."

"Hunh?" Lonnie blinked and sat up.

"Where's Daddy?" I asked.

"He won't be takin care of you all anymore during the day, and I have to go to work in a few minutes. And you all are big enough to stay home by yourselves."

Lonnie was overjoyed at the prospect of no father around to restrain him but I wasn't too happy about being left alone all day with him as my boss. Recalling the conversation I'd overheard Saturday night, I whispered, "Is Daddy comin back?"

"Of course he's comin back," said Mama impatiently. "What in the world is wrong with you, Amy?"

"He left yesterday, and now today."

"Yesterday Mr. Linwood and your father went to see Mr. Harry Thompson about a job he heard about and today he's goin to see if he can get it. And if he does, you all will be by yourselves for a while."

James was just as unhappy and confused. "Do I have to do what Amy says, too?"

"Your daddy said you are to mind Lonnie and Amy." Mama patted James on the head. "Will you be a good boy for Mama?"

James nodded.

Although my father was a strict guardian, he'd take a break from us once in a while to run a few errands, and during those times James always managed to fall and raise a lump on his head or scrape his knee. On those occasions Lonnie and I would rush him next door to Miss Edie, who provided a comforting lap as well as antiseptics, bandages, and cookies. Knowing what I knew now, I thought I should bring up the subject of Miss Edie before we committed a faux pas, so fixing my eyes on James, I said, "If James cuts himself or scrapes his knee, is he supposed to let me and Lonnie fix it?"

James pouted. "I don't want you to fix it. Miss Edie can, can't she, Mama?"

Poor boy. Mama lashed out at him so fiercely that tears jumped into his eyes. "No! You don't go to Miss Edie's anymore for anything! Do you hear me? If anything happens, bandages and peroxide will be right here on this shelf over the sink!" She turned to me, still fierce. "Do you understand, Amy?"

I understood more than she knew. I nodded and looked over at Lonnie, who refused to meet my eyes.

Mama took James on her lap and wiped his eyes. "I'm sorry I yelled at you, honey." She smoothed his hair down and hugged him. "But you try to be careful and not fall down. And Mama will bring you a Tootsie Roll when she comes home."

This emotional outburst from my mother was followed by a more violent one at the end of the week. I realized later that these fits of pique were related, but at the time it seemed as if she had drunk some kind of brew that transformed her into a wild-eyed crazy woman.

This second fit came about the day she hit the number.

# THREE

My mother and father played the numbers every day with a skinny bachelor named Mr. Chester Arthur who lived in a two-room shack not far from where we lived. It was Lonnie's job to take the number slips (wrapped around the money) to Mr. Arthur's house every day before one o'clock in the afternoon. When we were going to school, Lonnie would drop them off after lunch on our way back to school; when school was out for the summer, my father would send him every day about ten. Now that Daddy was away from home, there was no one to remind Lonnie to take the numbers, but Mama reminded me every morning. "Don't let Lonnie forget the numbers, Amy."

It was a task that Lonnie and I would never take lightly, especially after we'd inspected the welts on the back of Andrew Gates, a boy in Lonnie's class. His father had almost skinned him alive just before school was out because he forgot to turn in his father's slips.

Every evening that week when my mother came home from work, she'd open the gate to our front yard and ask us what the number was and look sadder and sadder because she didn't hit. "Well, I'll say a little prayer tonight. Maybe the Lord will help me see my way."

My father's luck was no better. He would shake his head and look very discouraged. But he asked no help from God. He was depending on a ship. "Well, I guess someday my ship will come in," he'd say, and run his hand back across his head. I wondered where this mysterious ship was coming from. I imagined that it was like a pirate's sloop, with a sleek body and full sails and trunks of money in the hold. I didn't understand that this ship was the embodiment of his dreams.

"People just stupid to play the numbers," said Lonnie one night as we swung lazily on the porch glider. "They're just suckers, that's all. Sometimes I get so mad when I go into Mr. Arthur's kitchen and see all them piles of dollars and fifty centses sittin there. And you know, some people put two and three dollars on one number!"

"Three whole dollars!" I said. "How much money would you get for three dollars?"

"Well," said Lonnie, "you get twenty-seven-fifty for a nickel and there's twenty nickels in a dollar and you multiply that by twenty-seven-fifty and that's what you get."

"For a dollar you get twenty nickels' worth?"

"Yup. Then take three times that and that's what you get."

"Gee."

"Will Mama get twenty-seven whole dollars?" said James.

"She played a dime on nine twenty-one. And she'll get fifty-five if she hits," said Lonnie. "But she probably won't hit. The whole thing's fixed if you ask me. It's all a racket."

"What's a racket?" said James.

"You know, like in the movies when somethin's against the law and then the crooks pay off the cops to let them alone."

"You mean Mr. Chester Arthur does that?" I said.

"He writes the numbers, don't he?" scoffed Lonnie. "Everybody knows he does, even the cops. So he must pay them off."

"Ooooh," said James.

I sat with my chin on my hand, staring into the dark, seeing Mama's sad face. "I'm gonna say a prayer for Mama tonight."

"You sure are goofy," said Lonnie. "God ain't gonna help nobody hit the numbers."

"Why not?"

" 'Cause it's wrong, that's why. It's illegal."

Illegal or not, I said a prayer that night for Mama. If it was wrong, God would know it. And she wanted to hit so badly. I included my father, too. I thought he would appreciate any help he could get, especially if he was depending on a sailboat.

On Friday morning my mother asked us to pick some dandelions for her. She wanted to make some wine. Not far from our house there was a field full of them, and as soon as we finished breakfast we headed for it. We zigzagged through the grassy meadow sprinkled with yellow and purple wildflowers, up to our ankles and knees in grass, with our brown paper carryall bags flapping at our sides. Ahead of me, James's head was thrown back as he screamed with laughter, his fat legs pumping as he tried to keep up with Lonnie.

I was tired of running, so I threw myself down in the tall grass and smelled the earth and the grass and the weeds, then I turned over on my back and gazed up at the cotton clouds, floating in wisps across the blue sky. I closed my eyes and basked in the warm sun, listened to the buzz of insects. Finally I stood up and looked around. No Lonnie or James or the sound of them. They had probably sneaked off to another part of the field. But I didn't mind being alone. I dropped to my knees and began to pull the dandelions, flower after flower, long green leaves enfolding yellow flowers, almost as large as a half dollar, atop fuzzy green stems. Soon I had a bag full. I stood up and looked around. I called for Lonnie and James. No answer.

They had left the field.

I hurried home and looked through the house for them to no avail. Lonnie had ducked me and taken James along with him. I was determined to find them. As I crossed the floor to go back outside, I kicked something. A small white lump. Even before I picked it up I knew what it was. The number slips. Somehow they had fallen from Lonnie's pocket. My heart stopped. I looked at the clock. Twelve-thirty. Still time. It was a short walk to Mr. Chester Arthur's house, but I couldn't go without my shoes. I'd gone out into the field bare-footed, but I would hear from my father if I went to Mr. Arthur's house that way.

After a frenzied hunt I found the shoes, slipped my feet in, and galloped up to Mr. Arthur's house. I yanked his screen door open and puffed into his kitchen.

"Well, well." Mr. Chester Arthur was lean and bent with wisps of hair that stood up like matted fuzz; he eyed me like a startled chicken. "Here's little Miss Beale today!" He blinked. "Where's Lonnie?"

"My mother told me to bring the numbers today." The lie slid smoothly off my tongue as I handed him the sweaty lump of paper.

"Well, you just in time." He unfolded the lump, rolled the coins onto the table, counted them, then quickly copied the numbers onto one of several white pads filled with figures. Finished, he waved me away.

When I got home, Lonnie, his face the color of putty, was sitting on the top step of the porch next to James. A pile of comic books sat by his side. Lonnie loved his comic books, and if he wasn't reading them he had to be extremely disturbed. Every extra penny he got he spent on Superman. He would read the books to James, and explain that Superman was extra strong, and helped the weak; he was the champion of truth, justice, and the American way. I think he truly believed it then.

I walked casually by them and dropped to the glider and began peppering them with questions. "What's the matter? Why're you so quiet? You got any new comic books? Where'd you go anyway? You didn't fall down, did you, James?"

No answers. James looked up at Lonnie, who just shrugged.

I swung for a few moments more, then I announced casually that I'd found the numbers and put them in and they both jumped up and hit the ground, whooping as if they had been saved from the devil's lash.

But Lonnie hadn't suffered enough for deserting me. I swung back and forth for a few more times, then said calmly, "Daddy's gonna beat you anyway." My father's belt was not the devil's lash, but it was just as effective.

Lonnie stopped prancing around. The smile left his face. "I guess you're gonna tell him about me losin the slip."

I shrugged. "You always sayin me and James got mouths like bell clappers."

"I ain't gonna tell, Lonnie," James said earnestly. "Not even if Daddy asks me."

Lonnie eyed me. "So you gonna tell him because me and James ducked you today."

"I don't have to tell him. Daddy always stops by Mr. Arthur's every night, and Mr. Arthur is gonna tell him that I brought the numbers today instead of you because he asked me where you were. Then Daddy's gonna ask you why you didn't take them."

Lonnie's shoulders fell. He returned to the porch. Finally he said, "No matter what we tell him, he's gonna be mad, anyway."

"You oughta be glad I found them," I continued airily, "because if I didn't and Daddy hit one, he'd leave more scars on your back than Andrew Gates got on his."

Lonnie shuddered.

Satisfied, I opened the book I'd been reading. Occasionally I looked over at Lonnie, sitting on the top step, still ignoring his pile of beloved comic books. Finally he got up and went into the house, something else he did only if he was depressed or worried. Later on in the afternoon he came back to the swing and stood humbly before me, saying that since I had taken the numbers to Mr. Arthur, maybe it would be better if I went back to find out what it was. Sighing, I put my shoes back on and left him and James looking sadly after me as I went up the road.

Mr. Arthur was waiting for me by his kitchen door. When he saw me, his wispy head wobbled on his scrawny neck; a grin spread across his face. "I had a hunch you'd bring your mama good luck today, you almost not gettin here on time. Yes, indeed. That number of hers come out straight as a arrow. Yes, indeed."

I shrieked and flew back down the road to tell Lonnie and James the good news, and when Mama came down the road that evening we ran out to greet her, screaming the good news, and she knelt in the dusty road and hugged us with tears in her eyes. Then she went to Mr. Arthur and got her money, and she gave Lonnie and James a dime, but to me a whole quarter because I had given her the lucky number.

That evening at the dinner table, still giddy over our mother's big hit, we were pushing mighty amounts of food into our mouths at a rapid clip when she broke the awful news. "Well, now we can move to that house in Hillsboro."

"Hillsboro!" said Lonnie. "Why are we gonna move?"

My mother nodded happily. "We need a house that has more room than this one."

Lonnie plunked his fork on the table. "I don't want to move!"

Apparently it had never occurred to Mama that any of us would object. Her smile faded. "Why not?"

Lonnie scowled. "I mean, I don't want to move to Hillsboro. Ain't hardly any colored people in that whole town. And they all live on Union Avenue like they segregated or somethin. Them white people probably don't even like colored people."

"We ain't movin there for them to like us."

"And all them kids on Union Avenue call you niggers and blackies and always want to fight."

"We ain't movin onto Union Avenue," said Mama.

"That's gonna be even worse!" And for the next few moments Lonnie argued with Mama so heatedly that James and I covered our ears.

Finally Mama became exasperated with him and appealed to me. "Amy, wouldn't you like to live someplace where you have your own bedroom and there's a bathroom inside, no goin to the outhouse in the cold or in the dark?"

I kept my eyes away from Lonnie and nodded.

James took his hands from his ears. "I know I would. Then I wouldn't have to worry about no bees when I go to the toilet."

Mama and I laughed, but Lonnie said, still sulking, "And we'll have to go to a white school."

"Lonnie, you went to a white school in Woodlynne for four years until you came up here. Now don't say you don't know how to get along with white children."

"That ain't it. Those teachers will put me back just because I went to a colored school for two years. That's what happened to Freddy Jenkins when he moved to Woodlynne."

"Freddy Jenkins was dumber than a tom turkey. That's why they put him back. Not because he went to a colored school."

Lonnie's eyes were shining with tears now and his voice was husky. "You and Daddy don't care about us losin our friends."

Mama made one last appeal. "Lonnie," she said softly, "we have to move. Your father has to be in Hillsboro for work at five o'clock in the morning and the trolley don't start running until five-thirty. He'd have to walk five miles to work every day." She reached over and touched his arm.

Lonnie jumped up. "I don't care if he got to walk ten miles to work and ten miles back! I hate that old nigger!"

Mama drew in her breath, then exploded like warm soda from a bottle. "You hate your father, do you!" She jumped up and faced Lonnie across the table. "People try to do their best for their children and the first thing they do when they get a little height on them is talk about hatin somebody! You ought to be glad you have a father!" Her face was mottled with rage. "Well, you hate him so much, stay here! Move in with your friends! Now get out of my sight! Do you hear me! Get out of my sight!" Her eyes were wild, her bosom was heaving, she was choking with anger.

Dumbfounded, Lonnie stared at her.

She raised her hand. "Get out of my sight before I . . . !"

Lonnie ran from the kitchen, up the steps to our bedroom. We heard him stomping across the room, the bed creak. We heard him crying.

I knew he was still remembering Miss Edie and the outhouse, and his anger had smoldered inside of him, then erupted when Mama and Daddy seemed so callous about disrupting his life, yet Mama was so willing to help Daddy, who seemed to him so unworthy.

Mama dropped down to the table and put her face in her hands. "That boy, that boy." She began to cry softly. "Maybe I should've whipped him when he was little. Lord, Lord. To jump at his mother like that. Maybe I should've whipped him."

James and I sat silent and miserable, afraid to move, not knowing what to say.

Finally Mama looked across at us and smiled. "Don't pay no attention to me." She wiped her face with her apron, then gave a little laugh. "I guess I had too much excitement today."

James went and stood in front of her. "When Daddy comes home, you can tell him, and Lonnie can get a beatin."

Mama hugged him. "Lonnie don't need a beatin, honey. He's just upset, that's all. Lord knows, we all get upset sometimes. And you don't need to tell your Daddy about it." She looked at me over James's head.

I reassured her that James nor I would mention it. "Else I ain't gonna give you any of my Tootsie Rolls, James." That would hold his tongue. He was crazy about Tootsie Rolls.

When my father got home he'd already learned of Mama's good news from Mr. Arthur. It had put him in a good mood, because he stepped onto the porch grinning widely. I assumed that Mr. Arthur, in his excitement, had not told him that I had taken in the numbers instead of Lonnie. Anyway, my father never mentioned it then or later, and that evening we had a little celebration on the porch: chocolate cake and peach ice cream.

# FOUR

We moved to Hillsboro one night during the last week of July. Just before midnight my mother made us climb onto a mattress in the back of the truck where, worn out from helping all day, we fell asleep. When we arrived at the house we straggled drunkenly from the truck and fell onto a mattress somewhere on the second floor and awakened the next morning in a strange room.

I woke up first. Someone had undressed us; we were in our underwear. Lonnie and James were slung out on their backs on a mattress next to me, mouths open, snoring fitfully. I sat up and looked around. We were in a large room, big as a bedroom. Across the room in one corner was a toilet; a sink stood next to it, and a claw-footed bathtub took up almost all of the end wall. Excited, I got to my knees and shook James, who woke with a grunt.

"Look!" I whispered. "A tub! And a sink and a toilet!" We went to investigate; I ran water in the sink while James urinated in the toilet and flushed it over and over.

Lonnie sat up with a growl. "Stop runnin that water, Amy. And stop flushin that toilet, James." He came over to the sink and splashed water on his face and surveyed the room as he patted it dry. "This must be the bathroom. Sure is big. We must be upstairs."

And with those statements he started out of the room to explore the house. James and I scampered after him. Down a long hallway from the bathroom we found a small bedroom. To the left of it was a staircase to a floor above. We climbed it and found an attic, a room large enough for the twin beds that someone had set up. "For me and James," Lonnie stated. "The one downstairs must be for you." I felt a thrill. A room all my own! No more sleeping with James and Lonnie! Across a narrow hall was a small room, large enough for a bed, but not much else. "We can put all our stuff in here," said Lonnie. "Me and James. Not you."

I galloped back down the steps to see if I had a closet. Yes, a narrow one at the end of the room. But more than ample for me, who had no closet at all in Westville. We had all hung our clothes on a rolling clothes hanger. I looked around. Nothing there in the room, just a forlorn-looking place with dust rolling across the floor. And a big water spot on the ceiling. But it was going to be mine.

Back down the hall we went, turned past the bathroom into another short hall that led to the living room. We raised a curtain on the wall to reveal another closet, deep and dusty, that went under the stairs. Lonnie dropped the curtain and we proceeded to another room. This one was large and airy with a long wide window at the end. The living room, we decided as soon as we saw the sofa and chairs from our other house.

My heart sank. If that bedroom was mine, where would my mother and father sleep? I posed the question to Lonnie.

"Maybe in the bathroom," he answered. "It's big enough to be a bedroom, too." He nodded toward the closet under the stairwell and laughed. "Or maybe in there. There's enough room for a cot."

"Can't nobody sleep in there! Ain't no windows."

"Don't need any." Lonnie looked at my face. "Aw, girl, I was just teasin. Mama and Daddy are probably gonna sleep right in here. There's the sofa bed, ain't it?"

I was relieved. Up in Westville my mother and father had often slept in the living room on the sofa bed when it got too hot in their little bedroom. "Yeah. And they'll have this whole room to themselves. It's real big."

The room was large enough to be divided into a step-down area near the stairwell. We crossed the room, ready to go down the steps, when we heard voices from below. Female voices. We dropped to the floor and lay on our stomachs, listening. I recognized immediately my mother's rapid speech. The other voice was low. Droning. I held my breath and looked over at Lonnie.

"That's Aunt Louise," I whispered.

Lonnie grunted. "I ain't goin down there until she goes."

"I'm hungry," said James.

I was, too. "Suppose she don't go right away?"

Lonnie put his finger to his lips, sat up, and started slowly down the steps. James and I followed. The stairway was dark and steep, but a crack of light came through a door at the bottom that was slightly ajar. We peeped through the crack for the face that went with that voice.

AUNT LOUISE lived on Union Avenue, and although my mother went to see her regularly, occasionally dragging us with her, our relationship with her had turned sour two years earlier during a stay at our house in Westville. The family had been quarantined when my mother and I came down with scarlet fever. For four weeks our house had become a clinic where Aunt Louise practiced the skills she had recently acquired at a Red Cross First Aid course at the Hillsboro Hospital. We children had always been leery of Aunt Louise, but during that forced confinement we discovered that our mother's sister was a she-dragon whose caustic tongue kept our father chewing his lip and us trembling in our beds begging God to restore our health as soon as His will be done.

That had been a stressful time, especially for me. During my illness, my hair, which had been long and fine, fell out and grew back still fine, but so kinky my mother couldn't comb or brush it. My hair combing sessions with her, which used to be a pleasant ritual of me standing between her legs as she brushed my hair and made water curls and tied them back with ribbons, became sessions filled with ooches and ouches and tears and shouting matches as she tried to unsnarl the kinks. In order to avoid the stress, my mother would comb my hair only on school days. On weekends, holidays, and vacations, I was allowed to comb it myself and ended up looking as if I had been caught in a windstorm.

The last time Aunt Louise had visited us was just after New Year's when my mother had become sick again, this time with appendicitis, and again Aunt Louise had come to nurse her after she came out of the hospital. Again we prayed, and God heard our pleas; she was there for only two days.

And now here she was in our kitchen.

My stomach growled. I pushed past Lonnie and jumped down the last two steps into the room.

Mama, at the sink, started toward me. "Amy! You gonna break your fool neck!" One of her long plaits had slipped from her head and she stopped to twist it up and anchor it there with a tortoiseshell hairpin.

"Hmph." Aunt Louise eyed Lonnie and James, who had stepped down behind me. "Where's your clothes?"

We shrugged, slipped around the table, and sat down.

"Too hot to wear any clothes," said Mama. "Must be ninety already and it ain't even nine o'clock yet." She put a box of cornflakes on the table. "Amy, look in that box over there in the corner and get the spoons and bowls so you all can eat."

I got up, happy to be out from under Aunt Louise's eyes. Lonnie and James had shrunk behind the table like jackrabbits downwind from a coyote, keeping their eyes hidden from the woman who was our jolly mother's sister, but so very different. She was coffee brown with a tad of cream, a surprising contrast to Mama's fair skin. Also, Aunt Louise was tall, lean, and angular, tough as half-cooked collard greens, my mother, shorter, and tender as new grass. But their manner of speaking, broadly Southern, was their most distinguishing characteristic. Aunt Louise spoke slowly with a nasal drawl, Mama quickly, like water rippling over stones in a stream.

As soon as I found the bowls and spoons I slid back into my seat; she eyed Lonnie, James, and me with her critical eye and ruminated on the vagaries of color in our family. "Now this sure is a mixture. A black one, a yallah one, and a red one." Silence from us, another long look from her—at Lonnie, stocky, green-eyed, dark-skinned and serious and hot tempered, and looking like my father (although Aunt Louise swore differently). At James, slight and caramel with curly hair and a sweet smile and a disposition just as sweet. And at me, coltish, biscuit tan, with my three red plaits which were always coming loose.

"Well," said Aunt Louise, "can't you little niggers speak? Where's your manners?"

"Mornin, Aunt Louise."

James, head cocked, squinted at her and said reprovingly, "Daddy gets mad if we say 'nigger.' "

"Oh, he do." Aunt Louise laughed. "Then don't you say it." She leaned toward him and ruffled his hair. He drew away, scowling, and she ruffled it again. "Look at him frownin. Lawd, Leatha, except for his color, if he ain't the spittin image of Jack Beale, skippy."

My mother smiled. "Like he spit him out his mouth."

"I guess he spit him out all right. Not out of his mouth, neither." Aunt Louise put her face closer to James's. "Where's your pappy, hunh?"

James's eyebrows were almost touching his nose. "Work," he grunted, then shoved a spoonful of cornflakes into his mouth.

"Work. Listen at him gruntin." She turned to Lonnie. "How you, Grandpap Ruther?"

Lonnie rolled his eyes toward the ceiling.

"I declare, Leatha, he look more like Papa every day, don't he?"

"Some," said Mama.

"You should've named him Ruther instead of Leonard."

"Well, Jack named him after Leona."

Aunt Louise grunted. "Let's hope he don't pick up none of her habits."

My turn was next. I braced myself for an onslaught of observations about my hair. Between Lonnie's constant teasing and Aunt Louise's comments it had become the bane of my existence.

"Now Amy, here, she don't look like nobody but herself." Aunt Louise tweaked my nose. "She must be you and Jack throwed together. She got his nose for sure. Spread out like a pancake." She closed one eye. "But that red hair. Tommy Scanlon sure marked her." She shook her head. "You oughta do somethin about that, Leatha. It's bad enough for the child to have a nappy head. But a nappy red head . . . mph, mph, mph."

"It ain't as red as it used to be," said Mama.

Aunt Louise was skeptical. "Get some strong black coffee and dye that stuff."

I gasped. "Do I have to, Mama?"

"No, child. My hair was bright red when I was little. It turned darker, and so will yours."

"Well, yours was straight. You need to saw off that stuff Amy got on her head. Look like a hoorah's nest."

Lonnie almost choked on his cornflakes. He'd been trying to get my eye for the past few minutes but I'd been studiously ignoring him. Now I looked his way, and he pointed at his hair and laughed silently. I rolled my eyes at him and turned my head.

"Amy's hair is just fine, that's all," Mama was saying. "It was all right until she had that scarlet fever that time and it fell out. Well, it's growing back fine."

"Hmph." Aunt Louise eyed me a moment longer, then gave up. "Well, talkin about them naps sure ain't gonna change 'em." She got up to get a cup of coffee. "What made the Bull decide to move anyway? I didn't think you'd ever get him out of Westville."

"We thought it was best, that's all," said Mama.

This lukewarm response from my mother did not satisfy Aunt Louise. She turned up the heat. "Well, it sure wasn't no atmosphere to be raisin children in. Gamblin and drinkin. Rent parties. And fightin the Battle of Bull Run. Hmph."

My mother's face was turning red. "Well, welfare sure ain't enough to pay no rent. And everybody can't pass for white like some colored men around here and get a good job."

"If you talkin about my husband, he don't pass for no white." Uncle Lee looked like an Italian and worked at the *Hillsboro Times*. "Everybody on his job know he's colored. Malcolm Lewis works there and he sure couldn't pass for no white. And there's plenty of colored men right on Union Avenue blacker than John Beale who got good jobs. Blackjack just want to make money his way or no way."

"Them parties put food in our mouths and clothes on our back. You can't blame a man for wantin to feed his children."

"Ain't nobody blamin nobody. There's plenty of people in the same circumstances. But it's the way we do things in this world that counts." Aunt Louise paused, then added pointedly, "Some things we do in this life create more problems than they're worth. And there is such a thing as a honest livin."

"Doin a day's work is an honest livin," said Mama. "But that don't mean I have to feel good about cleanin up behind white folks." She became very busy with a large box on the table, rattling paper as she unwrapped dishes and put them on a counter near the sink.

"But you still do it every day. Workin yourself to death every day because some fool would rather gamble away what money he do make."

"I don't work myself to death, Louise." Mama rattled more newspaper.

"That was Death knockin at your door in January when you had that miscarriage, in case you don't know it. And he wouldn't have knocked if you wasn't scrubbin and cookin and cleanin at home and at work and carryin a baby."

*Miscarriage.*

I didn't comprehend the full meaning of that word, but since I had seen no baby and she had been "carrying one" it could only mean one thing. She had "lost" a baby, as she had told Mr. Linwood that night of the party. And when you lost a baby, it made you sick. I slid a look at Lonnie but if he understood what Aunt Louise was saying, he gave no indication. He was pouring himself another bowl of cornflakes.

"The children have to have clean clothes and eat."

"If you had a man to help you instead of drinkin it up every weekend that the Lord sends—"

"He don't drink it all up, Louise."

"Lord, if you don't get more and more like Mumma every day. She spent her life makin excuses for Papa. Jackass drinkin every weekend and shootin up the house and us jumpin over bushes like jackrabbits and hidin in the dark until it was safe to come back in the house. Only reason that fool ain't dead is because your brothers left home when they got big enough so they wouldn't kill him."

"Jack ain't nothin like Papa."

"And a tadpole ain't nothin like a frog neither. Lord, when I sit here and listen to you takin up for that man I want to puke. Especially when I know that if he took that other job last winter when he knew you should've stayed home off your feet—"

"What job?" said Mama.

"And you standin here makin excuses for a man who didn't care enough—"

"What job?" said Mama, again.

"Oh, I know I shouldn't have said anything. But—well, that job that Joe Davis has, that's what. When they made that new addition to the high school, Harry Thompson, he's the janitor there you know, well, he needed some help, so knowin Jack and knowin you was pregnant, he thought Jack could use some extra money and asked him if he wanted a job part time with him. Assistant janitor. He could've worked four hours a night and made more in a night than you make in a week."

"That's just somethin you heard around on Union Avenue."

"Of course I heard it. Jack Beale sure didn't tell me. I heard it from Harry Thompson."

"Harry Thompson. That fool wouldn't tell the truth if he was hangin over hell on a spiderweb."

"Well, Harry Thompson may not be worth a quarter but he tells the truth sometimes. And the job sure must've been available, because Joe Davis sure works at that high school now. Five nights a week."

"Well, now I've heard it, all right?"

Mama wanted to hear no more, and Aunt Louise knew it. She sat in silence, sipped her coffee, and looked around the kitchen with eyes that scraped the walls. Lonnie and James and I sat slumped in our seats. We had finished eating, but unwilling to submit ourselves again to Aunt Louise's caustic observations if we asked for permission to leave, we waited silently for an opportune moment to slip out of our chairs and up the steps.

Aunt Louise finished her coffee and stood up and rubbed her hands on her hips. "Place looks like a rat's den."

"Walls just need some plaster," said my mother, obviously relieved that Aunt Louise had chosen a new subject.

"I see you got a new gas stove. Where'd you get it?"

"It was already here."

"That cracker must've just put it in then, 'cause it wasn't here when Avid Johnson lived here." Aunt Louise began moving around the kitchen. "That's one of the reasons she moved out. Got tired of choppin wood for that wood-burnin stove. Lazy bugger she was married to sure didn't chop none. Had a bad back. Not too bad to be turnin out Johnsons every nine months though." At the sink she turned on the spigot and let the water run over her finger. "No hot water. Hmph. Got to heat it on the stove, I guess. These white folks expect niggers to live like dogs and then charge them for it."

"Well, it's better'n what we had."

"Hmph. I guess anything's better'n what you had up in them bushes where you was." She turned from the sink, glanced around the kitchen again, and shook her head. "Dirt and grease piled up worse'n a pigsty. Well, I guess we better send these children outside so we can get started cleanin."

The words we had been waiting for. Lonnie and James slipped quickly up the steps, but before I could get around the table Aunt Louise grabbed my arm. "Leatha, I know you ain't gonna let this gal go outside with this head lookin like this. Bushier'n Orphan Annie's and full of lint."

My mother looked at my face and took pity on me. "Amy can comb her own hair. She's only goin out in the yard."

"Don't make no difference where she's goin." Aunt Louise pulled me to her. "And I've seen examples of Missy's hair combin. Rakin over the top. That's why it looks like it do right now."

In the next few moments she had gathered a jar of Dixie Peach hair grease, a brush with a comb stuck in the bristles, and three of my mother's tortoiseshell hairpins. I made one last attempt to gain my mother's intervention by letting a few tears slide down my face, but Aunt Louise pushed me onto my knees in front of her and began working on my hair. "Stop that whinin, Miss Mighty Lips, before I knock you upside your head with this brush. If I was your mother I'd plait these kinks up in so many little plaits you could go with them uncombed from Sunday to Sunday like a pickaninny. Hold your head up and keep still."

She began parting my hair into little sections, then inch by inch she greased my scalp. As she worked she talked. "It's about time you got out of that Westville . . . This stuff ain't so bad . . . Just need a little grease . . . Lincoln freed the slaves from their bonds but he couldn't free some of them from their ways . . . All bunched up together like they're on a plantation . . . and even got a colored school . . . And speakin of school, you know you gotta go register these children soon . . . They got to take a test, and if they don't they gonna put them back a whole year."

I had been staring listlessly at the floor, head bent, but alerted by the words *put back* I raised my head; Aunt Louise pushed it forward again and began to plait a section of my hair so tightly I felt as if she was going to pull my face off.

At the same time, my mother, who'd been bearing up halfheartedly under Aunt Louise's hypnotic drone, came to life. "Put back! I know ain't nobody puttin none of my children back!" Her words sputtered and popped like drops of water in a pan of hot grease.

"Calm down . . . calm down," said Aunt Louise.

"And I know damn well *Jack* ain't gonna let—"

"Jack!" Aunt Louise let out a loud snort. "Jack! What's old Black-jack Beale gonna say or do? Run up to that school and glare at them white folks with them bloodshot eyes of his is 'bout all he can do. Or breathe on 'em after one of them giant hangovers of his. He won't be messin with no bunch of niggers, and that's about all he *can* scare . . . and *you*. And it's his fault anyway. He could've got a house right here in Hillsboro when you all first got married. But no, he had to mess around movin from pillar to post, then end up in Westville sellin boot-leg whiskey and playin blackjack all night and get hisself a name. Well, I guess he ain't so popular now he ain't got no more money to gamble up. Got to get out and work like the rest of us poor niggers. And Lord. If that ain't a comedown for Jack Beale. A trashman. Up at five o'clock in the mornin." She threw her head back and her laugh crackled like cellophane. "Lord! I bet he ain't seen a sunrise in his life until now."

My mother sat down with a whoosh. "Well, I know . . . I'll see when I go up there. I know I ain't got no dumb children."

"They don't have to be *born* dumb. They can go to school and get dumb. Don't I know that Dr. Blount's child went to that same colored elementary school in Westville, and don't I know that when he went to the white junior high school that they said he didn't even know fourth-grade work and they looked at his records and had him tested and shook their heads because the boy's IQ or somethin went down 'stiddy up because he didn't learn nothin at that school? And I don't see how children can learn nothin noway when they got teachers like Charlotte Hobbes up there—drinkin like a fool and picklin her brain."

I drew in my breath. Miss Hobbes was Lonnie's teacher.

" 'Course, I don't understand them people up there lettin theirselves be segregated. They might as well stayed down South in the bushes than to come up here and act like they're down South in the bushes. Up there shootin and knifin and drinkin up their money as fast as they make it and pissin it out to make room for more."

"Well, I don't know about all that." My mother got up. "I just know they ain't puttin my children back." She slammed a pot into the sink.

"Pot ain't done nothin to you." Aunt Louise brought a last plait up to the side of my aching head and anchored it there with a hair pin. "There. That looks two hundred percent better."

I might have looked better, but I felt awful. My scalp was stinging, my knees were sore from kneeling on the patched linoleum, and the argument between Mama and Aunt Louise about "puttin back" had raised the hackles on my neck. I hadn't dared move or speak while Aunt Louise was wielding the hairbrush for fear she'd carry out her threat and knock me on the head. But now I twisted around and said hesitantly, "Are me and Lonnie gonna get put back, Aunt Louise?"

"Now see what you started, Louise," said Mama.

"Not if you smart enough," Aunt Louise replied sagely. "Now go on upstairs and wash and grease them rusty elbows and knees and put some shoes on them big Beale feet."

I pulled myself up and walked stiffly to the stairs. As I started up, Aunt Louise called after me. "Don't you say nothin to Lonnie about anything you just heard, you hear me?"

Her advice was unnecessary. I remembered the fit he'd had when my mother had told us we were moving, and I would rather have worried alone than subject my ears to more of that boy's rage. But the thought of repeating the fourth grade brought tears to my eyes.

# F I V E

The old part of Hillsboro was once a quarry. If you walk up Beech-wood from the train station, stop about halfway, and look up to your left, you'll see that part of town that resembles the smashed side of a three-tiered cake. On the top level, Hillcrest Avenue runs parallel to Beechwood and, like Beechwood, travels the length of the town. Middle-class residents live there in big old houses with backyards that drop off like the edge of a cliff and look down on Union Avenue, where most of the colored people in town live. Poor Irish used to live on the street, my father said. But during the twenties, a colored family from Virginia moved in and stayed in spite of the hostility of a few white people. The Irish eventually left and more colored people (friends and relatives from Mason County), moved in, among them my father's people and my mother's sister.

My mother's history we had learned at her knee; she was full of stories about her family and she weaned us on tales of her childhood days in that faraway place called Virginia. On the wall in the living room was a formal picture of her family when they were all together, from Papa Roo and Mama Callie down to the youngest child, Caroline, sitting on her mother's lap.

But I was unaware that the town of Hillsboro was where my father once lived, that he'd been born on the outskirts in a row of rickety houses near a lumberyard, that his mother later moved to Union Avenue, that he had fought and played with the children there, had at-

45

tended the public school, had left when he was a child with his mother and lived like a gypsy going from the house of uncle to uncle, finally returning to Hillsboro to live with his sister Leona after his mother died.

Union Avenue is one block long and rises in a hump, and the back-yards of the narrow houses drop off and look down on one block of Beechwood Avenue, where, when I was a child, many of the Italian residents lived. The only friction that arose between the two groups was on warm Friday evenings when the smell of hog maws and chitlins cooking in the kitchens on Union Avenue floated down to Beechwood Avenue and permeated their tiny backyard gardens; the Italians, out-raged by the foul odors drifting onto the statues of their blessed saints, would scream up, "You niggers stoppada cookin da shit up there!" And the indignant Union Avenue residents would scream down, "You wops come uppa for suppa! And don'ta forgetta spaghetti!"

Walk along Hillcrest and Beechwood Avenues and you would get a flavor of the town. Hillcrest: Orson's drugstore, where you got a double dip of ice cream for a nickel; the American Store, where customers were still served by a clerk with a long pole; Steuben's Bakery, from where the odor of the buns baked fresh every morning drew people like the Pied Piper to stand in long lines; the town hall, which included the police station, the jail, and the garages for the trash trucks; the Catholic church and the Catholic school where I passed in awe of the nuns and priests, unapproachable in black; the post office across the street from the church, a variety of small businesses and the tiny church where we attended Bible school, then, almost at the other end, the high school and the elementary school, a lumberyard, and finally, the railroad station.

Beechwood Avenue was more residential, with a few businesses scat-tered along the first two blocks. The health center, the shoe repair shop, a hardware store, two Chinese laundries, a carpenter shop, the fire-house, a blacksmith. In the center of town lived three Jewish families who owned businesses (a clothing store, a delicatessen, a tailor shop) and lived in apartments above them.

Highland Avenue was the main street. It ran directly into Philadelphia. Near the corner of Highland and Hillcrest Avenues was Woolworth's Five and Ten; the Highland Movies was almost directly in the center of town. And just as you left town you would pass the Hillsboro Public Library and the *Hillsboro Times* building and the Hillsboro golf course and country club for the newer residents in the newer part of town where the newer houses were larger with more space around them—three-story stone houses that sat back on cropped lawns. Along the sidewalks were oaks and maples and sycamores whose branches met in leafy arches over the streets on hot summer days and kept them shady and cool.

This was the Hillsboro we moved to that summer.

THE HOUSE we moved to was on Beechwood Avenue, just off of Highland Avenue and around the corner from Union Avenue. It was owned by a carpenter named Mr. Harrison who was acquainted with my father's family and had no reservations about renting it out to a colored man he knew. We got our first view of this house after we finally got past Aunt Louise's critical eye and stepped into the yard. By this time it was so hot outside that it seemed as if the earth had moved a little closer to the sun.

We had come to dismal surroundings. Our house stood on one side of a large square of hard, pebbly ground and stretched from the back shed, along the kitchen, which was the only entrance, down a driveway to Beechwood Avenue. Faded and gray, it sagged in the heat and regarded us wearily with windows as bleary as the eyes of a drunk after an extended binge. On the right, facing the driveway, were two other houses, equally faded, equally bleary. No one lived there, it seemed. Running along the yard across from our house was a snaggletoothed wooden fence with rotted slats, held by a rusty wire, that leaned forward or backward at will. The only green in the yard was the grass that sprouted in clumps along the fence. There was not one tree, no shade anywhere except the shadows thrown by the houses and the fence.

We stood in the hot sun, squinting and sweating, looking. At the driveway that led to the yard, at the end of our house where there was an opening. We went to inspect and found a cool alley, and beyond, the hot street. We sweated and looked.

"Let's go see what's out there," said Lonnie.

"Mama said don't go out the yard," I said.

"Aw, all we gonna do is go out this little alley and then walk around and come back up that driveway." Lonnie started through the alley. "Come on, James."

James looked up at me like a little bird. "Come on, Amy." When I didn't move, he started after Lonnie.

Lonnie knew I wasn't going to stay by myself so he went on. I followed them. But I didn't like the way things were going lately. When James was younger, Lonnie always left him with me. He didn't want to be bothered with him. But now that James was six, and starting school, Lonnie would get him on his side by telling him that boys did things together.

When we reached the street the heat bounced up from the sidewalk into our faces. We stood there squinting with our hands over our foreheads looking up and down the street. Sweating. Lonnie turned to his right. We followed.

When we got to the corner I called out in surprise. It was a street I recognized. Where we walked with our mother when we came on the trolley from Westville to go see Aunt Louise. "Hey! This is the way we go to Union Avenue!"

"Aw, I knew that, dummy!" said Lonnie.

He knew everything. I almost told him he'd know how smart he was when we got put back like Aunt Louise said, but I held back. That would just put him in a bad mood.

We walked down the block toward our driveway. A few houses. A shoe shop. And the front of our house, a sign. L. HARRISON, CARPENTER. The words were printed in black letters across a dirty window. We peeped in, but we saw no one.

Then the driveway. We stood looking up into the hot yard. Sweating and squinting.

After a while Lonnie said, "I got three cents. Let's go around to the Jew store. It's right around the corner."

"Mama said—"

"Aw, girl, shut up. I'm goin. Come on, James." Lonnie grabbed James's hand and pulled him down the street.

James wriggled his hand loose and ran back to me and took my hand. "Come on, Amy."

"No." Angry because Lonnie had told me to shut up.

James hesitated, looked at Lonnie who waved at him to come on, and let go of my hand and ran after Lonnie. When he caught up, they both stood waiting, but I was too stubborn to go. They turned and left and soon they became two little figures bobbing, then disappearing around the corner leaving me sweating in the hot sun.

I jerked forward and ran after them and, huffing, caught up with them just as they reached the corner of Union Avenue and Maple Street. And right there facing us was Weiner's delicatessen.

Lonnie grinned, hand on hip. "I thought you wasn't comin." Before he could rub it in, I cut him off. "I got a dime," I said. I sat down on the curb and took off my shoe and held it upside down and the dime clinked onto the sidewalk. Lonnie stooped and picked it up and I knew everything was all right then.

On the door of the store was a sign, a picture of a Coca-Cola bottle with fat drops of water sliding down the sides. They looked real enough to lick off. But there were three of us with just thirteen cents. We couldn't buy three Cokes at a nickel a bottle, and they were only six ounces each, not enough to share.

The bell tinkled as we entered. It was cool and dim inside and smelled like dill pickles and cheese and salami. Bread and rolls were piled on a shelf near the door and beneath the meat counter. Mops hung from the walls. Boxes were piled everywhere, leaving little room for people to stand. We stood in front of the candy counter and waited for Mr. Weiner, the proprietor. He came from behind the meat counter, a short, fat, balding man; he wore glasses with round, gold-rimmed lenses on his moon face. "Well, well." He wiped his hands on his white apron, leaving wide streaks of blood across his stomach. "Look who's here. The little Beales. And on a weekday, too. So what we heard must be true. You living here now?"

After he got as much news from us as he could, with Lonnie eyeing

James and me if we gave a civil answer, Lonnie said, "We want three long pretzels." He had my money, so he was doing the talking.

I rolled my eyes at him.

Mr. Weiner handed Lonnie the pretzels. "And what else?"

I thought of the Coke on the door. "A Coke." It was my dime, after all.

Lonnie scowled. "We only got thirteen cents and Cokes cost a nickel apiece."

Mr. Weiner winked. "For the new residents, perhaps we can drum up an extra Coke." He got them out from a cooler and opened them for us. "Nice and cold on such a hot day." Then he slid open the glass door on the cabinet and counted out six Tootsie Rolls. "And also two Tootsie Rolls to seal the bargain."

We thanked him elatedly and Lonnie handed him the thirteen cents and we turned to go.

"Just leave the bottles in the crate outside. And give my regards to your mama," said Mr. Weiner.

Outside again. The sun beat down on our heads; the heat smothered us.

We stood there and sweated and drank our Cokes and looked up into Union Avenue. Empty. The heat shimmering up from the black street in silver waves. Nothing in sight. No cats. No dogs. No cars. Nothing. No children outside to play with. We set the bottles in the crate and crossed the street and now back at Beechwood Avenue, we stopped. Instead of turning left and heading for home, Lonnie looked to his right.

"It sure looks cool down there."

Starting in the next block the trees formed a leafy tunnel of branches that swayed and beckoned. *Come, come, come,* they whispered.

"It sure is a long street," I said.

"A lonnnng street," said James.

With one mind we walked toward the tunnel, and soon we were in the cool green quiet. Down, down, we walked, silent, through the swaying arch until we finally reached the Hillsboro railroad station. We straggled up onto the platform and sank onto a bench.

I was worried. "Mama's gonna be wonderin where we are."

"I want to see a freight train," said James.

We waited. Finally one appeared. We watched it clackety-clack through the station as Lonnie read off the names. "New York Central. B and O. Lackawanna. Louisville and Nashville. Union Pacific."

"This whole country is covered by railroads, I bet," said James.

"I wish I could get on one of those trains and go all over the country," said Lonnie.

I stood up. "I'm goin."

"Go ahead," said Lonnie.

"You all better come on."

"We ain't ready yet."

I walked away. They jumped up and followed me. "Okay. But don't never come along with us anymore," said Lonnie.

All the way back up Beechwood Avenue I had to listen to him grouse about scaredy-cat big-mouth girls who didn't like a little adventure. "What we gonna do when we get back home? Sit in that ugly hot yard and listen to Aunt Louise if she's still there. And I don't feel like goin back until I think she's gone."

This last statement was enough to make me agree with them to walk completely around our block to see what was on the other side.

And we did.

Almost directly in back of our house, on Hillcrest Avenue, was the town hall, a little squatty white building that sat back on a manicured green lawn. A wide concrete walk led up to the front door. Legs apart, Lonnie crossed his arms and studied the building. Then, "Let's see what's inside."

I had no desire to go inside. I knew from conversations between my father and mother that the town hall was where my father reported for work every morning. I could see the spaces set aside for the trash trucks. One huge metal monster sat there waiting for the others.

But I followed Lonnie up to the building, up to the oak doors. We peeped through the windows. We could see a desk with an officer sitting behind it. When he saw us he came to the door, and, tall, young, smiling, asked us why we were there. Lonnie told him we wanted to see the station; he opened the door wider and let us in and escorted us around. When we told him our names he grinned. He knew our father. "Tell him you met Joe Donovan."

Lonnie and James wanted to see the jail. Daddy had been in the one up in Westville at least once, we knew, but we'd never seen one. It was a tiny cell with a cot and a striped pillow and a sink, dismal enough to make Lonnie swear off crime.

We ended our tour in the basement and saw the shop where toys were salvaged from the trash and repaired for delivery to poor children at Christmas. James saw a wagon and asked for it and I was so embarrassed I wanted to die. But Joe, that's what the policeman told us to call him, winked at James and said anything was possible. He then told us the trucks were due in soon and we could see our father.

I doubted that Daddy wanted us hanging around the place where he worked. He never mentioned his job to us, and after hearing Aunt Louise's assessment of the worth of a trashman that morning somehow I knew that he would be embarrassed if we saw him there. Lonnie and James had the same idea I did, I suppose. They didn't want to wait either. So we straggled back home.

Our mother had not even missed us. She and Aunt Louise were upstairs hanging curtains in the living room. "Well," said Aunt Louise after we huffed up the steps. "The wild bunch is back. Thought your mother told you not to go out the yard."

"It's hot out in that yard," said Lonnie. "We only went around the block."

"We went to the Jew store and Mr. Weiner gave us a Coke," said James.

"Must be gonna hail," said Aunt Louise.

"We went down and saw the freight train," James continued.

Aunt Louise fixed her eyes on Lonnie, then me, and said disapprovingly, "That sure was a long block."

"Well, the children have to have somethin to do," said Mama. She turned to me. "Did you play with any kids on Union Avenue?"

I shrugged. "We didn't see none."

"What makes you think those children are comin out in the hot sun to play?" said Aunt Louise. "You can't play in Union Avenue this time of year until late afternoon when the sun is almost ready to set."

Mama said we could go around there after dinner, but after dinner there were the dishes, and cleaning the kitchen, and my father made us wait until the following day.

The next day we met most of the kids on Union Avenue. Other children did live there, not just Lewises, as Lonnie had declared, but most of them were older boys in high school. The Lewises had no sisters. There was one other boy, Bumpsy, who was nine and fat and brown with a round face and a gap in his teeth. Lonnie became friendly with Malcolm (June) Lewis Junior. He was long and skinny with a head shaped like a football on a skinny neck. James became friendly with Bumpsy. And there was one girl. A cousin of the Lewises, my age, named Luetta Robey. In those first few seconds when I looked into her brown eyes, I knew that we would not be friends. We would play and fight and play, but we would not be friends. She was slightly taller than I, peanut butter brown, with a heart-shaped face and mouth that was pleasantly turned up at the corners, giving the lie to her eyes, which were looking at me hard from under a scowl. Her short hair was plaited in rows so that her scalp shone through like neat roads snaking through her head.

"You got your hair done in pickaninny plaits," said James.

Luetta sniffed. "These are French braids." She rolled her eyes and snorted like a bull ready to charge.

"James didn't mean nothin by what he said," said Lonnie. "Amy used to wear her hair like yours when it first fell out."

"My hair didn't look like that!" I said.

"Yes it did," said Lonnie. "Stop lyin."

"And you need to stop gettin upset, Luetta," said June Lewis. "You better make some friends because you ain't got none and this is the only other colored girl around near your age."

Luetta's lips went out, but in a few moments, after we eyed each other, she went and got her jump rope and we went down to a row of garages near the end of the block. There the concrete sidewalk was wide and smooth, perfect for drawing hopscotch squares or jumping rope. She tied one end of the rope to a handle on a garage door and we took turns turning and jumping. Later James and Bumpsy joined us and we played hopscotch.

In spite of myself I had fun that day and went home sweating and happy and back again in the evening to play with all the children: red rover, hide-and-seek, and red light until late in the cool night. By that time I thought that maybe I had misjudged Luetta. Maybe she would be fun to play with. And I went to bed looking forward to a summer of fun.

THE SECOND WEEK in August, Luetta and Bumpsy and all the Lewises—in fact, most of the children on Union Avenue—went down to the country for a few weeks, and Lonnie and James and I were left to fend for ourselves.

With no other children to play with, we reverted to our old habit of wandering. Little did we know of the trouble this would cause, for we were unaware that we were living among those humans most dangerous to independent, adventurous children—the idle, the pious, the righteous, those dutiful women one found in every small town at that time who were dedicated to the task of keeping order, which consisted mainly of keeping children in their place. We were unaware that we had to avoid Union Avenue. We knew that the street was guarded by three dragons—my aunt Leona on one corner, my aunt Louise in the middle, and on the opposite corner, across from the Jew store, in the spot most likely to cause me trouble, Miss Fanny Murray, a Sunday school teacher who wielded religion like a baseball bat. But we did not know that she and Aunt Leona made it a habit to sit on their porches most of the day and night and observe the goings-on of everyone who passed their corners.

So unaware, we would come through Union Avenue on our way home from a long day's play, dusty and sweaty from climbing trees and fences and wading in the creek, shoes tied together hanging over our shoulders, carryall bags filled with dandelions or berries for Mama's wine.

*Tch, tch, tch, little children ain't been home all day for a decent meal. Just running wild.* Those were the words whispered and carried on the winds of gossip.

Of course these whisperings did not sit too well with my father. One evening at dinner he came home through Union Avenue after we'd had a particularly long day. We had risen early that morning, made a few scrapple sandwiches, and taken off for the station and a blackberry patch we had stumbled upon in our travels. My mother had gone downtown on some kind of mysterious mission and was going to have a surprise for us in a few days, she'd told us, and warned us not to get into trouble.

We spent most of the day picking blackberries, watching trains and gathering tadpoles in the creek near the station. We must have been a sight, clothes stained, knees scraped, my hair loose on one side, we looked, as my mother later said, like country kids.

On our way home we dragged ourselves up Sycamore Street and started into Union Avenue; then, remembering how we looked, we decided to go home the long way and continued on up to Hillcrest. But as we passed her corner we caught the eye of Aunt Leona, who reported our condition to my father when he stopped by that day. When he got home from work that evening we got an earful at the dinner table. Of course, by then we were more presentable, but his sister's report led to a tug-of-war between him and my mother.

"How was they supposed to look," said Mama. "They been out pickin blackberries and runnin in the fields. They don't look any worse than we did when we was kids and out playin all day."

"Well, they ain't in the country now," said Daddy. "They're in a town, and they should keep their shoes on their feet."

"Amy was the only one who didn't have on no shoes," said Lonnie. "I told her to put them on before we started home."

"They hurt my feet," I muttered.

"Her shoes are too small," said Mama. "She need new ones. I was tryin to wait until school starts to get new ones."

Daddy's eyes went to my head. "And I guess you goin to wait for school to open before you see that her hair is properly combed? Leona said they came sneakin past Union Avenue and Amy's hair was a disgrace."

A dart pierced my chest. I ducked my head to hide the tears.

"It's too bad Leona ain't got nothin better to do. Perched on that sunporch of hers like a toad without a stool mindin everybody's business. And it wasn't nothin but one plait on Amy's head that came loose."

Daddy looked at me. "I can't understand why you can't plait your hair so it will stay, Amy."

"It always comes loose. Even when Mama plaits it."

Mama stared hard at Daddy. "Amy does all right with her hair. She has to learn. Boys get theirs cut off, so it looks neat all the time."

He returned her glare, but he made no comment. Just grunted and kept eating.

But Mama had been riled; she tossed her head. "If she took hair after me, she wouldn't have no trouble. It must be them Beale genes makin them plaits untwist when it ain't supposed to."

My father stopped chewing, looked at her through narrowed eyes, then away from her, and waved his hand for us to go outside.

Lonnie and James started throwing a ball against the fence. I sat in the shade near the door with my back against the house. I closed my eyes and drew my knees up and lowered my chin and folded my arms around my ears, trying to make myself small, trying to be a turtle, enclosing myself in a shell. Shielding myself against the words, the hard words that would follow. They would be at it again, batting words back and forth, sparring, slowly at first, but then soon it would get more intense and end up with my father walking out of the kitchen.

Again my father's voice, low. "Leatha, I'm not gonna sit here and listen to you run on about hair and—"

"No, but I guess I'm supposed to sit here and listen to you run on about your sister gettin upset over some hair. If she's so damned neat, why didn't she just call Amy and bring her up on the porch and comb her hair? Tie up the end herself? I'm sure she's used to workin with that kind of hair. Wouldn't be no problem for her. Instead she comes to you and runs your children down just because she's tryin to find fault with me."

"Find fault with you?" he echoed.

"I'm sure that's why she did it. I know if it had been *my* sister and she'd been dissatisfied with the kids, she'd have called them in and washed them if they was dirty and combed their hair if she thought it was messy. She sure wouldn't run to tell me about it. Or you neither."

"I don't know about that."

"That Leona ain't never liked me, but I don't care about that. You're her brother, and these children are part of her blood. And she need to act like it, instead of always findin fault with them. And if she need some children to watch, she need to get some of her own to take care of."

Silence. Then my father cleared his throat. "They need to stay in the yard till you come home from work."

"What do you expect them to do," said Mama. "Stay cooped up like animals in a pen?" Her voice sharpened. "You didn't mind if they went out of the yard up in Westville."

"I was there to watch them. And I saw to it they looked proper before they went out, too. And Amy's hair was always combed. Twice a day."

"And who was there to comb it?" said Mama, softly. "I was workin all day. And you sure didn't."

A barb referring to Miss Edie.

Another long silence, then my father's voice. "And I guess you waitin for school to start before the boys get a haircut, too? Well, tomorrow, I want them in that barber's chair." I heard him push his chair back. "And I'm goin around here now and tell Mr. Chauncey I'll see him at the end of the week."

Then the sound of pots being slammed around. "I got hold of Miss Minnie today, and she's said she'll come look after for me for a while. Then you won't have to worry about them wanderin around gettin on your sister's nerves."

The screen door opened and clapped shut. My father rushed past me and hurried down the driveway.

# SIX

Mr. Chauncey May's barbershop was a place for men, my father often said. It was not a place for young girls to sit around and listen to men talk. Therefore there was no reason for me to accompany Lonnie when he got a haircut. But it was a place where I wanted to be. A place where I imagined men sat around playing checkers, smoking, telling tales, teasing, laughing, slapping their knees as they relived old times and lied about new times. I was well acquainted with much of the talk that went on in there from Lonnie's tales when he returned almost baldheaded, reeking of bay rum and bursting with grown-up gossip and information pertinent to the colored community. "Negro teams got to have their own baseball league. Them white teams won't let them play. Man, they'd be crazy. The best players in baseball is in the Negro Leagues. Them white boys scared to let them on their teams. That Josh Gibson, he'd give 'em *all* a run for their money. He's the best I ever seen, and I been around a long time. Well, he ain't the only one. I ain't been around forever like you, Chauncey. Reverend Mickens up to his old tricks standin on the corner eyeballin them young girls. Eyeballs red as fire. Now leave the Rev alone. As long as that's the only ballin he's doin . . . Hee hee hee. Chauncey, you ain't a bit of good . . . B. O. Turner cooked a possum the other day. Man can cook a possum better'n anybody up here or down in Mason County, either. Seen that rascal George Tate down in North Philly last week drivin a big Packard with a pretty yallah gal all up next to him. The one he left Geneva for.

Funny how good a ugly man can look to a woman when he got a big car. Man, ain't no car in the world got that much magic."

That was the place I wanted to go.

So before my mother left for work that morning I begged her to let me go with Lonnie and James, but she must have been mindful of my father's interpretation of a young girl's place and so to avoid a confrontation refused to give her permission. At the breakfast table I regarded her with smoldering eyes, but to no avail. I was to wait at home while Lonnie and James got their hair cut. But as soon as she had left the house, I bribed Lonnie with two cents and before noon we all three were walking up the driveway to Mr. Chauncey's garage, long ago converted to Chauncey May's Barbershop and Poolroom.

An old man, bent at the shoulders, was sweeping the walk in front of the barbershop. We nodded a greeting and went inside. If I was looking for gossipers, I was disappointed. The place was empty except for Mr. Chauncey, who was sitting in a swivel chair reading the newspaper. He was a thin copper-colored man with a large mustache and a fringe of gray hair around the sides of his head. When the bell tinkled he rose and smiled and swept us in with a bow.

"Well, well, if it ain't the little Beales. Lonnie, and his little brother. And his sister. Amelia, isn't it? Named after your mother's sister. Oh, you prefer Amy. Well, that might be old-fashioned for a modern girl. Yes. And this is James. After your father's uncle James. Well, well. And he's to have a haircut today as well? Well, well." He ran his hand over James's head. "I know your mother don't want to see those curls cut off. But that's what we men got to do. Can't be runnin around lookin like girls now, can we, boys?" Wink, wink. He whisked a cloth from the back of the first swivel chair and held it out in the manner of a bullfighter. "Now, who's first? Let's do the big brother first so the little one can see that it don't hurt. And you two can sit over there and there and watch."

He pointed to the chairs lined up against the wall, but I wanted to sit in a swivel chair. Mr. Chauncey obliged with a grin that exposed a gap in his teeth on the left side of his smile. "I guess a girl is entitled to a ride in a chair. First time for you, honey?" I nodded and as he started on Lonnie I looked around.

On the wall opposite me were pictures of men and women modeling different styles of haircuts. In the center was a large picture of Joe Louis, the heavyweight champion of the world, his body bent forward, knees bent, boxing gloves raised to guard his face. Every colored kid in America knew about Joe Louis. His name was part of the conversation of every colored family; we huddled around the radio and cheered him on during each fight. "Knocked him out! You hear that! Knocked him out!" There were no other pictures; at the end of this wall was a door to the poolroom. I swiveled to my left and read a sign near the door. YOU HAVE TO PAY TODAY SO I CAN EAT TODAY.

I swiveled completely around to another long wall. A mirror extended the width and halfway down from the ceiling to end at a row of cabinets. On top of these rested the tools of the trade: hand mirrors, scissors, brushes, combs, boxes of powder, and bottles and jars from which those mysterious man smells emanated.

Mr. Chauncey's eye caught mine in the mirror. "You look just like Amelia, too. You never knew her. Died a while ago, now."

I didn't know much about her. My mother never mentioned her when she told us her stories about her childhood in the country. She seemed to have close ties only to Aunt Louise and a few of her brothers.

Lonnie's quick frown sent me a message in the mirror. Don't do any talkin, blabbermouth.

Mr. Chauncey caught it. But he pressed on. "How's your father?" Snip, snip.

"Fine," said Lonnie.

"And your mother?"

"Fine," said Lonnie.

"She told me she was comin by here to get her hair bobbed." Snip, snip.

"What's bobbed?" I said, avoiding Lonnie's gaze.

"Cut." Mr. Chauncey pointed to a picture of a woman. "Like one of the ladies up there. She used to get it cut once a year when she first come up from the country."

One of the ladies was in profile. Her hair was short in the back and longer in front and a piece of hair curled on her cheek. She looked like Miss Edie. "Like number one?" I said.

Mr. Chauncey nodded. "Most of the ladies like that one."

I didn't think I'd like it if Mama cut her hair. It was soft and long with reddish-brown ripples. Sometimes she let me brush it, but she was tender-headed and no matter how easy I tried to brush it she would wince.

Everything was quiet except for the snipping of the scissors that Mr. Chauncey's long fingers worked quickly across Lonnie's hair. Little burrs dropped to his shoulders and rolled down the cloth and dropped to the floor.

I sat back and swung around until I became dizzy. I heard the door open. I stopped and sat up. Two men, one tall and thin, one short and thin, had entered the shop. Maybe now, now, I would hear some man talk.

"Hey, Chauncey, how's things?" said the tall one.

"Can't complain," said Mr. Chauncey, still snipping.

The man pulled money from his pocket and counted it. "Guess I'll play a little game of pool. Jimbo in there?"

"Last time I looked he was."

He turned to go, then stopped. "What was it yesterday?"

"Don't nobody write no numbers in here. You see any signs saying get the number here?"

"Thought you might'a heard."

"Don't pass on no information like that."

The short man grinned and rubbed his hand across his nose. "Told you, man."

"I'd have every Negro in Hillsboro and every place around stoppin in here to find out the number. Hangin out, gettin on my nerves. I run a legitimate business here. And talk legitimate talk. Don't have no funny stuff in here, no sir."

"Gotcha." They went into the poolroom.

The door to the shop opened again, and a gray head appeared. "Mr. Chauncey, can you come out here a minute? I'm ready to lay this walk."

Mr. Chauncey turned, scissors stabbing the air. "Why can't you ask Sadie? You see I'm busy."

"Listen, last time I did what your wife said and you cussed me out. Now you comin or not? Or else I can go home now and come back tomorrow, you know."

Muttering, Mr. Chauncey hooked his scissors at his waist and strode across the floor. The screen door banged. Lonnie and James and I sat in the silence, waiting.

*Klick.*

James looked at me, big eyed. "What's that?"

Just as mystified, I shrugged.

It came from the poolroom, Lonnie informed us. The door had drifted open. We heard voices and the sound of the balls on the pool table. *Klick. Klick.* Voices. *Klick.* Then no sound. Ears open, I leaned back and stared at the ceiling and twirled around. Looked like I wasn't going to hear anything that day.

Now there were words louder and clearer. "... Yeah ... I heard about that ... Edie, right?"

"Hard to believe, ain't it?" *Klick.*

"Yeah, man ..." *Klick klick.* "Well, you know Jack Beale when he get a drink in him. Ain't no stoppin him."

I stopped twirling.

"I know him when he *ain't* got a drink in him, too."

*Klick.* "... in that little space got to be nuts."

In the mirror Lonnie's face was expressionless.

"I was wonderin why he moved ... he had a good thing goin on up there ... Edie and Arleatha ... good-lookin women."

"So was her sister Amelia. Used to go with her first."

"That black rascal." *Klick.* "He likes them yallah women."

"Now down here collectin trash." *Klick.* "Definitely not Jack's style." *Klick.* "I heard she gave him a year to shape up."

"Heh, heh, heh." *Klick.* "I'll give that nigger six months ..."

"Nah." *Klick.* "I'll give him a year. Won't cost me nothin."

We were saved from hearing anything else. Mr. Chauncey came in and heard the laughter from the poolroom and stepped over to the door and shut it tight.

"Got to keep that door shut when the ladies are present," he said, shaking his head and laughing. "Sometimes we get a little carried away with our language."

Had he heard anything? If so, his face didn't show it. "Sorry about that little delay." He returned to Lonnie and continued cutting his hair.

When he finished Lonnie slid from the chair and pushed the money for the haircuts into my hand.

"Wait a minute, son," said Mr. Chauncey. "What about your little brother here? Isn't he going to get his hair cut?"

"Amy's gonna wait for him. I gotta go." He turned and left.

Mr. Chauncey was puzzled. "You don't think he was mad about me takin time out from cuttin his hair?"

I shook my head. Even if he had been he wouldn't have dared offend Mr. Chauncey. I guessed that what the men said in the poolroom upset him so much he didn't care what happened to him if he left. James, who, as usual, was unaware of what was going on, climbed up gleefully into the chair, ready for his haircut. I stayed in my chair and swiveled miserably and wished I hadn't heard anything.

Whatever Lonnie thought about that conversation, he did not mention it that day. When James and I got home he acted as if nothing had happened. He was sitting against the fence drawing pictures from a Superman comic book. He did laugh when he saw James, as I had almost done when Mr. Chauncey whipped the cover cloth from around him. His hair was cropped close to his head, talcum powder was all around his neck and ears, which now stuck out prominently from his head. "Cut it kind of close, but your father wants it to last until school opens. It'll grow back in a week." James's eyes, which had seemed bigger in his small face, looked sorrowfully up at me, and I had merely smiled and agreed with Mr. Chauncey, and we stopped by the Jew store for a Tootsie Roll to ease his embarrassment. Tears came to Mama's eyes when she saw that James's curls were gone. She pulled him to her. "Mama's babies are all big children now. Everybody's goin to school. No more babies."

School. That day would be here soon. Mama wanted it to come soon so she could go to work regularly. She had been doing day's work once or twice a week since we'd left Westville, but it seemed that every time she went and left us on our own, we got into trouble, so now, she told us, we were going to have a woman named Miss Minnie live with us after school started, and she would come by the following week to meet us.

We were very curious about this woman who was going to stay with us and watch us and get in our way and report our every action to our father. Our mother tried to calm our fears. Miss Minnie was an old woman who needed a place to stay for a while; her husband had died and she was alone, except for her sister Eula in Philadelphia. Our father had known her when he was a child. Any objections we may have expressed to our mother we did not dare to bring up to our father, who at the table that evening reiterated what our mother had said. This woman, Miss Mineola Collins, who was going to take care of us, used to take care of him sometimes when his mother was away. Now she was old and needed help and we could use some help, too. And he looked each of us in the eye. There was to be no disrespect of any kind. It was only for five days a week, for Miss Collins would be with her sister on weekends.

We sat, heads lowered. Life was going to be hell.

The thought of Miss Collins flew from my mind at my mother's next statement: The following day we were going up to the school to register. The mention of school brought back Aunt Louise's dour prediction of being put back, and I certainly did not look forward to going there the next morning. Lonnie, even though I had not told him what Aunt Louise had said, still had his own premonition about repeating sixth grade, and when he and James and I went up to listen to the radio after dinner, he sat morosely on the sofa. "You wait. First thing's gonna happen when we get there," he muttered. "They gonna put us back. Just like they did Freddy Jenkins."

THE FOLLOWING MORNING we walked alongside of our mother to the school, listening carefully as she showed us the way to take. Down Beechwood, around through Union Avenue to the athletic field, across the field past the high school, then across the street to the elementary school. The old one had burned ten years before; this one was a modern one-story red-brick building with a white columned portico at the entrance, much different from the school we came from, a white clapboard building two stories high.

We followed the concrete walk to the oak doors. They stood open. Inside was a large foyer; an arrow on a sign facing us pointed to the office. We followed it to a small room with a counter; behind it a woman was at a desk typing. A long bench was by the door. My mother nodded for us to sit down and went up to the counter. After a moment the woman came to the counter and smiled at us and said just a moment, then she smiled at my mother and said, "May I help you?" and my mother said she was there to register her children. And the woman told her if she wanted to register her children she had to bring them with her so they could be tested. "Unless it's a child just going to kindergarten."

My mother's back stiffens. Her voice rises indignantly. Whose children do you think they are over there? she says, and the woman's face turns red and her hands flutter and she starts apologizing and saying she'll get the principal, Miss Duckett, and she rushes to a door near the end of the room . . .

We were used to the woman's reaction. To her my mother looked white. We looked like nothing but the colored children that we were, especially more so having spent the summer in the hot sun.

"These white people get on my nerves," said Mama. "She could see you all sitting there. Who did she think you came with?"

"Not with you," said Lonnie. Usually he laughed whenever we were in that situation. But not today. He just sat and scowled.

The woman was back, followed by a large woman who swirled toward us. Miss Duckett, the principal, was a tall, big-bosomed woman shaped like a capital P. She wore a flowered dress and gold-rimmed glasses. Her light brown hair was swept up away from her face. She reached the counter and her eyes pounced on us, then Mama, then on us, then back on Mama again. The children's names? she asked. Their ages? Their grades?

She was speaking to us, but Mama interrupted and gave her the information and then handed her our report cards.

Without even looking at them, Miss Duckett said James was to enter first grade; since he was new there was no problem. However, Lonnie and I were to stay in the same grade. Oh, I was sick when I heard that. Sick enough to faint. Lonnie, too, looked as if he would pass out.

Then Mama spoke up. "Is this because they went to a colored school?"

Miss Duckett turned red. "Not at all. But we've found that when we have children who enter our school from Westville, they have trouble keeping up."

"Well, my children ain't gonna have any trouble keepin up," said Mama, red as Miss Duckett. "You didn't even look at their report cards."

Others had come from Westville with high grades, but still they had trouble, said Miss Duckett. Then they failed to pass at the end of the year. "The work here is usually harder."

"Well, ain't there some kind of test for children who come from other schools? Suppose they came from Woodlynne? Would you put them back then?"

"The work at Woodlynne is comparable to that we do here."

"Well, before she knew these were my children here, the lady at the desk told me I had to bring them with me so they could be tested. Now you tell me they can't be tested. Well, my children went to Woodlynne before they went to Westville. That must count for somethin." Mama was adamant. "I want them to have a test."

Miss Duckett, now a deeper red, said nothing else. She twirled around and said to the woman, "Miss Garvin, take care of this, please." Then she swirled back into her office.

"That is what you said, ain't it?" said Mama to Miss Garvin.

Miss Garvin, now a pale pink, nodded and smiled and explained to Mama that she could test Lonnie and me that morning and we could wait for the results, or we could come back the next morning.

"They'll take it now and wait," said Mama.

After she and James left Miss Garvin took us to a long table near her desk, gave us two pencils and the test, and after explaining, left us to our work.

The tests were in reading and arithmetic. Miss Duckett came out twice to see how we were progressing, but she merely looked, said nothing. When we were finished, she took the test into her office, marked it, and called Miss Garvin, who returned to us with an envelope in her hand for our mother. She did not smile, so I presumed the news was bad and Lonnie and I left the building with our heads down. Luetta would be ahead of me, I thought. She was going to fifth grade. She would never stop teasing me. Never.

Out on the sidewalk, Lonnie turned the envelope over. It was sealed. He looked at me, then opened it. When he saw my look, he defended himself. "It's about us, ain't it? Mama won't care if we read it. It ain't a secret." He slipped the letter from the envelope. While he read it his face confirmed my fears. We were to repeat the grade.

"Are we put back?" I whispered.

Lonnie mumbled a reply, but his voice was so low I could not make out what he said. His mouth began to twist from trying to hold back from crying, and I knew something awful had occurred because Lonnie never cried. I was afraid to ask him again: I reached out and touched his arm in sympathy and he threw my hand off. "Aw, get away from me, girl."

He started walking down Hillcrest Avenue, away from home, and I followed him slowly. He could not hold back his sobs. His shoulders hunched up and he began eeeehing, his chest heaving as if he had the hiccups.

Worried, I asked him if we should go home.

He heaved and said, words garbled, "If you want to come with me, just shut your big mouth."

Silently I kept walking behind him, down down down to the railroad station, up the steps to the platform, down the steps through the underpass to the park on the other side, to sit on the grass near the creek. By then Lonnie had stopped crying. He stared straight ahead, not speaking. His face was streaked where he'd wiped the tears away. I stretched on my stomach and looked over at the station. I wondered what the letter said, but I was afraid to ask if I could see it. I gazed silently over at the station. Moments passed. A long streamliner clackety-clacked by. Then silence, so quiet I could hear the sound of water rippling softly over the rocks in the creek below.

Lonnie slumped forward, not moving, not speaking, just staring. Finally he spoke. "That old sloop-jawed, funky wench."

I said nothing for fear he might stop talking again. He started jerking out grass and throwing it, jerking and throwing, jerking and throwing.

Softly I ventured a question. "Because she put us back?"

This time when I said put *us* back, Lonnie didn't nod. His eyes filled with tears again. They spilled over and rolled down his face. He made no effort to wipe his face. I looked away, not talking, waiting for him to continue.

Then he blurted, "She didn't put *you* back." His face twisted.

My heart jumped up. I wasn't put back! I wanted to roll on the grass and laugh with joy, but I kept still and made every effort to keep a poker face so Lonnie wouldn't feel worse.

"Maybe it's like Aunt Louise said," I told him. I repeated what she had said in the kitchen that day about the segregated school in Westville and kids getting dumber if they went to school up there. I refrained from passing on her comments about his teacher, Miss Hobbes.

Lonnie wiped his face with his sleeve. "Aunt Louise don't know everything. You went to school there and you passed, didn't you? And if Mama hadn't made that old Miss Duckett give us a test, she would'a put you back, too. I told Mama they was gonna treat us mean. I told her we shouldn't move...." The tears slid down again, leaving big brown spots on his pants. "Now Aunt Louise will tell everybody I got put back just like she said, and sayin you're smarter than me and all that stuff ... and you will, too."

"No, I won't, Lonnie. Honest I won't."

"All the kids on Union Avenue will call me dumb...." Then he burst into sobs again. He turned his back to me and hunched over trying to hold them back but he couldn't and he heaved and heaved and between them he kept talking, saying things so muffled I could hardly understand him. "I got good marks on my report card. So did you. We passed and we should've been put in our right grade and if we couldn't do the work then they should keep us back. These white people just prejudiced, that's all ... and Daddy could go up there but he's scared of white people just like Aunt Louise said. All he wants to do is look big drinkin and fuckin and getting talked about and havin everybody laugh about us and Mama ... tryin to look big ... big for hisself but not for us ..."

He was beginning to frighten me. Lonnie never cursed. And this crying storm seemed as if it would break him apart. And I was helpless as the words poured out of him and the things he was saying I knew he had kept inside because they hurt, not because he hadn't wanted to talk about them with me. The events at the outhouse and in the barbershop had festered in a sac inside of him and the tension of today's insult had been too much. The sac, unable to resist the pressure, had burst, erupted. On the grass that day I saw the fragile body of a young boy twisting in pain. And I was not to see it again.

Finally he stopped crying and sat up and gave one final hiccup. He wiped his face with his shirttail, his sleeves were soaked and his eyes and lips were swollen as if from a thousand bee stings. He did not look at me, merely stood up and said, "Come on."

We went back through the underpass, and the white envelope was sticking out of his back pocket and when we reached the steps to go up I found the nerve to ask what the letter said.

He didn't turn, just kept going up, and said, "It just says you're in the fifth grade and I'm in the sixth and if Mama wants to discuss it to go back up to the school and see Miss Duckett."

"Maybe she will," I said.

Lonnie stopped and turned. "Daddy won't let her. Even if she wants to. You wait and see." His voice wobbled. "You wait and see." He kept on up. At the top he stopped, and turned and faced me. "When school starts and they tell us to salute the flag, you know what I'm gonna do?"

"What?"

"At the end I'm gonna say, 'with liberty and justice for all *white* people.'" He started walking again. "I am. You wait and see. Because that's what they mean when they say 'for all.' They don't mean for everybody. So I'm'a say 'for all white people.'"

"Out loud?"

"Yep."

"What if somebody hears you?"

"I don't care." He was walking faster. "And all them Superman comic books. I'm gonna throw them away. Talkin about some truth, justice, and the American way. Well, I found out what that is. And I ain't gonna buy them anymore."

His comic books. I hurried along behind him, trying to keep up. Saluting the flag and saying that at the end about white people, that was one thing, but throwing away his Superman comics. I couldn't bring myself to believe he would do that.

When we got home he threw the letter from Miss Duckett on the kitchen table and pounded up the steps. I sank into a chair, head down, while my mother, startled, picked up the letter. When she finished reading it, she pursed her lips, put the letter in her apron pocket. "It's good that you passed, Amy," she said quietly and went upstairs after Lonnie and I heard more crying, muffled, anguished; then at last it subsided and my mother came back down. She had been crying and wiped her eyes with her apron. "Poor child. Lord, Lord, Lord. Poor child." We sat quietly, staring at nothing for a while. Then she got up to start dinner.

At the dinner table Lonnie's eyes were still swollen, and my father asked him what was wrong, but Lonnie hung his head over his plate and did not answer. My mother told him about the letter, and my father pushed a forkful of greens into his mouth and slid them around to the side and said that was too bad. "You took the test and you didn't pass. It's a good thing you found out early that you need help in school."

"The letter said we could go up to the school and discuss it," said Mama. "And that Miss Duckett never did look at his report card. And he got good marks up in Westville."

My father kept eating. "Discuss what, Arleatha? The boy failed the test. You can't change that. And what's the use of havin good marks if they don't pay off? If he got good marks in readin and arithmetic why didn't he pass the test?" He nodded toward me. "Amy here did."

Lonnie looked so miserable I wished I had failed.

My father pointed his fork at Lonnie. "All you have to do is make sure it don't happen again. And lift that head up. After all, bein left down ain't the worst thing in the world. Not by a long shot."

He knew that from experience. But it was an experience he did not share with us at the table that evening. Or anytime soon. In fact, not until that day at my table when he was drinking that Wild Turkey.

*I stopped goin to school when I was about thirteen. You can't learn livin from place to place, stayin home off and on like I did, to take care of Granny. Mama didn't have no work, and her and me went to Brooklyn, New York, and stayed with my uncle in a big house. Up there my uncle made me go to school again. I learned more in Brooklyn in school than in any place. We had this white teacher, she had closets with trunks full of clothes. If you came to school dirty, she would write a note home. I'll never forget her name. Miss Derke. D-E-R-K-E. I think that's how you spell it. If she got no answer to her note, she'd send the monitor to your house. No nonsense in her class. No sittin up gigglin, no spitball throwin; when you read, stand up straight, perfect. If you got a star on your work, and she didn't give it to you if you didn't earn it, you'd go to the armory and listen to the marine band and the orchestra. That's where I learned to love music. The big bands. She was a fine teacher. And good. I enjoyed it there.*

*"When I was about thirteen I came back to Hillsboro for good. That's when I quit school for good, too. I had got so big I was ashamed to be in the seventh grade. I was in the eighth in Brooklyn, but they put me back in the seventh. But I was too big. You reach a point of shame, you know. So I quit. I was pretty good on reading but the main thing was fractions and there was nobody to help me like there was in New York. Leona had a little job and didn't have*

*time. There's a lot of difference when you don't have nobody to help you. And you feel the shame."*

❧

IF ONLY HE HAD told Lonnie that night. Would it have made a difference? If only he had laid his hand on Lonnie's and explained that he had felt the same kind of shame. Or had the shame been so deeply embedded, the pain still so great then, that he would have cried in front of his son as he did that afternoon on my porch when he told me that story over a glass of Wild Turkey.

But even if a man is willing to share his embarrassment, he cannot drink a glass of whiskey with a twelve-year-old boy and blubber and reveal his secrets and not expect to feel his contempt. Oh, that Wild Turkey can bring you to your knees if you drink too much of it. And my father always did.

As my father told Lonnie, it was not the worst thing in the world to repeat a grade, but it was like living in purgatory for James and me. It seemed that from that day on Lonnie had to be better than me in every other way because I had passed. I could understand that. But we were all subjected to his bossy behavior. "Put them dishes in the sink right now, Amy. You too, James. You'd better find all my marbles, boy, else I'm'a hurt you. Quit lookin over my shoulder, girl. Breathin down my neck. Make me sick." He sassed Mama, telling her one day, when she asked him to go to the store, that he wasn't any errand boy, to send me or James. Aunt Louise, who happened to be in the shed, rushed into the kitchen with her hand raised and told him she'd smack the black off him if she ever heard him talk to his mother like that again and he ran outside. He was just upset, Mama told her, and explained why, and Aunt Louise sniffed and said what could anybody expect; he was his father's son.

Lonnie even carried his air of bitterness around on Union Avenue. The following week Luetta and Bumpsy and June Lewis returned from their vacation in Virginia, sun-blackened and lively, and had to suffer Lonnie's barbs. "Look at this bunch of darkies! You all look like you been dipped in india ink." This started a verbal war, and the next few days we were chasing each other with rocks and sticks and slinging forbidden words at each other. "Niggers! Nappy heads! Blackies!" The war ended abruptly when Lonnie, apparently tiring of it all, stopped running from the Union Avenue gang at the end of the street, turned, and stood legs apart, arms folded, and declared he wanted a truce. Everyone agreed. And then, inexplicably, Lonnie turned that gang on me. With a sly grin, he informed them all if they got mad again, especially at me, they could call me "red, red, nappy head" if they wanted to. He wouldn't object. "She gets real mad if you call her that," he said, looking directly at Luetta.

She promptly mouthed the words at me, then yelled them aloud. "Red, red, nappy head!"

In a rage I ran around the corner, stopped, and turned. "I'm'a tell my father on you, too!"

"Go ahead! I don't care! Red nappy head! And after you do tell, just remember not to come around here to play!"

They fell on their knees laughing. I turned and ran, gritty-eyed, blinking quickly to hold back the tears. My life wouldn't be worth living if that old Luetta could see me cry. And that old Lonnie, I was glad he got left back. Old bastard.

I went into the kitchen and sat down. No one was home. My mother had gone to Philadelphia early that morning. She'd been in a hurry, had washed the dishes and left the pots for me to wash. Of course I had not done it yet. Since we had no hot running water, I had to heat it on the stove, and Lonnie and James had refused to wait for me. "Who's gonna wait for that old water to get hot?" They had run out and I ran out behind them. And now I eyed the cast-iron frying pan with its layer of bacon grease on the bottom and a steel pot with oatmeal encrusting the rim and a tall grizzled porcelain coffee pot with the grounds still inside. I threw myself down at the table and rested my chin in my hand and sulked. There was nothing I hated worse than washing pots.

I sat a moment brooding about Luetta, still stinging from her insult. Red nappy head. Oh, I hated my hair. The kinkiness of it. The redness of it. The snide, thoughtless comments from Lonnie or Aunt Louise ... mph, mph mph ... a redhead ... a nappy redhead ... I blinked quickly. They'd be sorry they teased me if I cut it off. But the thought left my head as soon as it entered. I'd probably get a whipping.

With a sigh, I got up and went to the stove, looked into the coffee pot. Some was left over. I stared at the black liquid in the pot. And from that place in our hearts where we store barbs and stones flung from careless slings, Aunt Louise's words rose up in a mist and made their way to my brain. *Strong black coffee. Need to dye that stuff with some coffee. Coffee.* I leaped into action, getting a bowl from the closet, a big bowl, big enough to dip my head in. I poured the coffee into it. It was strong all right. Black as coal.

Suspecting I'd be caught in the kitchen (Lonnie and James were always dashing through for a toilet break) I grabbed a cup and put it in the bowl with the coffee and slowly made my way up to my bedroom and set the bowl on a table near my window. I unbraided my hair and ooching and ouching and cursing I combed it to the top of my head, leaned over the bowl, and immersed my head in the coffee.

For a long time I worked at it, lifting my head to pour cup after cup of coffee over my hair or holding my head in the bowl breathing in the acrid fumes until finally the hairs in my nostrils dried and crackled like grass in the blazing sun and I dashed into the bathroom to splash cold water over my face. I inspected my hair in the mirror over the sink. Was it darker? It seemed so and should be, if the white towel in my hand, stained almost black, was any testament. I was ready to go back to the bowl for a final dip when I heard a sound . . . the kitchen door slamming . . . voices . . .

I sneaked into the living room and leaned over the banister, listening. Mama. And somebody was with her. I dashed back into my bedroom and slid the bowl, the towel, the cup under my bed, then back to the bathroom, stuck my head under the spigot in the tub to wash the coffee smell from my hair.

I could hear my mother coming up the stairs. "Whooooeeeee! Who's home?"

She had to hear the water running. I turned off the tap and threw another towel around my head and ran to the stairwell. "Me! I'm washin my hair!"

There she stood, looking up at me, wondering. "Washin your hair! It must be gonna hail!" She backed down the narrow steps. "Come down here. I want you to meet somebody."

An old lady was sitting at the kitchen table. Miss Mineola Collins, my mother explained. The woman who was to take care of us while my mother worked. The woman who was to watch us and keep us out of trouble.

I wanted to come to an understanding with this Miss Mineola so she would understand her role in my life, so I said, "James might need somebody to watch him. Me and Lonnie don't need anybody to watch us."

All children needed someone at home with them, countered my mother. Think of all the times the newspapers told about children falling out of windows or smothering in old iceboxes or setting the house on fire because no one was around to watch them.

Miss Mineola stood up and came around the table to meet me, and I carefully examined this person who was supposed to stop us from killing ourselves. She was bent at the shoulders, and as wrinkled as if she had been soaking in a tub of water for at least three days. White whiskers stuck out from her chin, and her brown scalp shone through the sparse white strands of hair combed back on her head. A blue voile dress with white polka dots reached down almost to her ankles, and I could see tan cotton stockings and black shoes with hooks and eyes, and strings that wound up and clasped the leather around her ankles. Her hands, crossed at her waist, were long and thin and bony with veins on the back like knotted brown vines. And she shook and shook and shook as if she had a permanent chill.

"Say hello to Miss Minnie," said Mama. "Miss Minnie, this is Amy."

I mumbled a greeting and shook Miss Minnie's hand and while Mama poured her a cup of tea James came in and Mama told her his name, and repeated to us both what my father had already told us a few days before, that we were to be good and not worry Miss Minnie.

"Who's gonna cook our dinner?" said James.

"Miss Minnie," said Mama.

I didn't know about that. From the way the teacup was shaking in

Miss Minnie's hand it didn't seem as if she'd be able to lift Mama's heavy iron pots to cook anything at all.

James informed us now that he had only come home to go to the bathroom and he ran upstairs, and Mama, who had been pleasant and smiling up to that point, now surveyed the pots on the stove. "Amy, I thought I told you to wash those pots. Then I bring a stranger home, and they still sittin on the stove and instead of washin them you upstairs washin your hair."

"I was just gettin ready to wash them when you came in."

"Why couldn't you wash your hair after you washed the pots, I'd like to know. And why are you washin your hair anyway? You ain't never washed it before. I declare, you children are enough to worry somebody to death."

"Now, Mrs. Beale," said Miss Minnie, in a surprisingly firm voice, soft, but not squeaky or weak as I had expected from someone so frail, "girls her age are just beginning to try things themselves. She was probably out there playing and got dirt in her hair. It's mighty hard to comb hair with dirt in it."

"Well, I guess I should be glad she's gettin to that age then," said Mama. "I been prayin for the day she could tackle that head herself." She frowned. "Well, let me get these pots done. When I came in here this kitchen smelled just like coffee. And I found the grounds in the sink. And you know don't nothin draw roaches like coffee grounds. Must be that strong smell."

I backed out of the kitchen and dashed back upstairs.

Lonnie met Miss Minnie later that afternoon, but he was surprisingly civil to her. Nodded and smiled and told her he was glad she was there to take care of his little brother and sister. I attributed his pleasantness to the warning my father had given us at the table that day. And my conclusion was reinforced that night at the dinner table when we all sat around the table and my father reiterated his statement. Miss Minnie was a guest. A welcome guest. He wanted to hear no complaints, and his hard look at each of us nailed the words in.

THE NEXT DAY was Friday, a hot day, but still the kind of day for playing outside. It was early afternoon and I was sitting on the stoop at the kitchen door, chin in my hand, angry because Lonnie and James had managed to sneak off without me. Mama and Miss Minnie were sitting in the shadow of the house to keep cool, sitting and talking as if Miss Minnie had been with us for a hundred years. Miss Minnie had put up a card table covered with a white cloth with napkins on top, along with a pitcher of iced tea, long spoons I had not been aware that my mother had, the sugar bowl, and slices of lemon on a saucer. I squinted over at her. She sure was a finicky woman.

"Do you want some iced tea, Amy?" asked Miss Minnie in her soft little voice.

"No." I kicked my foot against the step.

"Amy," said Mama, throwing me a look, "go over to the fence and pull me some mint. It's good in tea."

Miss Minnie's hand went against her chest. "Lord, Mrs. Beale, how you grow anything in this yard? All these rocks."

"I didn't grow it," said Mama. "It was here when I come."

The mint was growing in little green bunches along with some weeds. I pulled a few pieces and smelled it to make sure it was mint, then pulled more and went back over to Mama and gave her the mint and returned to my seat on the stoop.

"My mama told me that mint can grow just about anywhere there's some dirt," Mama was saying. "And that's good dirt over there by that fence." She pulled a few leaves from the stem and dropped them in her tea and stirred them around.

"Surely you're gonna wash it before you put it in your tea?"

"Shuh," said Mama, sipping her tea. "Take all the mintiness away. A little dirt never hurt nobody."

"Well, I have to wash mine," said Miss Minnie, drawing her mouth in primly. She picked up the mint. "You don't know if a cat or a dog been over at that fence."

Sure was a finicky woman.

She pushed past me into the kitchen, and in a few moments she was back talking again. She and Mama talking and drinking tea. Talk, talk, talk. I heaved a sigh.

Mama looked over at me. "Here, Amy." She reached into her apron pocket. "Go around to the Jew store and get me a loaf of bread and two yeast cakes. And you can take a nickel and get a soda. And tell that man to put my food in a bag." She handed me a quarter.

I bent down to put the coin in my shoe and flew out of the yard to Beechwood Avenue. As I turned the corner onto Maple Street, I stopped. A small group of white people was standing in front of one of the small row houses. When I saw them I crossed to the other side of the street. The crowd was mostly women and children, the women scowling and muttering to each other, the children sitting on their tricycles or on the wall in front of the house.

I walked by slowly and looked over at the angry crowd, and just as I got to the corner of Union Avenue, a colored man and woman stepped out of the house onto the little porch. A white man was behind them. The people on the sidewalk parted and let the colored people through without saying a word, but one of the men took the white man by the arm, and then a woman joined in and then the whole crowd began talking loudly and waving their arms.

Something ugly was happening, I knew, and instead of going into the Jew store or back past the crowd, I dashed by the store and ran up Maple Street to Hillcrest Avenue and took the long way home. A moment later I ran puffing through the back alley into the yard where my mother and Miss Minnie were still sitting.

"Mama—" I gasped for breath.

"Amy!" My mother jumped up, her eyes big. "What is the matter with you?"

"Nothin!" Panting, my hand against my chest.

"What you runnin like that for?"

"In all this heat, too, child," said Miss Minnie. "You gonna fall out running in all this heat!"

"Where's the bread?" said Mama. "Now don't tell me you lost the money—"

"No!" Another gasp and I fell into a chair. "There's a big crowd of white people standin around on Maple Street and they were watchin these colored people that came out of one of those houses across from Miss Fanny Murray's!"

My mother sat back down and settled herself. "Shuh. Is *that* all. Ain't nobody but that old Joe Davis round there with his simple self. Everybody know *that* was gonna start some trouble."

"Yes, indeedy," said Miss Minnie. She too sat back and began fanning herself with a folded-up newspaper.

"Louise told Ruby Davis not to go lookin at that house," said Mama. "There's a perfectly good house right there on the corner of Union Avenue right across from Leona that she can get. Only has two bedrooms else we'd'a got it. And it won't start no trouble and nearer to his job at the high school, too. All Joe Davis would have to do is step out his back door and walk across the field to the school. But that fool always did want to be white. Maybe he think livin next to some white folks will rub off on him." She sniffed and poured more tea.

"Well, I'm surprised at Ruby," said Miss Minnie, fanning.

"I don't know what they thinkin about," said my mother, stirring her tea. "Must be tryin to start a riot. They know those poor white trash on Maple Street don't want no colored people livin there. Or Jews neither. They give poor Mr. Weiner a hard time when he tried to move in a house across the street from his store. They don't even want no Eyetalians. I remember when Mr. Tivoli tried to get a house in that same block not even two years ago. Wanted to get a house near his shoe shop. Called him all kinds of wops and dagos. And him Catholic like they are. Hmph. Poor Irish trash ain't even off the boat good and tellin people where they can live ..." She looked over at me sitting there listening. "Go get that bread and them yeast cakes, Amy."

I got up and headed for the alley at the back of the house.

"Why are you goin that way?" said Mama. "You go the front way. Down Beechwood. That's the shortest way."

"I don't want to go back around there and walk past those people. They're mad."

"Listen here," said Mama. "Them poor trash might think they can tell me where I can live, but they damn sure ain't gonna tell me what street I can walk on. I said go back there and get that bread. Down Beechwood and up Maple like you always do."

"Ain't nothing gonna happen to you, child," said Miss Minnie in her soft little voice. "Go ahead and get the bread for your mother."

And nothing did happen. When I turned the corner, everyone had disappeared. The hot sun was shining on an empty street.

※

A FEW DAYS LATER I had the opportunity to see the Davises again. I was in the kitchen with Miss Minnie, fussing about Luetta. She and Bumpsy Lewis had just chased me home and one of my plaits had come undone and Miss Minnie was braiding it again.

"It's bad to live someplace where there's only one girl to play with," I complained. "Then when she gets mad at you, you don't have anybody to play with."

"Child, you've got to stop running in this heat. And when they chase you, don't you call them those names I heard you calling them when you ran up into the yard."

"They call me names!"

Miss Minnie shook her head. "Two wrongs have never made a right. 'Sticks and stones—' "

" '—may break your bones but names will never hurt you.' I know. That Bumpsy and Luetta say that, too. But they'll still call you a nigger in a minute."

"Well, you know what your father would do if he heard you saying those words. 'Nigger' and 'black.' "

She might have been doing her duty to remind me of my father's temper, but I became angrier and jerked my head away from her hands.

"Child, a hard head don't do nothing but land you in trouble."

I stomped upstairs to the living room and sat on the window seat and stared out of the window. I was very good at feeling sorry for myself and a tear leaked out. Soon I heard Miss Minnie coming up the steps and I wiped my face.

"Amy," she called from the top of the stairs.

"What?"

"Don't act like that, child." I could see her head just above the landing. "I'm going around to see Miss Ruby Davis. She moved into that house on Union Avenue today and she has a child about your age. Do you want to go with me?"

I nodded.

"Then go wash your face, child," she said, and disappeared.

Wash your face. Wash your face. She was worse than Aunt Louise. But I ran into the bathroom and splashed cold water on my face. I would have taken a bath in ice water if I thought I would meet someone to play with other than that Luetta.

While Miss Minnie and I were standing on the steps of Miss Ruby's house I saw Aunt Leona's venetian blinds open and close, and I was sorry that this new friend lived across the street from her. Aunt Louise was our nemesis, and Aunt Leona was her short, fat twin. My father dragged us around to her house for a visit every Christmas, and she would draw her chin back, fold her arms across her fat stomach, and regard me as if I were an untouchable. Now I could feel her eyes burning my back right between the shoulder blades and I wished I was brave enough to do a jig on the doorstep. At that moment the curtains on Miss Ruby Davis's door parted. It opened and Miss Minnie and I stepped into a living room that was cool and dark and empty and smelled like cabbage. Miss Ruby was thin with protruding eyes. Her hair was rolled up in curlers, and she clutched a chenille bathrobe around her narrow waist. While she and Miss Minnie talked for a minute, I looked around, but no one else was in sight.

Then Miss Minnie introduced us, and Miss Ruby said, "Well, she's just about Marvin's age."

Marvin! Another boy! I wanted to bolt from the house. Were any girls ever going to move to Hillsboro? "He's out back," announced Miss Ruby. We followed her through to the shed kitchen where she held the screen door open and I stepped onto a small back porch. "Marvin, this is Amy," she said, and shut the door and left us alone.

Marvin, like his mother, was skinny with poppy eyes that were fixed on me as if I had risen from the dead. I returned his stare and we looked at each other for a few moments, then he walked over to me and said, "Do you want to play hospital?"

I played many games with my brothers, but I'd never played that, I told him. However, I was willing to try. Since there were only two of us, it seemed we had to act out the parts of the nurse or the doctor or the patients who came to the hospital and we could make up what they'd say and we could have bandages and a cane and an operating table. He indicated a table at the end of the porch. "That's the operating table." Then he went into the house and was back in a few moments with a mop and some rags. He unscrewed the mop handle and handed it to me. "This can be a cane."

I took it.

He took the mop and plopped it on his head. "And this can be the nurse's hair."

My mouth fell open. How could he be the nurse? He was a boy! And didn't he look silly with all those gray strings falling over his face. "You can't be the nurse," I said. "I'm a girl so I'm the nurse. You have to be the doctor."

Well, Marvin flounced over to the top step and sat down and yanked the mop from his head and threw it into the yard. He wasn't going to play if he couldn't be the nurse. I didn't know what to do. If I had been alone I would have gone home, but I had to stay until Miss Minnie was ready to go. I waited a few moments and stared at the back of Marvin's head. He was in a real snit, breathing hard and tapping his foot. Finally I thought of a compromise. "All right. You be the nurse now, and I'll be the nurse next time."

He looked around at me and smiled, then got up and went to get the mop and he was the nurse and I was the patient and I was very good at it because, as I informed Marvin, my aunt had nursed me when I had scarlet fever for two weeks, and Marvin was a good nurse, kind and thoughtful. "Where do you hurt, dearie?" he'd say, and pressing the area of pretend pain, add, "Now tell me if I'm hurting you." He was also good at small talk. He was in the fourth grade and was going to the Catholic school and his mother was from Virginia, like my mother. And he could talk like her, too.

When I got home and told Lonnie and James about Marvin and the mop, Lonnie rolled on the hard dirt in the yard, laughing. "He's a sissy! And livin on Union Avenue, he better watch out! He's gonna get beat up good!"

"You're always makin fun of somebody," I retorted. "You're not perfect." He knew what I meant. He flunked. I stared at him, and he stopped laughing and stared back, probably trying to think of a withering answer. But I didn't give him a chance. I turned and hurried into the kitchen, letting the screen door bang in his face.

# EIGHT

꧁

Since Miss Minnie went to Philadelphia on weekends, my mother made arrangements for James to be under someone's guardianship on Saturday mornings when she worked. Lonnie and I were big enough to be left on our own for half a day, but she wanted James under the supervision of an adult. And since James balked about being left with Aunt Louise, she enlisted the help of Mr. Tivoli, the shoemaker who had his shop a block up the street from our house.

My mother knew the Tivolis from the time she'd first come to Hillsboro, and we knew him, too. His shop was directly across from the Hillsboro Health Center and whenever my mother took us from Westville for shots and a checkup, she would leave us with Mr. Tivoli for a few hours while she went shopping. "Now sit right here on this bench until I come back," she'd tell James and me. Lonnie always went with her to carry groceries; I remained behind with James who at that time was only three years old. I was six.

So when she asked Mr. Tivoli for the favor after we moved to Hillsboro, he was agreeable, and that's where I took James on Saturday mornings. Mr. Tivoli's shop reeked with smells and reverberated with sounds. There was the musty odor of shoe leather and the heady whiff of shoemaker's glue mixed in with the smell of the garlic and peppers and onions that Mrs. Tivoli was usually cooking; we heard the whirring wheel as he shaped and sanded the leather, the tapping hammer as he applied tacks to the soles, and the music of the Italian operas that were continually streaming from his Victrola.

He kept a few tacks between his lips and would answer our questions: "Now I'm gonna take the leather, see? And I'm gonna cut it like this, a little longer and wider than the shoe. Now I'm gonna draw the sole. Then I'm gonna cut it out like this, see? Then I'm gonna glue it to the shoe, like this." And on and on he'd go, until he had a sole on a shoe.

Mr. Tivoli had a son who was seven. His name was Alfred. He went to the Catholic school. Alfred would come out from behind a curtain (they lived in the rear of the shop) and he and James would disappear, to play either in the back of the shop or out in the little yard beyond. I would accompany them once in a while.

They had a huge player piano in the dining room and Mrs. Tivoli would sometimes let us play it. I would sit on the couch and listen to the piano or Mr. Tivoli's operas. And James and I would come home and play opera singers and drive my mother crazy.

So the month of August passed and soon it was Labor Day. The last warm holiday of the year and the last of Aunt Leona's backyard parties. She had a few every year. One on Memorial Day, one on the Fourth of July, and one on Labor Day. And a few in between. Everyone who was anyone went, I heard. I'd never experienced one, since her parties were not the kind where children were welcome. They were like my father's. For adults only.

But this Labor Day I was to go to one of her parties for the first time. My mother and Aunt Louise had gone to Potter's Grove to see about my grandfather who was sick. My mother had taken James along with her and left Lonnie and me in the care of my father. They left on Sunday and were to return on Tuesday.

My mother almost didn't go.

Early Friday evening she was cleaning the stove and I was ironing a dress when Aunt Louise stopped by to tell Mama the news about our grandfather, and after Mama cried a little, she wiped her eyes and asked Aunt Louise when she was going down to see him and Aunt Louise told Mama she had to go too because he might die and Mama said she didn't have the money. Aunt Louise said she'd guessed that and she had the money for both of them. And Mama said who would take care of the kids.

"I thought you had Miss Minnie here to do that," said Aunt Louise.

"She stays here durin the week," said Mama. "On Saturdays and Sundays she goes downtown to visit with her sister. She's sick, too."

"I guess that's best for Miss Minnie. She needs a break from these devils." Aunt Louise thought a moment. "Well, there ain't nothin for you to do but leave them with their father. Just have to cramp his style."

"I guess I'll take James with me. Papa's never seen James."

"And where's Jack at anyway? Probably up there in Westville at the weddin."

"Weddin," said Mama, frowning.

"I know you know what weddin."

"If I did I wouldn't ask."

"Now you know that oldest Lewis boy, Marshall, gettin married today to one of them tight-headed Wyatts. Your former next-door neighbor's niece. The oldest one, whatever her name is."

Miss Edie's niece. I knew her. Rose. I ironed my sleeve and avoided looking at Mama so I wouldn't see the look on her face.

"The oldest one's only about sixteen," said Mama.

"Sixteen. What's that got to do with it. Old enough to get babies, old enough to get married. And that's the one. The oldest one . . . now, Ruby Davis just told me her name."

"Rose."

"That's right. Rose. And she look like a rose. Ugliest yallah gal I ever seen. Seen her last week up on Highland Avenue, belly out a mile and that head nappy as a sheep's back. Oughta be taxed comin out in the street lookin like that. Heels like unwashed potatoes stickin out of them sandals and corns on every toe, big and hard as acorns."

"And she havin a weddin with her belly out," said Mama.

"Hmph. Seem like that's the new shape for brides these days. And I guess she ain't the first and won't be the last."

Mama polished the stove silently. Aunt Louise watched her. I ironed. Finally Aunt Louise got up. "Well, we're leavin Sunday afternoon. I guess Jack will be back by then. You just get yourself ready to go."

She looked at me. "I'm sure you and Lonnie can take care of yourselves until we get back. When you get hungry, go around and see your uncle Lee. He'll feed you."

"I can fix somethin for them," said Mama. "I ain't worried about them not eatin. Jack's a good cook."

"If he's here *to* cook." Aunt Louise's parting shot.

EARLY SATURDAY morning before dawn I heard my father come in, cursing each time he banged his shin or missed a step. There was a sound of someone falling. I sat up and listened. Lonnie and James, up on the third floor, probably didn't hear him. After that I heard no sounds. I went back to sleep.

About an hour later when my mother got up I did too, and I followed her down to the kitchen. My father was lying on the kitchen table, on his side, knees drawn up almost to his chin, mouth hanging open, spit dribbling from the side of his mouth. The funky smell of stale whiskey filled the room. My mother opened the door, then rolled my father over and felt in his pockets. In one she found a handkerchief glued together with dried snot. Disgusted, she threw it into the trash. In the other pocket she found a roll of bills, counted some off, and returned the rest to his pocket.

I sat on the bottom step and watched as she banged pots around hoping to awaken him. No luck. She went over and rolled him off the table and he slid to the floor with a bump, grunted, and shook his head. He looked up, saw us, then, wiping his hand across his mouth, held onto the table, pulled himself up, and went stumbling toward the steps. "Sorry," he muttered, and made his way up.

"Look at him, tryin to act sheepish," said Mama, banging pots, "as if a damn black drunk can look sheepish."

He slept all day. That night he didn't go out, and I heard them talking, arguing. His voice was always soft, so as not to be overheard, Mama's louder, as if she didn't care. I shrank down in my bed and pulled the blanket over my head. Suddenly there was a thump, then more thumps, down the hall now to my room.

The door opened. "Amy?"

I felt my mother's hand on my arm. I mumbled, then I felt the bed sink down as she got in next to me. She had not got in the bed with me before, but I had never slept alone before. I'd always been in a room with Lonnie and James. Probably if they had been in the room, she would not have climbed in with me that night. Somehow I was glad. I turned on my side and pressed my back against her. She was soft and warm. I lay there awhile listening as she cried softly.

Oh, I hated that man then and the hatred burned in my chest like a hot coal. I stared into the dark for a long time and it kept easing and after a while I fell into a deep sleep.

On Sunday afternoon Mama and James and Aunt Louise left for Virginia. I felt alone right after they left, then I went upstairs and looked at the picture of her family that hung on the wall in the living room. It was cracked and faded, but I knew all the faces. I looked at the picture a long time, and somehow I got over the feeling of being lonely.

Mama had left a good dinner for us: stewed chicken and dumplings and carrots. Lonnie and my father and I ate in silence and then Lonnie and I went around to Union Avenue to play.

On Monday my father disappeared right after breakfast after instructing Lonnie and me to go to Aunt Leona's for dinner. Lonnie swore he'd eat baloney sandwiches and candy bars first. About four o'clock I decided to take up Aunt Louise's invitation to have dinner with Uncle Lee. On my way there I met Marvin Davis and agreed to play a couple of games of checkers with him, but Aunt Leona caught me just as we got to his house. I was hoping she'd be in her backyard with her guests, but she was on her front stoop talking to one of the ladies at her party and that's when she saw me and waved me over and asked me where I'd been, that my father told her to expect Lonnie and me for dinner. And where was he? she wanted to know. I had no idea. Lonnie had left home right after lunch. But I told her he was over in the field playing baseball.

She looked me over carefully. My hair had been looking decent the last few days thanks to Miss Minnie, whose constant brushing had made it easier for me to comb. So, since I had met Aunt Leona's standards, she dragged me around the side of the house to the backyard and sat me in a corner to wait for my food.

I had never been in her yard and I looked around in wonder. The lawn had been cut close like a green velvet square and part of it was covered with a wooden platform so it resembled a large patio. Along three sides flowers grew: red roses on one side growing up a white trellis; at the rear, where I was sitting, a riot of wildflowers, purple, pink, yellow, lavender, red, tall enough to screen out the alley behind the yard. On the side across from the roses was a green vine climbing another trellis, meant to screen out the sidewalk traffic. On the ground along the length of the yard, in front of the vine, were pots of geraniums. And throughout the yard a faint, wonderful odor, as if someone had crushed a basket of the roses and scattered them around. Placed through the yard were tables, one or two with yellow and white umbrellas to block the sun. Some people sat at the tables laughing and talking and drinking and playing cards; others moved around on the platform, dancing and talking to those at the tables. Music from a Victrola under the steps drifted through the air. A short fat man seemed to be in charge of the music; people were going over telling him which records they wanted to hear.

After a few moments Aunt Leona brought me my dinner: orange soda, a plate of fried chicken and potato salad and collard greens. There was also a slice of chocolate cake. I picked at the food and looked around. Some of the people were the ones who attended my father's parties in Westville. A few of them saw me and came over to speak—Well, Amy, aren't you growing, how's your mother—and clucked their tongues in sympathy when I told them where she went. A bouncy tune came on, "Don't Get Around Much Anymore." The crowd really liked it; they laughed their approval and a lot of them jumped up to dance. I tapped my foot to the beat. Then it was over and a softer song came on. Bluesy. A woman singing one of the songs Mama hummed around the house.

*Never treats me sweet and gentle the way he should. . . .*

Suddenly the back door opened and my father stepped out into the yard. And behind him was Miss Edie. They smiled and greeted the people near them, and a couple of the men standing near the door laughed and slapped him on the back, and he put his arm around Miss Edie's waist and they swung around to dance.

*My poor heart is sentimental, not made of wood. . . .*

I wanted to shrink. I wanted to run and hide. That was not my father out there. That was a man courting a woman, the way he was holding her, the way he was smiling down at her and the way she was hanging onto him. They were still, then swinging around, then still, then swinging; the music seemed to be part of them. I watched them, and that night up in Westville came back to me in a rush, my mother's anguished words, my father's anguished voice . . . I stared across the yard and thought of that night and he glanced across the yard and his eyes met mine. And for a moment time stopped.

*He don't love me like I love him . . . nobody could. . . .*

Was he remembering the words he'd told me in our kitchen? They rang in my head clear as a bell. *Sometimes men do things when they get a few drinks in them that they wouldn't do otherwise. Do you understand?*

*I got it bad and that ain't good.*

He stopped dancing, said something to Miss Edie, still looking across the yard at me.

He starts toward me and I want to get up and leave but I just look down and then I look up because he's at the table speaking to me. Then he sits down and I don't look at him and I don't know what to say. I keep on watching the people dance and Miss Edie's looking over now and she comes over too and she's smiling at me and opens her arms and I smile and stand up and she hugs me and I smell her perfume. And she sits down and asks me about Lonnie and James and I tell her and wonder how she and my father can sit there acting as if I can't see and can't know about them and everything and I'm acting as if nothing is wrong when I want to throw my orange soda all over her dress. So I bend my head because I don't want to look at her smiling face and I see my father's pointy-toed black shoes and her open-toed sandals and her painted toenails and then I know that it was his hand on her thigh under the table that night.

And that man is playing that stupid old song again.

As soon as I could I got out of there, but not before my father gave me a dollar and told me to tell Lonnie to come and get something to eat, but instead I went over to Marvin's house and played checkers and let him win a couple of games and then we looked at his new school clothes and he showed me his new composition books and Miss Ruby gave me a pack of pencils as a gift to start me off right at my new school.

MY MOTHER and James returned early Tuesday afternoon. Her father was getting better, she told Miss Minnie. Pickled in body and mind. Probably last another forty years. In the press of getting ready for our first day of school the next day there was not much time for her to talk to me alone, and I was glad because I knew she would question me about my father. Things that perhaps one female would ask another, for she never asked Lonnie and James the same questions she asked me. What time did your father come home last night? she asked. How long was he home with you? I didn't want to talk about him because I would not lie for him. But I answered her questions. He'd come home about two in the morning. Drunk. He had spent no time with us. I wanted to shout, *"He danced with Miss Edie at Aunt Leona's!"* But I could not tell her that because I didn't belong there in the first place. I was supposed to eat the meal Aunt Louise had prepared for us. But she questioned Lonnie about that. How the meal had gone with Uncle Lee. Lonnie was reluctant to talk, too. Even though he had not been with me in Aunt Leona's backyard to witness my father's indiscretion, he too had not obeyed her orders to eat dinner at Aunt Louise's with Uncle Lee and he didn't want to give the impression that he and I had been flying around as free as gypsies.

We spent the rest of the afternoon at the Ladies' Exchange looking for a dress for me, at the Goodwill looking for underwear and socks for Lonnie and James, and at Levy's shoe store where we used the welfare coupons to buy the first pair of shoes for the year. We ended up at Woolworth's buying pencils and notebooks and finally ended up at home to find Aunt Louise in the kitchen talking to Miss Minnie.

Uh, oh, I thought when I felt Aunt Louise's baleful look.

As soon as Lonnie saw her, he dropped our packages onto the floor and backed out of the kitchen and took off, James right behind him. Aunt Louise grabbed me by the arm and dragged me in front of her. "Mmm-hmmmm. What you got to say for yourself, you nasty stinkin little hussy."

Miss Minnie cringed. "Oh, my, Miss Louise."

"Louise, what is wrong with you?" said Mama.

"I fix dinner for these little niggers and they don't even go around there to eat it. I guess they ain't told you that yet."

"No, they ain't," said Mama. "But that ain't no reason to call her all them names."

"Names. She need to have her tail whipped. People cookin food and waitin dinner for them and they don't appreciate it."

"Lonnie didn't go and ain't nobody said nothin to him," I said.

"You ain't as fast on your feet as he is, the little skunk. And the skin will be hangin off both your bones before I offer to feed you again."

"Where did you eat, Amy?" said Mama.

Trouble now. I hesitated.

"Oh, I *know* where she ate," said Aunt Louise.

"Hush up, Louise," said Mama. "Where did you eat, I said."

"Daddy told us to eat around Aunt Leona's house."

Mama and Aunt Louise spoke together. "And where did we tell you to eat?"

"I *was* going to eat with Uncle Lee!"

"What do you mean, you was?" said Mama.

"I was gonna play checkers with Marvin and then when I was goin in his house Aunt Leona seen me and made me eat at her house."

I moved from in front of Aunt Louise and plopped into a chair while she and Mama digested and redigested this piece of news. Then they flung a series of questions at me. Where was your father? Where was Lonnie? Why didn't you stop by and tell your Uncle Lee what happened?

The last two questions I answered. Lonnie was in the baseball field. I was scared to tell Uncle Lee because I thought he'd be mad. They didn't ask me the first one again.

"Mmm-hmmmm," said Aunt Louise, giving my mother a look that signified more. "I heard somethin about it."

"Amy, go on outside," said Mama.

"I'm goin upstairs," I said. And I went up and lay on the floor at the top of the stairway and listened to Aunt Louise tell my mother what she had heard.

Ruby Davis had told *her* that *she* saw Jack go into Leona's house to the party and that Ruby had also seen *Edie* go in there. Of course they didn't go in together, but what do that matter, of course, and that at the party Jack had been drinking, and name a time when he ain't, and they (him and Edie) was dancing and acting the fool in front of the child (Amy, that's who) and that the child looked like she was going to bust out crying right there.

My hand went over my mouth. People had been watching me!

"Amy done seen her father act like the fool before," said Mama. "That ain't nothin new."

Miss Minnie's voice: "Will you excuse me, Mrs. Beale? I think I'm going outside and sit in the shade and catch a breeze."

"Certainly, Miss Minnie," said Mama.

There was a small silence while she did this, I guess, then, Aunt Louise again. "Ain't nobody said nothin about nothin new. I'm just tellin you what happened, because I know the child ain't. And him supposed to be down here in Hillsboro turnin over a new leaf. And I understand he's up in Westville every mornin. Now what he's up there for, I'd like to know."

"He gets a ride up there to play his numbers."

"Like there ain't no number writer here in Hillsboro and Geneva Tate up on that wall rakin in the money every day."

"Well, I guess he like to play with Mr. Arthur. Some people think they lose their luck if they change."

"You can call it luck if you want. Ain't no sense in somebody ridin five miles at lunchtime to play a number. And Jack Beale may be a rogue, but he ain't lackin in common sense."

Mama started slamming pots around. "Well, I sure am goin to ask him about all this when he gits home from work."

"Well, don't tell him you got it from *me,*" said Aunt Louise.

More slamming of pots.

THE REST OF the afternoon my stomach lurched around as if I had swallowed a handful of jumping beans. If my mother told my father about his transgressions, and didn't tell him that Aunt Louise was the source of her information, wouldn't he naturally think that I was the one who told? That he would think of me as a snitch or a traitor? Lonnie would've called me that and more.

But my mother must have had all that figured out. For at the table that night, when dinner was almost over, she brought up the subject in my presence. "Louise was around here this afternoon," she said, each word hard as a pebble.

My father's fork stopped in the air, then continued down to his plate. "Oh?" he looked around at Lonnie, James, and me. "You all finished?"

We nodded and excused ourselves from the table and went out into the yard. And I heard no more about *l'affaire* Edie or anything else that took place on Labor Day.

But one change did come about. My father stopped going to Westville to play his numbers. From then on, like my mother, he played them with Miss Geneva Tate.

# N I N E

The first day of school. James and I were up early, anxious to go, but Lonnie took his time. We waited impatiently for him in the yard. My hair was now long enough for Miss Minnie to make three decent plaits, one twisted and anchored on top of my head with a tortoiseshell hairpin and one on each side tied on the ends with a red bow. She had generously applied Dixie Peach and water to my hair, and in spite of my grumbling, had brushed it until it was plastered against my head and now the plaits dangled against my neck. I drew a hopscotch in the yard and hopped into the blocks straining my neck, turning to see if my plaits would bounce. They didn't. James was especially anxious since this would be his first day ever at school, and he too was hopping around the yard working off some of his nervous energy.

Miss Minnie fretted around the kitchen washing the breakfast dishes as she kept her eye on the clock, and once we heard her calling up to Lonnie, who answered, "What!" in a tone that should have gotten him a bloody lip.

Finally he was there in the yard, scowling at us. "Okay. Come on." We stopped hopping and walked over to him, and stood straight and still. "And I ain't walkin to school with nobody runnin and skippin ahead of me. Mama said I have to take you to school, but if you two start actin simple, you ain't goin nowhere with me."

Everything inside of me was dancing so I could hardly keep my feet still, but I stood quietly while Lonnie checked his pocket to make sure he had the key so we could get in if Miss Minnie decided to go out. "Okay. I'm ready. Come on." He started down the drive.

"Yippee!" I said. It slipped out. I stopped short and covered my mouth.

Lonnie turned. "What did I just say?" Two moments of silence and a green-eyed stare. "Now take James's hand and walk like you got some sense."

Beechwood Avenue was cool and sunny. As we turned the corner onto Union Avenue we met the blinding rays of sun that slanted across the rooftops of the weatherworn houses rising from the lumpy brick sidewalks and sparkled on the bottles of milk in the crates sitting in front of the Jew store. We squinted, covered our eyes, and were halfway up the street when I looked to my right and saw a strange sight.

A boy was walking down from the sky. James and I stopped; I tightened my grip on his hand. As I stared, I saw that the boy was coming down steps that were built into a wall, a wall covered with green vines. I had seen that wall many times when I was playing in Union Avenue, but I had never noticed the steps.

The boy was now down on the street. I could not determine his age, but he was not as tall as Lonnie, and I assumed he was older than I. He was wearing a white shirt, a blue tie, and gray pants. And on his feet were a pair of black leather shoes with extra thick soles. A pair of steel-rimmed glasses framed his round face. He scowled at us and crossed his arms.

My heart jumped. James froze.

Now Union Avenue was a crooked street and ran up in a little hill and bent around from the top so you could not see down to the other side where it ended at Sycamore Street. Lonnie, who had kept on walking ahead, had gone down the other side of the hill, and now realizing that James and I were not behind him ran back to the top and called to us. "Come on! What's the matter?"

James started forward with a jerk. I followed him, keeping my eye on the boy, who stepped into the street when we moved. I took a quick look back and saw the boy bending over. That meant one thing. A stone.

Lonnie saw him too. "Run!"

I reached James, grabbed his hand and dashed for the top. A stone passed my head and rattled on the street in front of us. I shrieked and released James's hand and flew down to the end of the street. The hairpin that anchored my plait to the top of my head dropped out and the plait bounced in front of my nose. James ran screeching behind me and Lonnie loped along behind him. For a moment we stood panting, waiting, looking back at the top of the hill. But the boy did not appear.

A quick glance at Aunt Leona's house assured us that she had not witnessed our mad dash, and we crossed Sycamore Street to the athletic field that adjoined the high school. From there it was a sprint across to the elementary school. A long, high cyclone fence surrounded the field, but there was a gate which was open all summer. To our surprise that morning it was locked. We had to go the long way, up to Hillcrest and down to the school. And sitting on a wall in front of the high school were June Lewis, Luetta, Bumpsy, and other kids from Union Avenue. James pulled himself up next to Bumpsy and immediately began telling everyone about the gate. That gate was always closed the first day of school, Bumpsy haughtily informed him. That was so they could clean up the field and draw lines for the hockey team and the football team.

That conversation held no interest for me. I was staring at Luetta. The moment I saw her I raised my hand to my plait. Her hair! The little braids were gone, and in their place was a riot of black curls that covered her head like little fat sausages. And her dress! My plaid dress was secondhand, purchased at the Ladies' Exchange. Luetta's blue dress was unmistakably new and crisp; it did not have that weary look of many washings and ironings. And on her feet were new patent leather Mary Janes without a scuff mark on them, not brown leather oxfords like mine, sturdy enough to last all year through wind and rain and snow if I were careful.

Luetta tossed her head. Her curls bounced and gleamed. I rolled my eyes and drew away from her and sat on the wall next to Lonnie. But she was not to be thwarted in her attempt to crow. She came over and sat next to me. "Your plait comin loose, Amy." Another toss of the head.

"I know it." Time for me to mention her hair, I supposed. But I would never acknowledge those saucy curls. I merely said, "My hairpin fell out." I braided the end of the plait and pushed it underneath the hair on top.

"It come out when we was runnin from that boy," said James.

"What boy?" said Bumpsy.

James shrugged. Then Lonnie took over and told June Lewis about the incident on Union Avenue. June nodded, and grinning, told us about the boy. His name was Asbury Tate and he lived in a house at the top of the wall. He was the son of Geneva Tate. We hadn't met him because his mother sent him down South every summer to be with her mother in the country. "She think her precious little angel is too good to play with the kids in Union Avenue. When he comes back to go to school she keeps him up there in the yard. He ain't no harm in a fistfight, but he can *throw* some rocks. He gits up on that wall and throws them down and we can't git him back good because he ducks back. But once in a while when he goes to the Jew store or somethin we get him down in the street. Good. Then he goes whinin to his mother and she sure don't like it when you lay a finger on that little sucker . . . and she seen him this mornin. She sees everything. Right from her window. She keeps lookout there all day long, 'cept when she's in the kitchen writin the numbers. . . . Your father play the numbers?"

Lonnie nodded. "Yeah."

"Well, she sure will tell him if she sees you doin anything to Asbury." June shook his head. "All the grown-ups who play with Miss Geneva got to keep on her good side or she won't let them play on credit. No more 'See you payday.' Not if your kids touch Ass-bury."

We giggled. "Ass-bury. Ass-bury."

"I'm sure glad my pop don't play no numbers," June continued. "That Asbury knows if he messes with me or my little brother, I'll kick his butt."

"Well, ain't he scared to come to school with everybody mad at him?" I said.

"He don't come to our school. He goes to the Catholic school. That's why he can wait for you. He's only got to go right down the street. So if you want to get by him and not go the long way around, you have to come earlier than you did today."

SINCE LONNIE and I were new to the school, we reported to the office at eight-thirty to wait for our teachers. Mine came first. Miss Quinlan was her name. She was a tall, beefy, pink-faced white woman who wore her thick white hair cut short, and round wire-rimmed glasses. A ruffled organza collar attached to a lavender dress seemed out of place around such a thick neck. With a nod at me, unsmiling, she took me to her room and sat me in a chair by her desk, where I sat nervously until she returned leading her class in from the schoolyard.

She told me to stand, introduced me, stood by me overlooking the class, and asked me to say a few words—my name, where I went to school the year before, if I had brothers and sisters, other questions that teachers seem to think children need to know about other children in their class. I spoke through a haze of discomfort. Not because the children were white. I would have been just as embarrassed standing for the first time in front of a group of colored children in Westville. It was because I felt so much poorer than everyone. In front of me sat a group of children who lived in houses like those where my mother worked; I had seen enough children like them in school and in their homes when I had lived in Woodlynne to know they were children of privilege. Just from seeing them glance at me as they entered the room and took their seats, their wide-eyed attentiveness as I stood there talking, I sensed the air of self-confidence that would intimidate any stranger. I hurried through my recitation and with a sigh of relief took the seat assigned to me by Miss Quinlan. Amy Beale: just behind Judy Anderson. Second seat in the row by the window. I slumped and bent my head.

Since it was the first day, school was in session only until eleven o'clock, but Miss Quinlan kept me for an hour to check out my skills. She was pleased with the results of my reading and arithmetic tests, but there were more practical ones for her to consider. Handwriting, for instance. And spelling. And long division, which the class had already mastered.

We started that day with handwriting. Miss Quinlan printed the first sentence from the Gettysburg Address on the blackboard and asked me to copy in cursive writing. She sat at her desk as I wrote. *Four score and seven years ago, our fathers brought forth on this continent a new nation, conceived in liberty and dedicated to the proposition that all men are created equal.* When I finished I sat back and regarded the neat cursive writing that I had learned in Westville. A neat, utilitarian style that emphasized hooking the letters together with as little fanfare as possible.

Miss Quinlan regarded my paper stoically. In Hillsboro Elementary School we use the Palmer Method, she informed me, as she took out paper and pen and ink. She placed on my desk an example of writing that consisted of swoops and curlicues that I thought I could never do. She continued her explanation of writing. We write to communicate, yes, but we are creating a work of art as well as producing a piece of writing. The letters should flow across the paper. She wrote a sentence on a sheet of paper and that beefy hand produced words so beautiful they might have been drawn by Leonardo da Vinci.

"Now," she said, smiling at my look of amazement. "We'll have you doing the same thing in a few weeks." She looked at her watch. "Time to go."

AT LUNCHTIME Miss Minnie always left us to eat alone, and after reminding Lonnie that the numbers had to go around to Miss Geneva, she went upstairs to make up beds. She or my father had been taking them around up to the day that school opened, but since we passed by there on our way back to school after lunch, one of us was to take them up.

Lonnie got the number slip from the mantel. Now my mother always wrapped her number slip around her money, but when Lonnie unfolded it there were two slips. One was a note. He read it and laughed and handed it to me. I read it. "Amy, take my number slip and your father's around to Miss Geneva when you come home at lunchtime."

I almost choked on my baloney sandwich. Then I exploded. I jumped up and kicked my chair and slammed my dish into the sink. The noise brought Miss Minnie rushing back down to the kitchen.

"Child, I thought you had fallen off a chair or something! What in the world is wrong with you!"

"I'm not takin no numbers around to that lady's house! That old boy around there throwin rocks at people! And I'm not supposed to do it anyway! Lonnie is!"

"Me! Why me!"

"You did it up in Westville!"

"This ain't Westville! And Mama said for you to do it!"

Miss Minnie threw her hands into the air. "Child, do what your mother tells you and stop fussing." She went back upstairs.

I burst into tears. Lonnie was expected to take the numbers around. It was his job. He was still trying to get even with me because I passed and he didn't. And I said so. "You're just mad because you got left down!"

Lonnie threw a chair out of his way and stomped up the steps. James, who had been watching us solemnly, said quietly, "I'll take them up for you, Amy."

I looked at him through watery eyes. "Will you, James? I'll go around there with you if you take them up."

James nodded and kept on eating. I wanted to jump up and hug him but he didn't like that now that he'd started school.

In a few moments Lonnie came back downstairs to a silent kitchen. I didn't even look at him, just went outside and sat in the yard. I heard him talking to James, then he came outside. "I'll take the number money up," he said gruffly. Then he started out of the yard.

James came out of the house and we started after him. "What did he say?" I whispered to James. "Why is he takin it?"

James shrugged. "I think Miss Minnie said somethin to him."

"Maybe she said she was gonna tell Daddy," I said. I couldn't think of another reason why he would change his mind.

James and I trailed along behind Lonnie, but he did not acknowledge us. Up the stony steps we climbed; I expected to see Asbury any moment. But he didn't appear. James and I waited at the landing as Lonnie climbed a flight of rickety wooden steps up to the door in what seemed like a turret. It was a peculiar feeling to be up there high above Union Avenue. And why was this house up so high, I wondered, but still on Union Avenue?

We heard footsteps. Someone was coming down the stone wall. Mr. Benjamin Otis Turner, a big man whose nickname, B.O., stood not for his initials but his distinctive body odor. He was Aunt Louise's boarder, and she constantly reminded him that he had ruined her good bed from John Wanamaker by watering it every night "like he some hot-house flower." In spite of such shortcomings, he deserved, as all adults we knew, our respect. To us, he was *Mr.* B.O.

Mr. B.O.'s eyeballs were muddy yellow. He was old, slow moving, with wrinkled clothes too big for him that sagged at the behind as if they had been stretched to fit an elephant, and he had a kind, mellow disposition. "Well, children, what are you doin up here?" he said when he saw us.

Waiting for Lonnie, we told him. We assumed he had come up to play a number, but no, he explained, he came up every day to rest in the swing. He nodded toward some bushes near the house. Curious, James and I followed him around the side yard which was long and green-grassed, to a secluded area where a garden swing rested, a swing with a striped awning above it. Mr. B.O. ambled over to it and sat down with a sigh. We walked to the back of the house where we saw that the house was on posts, like stilts. We looked around and could see the back porches of the houses on Hillcrest Avenue.

We learned later from our father that the house had once been a stable for horses for the big house in front. Miss Geneva had worked for the family who owned it and they had deeded it to her when they moved. Since it was so far back from Hillcrest Avenue, none of the white people had minded, and a stairway had been formed along the wall so she could enter on Union Avenue. We walked back to the yard. Mr. B.O. was leaning to the side, asleep, as the leaves rustled overhead and whispered a lullaby.

James and I walked back to the edge of the wall and got a bird's-eye view of Union Avenue.

"Gee," said James, "this street sure looks tacky from up here. Look at the houses leanin like they're gonna fall down."

"Yeah. And look at how many of those bricks are out of the sidewalk. Funny you don't see all that when you're right down there on them, ain't it? And there ain't one tree on this whole end of the street. No wonder it's so hot down there."

"And look! you can see in some rooms, too! I can see a bureau in somebody's room in the Lewises' house!"

"Hey, James, look." I pointed down at Bumpsy Lewis who was coming off his front porch.

James grinned. "Wonder what would happen if I threw a rock down at him?"

We never found out. Just then we heard Lonnie clomping down the steps from Miss Geneva's kitchen, and we ran down the wall to catch up with Bumpsy.

The next morning we started out for school earlier. So early I thought Asbury might not even be up. But as we walked up the street, we saw him sitting on the bottom step. He rose and went to the middle of the street and stood with his feet apart like Billy Goat Gruff daring the frightened little kids to pass over the bridge. As we got nearer, he swaggered toward us, hands in his pockets. My knees grew weak, I tightened my grip on James's hand. I didn't stop.

Asbury came on. Lonnie, in front of us, hands in his pockets, looked straight ahead and kept walking toward him. When Asbury reached Lonnie they bumped shoulders. Asbury glared at Lonnie. James and I stopped.

"You tryin to take up the whole street?" said Asbury.

"You got plenty of room," said Lonnie, taking his hands from his pockets.

"And so do you," said Asbury, freeing his hands up, too. "And anyway, this ain't your street, so what you doin on it anyway?"

"None of your beeswax, that's what," Lonnie said softly.

Then Asbury, probably thinking Lonnie's soft answer came from the mouth of a coward, tapped him on the chest. "I said this ain't—"

I drew in my breath. Lonnie couldn't stand for anyone to touch him. Quicker than the eye could follow, he reached out and grabbed Asbury's necktie, and they were both on the ground punching, pulling, and kicking, out there in the middle of Union Avenue in their school clothes, Asbury on top one minute, Lonnie on top the next, while James and I jumped up and down squeaking behind our hands to muffle our screams. "Git 'im, Lonnie! Git 'im!"

Finally Lonnie was on top pinning Asbury's arms to the ground until he stopped struggling. Then Lonnie jumped up and Asbury scrambled around on the ground looking for his glasses. He found them and put them on and screeched, "You broke my glasses! And you're gonna pay for them, too!"

We laughed. Whoever heard of paying for glasses that got broken when you were fighting, especially if you started the fight. Besides, nobody told when they got into a fight. They were most likely to get a whipping for that. At least, that's the way it was in Westville.

But June Lewis's words were nuggets of wisdom. At the dinner table that night my father laid down the law. "Here that boy's mother tryin to fix him up a little and you all tryin to tear him up. People workin to make things better and other children makin them worse. Money don't grow on trees. I don't make enough money to keep us in food, much less be payin for broken glasses. And if it happens again, *I'm* gonna break something, and it won't be glasses, either."

"Well, I can't see payin for no glasses when that boy started the fight," said my mother. "Everybody on Union Avenue know that Asbury's a devil."

"They don't have to go through Union Avenue to go to school, Arleatha. If they have to fight, go around."

"Did Asbury bother you when you took that number money up there, Amy?"

"Well . . ." I was going to explain about Lonnie taking the numbers up, but he interrupted.

"He wasn't even in sight."

Mama sniffed. "I guess not. Might interfere with Geneva makin some money. So if they don't have no trouble at lunchtime, why should they have to go around in the mornin? Why can't Geneva Tate make that boy behave then? Even if she have to get up off her bony behind and come down those steps every morning with him and watch him until he gets out of her sight."

My father glowered, but he said no more.

After dinner when we were upstairs on the living room floor listening to the radio, Lonnie gave his opinion about the argument at the table. "Daddy didn't even ask *us* what happened. He just listened to what Miss Geneva said. He won't even stick up for his own children. And he gets mad at Mama if she sticks up for us." His eyes grew moist. "You wait. Someday . . . someday when I get big . . . you wait."

I got up and went into my room. I was tired of fights and threats and grumpy people.

Before she had dismissed me, Miss Quinlan had pushed three books at me. She wanted me to develop a reading habit and these would be good to start. *A Little Princess. Little Lord Fauntleroy. Little House in the Big Woods.* The children had read them in fourth grade and she thought I should read them if I hadn't. I chose *A Little Princess* and lay across my bed to read, but thoughts of Luetta kept interfering with the words on the page. Curls. Well, they wouldn't last long. In a couple of days she'd have those teeny plaits right back again.

Oh, if only I could find a friend. A girl friend. Marvin was all right to play with, but there were things girls liked to talk about . . . things they couldn't talk about to boys. Moving around so much made it hard.

When we were younger, Lonnie and I had been constant companions. We went everywhere together. To school, played together after school; then when we moved to Westville, I was seven and he was nine, and he found a lot of friends. It seemed that in Westville, like Hillsboro, the families ran to boys. There were not any girls my age. But even in Westville I had not felt isolated as I did now. Just as Lonnie had felt the need to be with boys, and now James, too, playing with his friends on Union Avenue, I longed for the companionship of a girl who didn't base her friendship on moods, like Luetta. Friends when she felt friendly, lonely when she didn't feel friendly. I sighed. At times like this I wished I were a boy.

# TEN

The next few weeks were busy ones for me. Handwriting and long division after school with Miss Quinlan. Catching up on my reading. James would wait for me after school and sometimes Luetta would wait with him, and I resigned myself to the fact that like it or not, she was to be my only girl friend in Hillsboro.

But at the end of September a family moved into the empty house on Maple Street. The very house among those surly neighbors who had given Ruby and Joe Davis such a hard time. After witnessing the reactions of those people to having colored people around them, I would never have suspected I might find a friend among those people whom my mother considered trash.

People who seemed to be one extended family. Like a clan. Certain characteristics were common to every family on the block. No chins. Lips like lines drawn against the face. Skin a pale white that wouldn't tan. Stringy, greasy hair, blond or red. Their laundry: tattletale gray wash hung out in the narrow backyards with holes large enough to pass an arm or a finger through. Dirty, my mother once sniffed as we passed by on a laundry day. I wondered how that could be. It seemed to me that women in those houses were always cleaning. Nearly every morning on our way to school we would see them on their little front porches with a mop and a bucket, sloshing water over the boards. If they weren't on their porches, they were upstairs at a window shaking out a blanket or a dust cloth. If they were not cleaning they were conversing with each other over the porch railings or out of the windows, their bobbing heads cluttered with brown paper curlers; they chatted over their brooms as they swept litter from the cracked sidewalks. They even swept the tiny crabgrass lawns in front of each house.

There were many children who tumbled forth every day to play on those sidewalks—to toddle, ride their scooters or tricycles up and down and stop and scowl at us as we passed by on the other side, glowering as if we needed a douse of some of that dirty water their mothers were sloshing on the porches.

The family that moved in was that of Joe Donovan, the policeman we met our first day in town. When he got the job he'd been living in Mayfield, a farm community about twenty miles to the north, but he'd been required to move to Hillsboro within a year. His older children had moved out, and at home now were two little boys, two and three, and a girl about my age who was unique among the children on the street: She attended public school. She appeared one afternoon in front of our class. Miss Quinlan, who wore her glasses only on important occasions, raised them from her chest and introduced her to us.

Her name was Mary Katharine Donovan.

Mary Katharine was wearing a plaid jumper and white socks and sturdy brown oxfords and she stood with one leg crossed over the other. She had long red hair that was parted in the middle and on each side of her head was a barrette to hold the hair back from a face sprinkled from chin to forehead with cinnamon freckles.

The class stared and whispered as they had when I had stood there a few weeks before. But this girl did not twist a foot or a hand or turn pink. She was composed, serene. After the introduction she went to the seat that Miss Quinlan pointed out. Since I was near the front I did not dare look around. Miss Quinlan was a hard taskmistress. Looking around could be considered being inattentive, especially since she was ready to review the answers to the arithmetic test, and she considered the review of the answers as important as taking the test. Inattentiveness could lead to an indoor recess, or worse, lunch with her in the classroom.

At afternoon recess the girls in my class gathered around Mary Katharine to find out where she lived. When I heard that her family had moved into the empty house on Maple Street, I remembered the women and the way they had acted and I knew this new girl would not have much to say to me.

I drifted away from the group and went over to the swings and sat on one and watched the girls jump rope. They jumped single, and were awkward jumpers, arms flailing and hopping up and down as if they were splashing around in hot water, unlike the girls in Westville, who jumped double Dutch, arms at sides, still, or moving in rhythm as they pranced like fillies on parade, their toes lightly touching the ground between the two ropes slapping at their feet. I was not good at double Dutch, but after a week with the girls in my class, I became bored with the slow pace and had retreated to the swings. Then, too, most of the girls had been together since first grade and knew each other very well and had their own secrets and jokes, and I hated being around girls who were always whispering and making fun of less popular girls.

They asked the new girl to jump rope. She laughed and shook her head and looked around. When she saw me she walked over and sat on the swing next to me.

"Hi," she said.

"Hi." I touched my toe to the ground.

"I'm in your class, right? What's your name?"

I wasn't surprised that she knew I was in her class. I was the only colored girl in the room, so she couldn't miss seeing me. I told her my name and added, "I'm new here, too. We just moved here this summer."

"Gee, we got somethin in common already," she said.

We had something else in common. Red hair. But mine was darker than hers and arranged so differently that I supposed she had not noticed. She took one of the barrettes from her hair and shook her head, and her hair, sunlit, silky, smooth, fell toward her face and she shook it back. "These barrettes hurt my head when I keep them on too long." She rubbed the tender spot with her finger, then pushed her hair back and anchored it again. I touched one of my stiff plaits, and if a fairy had given me three wishes my first one would have been for hair that swung free when it was loose.

"Where do you live?" she asked me.

"On Beechwood Avenue. In back of the carpenter's shop."

"I know where that is! We can walk home together!" She pushed her swing back and swung forward. "You ever go over the bumps?"

I had. Up, up in the air so high that the swing jerked and pulled me back and left my stomach behind. I hadn't tried it since. "Lots of times," I said. I wasn't going to tell her it made me sick in the stomach.

"Well, come on! I'll beat ya!"

We were off, furiously pumping our bodies back and forth trying to be the first to hit the bumps but I could hardly push myself for watching her as she swayed back and forth with her red hair streaming behind her then whipping forward across her face.

"I'm winning, Amy! I'm winning!"

I didn't care. Somehow I knew that I had found a friend. Hadn't she told me we would walk home together? And I was certain when she told me in line that I should call her Kitty.

Since Kitty was new and I lived near her, Miss Quinlan let me go home early that day. Lonnie and June Lewis had gone on ahead to the athletic field because they were playing touch football there nearly every afternoon. That meant that James and I and Luetta and some of the smaller kids from Union Avenue would walk home without the supervision of the older boys, and Luetta had assumed the job of overseer.

As Kitty and I strolled along behind them, I turned from Hillcrest Avenue into Green Street to follow them across the athletic field. Kitty was puzzled. "Why are you going that way?"

"This is Green Street. It's a shortcut to the athletic field. We can cross through there to Sycamore Street and then go through Union Avenue. Then we'll be right in front of your house." Even as I spoke my heart was sliding down to my stomach. As soon as I'd said Union Avenue her face told me something was wrong.

Now she was looking down, digging a little hole with her shoe in the grass strip next to the pavement. "I can't go through there." Her voice was low.

"Through the athletic field?" I said. A lot of white kids went that way. "Everybody goes that way to Sycamore Street."

"I mean through Union Avenue," whispered Kitty. Her freckles disappeared in a crimson blush.

At the same time the blood rushed to my face and I was so embarrassed I wanted to disappear myself. She hadn't said so, but I suspected she couldn't go through Union Avenue because only colored people lived on it.

After a moment, she looked up and shrugged. "My mom told me to go up Hillcrest Avenue. And you can walk home that way, too. It's not that much longer."

Oh, I knew I *could* walk that way. And a few times in order to avoid Asbury in the morning, I *had* walked that way. But that afternoon I knew I *wouldn't,* for I had looked up the street and seen James and Luetta waiting for me at the gate to the athletic field. Luetta would never let me forget that I walked home with a white girl instead of her and James. Oh, James wouldn't care. But Luetta would call me a white man's nigger every time she saw me. And there she stood, waving at me to hurry, as if we were best friends.

Kitty had seen Luetta. We looked at each other. And we both knew what we were going to do. She spoke first. "I'll see you tomorrow, okay?"

"Okay." I blinked quickly, then we both turned and started running.

When I caught up to James and Luetta, she looked across at me and her nostrils flared. "We thought you was gonna walk home with that white girl, didn't we, James?"

*Didn't we, James?* Oh, I wished I had nerve enough to push my fist into that simpering, sneering face.

"It don't make no difference to me," said James. "I know my way home."

That shut her up. She sniffed and walked ahead of us, nose in the air, then ran to catch up with Bumpsy. I leaned over and hugged James. I was so happy he spoke up that I stopped in the Jew store and with my last two cents bought him two Tootsie Rolls.

The next morning I thought Kitty might have changed in her behavior toward me, but as I passed her house she was sitting on her stoop waiting for me. She would walk to school with me, she said, but she had to stay with her little brothers until her mom got home from work in the mornings. She was a nurse. She worked nights.

At morning recess Kitty came over to the swing and sat down, saying nothing, merely looked at the ground and twisted the swing. Finally she looked up at me and said, "I got an idea."

"What?" I said. We started swinging slow and easy.

"My mom told me not to go through Union Avenue. She didn't say I couldn't go through Green Street or the athletic field."

We looked at each other and laughed, and then we started swinging so fast and so high that I went over the bumps and didn't feel sick at all.

That afternoon Kitty turned onto Green Street with me. When Luetta saw her, she rolled her eyes, but she pushed the Union Avenue kids in front of her and we followed her along the edge of the athletic field and watched the boys playing football. The kids wanted to stop. "No!" said Luetta. "We ain't got time to watch them now! We gotta go home and change our clothes first!"

They scuttled ahead with Luetta nipping at their heels, wanting to linger but afraid to stay. Luetta could be pretty mean, but she and June were charged with getting the kids to and from school safely, and she took the job seriously.

"Whyn't you let 'em watch a little bit?" said Kitty. "They can't get dirty just lookin."

Luetta turned and scowled and threw a look that should have rooted Kitty to the ground. Then she turned and we all headed for Sycamore Street. Now Luetta probably thought her scowl would discourage Kitty from walking with us. I would've stayed behind if she'd glared at me like that. But not Kitty. She walked right along with us, laughing and talking. Then out on the street Luetta decided to make a stand. Just as we all passed through the gate, she turned to Kitty. "Why you got to come along with us anyway?"

Kitty stopped. "I'm walkin with Amy."

Luetta looked at me but I looked away and she leaned toward Kitty. "You better not come into my street!"

*Her* street. I wanted to ask her how it got to be her street but I didn't. I just kept quiet.

Kitty tossed her head. "I ain't comin into that old street. But I can if I want to!"

Luetta leaned closer. "You better not, white girl!"

Kitty's face paled; the freckles on her nose and cheeks were as red as drops of blood.

Luetta pressed on, repeated her words. "White girl!"

Kitty recovered and leaned into Luetta so they were almost nose to nose. "Yeah, I'm a white girl! So what!"

Luetta blinked; she stepped back. The Union Avenue kids she had herded through the athletic field threw their heads back and laughed in sharp little barks like lion cubs excited by the smell of blood.

James jumped around screeching and pulling on my arm. I tried to contain myself. But when I saw Luetta's face, I laughed so hard that water rolled from my eyes.

Oh, the sight of Kitty that day, red faced, defiant, gave me courage enough to last a lifetime. I could never have done that, been the only colored girl among a group of white kids and challenged them if they called me names. But Kitty, I was going to discover, was a redhead with an attitude; at her tender age she had mastered the art of the "woof."

Luetta came to herself after a moment. She looked around at us all laughing; when her eyes met mine, I stopped.

Kitty, as if nothing had happened, turned to me. "I'll meet you at my end of Union Avenue, Ame. Okay?"

I nodded.

She grinned. "I bet I beat ya!" And she started running up Sycamore Street to Hillcrest Avenue.

I didn't run. I knew she couldn't beat me there. Since I was right at Union Avenue, I merely had the base of a square to run, whereas she had the sides and the top.

We all started walking again, Luetta now walking beside me, the Union Avenue kids trailing, her mouth poked out. "I betcha that old white girl better not walk on Union Avenue." Poor Luetta. She was unaware of her new status in the group now. Even I, who before that day would have said nothing to her, found the courage to speak up.

"What you gonna do if she does? Throw rocks at her like Asbury Tate?"

The little kids also found their voices. They giggled, but they stopped when Luetta stopped and gave us her stare, reinforced with her hands on her hips. I returned the look, but only for a moment. She had a glare almost as powerful as my father's. Holding her eyes, I walked by. I knew she would win if I looked away.

James and I waited at the end of Union Avenue and Kitty soon came puffing into sight. We sat on her step a moment, talking; James pulled a nickel from his pocket and asked us if we wanted a pretzel from the Jew store. I didn't want a pretzel so I said maybe we could all go and get a piece of candy.

"I can't go over there," said Kitty.

Thinking this was part of her mother's injunction against going through Union Avenue I said, "But the Jew store isn't really on Union Avenue. It's on the corner."

"Yeah, but it's a Jew store," said Kitty with a shrug. "Nobody over here goes in there."

"Well, I'm goin over there," said James. He ran across the street.

I frowned. I didn't understand what Kitty meant, but I didn't want to keep asking her about it. I might make her angry and I certainly didn't want to do that. And if she hadn't answered me when I had asked her why she couldn't go through Union Avenue, she probably wouldn't tell me now why she couldn't go into the Jew store.

We were having a spelling test the next day and she pulled out her list of words and we called them out to each other. By that time James was back and the kids on Kitty's side of the street were coming out to play. A few stopped to stare at us. I stood up nervously. "I think me and James better go."

Kitty had also noticed the kids. She stood up and brushed down her skirt. "Ah, don't let 'em bother you. They don't like me neither." She stuck her tongue out at a boy who was staring boldly at us. "What're you lookin at?" She hopped up her steps and waved good-bye from her doorway. "See you tomorrow." Again a quick poke of her tongue at the boy and she was gone.

Just as James and I started down the street we heard a voice. "Amy

Beale! James Beale!" I looked around. Miss Fanny Murray was on her porch beckoning us.

I took James's hand and crossed over to her. Since we had moved to Hillsboro, we had been aware of her watching us from her porch. Since she lived directly across from Weiner's delicatessen, she had probably seen us every day, going to school, going into Union Avenue to play, but she had never spoken to us about our behavior. Until that moment. As we climbed the steps she went over to her chair and sat down and fanned herself with a church fan with a picture of Jesus pasted on one side.

Miss Fanny and I were well acquainted with each other. She was in charge of the primary Sunday school class at the Jeroboam Baptist Church which I had attended when we lived in Woodlynne. For one long year I languished in her class while she injected the fear of God and hell into us with the fervor of a nurse inoculating the sick during a smallpox epidemic. Every week I regarded her from a corner with a scowl on my face and my thumb in my mouth as she read to us from little pamphlets with little blue-eyed, blond, winged cherubs on the cover. One Sunday she tried to pull my thumb out. The more she pulled, the harder I sucked. She tired first and warned me that bad little girls like me would never get to heaven. Having observed that every saint or disciple or angel in her books was white, I informed her that I didn't care. There weren't any colored angels anyway. She wrote a note to my mother who said I musn't be sassy to grown-ups. The following year we moved to Westville, and I hadn't exchanged words with Miss Fanny Murray again until that moment when she sat scowling up at James and me. "What are you two doin over there on that side of the street?" She swept Jesus slowly to the left, then the right.

I shrugged. "Nothin. We was just talkin with a girl in my class at school."

"Yeah, we was just talkin," echoed James.

Jesus was passing quickly back and forth across her face. "Well, stay away from over there. Them people don't want you over there playin with their children."

"But we wasn't playing with anybody. We was only talkin."

She stood up and pointed Jesus straight at me. "Amy Beale, you always did have too much to say. Now git on home, both of you."

We got. Without a backward glance, we got.

That evening when we were doing our homework, to my annoyance James told Lonnie about Miss Fanny calling us over.

Lonnie looked up. "Miss Fanny's right this time. Those people don't like no colored kids. Don't you go over there, James. Amy already said Kitty's mother don't want her walkin through Union Avenue. And you see the way those kids look at us when we go by. So you just stay away from that side of the street. If Amy wants to go over there and get called a lot of names, let her."

"And Kitty can't go into the Jew store," said James.

Lonnie put his pencil down. "I bet she didn't say why." He looked at me. "Did she?"

I shook my head. I knew they didn't like colored people because our skin was darker than theirs. But Mr. Weiner looked white to me.

"Well, it's because of religion," said Lonnie.

I frowned. Lonnie brought a lot of wisdom home from the barber shop, so I knew it must be true, although I didn't understand what he meant. "Religion," I said.

"We go to Bible school and Sunday school and I bet you don't even know what religion you are. What are you?"

I shrugged. "Baptist?"

"That ain't your religion. That's the kind of church you go to. Like some people go to Catholic churches. You're a Christian."

"Why?"

"Girl. All the colored people we know are Christians. And the white people, too."

"What's a Christian?"

"People who believe in Jesus Christ. And Mr. Weiner don't. So he's not a Christian. He's a Jew."

"Well, who does he believe in?"

"God."

Now I was really confused. "Well, we believe in God."

"Yeah. But we believe in God *and* Jesus, and they only believe in God."

"And that's why they don't like Jews?"

"Well, you see all them pictures of Jesus dyin on the cross? They say it was because of the Jews."

"But I remember in Sunday school Miss Fanny Murray said Jesus was King of the Jews. So wasn't He a Jew?"

Lonnie picked up his pencil in disgust. "Girl, you asked me why Kitty don't go into the Jew store and I told you. If you want to know more than that, ask Mama."

But I didn't. Instead of making things clearer, grown-ups always made things more confusing.

AFTER MISS QUINLAN introduced me to the Palmer Method of writing, I spent four afternoons a week learning to produce a "work of art." And I was succeeding. The secret of my success was due mostly to her efforts; she had Palmer on the brain. Practice, practice, practice. The correct posture. The exact positioning of the arm, the hand, which must barely skim the surface and swoop lightly over the paper . . . move the entire arm, not the wrist . . . the arm must not hamper, it must aid, the entire process. This required hours of sitting with a straight back while I practiced, much like a young ballerina mastering the skills of the dance under the watchful eye of a grand mistress. And master them I must, for one of Miss Quinlan's pupils was always the winner of the annual handwriting contest which would take place in April. And Miss Quinlan had fixated upon me as one of the more likely prospects in the class.

I suppose that Miss Quinlan was partly responsible for the development of the friendship between Kitty and me. The very day after Kitty arrived she joined my after-school sessions. "Well! You were taught the Palmer Method!" said Miss Quinlan after Kitty copied her "Four Score" sentence, and immediately raised her a few notches on her Ladder of Skills Accomplished. "But your long division is weak." So Kitty would have to work on her long division and spelling. And of course, she would have to make up all the tests she'd missed in social studies and science and reading since the beginning of the year.

"Now as to the fact that your mother wishes you to come home right after school because you have to watch your brothers." said Miss Quinlan. "You need to come after school for about two months to make up work, and I will write your mother a note to the effect that school is the most important duty you have at this time of your life."

Kitty gave me her assessment of Miss Quinlan on our way home. "Wow. That lady's a witch."

Kitty's mother made arrangements with her married sister, Maureen, and Kitty stayed after school from then on until Miss Quinlan felt we no longer needed to come. She kept us about an hour for each session, and I was relieved of the stress of facing Luetta every afternoon since I walked home the long way with Kitty, and in spite of Lonnie's lecture and Miss Fanny Murray's warning, I walked on Kitty's side of Maple Street. As the children got used to me, they stopped staring, and I would even sit on Kitty's step and we would review the spelling lists together. Maureen would dash out as soon as Kitty appeared and Francis and Matthew, her little brothers, would come out and play on the sidewalk in front of us. And that's how it was for a while.

# ELEVEN

Since I was walking home with Kitty in the afternoons, I only saw Luetta in the mornings, and between her taunts of being a "white man's nigger" and fighting the Battle of Union Avenue with Asbury, I was sinking into a state of depression. Those daily skirmishes had become worse for James and me since Luetta and Bumpsy, once our allies, had turned on us, leaving for school extra early or hiding in the house until we went by or running ahead when they spied us turning the corner into Union Avenue.

Of course it would have been different if Lonnie walked with us every day, but sometimes he left early to be with June Lewis and the older boys. They never walked with their little sisters or brothers. Asbury Tate was like a toothache: The only way to get rid of it was to get rid of the tooth. And Lonnie had thrown down the gauntlet: James and I would have to leave earlier with him or make it through Union Avenue the best way we could. Or go the long way. But something inside of me rejected that solution. I was not going to let Luetta Robey or Asbury Tate stop me from going through Union Avenue in the mornings.

One Monday I got up later than usual and dragged myself down to the kitchen, sick to my stomach at the thought of going to school. Lonnie and James had finished eating and were waiting impatiently at the table.

"Girl, you better hurry up and eat," said Lonnie. "I ain't gonna be late on account of you."

"If you late Miss Duckett hit you with her rubber hose," said James. Bumpsy had impressed James with the account of a smacking he'd got for that transgression.

The clock said eight o'clock. "We ain't gonna be late."

"Well, I want to be *early*," said Lonnie. "If it wasn't Monday and Miss Minnie was here me and James would've left you and you could go to school by yourself."

"Go ahead. I ain't scared to go by myself."

"I would go. But Miss Minnie would probably come before you leave and tell Daddy we left you here by yourself. And I ain't gettin no beatin because you scared to run into Luetta."

The very mention of her name and I jumped up and blasted off at Lonnie. "I ain't scared of no Luetta!"

Lonnie calmly folded his arms. "Yes you are. That's why you didn't go outside all day yesterday. Sittin around here with your mouth stuck out. Well, you better go with us so we can help you out in case Luetta decide to smack you upside your head!"

I erupted and threw the spoon across the table at him. He ducked and the spoon hit the door.

"You crazy! I bet I'm'a tell Daddy on you, girl!"

"I don't care! I don't care!"

The door swung open and a gust of fresh air blew into the heated atmosphere. Miss Minnie, satchel in hand, stood in the doorway gaping at us. Then she looked down at the spoon at her feet. "What has got into you children so early in the morning! Why ain't you all headed for school?"

"This dumb girl's afraid to go to school!" said Lonnie.

James, his arms and mouth flapping like a hungry baby bird, grabbed Miss Minnie's hand. "Amy scared to go through Union Avenue!"

"You big blabbermouth!" My rage uncoiled and swung me around and I stumbled to the steps. "I hate you all! I hate everybody!"

I dashed up to my room where the outburst, like a summer storm, was over as suddenly as it appeared. I sat on the side of my bed in sullen silence, embarrassed, wondering what to do. Then I heard Miss Minnie's footsteps and then saw her face peeping through my doorway.

Seeing I was calmer, she came in and sat next to me. "Now you have to go to school, Amy."

Not a peep from me.

"Did you tell your mother about the girl?"

I shrugged, got up, picked up my books. I was reluctant to explain my problems to Miss Minnie. She was a grown-up. Grown-ups just wanted kids to be quiet, keep out of their way. Be good.

"When I told my mother things, of course not *everything,* she was a big help sometimes."

I was on my way out of the door. I stopped. Maybe if I told her . . . I said without turning, "I didn't tell Mama because she'd get mad and then tell Daddy and they'd start fussin. . . ."

"I understand."

I didn't think she did but I didn't say so.

"This Luetta . . . she said something . . . teased you . . . that's what Lonnie said."

"She calls me a white man's nigger and nappy redhead."

"Name calling. That happens to us all at some time or other. But the best thing to do is face her. No matter how afraid you might be, or embarrassed . . . you have to face things. Now the best thing for you to do is not listen to my mouth this morning . . ." She was escorting me from my room, down the steps. "You have to get to school. . . . Don't go through Union Avenue if that's where this Luetta lives . . . just go around the long way . . . and you might not even see her in school . . . and come back home the same way. . . . She's not going to follow you home." By this time we were at the door. "And you better hurry. You have about ten minutes. And I'll see you when you get home."

When you get home. Those words sounded strange, yet comforting. I took her advice and went to school the long way that morning.

As soon as I got to the classroom I had to jump in line for assembly. We were in alphabetical order and Kitty was three people away, but she managed to move behind me as we made our way to the assembly hall so we could sit next to each other in the auditorium.

We had already been there several times to be informed of the business of the school: school rules; the introduction of the teachers, the principal, the nurse; the programs we could expect throughout the year on the holidays: Armistice Day, the Thanksgiving pageant, the Christmas program, Color Day; and singing assemblies once a month. Today the class was excited because this was the day of the first singing assembly.

I was familiar with singing assemblies. Once a month in Westville classes in every grade would sing songs that they'd learned in class or songs that were to be taught to us in the assembly by the music teacher. The music teacher at Hillsboro was Mr. Kunstler, intense, tall, with thin blond hair and thin, elongated arms like the sleeves on a wet sweater hung up at the wrists. He was in charge of the choir and the orchestra, and I had met him the previous week when I tried out for the upper grade choir. I could not read music, but I had a strong alto voice and could carry a tune, which seemed to be two prime criteria for an elementary school choir. Not only that, but his raised eyebrows indicated he was impressed when I sang in harmony to any tune he played on his piano.

In Westville we had sung a variety of songs. "The Old Oaken Bucket." "Home on the Range." "Jeannie with the Light Brown Hair." "You Are My Sunshine" and many others that I loved. I expected to sing those same songs at Hillsboro, and I was looking forward to the singing as we filed into our seats. Since we were fifth graders we sat near the back; the last seats were assigned to the tallest students in the school, the sixth graders.

When we were all seated and quiet, Miss Edwards, James's teacher, was on the stage, and she went up to the podium and read the Bible. After that we pledged allegiance to the flag and sang the National Anthem. At our first assembly I had looked for Lonnie to see if he was going to do what he said about adding "white people" after "justice for all." Since he was a grade ahead of me his class sat behind mine, but he was across the aisle and I could see his face. As we were saying "and justice for all" I sneaked a look his way. Instead of stopping at the end, his lips kept moving and he said "white people." The only way I knew what he said was because he had told me. Otherwise, I wouldn't have noticed a thing. But Miss Quinlan had noticed me and she took me aside after assembly and told me I must be attentive and respect my flag. I had shown the proper amount of penitence (a few tears) and she had smiled and patted me on the shoulder and sent me to the lavatory to wipe my eyes before I returned to class.

Now from an aisle seat her eyes swept our class continuously, and whenever I looked her way my eyes met hers. Finally Mr. Kunstler walked onto the stage, gave us the page number of the first song, brought our chins up to attention, his arms down as a signal to begin, and we were off with "Home on the Range." Kitty, on my left, dug me in the ribs and sang loudly.

> *Home, home on the ray-hay-hay-hange*
> *Where the deer and the antelope play-hay-hay-hay . . .*

This song, Mr. Kunstler had reminded us, was a song of the Old West, to be sung as if we were cowboys dreaming about home. Not the way Kitty was singing it, head back as if she were baying at the moon. I leaned past her to see if Miss Quinlan noticed but her eyes were on Mr. Kunstler. I looked at the board in front of the auditorium for the page number of the next song, then flipped through the book. At the top of the page was a picture. My heart sank. Two inky black children, white eyeballs popping, were sitting in a large bed. Their hair was twisted into teeny plaits all over their heads. One child had white bows on each plait.

*Pickaninnies.* My first-grade teacher at Woodlynne had read to us about Topsy, a pickaninny on a slave plantation. What the significance of that lesson was I have never been sure. But the children in the class had laughed at me and whispered, and shame had washed over me as I stared at the picture she'd held up for us. I was affected the same way now as I looked down on this picture. I kept my eyes on the book and listened to Mr. Kunstler. "Boys and girls, now in contrast to the song we've just sung, this song is sung in a southern dialect. And we soften the r's. We say 'dah-kee,' not 'darky.' 'Shoat-nin.' Not 'shortening.' " He sang a line for us. " 'Two li'l dahkees lyin in dee baid, One ob'um sick and dee uddah half daid.' If you look at the top of the page you'll see the word 'sprightly.' Sprightly means lilting, happy, lively. Like this." He sang again, this time smiling broadly, tapping his foot, and bobbing his head. " 'Call foe dee doctuh, dee doctuh said, feed dem dahkees some shoatnin bread.' " Then he brought down his baton for us to begin and the voices in the auditorium sprang to life, with bobbing heads, tapping feet.

Sitting here now, thinking about that time, I still feel the flush of shame that came over me and I knew that my brothers would feel it too. I remember looking back at Lonnie; he seemed turned to stone, lips not moving, staring ahead, as he had that day in the barber shop when we had overheard the men talking about our father. I remember sliding a look at Kitty, smiling, singing, head bobbing as she followed Mr. Kunstler's instructions. And I remember that feeling of guilt that came over me when I wanted to tap my foot and sing, too. I remember looking around to see if any children would be looking at me or Lonnie since the song was making fun of colored people.

A boy in the row ahead of me nudged the boy next to him. They giggled softly. If you weren't expecting it you wouldn't have noticed them. The first boy whispered to his friend and they turned and looked toward Lonnie. I looked away, lowered my eyes. I looked at the picture, at the girl with the ribbons. If she got caught in a big wind, they'd whirl around like propellers and she'd take off up into the air. And those eyes bugging out of her head. She looked like Luetta when Kitty had screeched at her that day at the corner of Union Avenue. I controlled an urge to laugh. I stretched my eyes and pressed my lips together and looked up. The boys in the row ahead were singing now, eyes on Mr. Kunstler energetically wielding his baton as if he were leading the audience in a rendition of the Hallelujah Chorus.

*Mammy's little baby likes shoatnin, shoatnin*

I hummed and tapped my foot.

*Mammy's little baby likes shoatnin bread.*

Head bobbing, I began to sing.

# TWELVE

Perhaps the purpose of these songs was to provide a multicultural experience for the children in the school. Hillsboro, as I remember it, was heavily invested in "Learning by Doing." James's first-grade class went to a farm to see the cows and their udders and learn where the milk came from; the children squeezed the teats to see the milk foam in the buckets. They had learned a poem in class: "How now brown cow, what makes you look so sad?" combining pronunciation (learning to round their o's) with this class activity, and they stood on the bottom rail of the fence and said the lines as they patted some cows. They brought milk back to the school and churned it into butter and brought buttermilk and butter home so we could taste it.

This same impulse behind the improvement of our minds was extended to the amelioration of our souls—the aim being, I suppose, to produce God-fearing and God-loving children. The God we were exposed to was a benevolent, Protestant God and He was presented to us just as reverently as I'm sure He was in the parochial school. Along with praising Him in the assemblies, we heard Him praised in the mornings when the teacher read ten verses from the Old Testament of the Bible. To supplement these activities, once a week at one o'clock all the children attended Bible school at a church on Hillcrest Avenue that was a block up the street from the elementary school. It was not a large church, and I can't remember the name. I do recall it was a Baptist church and it sat on a little hill in the center of a neat green plot of ground and it was surrounded by a black wrought-iron fence, whether to keep God in or the Devil out I wouldn't know.

Every class was assigned a different day. James, a first-grader, attended on Mondays along with the second-graders, I and the other fifth-graders on Thursdays, and Lonnie, a sixth-grader, on Fridays. Third- and fourth-graders attended on Tuesdays and Wednesdays. On those days after lunch we lined up at the iron gate and were led into the church by a tall man in a black suit, one of the assistant pastors, named Mr. Goins; he had a ruddy face and blond hair that was thinning on the top. We would walk down the hallway and smell the church smells and enter a long room with tall ceilings and oak woodwork. There were two long tables and a piano. We would sit around the table and the pastor would read stories about the Garden of Eden and Moses in the bullrushes and, in a deep voice that rumbled up from his chest, he would lead us in hymns about Jesus and His love, faith and duty and friendship. I think back to those days and I now know that I drew strength to face Luetta from the words of those songs that we sang every week. One song especially brought me comfort.

> *Earthly friends may prove untrue,*
> *Doubts and fears assail.*
> *One still loves and cares for you,*
> *One who will not fail.*
> *Jesus never fails, Jesus never fails,*
> *Heav'n and earth will pass away*
> *But Jesus never fails.*

Those words made a lasting impression on that melancholy child who sat at her window and sang them whenever she was depressed.

As I grew older, in the business of living I forgot those words, that song. And then one day recently I was leafing through a hymnal and came upon it. "Jesus Never Fails." And as I picked out the tune on my piano, I was so overcome by the memory of those days that I wept.

I came to know the meaning of that word, for I have cried and wailed many times in my life, but I have never wept. For *wept* implies such a deep, an uncontrollable seeping of water from the eyes, and dry them as we might, it seeps until the emotion subsides and rests in a lump at the base of the throat. The tears dropped down the front of my dress and I wiped my eyes, wondering at such foolishness. A hymn. Bringing tears. A hymn. And it came to me then the power that music has in shaping the lives of the people we are to become.

Lonnie had a different memory of Bible school, for an incident occurred there that led him to have a meeting with the fearful Miss Duckett. I forgot about it and never learned the full story until he was almost thirty years old and he was thumping on my kitchen table ranting about the ludicrousness of black men hanging pictures of a white man on their walls and calling him their savior.

"JESUS WASN'T WHITE anyway. That's what these white folks want you to believe. Jesus was a Jew. And Jews weren't no way white two thousand years ago. And they sure didn't have no blue eyes. It's enough to make you sick . . . all these black folks suckin up to Jesus."

"I don't think they'd think of it as 'sucking up.' 'Worshiping' is what they call it, I believe."

"And what does that mean?" (One of my father's favorite phrases.)

"Believing in Him. Following His precepts," I said.

"Who did you know that did? Mama? Daddy? Aunt Louise? Aunt Leona?"

"Well, I don't think Daddy did."

"You don't think. You don't think. You know he didn't. Not the way that man carried on in his life." He sipped his tea. Tea sweetened with honey. "But maybe the Lord will forgive him. I know I won't."

He was silent a moment. Staring into a corner. I didn't know what brought him to my house that day. But I now suspect that it was because he was soul searching—wanting to verify his reasons for hating his father, to acquaint me with his changing beliefs, I don't know. Lonnie had been searching for his kind of God for a long time.

I was at the other end of the table sewing, nodding at the appropriate moments. I was busy making costumes for the assembly my seventh-grade class was going to put on the following week. I didn't have time to talk, but I suspected he wanted me just to listen, anyway. Not offer advice. Just listen.

" 'Honor thy father.' Hmph. How can you honor your father if he don't honor you? Or your mother? I swear I don't remember one time that man took our side in anything. Not one time. Or let Mama take our side. And I will never forget that time—do you remember that time when I was in the sixth grade and I got in trouble at Bible school?"

I nodded. "Billy Whitman called you a nigger."

"No. Not a nigger. Darky. Darky. And you know where he got *that*. From those damned songs we used to sing in the auditorium. That faggot Kunstler up there on the stage showin them how to say it: Dah-kee. Dah . . . kee. And then the very next afternoon that Billy Whitman tried to get in front of me when Mr. Goins told us to line up and I wouldn't let him in front of me and he pushed me . . . and called me a darky. And I knocked his ass right on the ground. And we were rolling around. Mr. Goins stopped us or I would've beat him to a pulp, that's how mad I was. And by the end of Bible school, we were okay. Mr. Goins made us shake hands. And we were okay. Until that afternoon."

That afternoon came back after he reminded me. Just as school let out Kitty had pulled me aside and told me that Miss Duckett had sent for Lonnie. Kitty had been the office messenger, had delivered a note to Miss Early, Lonnie's teacher. It wasn't stapled, so she'd read it. "Send Lonnie to the office immediately." And Lonnie looked scared, she'd whispered.

He couldn't have been dismissed yet, so we waited, James and I. Kitty had to go home right away to be with her brothers, so we sat on the wall and waited. And soon we saw Lonnie coming out of the double doors. Head down. When he saw us, he straightened up. When he reached us his eyes were shining, as if he'd been crying, but he merely said gruffly, "Come on," and we tagged along.

I remembered that other day, the day he'd been left down, and I knew something serious must have taken place in Miss Duckett's office.

I knew better than to ask about it, but James didn't. "What's the matter, Lonnie? What's the matter?" He ran up beside him to look at his face. I stayed behind. Maybe he'd tell James if I wasn't up next to him.

"Nothin. Just that old Miss Duckett, that's all."

Of course no one ever went to see Miss Duckett except for one thing. The Rubber Hose. "Did she beat you with her rubber hose?" said James.

"No. She just hit me on the hand with that ruler of hers," said Lonnie. "Old prune-faced bitch. She never did like us ever since we got to this school and Mama made her test us."

That's how Lonnie felt when he was twelve, and he was still bitter when he was thirty.

I made myself a cup of tea. "I was late for school once, but Miss Duckett never hit me."

"Because you were a girl. These white people, they want to keep black boys down. Then, and now. Every chance they get they got to show their power over them. Especially white women. When they see a black boy in front of them they see a black man, and the first thing they think of is rape. Mr. Goins said everything was okay. But I get back to the school and then she sends for me with a note. Tellin me that she heard I was in a fight and I punched a boy and that couldn't happen in Hillsboro. And she didn't send for Billy Whitman. No. He was right in my class and when he saw me go, I know he expected to go to the office, too. But she didn't call for him. Didn't say nothin to him. Callin me a name wasn't important."

"Did you tell her about him callin you a darky?"

"Sure I told her. I looked her right in her face and when she asked me why I hit him, I told her. Right to her face. And she just kept lookin at me and then turned red, and reached in her drawer and pulled out that long ruler and told me to hold out my hand and hit me twice. Talkin all the time about 'sticks and stones will hurt your bones but names will never hurt you.' But I know why she really hit me. She hit me because I wouldn't look away from her. Looked her in the eye. Didn't know my place. That's *really* why she hit me. And what did that father of mine do when he heard about it? Nothin. Nothin." He stopped. Thought. Then, "It's enough to drive a man crazy, thinkin about all the shit they put colored kids through in school."

I REMEMBER my father's reaction at the dinner table that night. James let the story of the fight and Lonnie's ensuing punishment slip out. My mother had a fit, at least as much of a fit as she would have in front of my father. Miss Minnie, who did not like to see my mother or father get upset, drew her shoulders forward as if she were trying to curl into herself and disappear.

"It would've been different if he was fightin more than once," said Mama. "The first time he should've been warned. Up in Westville they sent a note home if a child caused trouble. And why didn't she call that white boy in with Lonnie and let them both tell their story together? I betcha if they was little white children fightin she would've done that. And she wouldn't have hit *them*, and I'm gonna make it my business to go up there tomorrow to find out about *this*."

My father disagreed. "The boy was wrong, Arleatha. Don't make no difference if he is colored. You can't go stompin up to that school gettin all excited over something you can't prove. He ain't *maimed* or nothin. Lonnie knows he ain't got no business fightin at school."

Lonnie stared into his plate and muttered, "I ain't gonna let no white boy call me a darky and get away with it."

"Look at me." My father leaned across the table and held Lonnie's eyes like a snake charmer; he tapped his finger and spoke softly. "You gonna be called that and worse before you get through this life." (Tap.) "And school ain't no place to prove how *bad* you think you are." (Tap.) "You go there to learn, not to give no trouble, and I don't want to hear about no more trouble." Then he tapped out each word. *"You hear me?"* Lonnie nodded. "And if I *do,* you gonna find out who's really *bad.* Understand?"

"Yes," muttered Lonnie.

Then my father looked at James and me as well, and we answered with solemn nods.

Later that night Lonnie told James that he had a mouth like a bell clapper. He was worse than me, he told him. And poor James cried. I flounced to my room, but not before he sent a barb after me. "And I ain't lettin you walk to school with me no more, either!"

The next morning he didn't let me walk with him. James stayed behind to walk with me. And an incident occurred that would not have taken place if Lonnie had been with us. Union Avenue was empty that morning when we turned the corner. Heart thudding, I took James's hand and we started up the street. When we got past Mr. Chauncey's barbershop we stopped. I looked up at Asbury's wall, then at the top. Nothing. No one in sight. We dashed up the middle of the street thinking we were safe. Then out jumped Asbury. He had hidden behind a recess in the wall and had waited until we were almost up to him and was in a crouch running toward us. I shrieked and dragged James up the hill and down the other side, where we stopped halfway down. We felt safe there, for we had noticed that he never came over the top of the hill.

He was up there doubled over laughing and pointing at us. James teased him with a little jig and a dance. I followed along, shaking my hips and sticking my fingers in my ears and wagging my fingers at that devil up there. Asbury threw a stone. We ducked over to the pavement and the rock clattered down the street and James cupped his hands around his mouth and yelled, "You can't even see how to throw straight, you four-eyed darky!"

I gasped and looked around to see if anyone had heard him. But no head peeped out from a door. No window went up. As usual, the houses were silent as coffins. This time when Asbury bent to find a stone we flew down to the corner and slowed to a walk when we got to Miss Ruby Davis's house. As we turned onto Sycamore Street, I breathed a sigh of relief. Aunt Leona had not seen us.

But Miss Ruby Davis had. "Amy!" She poked a head full of brown paper curlers out of her shed door.

I went over to her hedge. "Yes?"

"Why were you two runnin down the street?"

I shrugged.

"Were you runnin from that boy up the street? That Asbury?"

Something in the tone of her voice told me she wasn't going to scold us, so I nodded. "He chases us all the time."

Miss Ruby nodded grimly and told me to wait out front. James and I went back around and waited. I kept a nervous eye on Aunt Leona's porch fearing I'd be called any moment, but in a few seconds Miss Ruby came out wearing a scarf tied over her head, her chenille bathrobe and chenille flip-flops. Marvin was behind her. He was dressed for school and carrying his books, which were held together with a wide leather belt. He spoke to James and me as he followed his mother down the steps. She pulled her robe closely around her and without a word, started up Union Avenue, Marvin close behind, head sunk to his chest.

I stood there wondering why she had called me. When she looked back and saw that James and I weren't following, she called, "Come on here, you two."

"We might be late for school," I said.

"No you won't. It's only fifteen past eight. You got plenty of time."

She turned and hurried up Union Avenue, Marvin and James and I close behind. Not talking. Just walking fast. At the top of the hill, we stopped and looked down the street. By this time, I had guessed she was looking for Asbury. But he was not in sight.

Miss Ruby's hands went to her hips. "Gone, hunh. Well, it's a good thing. I don't want to have to kill nobody's child out here this mornin. Chasin my child home with stones." She pushed Marvin in front of her. "You go on to school. And if you see that boy and he bothers you, you come on back home, you hear?"

It seemed that Miss Ruby Davis, like Mr. Malcolm Lewis, was an independent soul who had no reason to fear arousing Miss Geneva Tate's ire. After watching Marvin safely to the corner, she strode back down to her house with us scuttling behind her. "I don't know how a child is allowed to pick on other children like that. I been to see his mother once. Now I guess I'm gonna have to take care of Mr. Asbury myself since his mother won't control him. I'll wrap my hands around that little nigger's neck and choke him so hard he'll speak in a permanent whisper." She jerked her belt to tie it tighter with big hands made strong by wringing out towels and sheets and bedspreads as I had seen her often do when I was playing with Marvin. She stepped up to her door. "If he bothers you again, just knock on my door."

As soon as we turned to go, I heard my name again. This time Aunt Leona. She was at the door of her sunporch. "Amy!"

I shuddered. "Yes?"

"What are you and James doing over there?"

Resigned, James and I climbed the steps to her house and she pulled us inside so Miss Ruby wouldn't see her talking to us, trying, as Miss Ruby would interpret it, to get into other people's business. She stood arms folded, looking down at us, nostrils flaring like those of a mare in heat.

I told her the truth. That we weren't doing anything over there. That Miss Ruby had called us to find out the name of the boy who was bothering Marvin. I was crossing one leg in front of the other because I had slipped away without greasing them like Miss Minnie had told me but Aunt Leona's eyes were on my hair. I reached up and felt my plaits. The top one had come loose, I suspected, when I had done that wild waggle in the street. I plaited it and, since the rubber band was gone, tucked the end in. I sneaked a look at James, who looked neat and innocent as usual. Having nothing else to tell, I mumbled something about Daddy not wanting us to be late for school and we rushed out of the sunporch and galloped down the steps and didn't stop running until we got to the schoolyard.

At lunchtime Miss Minnie's hands flew up in consternation. "Child, what in the world do you do between breakfast and lunch to get your hair looking like this! When you left here this morning it was perfectly fine. Your father would skin you alive if he knew you were in school looking like this!" She snatched me with surprising strength for someone so skinny.

"She look like a chicken runnin from a fox," said Lonnie.

James came to my defense. "We was runnin from Asbury."

"Asbury!" Miss Minnie rebraided the willful top plait. "Is that boy still plaguin you all?"

We told her about the trick he had pulled on us that morning. She shook her head. "Well, if his mother don't pay no attention to Miss Ruby Davis, she must not have a good grip on his behavior. You might have to go to school the other way if he keeps botherin you." She searched in a drawer and found two rubber bands and twisted one on the end of my plait and one next to my skull so that the braid rose up from my head like a geyser, much to the amusement of Lonnie and James. "Now these ought to hold this hair until you get back." In spite of my protests she sent me back to school with a warning to walk, not run.

At dinnertime I came to the table apprehensively, thinking that my father would say something about my hair. Aunt Leona must have said something about it because he looked at me sharply when I sat down, but he didn't say anything to me then. No, not then in front of the family. I was to hear about it in private, later.

After dinner we followed a set routine. If my father stayed home instead of going around to Union Avenue, Lonnie and I would take turns washing the dishes. James was now big enough to dry them. So we four would be in the kitchen while Mama and Miss Minnie sat in the yard or upstairs talking, free of our company for at least an hour. If my father went out, Miss Minnie and Mama would wash the dishes and afterward they would sit downstairs and talk while we did our homework upstairs in the living room. This evening my father sent us upstairs to finish our homework.

As I went up I heard my father's voice. Harsh. Questioning. A moment later Miss Minnie came upstairs and said, voice quavering, "Lord, your father and mother down there talking. Oh, that man makes me so nervous sometimes."

That meant they were getting ready to argue, and I suspected it was about me. I waited a moment while Miss Minnie went around to her little cot in the bathroom, until Lonnie and James were stretched on the floor listening to *The Green Hornet*, then I tipped to the top of the stairs and lay on the floor and wiggled forward until my head was hanging over the top step. The door was slightly ajar. I could hear my mother's voice.

". . . got the hair on her head that God gave her."

Then my father's voice. ". . . seems you could. . . ."

Yes, they were talking about me. I hitched myself forward and turned my ear to the door.

My father now. ". . . straighten . . ."

". . . too young . . . hot comb all the time . . ."

Then my father mumbled something I didn't understand and my mother's voice got louder and I could hear all the words.

"I never *had* to learn to straighten hair. *Mine* don't need it."

"What does that mean?"

"Just what I said."

I knew what she meant. That if I had straight hair like hers instead of kinky hair like my father's they wouldn't be arguing about it. Oh, if only I were bald-headed.

"There's nothin wrong with Amy's hair," said Mama. "And if you and your sister keep it up, she'll end up with a complex."

"A complex. How?"

"Well, Leona keeps talkin about Amy's hair, don't she? That time Amy come home from playin with Lonnie and James, Leona had to say somethin. I can just hear her now. 'Now Jawhn, you *must* do somethin about your daughter's hair. It's tew, tew nappy.' Hmph."

I put my hand over my mouth to press back a laugh.

"Well," Mama continued, "it ain't everything in the world to have straight hair. Instead of criticizin Amy's hair, you oughta be tellin her how good she combs it. And her hair sure don't look no worse than most other colored girls' when their mothers leave it alone. Burnin the little girls' heads and ears tryin to give them Shirley Temple curls."

"What's wrong with people wanting to make their children's hair look nice?"

"Nothin. It's just that most colored women don't think hair looks nice unless it's fried till it's crisp. As long as it's neat and clean, that's all they ought to care about. And don't nobody go around straightenin little boys' hair. Then some colored men, they just got the idea that colored women can't be pretty unless their hair's straight. A woman can be ugly and mean as the devil, but as long as she got straight hair she's all right. And if she *light-skinned* with straight hair, whoooeeeee!"

A chair scraped against the floor. Heavy footsteps approached the stairway. I rolled away from the top of the stairway and ran back to the living room as my father's voice roared up the steps. "All right, whose turn is it to do these dishes?"

I ran back over to the stairway. "Mine!"

I started down the steps. Miss Minnie was right behind me. As we stepped into the kitchen the door banged.

My father was gone. My mother was at the sink, muttering. "Straighten some hair. Hmph. Better take care of her own hair."

I flopped into a chair.

"What's that, Mrs. Beale?" said Miss Minnie.

"Nothin," said Mama. She placed two cups on the table and poured coffee, then sat down and repeated the conversation she'd had with my father.

Miss Minnie put a teaspoon of sugar in her coffee. "Lord, Mrs. Beale, that's why I go upstairs when you and Mr. Jack are down here together. He makes me so nervous, jumping on every word anybody says. I declare, a person's scared to open their mouth around him."

"He gets worse as the days go by. Round there gamblin and drinkin at Leona's every night. Alcohol must be picklin his brain. And that sister of his is just as bad as he is. Fillin his head full of junk. Tellin him Amy's hair need to be straightened. Just like her word is gospel."

"Well," Miss Minnie said, stirring her coffee. "You know I've knowed Mr. Jack ever since he was a little boy. And Leona, too." She took a sip.

I gazed at Miss Minnie, trying to picture this withered person as a young woman with no wrinkles, no gray hair, no trembling hands.

"Yes. I know you used to live next door to him when he was little," said Mama.

"Yes. Right next to that house where Leona lives now. That's where their mother and father lived. Off and on. They were both from Virginia. He came up here first, then she came. He was working on the railroad but he gave that up when he had the kids. Then they lived up the block, then back to that house again. Then he died. Stroke, they say. And times were hard for them after he died. Mrs. Beale had to go back home with her mother, then when the mother died, she had to come back here and get work, and it was hard to keep an eye on Jack . . . you know a boy at that age. She and Mr. Jack went to New York to stay with her brother a while. Then she came back here and took in wash and her and Leona come back to that house. And then she got sick and Mr. Jack came home and stayed with them until she died. I guess he must've been about fifteen by then. I know he had a little job cutting grass."

"What was Daddy's father like?" I said, leaning on the table with my chin on my hands.

"Oh, he was a big, dark man. And he was a nice man, John Beale Senior. A nice man. Hard working. Had two jobs. A janitor in the Presbyterian church over in Woodlynne, that he did in the evenings. Then delivered ice during the day."

"How old was Daddy when his father died?"

"Oh, he must've been about four or a little younger."

"Was his mother nice?"

"Amy, stop askin so many questions," said Mama.

"Now, Mrs. Beale. It's natural for the child to ask," said Miss Minnie. "Well, she was hard working. Made them children clean and iron as soon as they were big enough to hold a mop and see the top of an ironing board. They didn't go out to play much with the other kids. Poor little things. Sometimes they would sit outside in the yard or on the front porch."

Mama snorted. "I guess that's where Leona picked up that porchsittin habit."

"But they were always neat and clean—and people said she was mean . . . mean . . ." Miss Minnie shook her head on those last two words.

"And she passed it on, too," said Mama, sipping her coffee.

" 'Deed, I declare, I guess she did. Beat them children so bad sometimes you could hear them hollerin up and down the whole street. Mean . . . mean . . ."

Mama sniffed. "Crazy is more like it. My papa was the same way. Mean and evil. Always beatin on somebody like he was crazy."

Miss Minnie got up and took her cup to the sink. "Then those little children up and down Union Avenue used to make fun of them a lot. They were the darkest ones on the street and they were quiet and scared of their mother so they wouldn't fight. I used to have to go out practically every day in the summer and chase those mean little devils. Throwing rocks and calling them names." She stopped to wipe the table and she was silent so long I thought she wasn't going to tell any more about my father so I said, "What kind of names, Miss Minnie?"

"Indeed, what kind of names do colored children call each other? Niggers. Blackies. Anything mean that comes into them empty heads. Then one time Mr. Jack got so mad he started hitting one of them with a stick. If I hadn't run out there and pulled him off that boy he'd'a killed him sure. Or maimed him, anyway. Mr. Jack's always had a terrible temper, you know."

"Hmph," said Mama.

"Then you know the children laughed at Leona because she had short hair and her mama put it in corn rows. To keep it neat, I guess. That ain't so bad when they're little, but when they get bigger they should plait it some other way."

"What's a corn row?" I said.

"Hush, Amy, and stop interruptin," Mama said sharply. Then, seeing my embarrassment, she added, "Like Luetta wears her hair."

"She says they're French braids," I said.

"And she's French," said Mama.

Miss Minnie started washing dishes. "Looking back, I guess that's why Leona and Jack are so sensitive about hair and color."

"That ain't nothin new," said Mama. "When I was little and went to school, these little dark girls named Sheltons used to wait for me and my sisters after school every afternoon. And they picked on us because we was light and had long hair."

"Aunt Louise ain't light," I said.

"She wasn't as dark as they was, and that's all they needed. And we had to fight our way home every day with sticks and rocks and anything else we could find to throw. And sometimes they'd catch us and pull our hair almost out of our heads. Just because it was long. They was too many for us to beat. Lord, if we didn't have a time! Sometimes they'd chase us right up to Papa's fence, callin us yallah hussies, and we'd get up on the fence and yell at them then, because we were safe. They were scared to come near us because we had a big old collie named Tom we'd sic on them. And would we yell! 'If you light you all right! If you black get back! If you brown stick around!' Oh, we'd be hollerin at the top of our voice, and they'd throw stones and yell back, 'The blacker the berry the sweeter the juice!' And we'd holler back, 'But when it's too black it ain't no use!' Oh, many's the day I went home with a headache after fightin them ugly shorthaired girls. Sometimes we were scared to go to school, but my mama would make us go . . ." Mama sipped her coffee and stared at the wall as if she were viewing some scene from the past. The water sloshed and the dishes clattered as Miss Minnie placed them on the counter.

I sat silent, chin resting on my hands. I could easily picture my mother as a little girl running home from school and fighting. But it was strange to learn that my father had been a little boy whom other children teased.

Miss Minnie called me to dry the dishes and I jumped up to get the dish towel. "Well, Mrs. Beale," she said, musing, "I've lived long enough to know one thing, and that is this." She handed me a dish. "Sometimes Negroes are their own worst enemy. Name calling. Fighting over color, getting excited over hair. Looking at the outside, not worried about the inside." She sighed. "When God made Negroes, he should have made us all the same color with the same kind of hair. Then there wouldn't be nothing to argue about."

Mama snorted. "He did, Miss Minnie. Then the white man started messin with our mothers."

"Hee hee," said Miss Minnie. "I declare, Mrs. Beale, you always got an answer for everything. Hee hee."

"It's the truth."

"Well, I pray for Mr. Jack." Miss Minnie shook her head. "Yes, I pray for Mr. Jack."

"Jack Beale need more than prayers," said Mama.

I took Miss Minnie at her word and I mentioned him twice in mine that night with three extra pleases. It had worked with the numbers when Mama wanted to move, hadn't it? Perhaps if I asked very hard it would be twice as effective.

BUT I BEGAN to doubt whether even prayers would work as I listened to the conversation between Aunt Louise and my mother one afternoon later in the week. We were in the living room. I was doing my homework. My mother was pressing the new priscilla curtains she'd bought for the front windows.

"The cops raided Leona's house last night," said Aunt Louise, settling into the sofa and folding her arms across her chest. "And it's about time they cleaned out that nest of niggers. Carried out a van full of them. I thought Jack might've been in the bunch but he wasn't."

Mama shifted the curtain forward.

Aunt Louise recrossed her arms and shifted her haunches. "Don't know how Jack's gonna keep his job if he keeps hangin around Leona's playin blackjack and poker every night."

"Who says he's around there every night."

"He ain't got no twin, and I can sure see him sittin on Leona's back porch most nights under that gambler's light drawing all them bugs. She's only five houses down."

"That must be somethin," said Mama, turning the curtain over. "You on your back porch spyin all night and Leona on her front porch spyin all day."

"And he's down there most afternoons, too."

"And who says that?"

"*I'm* sayin that. Harry Thompson lives next door to me and he sure works on the same truck as Jack and when he comes home from work in the afternoon Jack is right there with him. 'Course, Harry comes right home after work. I can set my clock by him. Four-thirty every day he walks right up them front steps to his house. And Jack keeps right on down the street to Leona's. At least, he walks that *way,* so naturally I assume that's where he goes."

"She's his sister. I guess he thinks he has a right to see her whenever he wants."

"Sister-fister. Don't make no difference. She know he's a married man with a family and she know you work all day and half the night. If he was my brother I'd send his behind on home instead of lettin him sit in my house drinkin and runnin his mouth. I don't understand these women lettin these men sit up in their houses drinkin and talkin."

"Maybe she's lonely. Maybe she might want some company."

"Company! What kind of woman knows a man is married, even if she is his sister, and lets him sit up in her house wastin his time instead of bein home fixin up his house and takin care of his children if his wife is workin? And as for company, she ought to be restin up for the night for them 'friends' of hers that come around there practically every night. If I was a suspicious woman, I'd say she was tryin to break up her brother's home."

"Well, she ain't alone," said Mama, seemingly unperturbed. "I believe there's somethin to that old sayin about what you don't know don't hurt you."

Aunt Louise looked at her sharply, then changed the subject.

※

BY THE END of the week my father had said nothing to me about my conversation with Aunt Leona, and I thought he might have forgotten about it in the excitement of her arrest. But things were back to normal by Friday night. Before my father went out he told my mother he was going around to Leona's. Just before he left, my mother, still smoldering from Aunt Louise's revelations of a few days before, told him that he had promised to put another cabinet up in the kitchen so she could have more room for her dishes. Miss Minnie and I were in the kitchen at the time, and she began to shake, but my father held his temper and said softly that he would do it the next morning.

On Saturday morning my mother and Aunt Louise accompanied Miss Minnie to Philadelphia. It had something to do with helping her clean her sister's house. After placing the seal of approval upon my appearance, they left me in the kitchen with three dimes in my hand with a warning to keep out of trouble and a mandate to deliver that message and two dimes to Lonnie and James, who were still upstairs asleep.

They always got up late on Saturdays unless they were trying to sneak away from me. But they weren't sneaking away today; my father was going to be home. He'd been downstairs earlier to tell Mama what he had to do: brick up a window facing the alley between our house and the building next door. No light came in; it would be a good place for a cabinet. Earlier he had gone around to the lumberyard store to get lathes and plaster, and just as Mama and Aunt Louise left I heard him come into the shed. When he came into the kitchen he poured himself a bowl of cornflakes and sat down across from me. I sat nervously, finishing mine. It had been a while since I'd seen my father at the breakfast table. I was almost overwhelmed sitting there alone with him.

After a few minutes he said, "Well, how's school?"

I was surprised. He'd never asked me about school. Not in my whole life. "Fine," I said. And I swung my feet, feeling good. I was always ready to talk about school. While he got up to turn on the tea kettle I continued. "Miss Quinlan says if I keep practicin I might be the best handwriter in my class, and I'm gonna be in the choir, and I'm catching up with all the books the kids read last year. I had ten to read, and I'm up to four." Oh, I was ready for a long chat.

"That's good." He put a tea bag into his cup and added the water. No sugar. My father was not by nature a tea drinker; he preferred coffee, but he could never make it to his own satisfaction.

"I got a hundred on my spelling test," I said.

"That's good." The casual answer revealed that he had no idea of the time and effort I spent studying to get a perfect score on Miss Quinlan's spelling tests. She tested not only on the current list, but on "demons" from the previous grades. The tea kettle whistled and he got up; while his back was to me he said, "Who combs your hair in the morning, Amy? Before you leave for school, I mean."

I would have felt less pain if he'd turned and thrown the boiling water in my face. Oh, silly girl. To think that my father would have a conversation with me about anything of interest to a ten-year-old. The only subjects he thought worth talking to me about, besides how I combed my hair, were greasing my legs or getting his numbers in on time or being respectful to nosy old people like Miss Fanny Murray.

I didn't answer. He turned toward me. "What's the matter?"

I stared down at my empty cereal bowl. "Nothin." How could I tell him? How could I tell him that when he looked at me, he didn't see me, just my hair? To my horror, tears filled my eyes.

He sighed and sat down. "You can't cry every time somebody asks you something, Amy."

I took a deep breath. "I don't always—well, I don't know why people keep lookin at my hair and sayin somethin's wrong with it. I try to comb it right."

"Now, nothing's wrong with your hair, Amy. Your Aunt Leona was asking me the other day if you would like to get it straightened. That's why I asked."

Aunt Leona. I knew it. I knew it. I didn't want to hear any more. I jumped up, ran up to my room, and slammed the door. I was afraid my father would follow me and yell at me, but he didn't, and I sat on my bed crying and hating him and Aunt Leona.

And my hair.

# FOURTEEN

When I finally clumped back down to the kitchen it was after twelve o'clock and my father, at the window plastering, sent me to Weiner's for lunch meat. I passed Lonnie and James in the yard playing marbles. I swelled with resentment. Was I the only one in this family with legs? Or was it that only girls were good for running errands? If I hadn't come down to the kitchen when I did my father would probably have called me. He wouldn't have asked *them*. They were doing something important. *Playing.* I was just doing something *stupid. Reading.*

And look at old Maple Street. Empty. Not a soul outside. All probably inside eating lunch getting ready to go to the movies. No. We couldn't go to the movies. Had to stay inside under my father's eye. By the time I left the store, resentment was burning and bubbling, steaming from my nostrils. I crossed over and walked on Kitty's side of the street, hoping one of those old women *would* come out of one of those raggedy, teeny houses and say something to me. Hunh. It wasn't *their* street. But the houses sat dumpily silent as I marched by.

I turned the corner and almost knocked Kitty down. "Girl! What's wrong with you! Always jumpin out from someplace!"

Kitty laughed so hard her face turned pink. "Scared ya, didn't I?" She leaned toward me, and pushing her hair behind her ear, she held a dirty fist up to my nose. "Look."

I pushed her hand aside. "I can't see through no fist." I started walking. "I got to get this baloney home for lunch."

Kitty hurried beside me and stuck out her open hand. On her palm was a crumpled cigarette. "See?"

"Yeah, I see."

She closed her hand and dropped it to her side. "You ever smoke one?"

"Nope."

"Want to try one?"

"Nope."

"I did."

"I ain't you."

"You're just afraid."

"No I ain't. I puffed a cigar once." (A lie.) "And all those things taste nasty."

We had reached my driveway. Lonnie and James were standing in the yard looking our way, and when they saw Kitty, Lonnie ran toward us. "Girl, Daddy said you better hurry up with that baloney."

"See you, Kitty." I followed him up the driveway.

"I'll wait out here for ya!" she called.

"Okay! I gotta eat first!"

After making a pile of sandwiches and putting them on a plate I watched Lonnie and James wolf them down and run out ahead of me, leaving me to do the dishes. There were only a few, my father had said when I complained. I washed and dried them quickly, fearing he might initiate another tête-à-tête. But he let me go as soon as I hung up the dish towel and told me to tell Lonnie and James not to leave the yard because he might need a little help with the plaster.

My brothers weren't in the yard. I ran over to the driveway and looked down, expecting to see them talking to Kitty, but they weren't there, either. I ran to the back alley. There they were, standing on the sidewalk at the end of the alley looking into Kitty's outstretched hand.

I approached them nonchalantly. "What you doin?"

"Kitty got a cigarette," said James, bug-eyed.

"Aw, boy, you worse than Amy. Blabbin things," said Lonnie.

"Worse than me!" I was incensed. "I knew she had that old cigarette when I came home, but I didn't tell you, did I?" I turned to Kitty. "Come on, Kitty. Where we gonna smoke it?"

After much discussion, Lonnie decided on a little airless passageway between our house and the building next to it, but I cautioned against it. "Daddy's in the kitchen."

"Aw, he ain't gonna hear us," scoffed Lonnie. "All that noise he's makin hammerin and scrapin. And we ain't gonna talk. We gonna smoke."

In the passageway we sat on a narrow concrete ledge jutting from the building next to our house. Kitty took a book of matches from her pocket.

"Aw, we ain't supposed to have matches," said James.

"We're only gonna strike *one*." Lonnie took the matches from Kitty. "We can't smoke unless we strike a match. You gonna smoke, ain't you, Amy?"

Kitty was looking at me. I nodded.

"You want to smoke, don't you, James?" said Lonnie.

James nodded, and assured that the decision was unanimous, Lonnie put the cigarette between his lips, pulled back the matchbook cover, took out a match, and struck it. It sputtered, then the flame caught on and Lonnie held the flame against the tip of the cigarette. He sucked it, then puffed quickly two or three times and the tip began to glow. He threw the match on the ground, stamped it a few times, puffed three more times, then handed the cigarette to Kitty. She took it gingerly between her first finger and her thumb, and I watched, goggle-eyed, as she puffed it once, took a long drag, then another without choking or gagging. Then she handed it to me.

I took the crumpled cigarette and put it between my lips. The paper was damp; the moist tobacco stung my tongue. "Eewww." I pushed it from my mouth. Kitty giggled and showed me with her lips and fingers how to smoke the nasty thing. I tried again. I drew in a deep breath and the smoke went into my mouth and up my nostrils. I was afraid to cough or make any kind of sound. The water ran out of my eyes. I bent over and wiped them with the hem of my dress. As I raised my head I looked at the end of the passageway and dropped the cigarette. Standing there was my father with a trowel in his hand. The others saw him too. How long he'd been standing there I didn't know.

He didn't yell. He just stood there, his face and hands and clothes covered with a fine white powder looking like a zombie arisen from a dusty grave. For a long moment we stared at each other, then he jerked his head and said, "Come out of there."

We straggled into the yard, into the bright sunlight where we stood as my father looked us over one by one.

Finally he spoke. "Who's got the matches?"

Kitty held out her hand. The matchbook lay on her palm.

My father took it. "You go home, young lady."

She flew down the driveway as if six demons were after her.

My father turned to Lonnie. "Where did you get that cigarette?" His voice was soft, silky.

"I found it," whispered Lonnie.

"Go get it," said my father.

In a few seconds Lonnie was back with it curled in his fingers.

"It's still smoldering. Do you know what that means?"

Lonnie didn't answer.

"You could've burned this house down, that's what."

No answer.

My father studied him a few seconds. Then, "I asked you before. Where did you get it?"

But Lonnie wouldn't tell on Kitty. "I *found* it," he said stubbornly, studying the ground.

"Look up at me when I'm talking to you!" roared my father. We jumped. He only yelled when he was really angry. "*Where* did you find it!"

Lonnie looked up with shining eyes. "In the gutter."

"In the gutter! Then you didn't *find* it." His voice was soft, now. "You were *looking* for it. Out in the street looking in the gutter for cigarettes." He bit his lip. Waited. Then, "Didn't Amy tell you I said to stay in the yard?"

I hadn't remembered until that moment. I almost fainted. But still no answer from Lonnie. There was a silence while my father thought, chewed his lip, thought. Then he said, "I've been warning you all about your behavior. Mmmm-hmmmm. Well, I see now that talking ain't enough. I been promising you a whipping. And I see that my promises don't matter to you either. You're getting worse every day. Well, we'll see. Now get up those stairs."

As we scuttled toward the kitchen, he headed for the tall privet hedge at the back of the yard. We galloped up the steps and ran to the sofa and sat down and folded our hands to wait for him. Waited for our first whipping since we'd moved to Hillsboro. I expected it to be more serious than those he'd given us up in Westville. Up there it had been for silly things: Lonnie threw my doll down the cellar steps and broke it up; James peed on a bush; I sat on James's toy piano and broke it; James drew on the wall in the living room; we sassed an adult on our way home from school; just before we moved we broke the sofa playing swimming and diving. Depending on the case he'd smacked us on the tail with his bare hand, or lashed us on the legs with a switch or his belt, but once Lonnie had run from him and he'd taken a stick and cracked him across the shoulders a few times.

Most of the children we knew in Westville or on Union Avenue got whippings. We entertained each other in the schoolyard with our tales of whackings by our parents. June and Bumpsy Lewis's descriptions of the screams and bruises were enough to curdle the blood. And just the week before in the schoolyard Kitty had shown me the results of her whacks. As we got off the swings at morning recess her dress got hiked up by the chain attached to the seat and revealed a dark mark on her thigh.

"You got dirt on the back of your leg," I said.

Kitty twisted around and looked. "Ah, that ain't dirt." She touched the mark. "I got a beatin." She lifted her dress and showed me marks on her other leg as if they were badges of bravery. "See?"

I reached out and touched them. "Gee. Don't they hurt?"

"Nah. Not now. I wouldn't cry so my mom beat me harder. She don't like it if I don't cry. But I didn't. So this is what I got." She lowered her dress.

"Your *mother* beats you?" I was shocked. All the children I knew had one beater in the family. The father. My mother would yell at us, yes, but she would never hit us.

"Sure. Don't yours?"

"No. Just my father."

*"When I took care of grandmom Lotty she was over a hundred years old. And evil and mean. She couldn't get along with none of her sons' wives. My mother's brothers' wives. When me and Mama was in Virginia they would fight and carry on. Somebody had to stay home from work to watch her. She was senile then, you know. That's why I first fell behind in school. They kept me home to watch her. She would wander away from the house, so they tied her to the pump with a long rope. She would call me over—I was only eight or nine—she would call me over and make me bring matches and light her pipe. She almost burned the house down one time and wasn't allowed to have no matches. She would ask me to bring her some and if I didn't she would take a switch to me. If her pipe wouldn't light she would take a switch to me. . . . She was a mean woman. When she was younger she would beat my uncles every day, even when they was big enough to be men. My Uncle James (her brother) would say, 'Sister (her name was Charlotte, but they called her Sister), Sister, why you beat them boys every day? They didn't do nothing.' And she would say, 'They might've done something I didn't see them do.' That's why she beat her boys so bad. For what they might've done. And me too. Whipped me for nothing . . . They didn't treat me right down there. No, they didn't treat me right."*

When my father came toward us with the switches in his fist, James and I started sniffling. My father, iron faced, ordered him and Lonnie to take off their pants. They stood before him in their underwear, shaking, and poor James broke into loud sobs. I, on the sofa, began twisting my hands and wailing in sympathy.

He whipped Lonnie first, grabbed him and held him in the crook of his arm and slashed the switches across his legs. Lonnie screamed and thrashed his legs and kicked against my father and tried to wiggle loose. But he just gripped him tighter and the switches whooshed through the air three more times before he let Lonnie go. He scuttled over to the couch and then my father called me and I screamed and tried to run but I slipped and fell and he grabbed my arm and I scrambled on the floor and screamed and kicked and hollered Oh, Daddy,

Oh, Daddy and he snatched me and lifted me up and I felt three sharp stings on my thighs and I gasped and screamed once, loud and long, and before I could get my breath and scream again it was all over. I ran over and sat beside Lonnie and wiped my arm across my face. I heard James scream two times. Then silence. I peeped from under my arm and my father's chest was heaving. He wiped the sweat from his face with his shirtsleeve and said in a hoarse voice, "Now sit there and don't make a sound."

I held my breath. James sank against me, sniffling. Lonnie sat as if dead. My father stood there a few minutes, eyes narrow, biting his lip, then he turned and crossed the floor and disappeared down the stairwell.

As soon as the top of his head vanished, we moved. Looked at each other with swollen eyes. Then for some unaccountable reason we started gasping and giggling; words poured out through the gulps. "Lonnie's legs were pumpin like he was ridin a bike. Amy got a scream like a hoorah. And James squeaks like a mouse."

We giggled out. Sat quiet. Then, "It didn't hurt all that much," said Lonnie. "I hollered real loud though. June Lewis said if you holler real loud it doesn't hurt as much. And then your father thinks he's really hurtin you and he don't beat you so hard."

"Kitty's mom beats her," I said. "She don't cry at all."

"Her mother. She's crazy," said Lonnie.

"Here's how Lonnie went." James got up and turned around and around and pumped his knees and we laughed so hard we slipped onto our knees, holding our stomachs with one hand and our mouths with the other so our father wouldn't hear us. Finally we flopped onto our backs, laughing so hard we were too weak to move.

We pulled ourselves up and sat silent, staring at the walls, the window, listening to the sounds of scraping from the kitchen. We were leaning and drowsing when at last our father came up the stairs. We sprang to attention. "You all go to your rooms," he called from the stairway.

About an hour later he came to my room, hair slicked back and smelling of Noxzema. He called Lonnie and James down from their room, gave us a dime apiece, and told us to stay in the house until our mother came back. Lonnie and James gave him a few moments head start, then they dashed out behind him to run to the store and spend their money.

I thought this would be a good time to try my coffee dye again, and I had just poured the last cup of coffee over my head when I heard the kitchen door bang, then footsteps running up past my room. Lonnie and James going to their room. I locked my door and threw a towel over my head and hid the bowl and cup under my bed, then jumped back on my bed with a book in my hand just as footsteps pounded down the stairs. My doorknob turned.

"Amy? Why you got your door locked?" It was Lonnie.

"Because I want to, that's why."

"Come on, girl, open the door."

"What for?"

"I got you a soda."

I opened the door and stood there. Lonnie brushed by me.

"Who told you to come in here?" I went and flopped on my bed.

Lonnie said nothing. Just eyed me, looked around. Sniffed. "It smells funny in here. Like coffee." He eyed the towel on my head. "What you doin with coffee?"

The game was over, I knew. "Just dyeing my hair, that's all."

I got onto my knees and pulled the bowl from under my bed. I didn't want to see Lonnie's face when he laughed. But he didn't laugh. I looked up at him.

He was looking down at me with a peculiar look on his face. He didn't ask me why, he seemed to know. He shrugged. "Girl, your hair's gonna turn darker. Mama said so, didn't she?"

"I want it dark now," I said. I stood up with the bowl.

Lonnie shrugged. "Suit yourself." He started for the door. "Want to play some Monopoly with me and James?"

After I rinsed the coffee from my hair we sprawled on the floor in the living room and drank soda and played Monopoly. At the end of three games James got tired of losing and jumped up. "You and Lonnie always win." I suggested Parcheesi, but that was not the type of game he had in mind. Lonnie and I always beat him in those games because we were older. James wanted to do something physical. Like play Boogie Man, a game we played up in Westville. There were many places in our old house to hide in and jump out and scare each other. Here there was only one deep closet and no cellar steps to hide under. Even their room in the attic, long and bare, had no good hiding places.

Children have always made up games about the adults around them, and we were no exception. Doctor. Throw the dolls down the steps and rush them to the hospital or pull out the stethoscope and examine them. School. Sit the pupils on the steps and smack their hands if they talked. We made up many little plays about our teachers and our parents. I would be the mother, Lonnie the father, and James would be the child. Lonnie would fuss at him when he didn't eat, spank him with a little switch when he disobeyed, and James would cry. No hugs. No kisses. No forgiveness. The plays we created began with what we knew, and we knew none of that. And now Lonnie proposed an updated version of this game. He would be the father, James and I would be the children.

"In this game," he explained, "I get my belt. And it starts out with you and James beggin me not to beat you. And you have to think of some reasons for me not to beat you. Like, Amy, you can say, 'Oh, Daddy, don't beat me, that cigarette just jumped in my hand!' " James and I fell on the floor laughing. "Or James can say, 'Oh, Daddy, don't beat me! I didn't take the numbers around because I spent the money on Tootsie Rolls!' " Squeals from James and me. "You know, you think of something that Daddy can beat you for and then I'll be Daddy and I'll beat you anyway no matter how hard you beg. And I won't hit you hard . . ."

And so we played. And James went first and he was on the floor grabbing Lonnie's ankle, and Lonnie dragged him all over the floor all the time slapping at him with one of my father's leather belts, and we were laughing and screaming and Lonnie was hitting James and James was yelling, "Oh please don't beat me Daddy, oh *please* don't beat me you big black Daddy!" And when he said that we stretched out screaming and weak.

And that's what we named our game.

Big Black Daddy.

We must have played it about an hour, then Lonnie got carried away and hit me once too hard and I told him I wasn't playing unless I could be Daddy. But he said no, and it wasn't fun anymore. So I went to my room to read. Lonnie was angry, but I didn't care. I didn't need any more welts on my legs.

※

"WHOEEE!" Mama.

I dropped my book and ran up the third-floor steps to the attic where Lonnie and James were flopped on their bed, mouths wide open. "Mama's home!"

They sprang awake. I galloped down two flights of stairs with them at my heels. We fell into the kitchen.

"My Lord!" Aunt Louise was slipping off her shoes. "Is you all crazy! Fall down them steps you'll kill yourselves!"

James ran over and jumped into my mother's lap.

Lonnie and I stood by the table, sober, silent.

Aunt Louise rubbed one foot with the other. "Sure is good to get off my feet. I worked harder today workin for Miss Minnie than I do for white folks."

A look at James's face, then ours, and the smile on my mother's face disappeared. "What's the matter with you all?"

"We got a beatin and I didn't even do nothin!" wailed James.

Then we were all three talking at the same time. Lonnie prevailed since his voice was the loudest. As he talked, James and I nodded our affirmation, and James pulled down his pants and displayed the red welts on his legs. I raised my dress and showed her the thigh with the angriest marks. Lonnie had no red marks to show, just swellings, as if leeches had burrowed under his skin.

The sight inflamed Mama. "Beatin children don't mean they're gonna do right! If it did the world would be full of saints!"

Aunt Louise sucked her teeth. "Jack should've skinned these little niggers alive. Out in the alley smokin. They could've burned up the whole block, much less theirselves."

"It was Kitty Donovan who had the cigarette. Not us," said James. "She was showin Amy how to smoke."

I glared at the little rat.

"Kitty Donovan!" Mama shook her finger in my face. "Listen, didn't I tell you to keep away from that poor white Irish trash and their trashy ways?"

I was dumbfounded. She had never mentioned poor white trash to me. Or trashy ways. Or Kitty Donovan. I wasn't aware she'd even heard of Kitty Donovan.

"Oh, I know about that time Miss Fanny Murray told you to stay away from her side of the street. I just never said anything, that's all."

"Trash or not," said Aunt Louise, "that white gal didn't take a gun to these niggers' heads. They smoked because they wanted to."

"Hmph. Them Donovans is just a bunch of scum. All of them. Joe drinks like a fish. And him a cop. And his wife, too. Got throwed out of that last house they was livin in over in Mayfield. Noise and dirt. Livin like a bunch of gypsies, movin from house to house with them snotty-nosed kids tearin them down worse than they was. And round here spreadin *knowledge*. Keep it up, they won't be livin there where they are too long, neither." She reached up on the shelf over the sink for a jar of Noxzema. "Come over here." She moved James aside and I moved to her side and she rubbed the Noxzema on my thighs and when she finished, "You stay away from that girl. All she's gonna do is get you in trouble."

I moved away from the table, and pants around his ankles, James waggled over to her next. "Poor little boy." She rubbed the ointment in and looked around for Lonnie, but he had slipped out of the kitchen.

# FIFTEEN

October. The world was turning red and yellow and the smell of dying leaves was in the air. They dropped from the trees and floated to our feet and Kitty and I mashed them under our feet or picked them up to make leafy bouquets for Miss Quinlan's desk. We were growing accustomed to the after-school sessions with Miss Quinlan and developing the pride that children feel when a stern teacher praises them for a job well done. I was mastering long division; Kitty was conquering the spelling demons.

We reached her house. "Come sit on my step with me, Ame." "Nah. I gotta go home." "Ah, I'm tired of nobody to talk to in the afternoon just watchin my little brothers." I thought of my mother's warning, saw Miss Fanny Murray sitting on her porch; I looked at the women of Maple Avenue who were sitting on their porches enjoying the late afternoon sun. They didn't seem to mind that I was there. I looked at Kitty who was gazing at me like a puppy wanting to play, and I relented and sat on her stoop and we opened our spelling books and I called the words to her first and she called them to me. And after we finished the spelling words we sat back on our elbows and basked in the warm sun, one leg crossed over the other, wiggling one foot, watching the little kids play on the sidewalk.

In front of us Kitty's little brother Francis was playing with one of the boys from up the street. Francis was a friendly little one. He was always smiling, always polite. Sometimes I gave him candy, he held out his dirty little hand and thanked me without prompting. So he and this little boy were squatting on the sidewalk, digging into the cracks on the sidewalk with sticks. Just digging, as little children like to do.

Then another boy marched up. He stood looking down at Francis and his friend digging. They paid him no attention. They were concentrating on their digging. And the latecomer walked over and hit Francis. Why, we never found out. Who can fathom the motives of a four-year-old?

Francis stood up and began to cry.

"Hit him back, Francis," said Kitty.

But Francis just stood there crying, his big red sweater hanging off his shoulders, crying and rubbing his dirty hand across his face and leaving dark brown streaks. So Kitty went over to him and took his hand and hit the boy with it. The boy hit Francis again. Then Francis put out both hands and pushed the boy. Plop! To the sidewalk he dropped, not hurt, not crying, his mouth and eyes open as wide as a baby bird's. Kitty and I burst out laughing.

His mother, who must have been watching, swooped down on us with a broom. When the child saw her, he burst into tears and screamed as if he'd been jammed with a hatpin. And the mother! She flew at us, her hair and dress streaming behind her like the wicked witch from *The Wizard of Oz*. She shook her broom at Kitty. "You goddamn Donovans better keep your dirty hands off my kid!"

Kitty held her hands out in front of her and turned them over to look carefully at each side, then held them up to her face, then looked at the woman and said, "My hands aren't dirty."

"You black-Irish brat! You make trouble wherever you go!" She swung around to me. "And you. What were you laughing at?"

I back away from her.

"What's a *nigger* doin over here anyway? You don't belong over here!" She pointed her broom at Union Avenue. "That's where you belong! You and all your kind!"

Then she swung at me and I ducked and scooted across the street to stand in front of Miss Fanny Murray's house. I looked back across the street. Kitty and Francis had disappeared. Only the mothers and a few children were standing together, looking over at me, gabbing and nodding. The word *nigger* drifted over and I swelled up. What had I done wrong? Nothing. I was going to yell that across the street when I heard Miss Fanny's voice behind me.

"What are you starting over there, Amy Beale?"

I turned and looked up at her. "Nothin."

"Come up here."

I clomped up onto her porch.

She nodded her head in the direction of the people across the street. "Didn't I tell you the people over there don't want you playin with their children?"

"I was only talkin—"

"From what I just seen, you don't need to be over there *period*. Talkin or anything else. Oughta be home doin somethin constructive. And this time I'm goin to tell your father when he pass by here today." She waved me away with a skinny brown arm. "Now get on home." She followed me to the edge of her porch. "And I'm gonna stand right here until I see you turn that corner."

I ran down the steps. Tears stung my eyes. I didn't know who I hated most. Those women or Miss Fanny Murray.

MY FATHER came home earlier than usual. Miss Minnie was apprehensive because I had told her about the incident when I came home and she liked a peaceful dinner. But my father did not broach the subject at the table. He merely asked where my mother was. Miss Minnie told him she was going to stop by Aunt Rachel's and would be a little late. We ate in silence, something we often did when he was home for fear that we'd let something slip that we shouldn't and get a lecture. That evening I said nothing at all.

After dinner he sent Lonnie and James upstairs and told me to stay at the table. Miss Minnie followed them up. I knew now that Miss Fanny had told him, and I braced myself.

He got up and tied a dish towel around his waist. "Amy, I want to talk to you and I don't want no crying." He started clearing the table.

My right leg began to jitter.

He removed my plate. "What's this I hear about you giving Miss Fanny Murray some trouble? Talking back and not doing what she tells you? And what are you doing starting trouble with those white people on Maple Street?"

*Talking back. Starting trouble.* Now both legs were jittering. "I was only just talkin to some girl." Why did I have to explain this over and over and over?

I was only a child and I knew that I was not supposed to argue with Miss Fanny Murray, but in spite of her warnings I sensed the *unright-ness* of what she was telling me. I remembered my mother telling Miss Minnie that day in the yard that *nobody* could tell her what side of the street to walk on. So I stubbornly clung to the idea that I wasn't doing anything *wrong* by sitting on Kitty's step. Miss Fanny Murray and that mother were wrong and my father would have to agree with me if I explained it to him.

"I only just stopped to talk to Kitty Donovan after I came out of the Jew store."

"The *what*?" said Daddy. He stopped, dishes in midair.

What had I said wrong? I hesitated, my heart racing, afraid to repeat my words. He must have realized he had frightened me into silence and if he wanted an answer without a bucket of tears he would have to take a different approach.

He placed the dishes on the sink and turned to me and kept his voice low and even. "Now, you said you were comin out of the Jew store."

Those were my words. I nodded.

"Mr. Weiner's delicatessen?"

I nodded again.

"Who do you hear call it the Jew store?"

Lonnie. Luetta. Kitty. *Mama.* I knew better than to mention names. I tried to get around it. "Lots of people."

"Lots of people." The answer didn't please him.

My eyes began to water.

He looked away from me. "Amy, I don't know if I can explain this too good." He looked at me again and his voice was soft. "Now when we lived in Westville there was only colored people. And we didn't see the way anybody was treated mean and called names except colored people. But here in Hillsboro there's a lot of different kind of people and you're gonna come across a lot of name callin. Now if a colored man owned a store and you went there, would you call it 'the colored store' or 'the negro store'? Some people might even say 'the nigger store.' Do you think that would be right?"

I shook my head.

"Well, it's the same for Mr. Weiner. Now, I've known him a long time, and I've always called his store 'Weiner's delicatessen' or 'Weiner's.' And that's what nice people still call it. Not 'the Jew store.' And that's what I want you to call it."

"Is 'Jew' a bad word?" I asked.

"No. It's the way it's used that makes it bad."

"Like 'nigger.' "

" 'Nigger' is a bad word. Period."

"Why does everybody say it?"

"It's just a bad habit some people have. Not everybody says it." Then his voice softened. "Amy, words are like . . . like clothing. If you're poor, you can dress in rags and be dirty, or you can dress in rags and be clean. Just because you're poor, you don't have to be dirty. People judge you by the dirt on you and the dirt that comes out of your mouth. I want you to remember that."

"I will," I whispered.

He waited a minute. "Now I want to talk to you about how you got in trouble with Miss Fanny Murray. Why were you playin with this little girl? You said her name is Kitty."

"Kitty Donovan. She's in my room at school."

Daddy turned away from the sink. "You mean that little girl who was around here the other day smokin?"

I nodded. Oh, I knew just what he was going to say. Keep away from her.

But he said nothing for a moment, then, "Can't you find nobody else to play with?"

"Only Luetta Robey and she's always fightin and callin me names."

Silence.

"No other girls your age on Union Avenue?"

"No. And only Kitty lives near us." I stared down at my shoe.

Silence. I felt his eyes on me.

Into that silence, without raising my eyes, voice trembling, I found the courage to speak. The words knocked at each other as I tried to express my frustration. "Lonnie and James, they have friends because all boys live around on Union Avenue, and in school, there ain't nobody colored in my class, and so I have to play with Luetta, and then when Kitty came to my class, me and her started walkin home together and then Luetta called me a white man's nigger. But I didn't care about that. And then Kitty, lots of times she has to watch her little brothers after school until her mother comes home, and she could come into Union Avenue to play, probably, but her mother won't let her, and that's where we play most of the time, down by the Jew—I mean by Mr. Weiner's garages. She can't even walk home through Union Avenue with us after school, and I was only talkin, that's all we do is talk, and we were studyin our spellin and Miss Fanny Murray told me to stay away from that side of the street. Why? We only talk and study our spellin and then today this mother she got mad because Kitty's little brother pushed her little boy and she called me a nigger and she came after me with her old broom and Miss Fanny said she was goin to tell you." I wound down. "And we were only talkin."

My father said nothing for a long time. I kept looking down at my shoe. Finally he came and sat near me. "Well, I see Joe Donovan every day. Maybe I'll talk to him, see if she can come around here and play sometime. Would you like that?"

I looked up at him. He met my eyes. I nodded. "But Mama don't want me to play with her. She says she's poor white trash and will only get me in trouble."

He got up and went back to the sink. "Poor white trash, hunh. Well, that's a good example of sayin things that you shouldn't. Sometimes your mother says things without thinkin."

I wanted to pull my tongue out. They'd probably start arguing and it would be my fault. But I was too happy to dwell on that thought. He was going to see if Kitty could come and play with me. I sat quietly, waiting for him to dismiss me. Finally he said, "Well, we'll see."

*We'll see.* The hope that was rising in me disappeared. Whenever my father said that, whatever he was promising usually didn't happen.

"You go on upstairs and do your homework," he said. "I'll finish the dishes tonight."

When I got to my room Lonnie was waiting for me. "Hmph," he said, arms crossed, leaning against the doorjamb. "Mama told you Kitty was gonna get you in trouble. But no, you couldn't listen. Mmmmm-hmmmm. Hardheaded. Well, I guess you know now. They looked at you hard but you still kept goin over there so they called you a nigger to make you understand. And Kitty will probably do the same thing one day when she gets mad at you. Call you a nigger. She's just as poor white as they are."

I flared up. "Kitty's not like that! She likes everybody!" I looked away from him and bent over my composition book.

"She don't like Jews. James told me about her not goin into the Jew store for candy because Mr. Weiner is a Jew."

I kept my head bent. "She just said that's why her mother wouldn't let her go into Mr. Weiner's store. She didn't say she didn't like him."

Lonnie snorted. "You better wake up, girl. All these white kids here in Hillsboro are prejudiced. You oughta hear those white boys in the schoolyard talkin about hatin Jews and Catholics and wops. They say all that stuff in front of me because I'm colored and they don't think I care, but I know as soon as I go away they add niggers to the list of people they hate. And Kitty is probably just like them. But you don't want to believe it so you'll have somebody to play with besides Luetta."

THE NEXT FEW DAYS, wary of walking on Maple Street, I took the long way to and from school and stayed home after school instead of going into Union Avenue to play. Miss Minnie regarded me with a furrowed brow, but she said nothing. I stayed up in my room and practiced my handwriting and was especially quiet at dinnertime. My mother was working later now, since she'd found five steady jobs. Two of them included cooking dinner. So at our table now were us and

Miss Minnie and my father, and everyone was talking in muted tones as if there had been a sudden death in the family. Finally on the third day, Luetta approached me almost timidly after school and asked me to come and jump rope.

And there we were at the garages jumping rope, Bumpsy and I turning and Luetta jumping, when Kitty came to her corner, and to the surprise of us all, she came across Maple Street into Union Avenue. Bumpsy and I stopped turning, mouths open. Luetta stopped jumping and stared. Kitty's face flamed but she came right up to us and said, "Can I jump with you?"

I closed my eyes. Please let Luetta be nice to Kitty, a little voice whispered. But I needn't have worried. Luetta was overjoyed to have another girl so we could jump double Dutch.

"I'm not sure I can turn double Dutch," said Kitty.

"Aw, it's easy," said Luetta. She snatched the rope from Bumpsy, doubled it, and she and I proceeded to show Kitty how simple it was. "You just turn like this, one hand, then the other hand, and this hand, then the other hand," and after watching us a few minutes Kitty was able to turn alone and she and I stood at each end of the rope turning and grinning at each other while Luetta jumped to her heart's content. Once, between jumps, she said breathlessly to Kitty, "Can you come whenever you want?"

"Yep," said Kitty.

Luetta grinned and jumped more furiously.

And me, my heart was singing.

When it was time for me to go home, Kitty walked with me up Maple Street to Hillcrest Avenue. Though the children on the sidewalk at her end seemed to take no notice of us while we were playing, I was still wary of passing by her house even with the width of the street dividing us.

All the time we were jumping rope I wondered how this miracle had come about. Had Daddy really said something to her father? Was this their doing? Now I dove in and asked her the question I hadn't wanted to ask in front of Luetta. "How come you can come into Union Avenue?"

Kitty shook her head slowly. "I dunno. My mom just changed her mind."

"Why?"

"I dunno. She was off from work today and she saw you playin rope over here and she asked me if I'd like to come out and play with you for a little while since we were friends. She's weird. I been askin her for weeks, and it was no, no, no. Stop askin me. Then today—wham— she says that I can go into Union Avenue to play with you today, and every other day."

"Who's gonna watch your little brothers?"

"My sister. Mom says maybe they need somebody older, especially after what happened the other day. You know." She leaned forward and whispered, "Those bitches actin like that. Sayin all that stuff to you."

"Wow!"

"And she says I can walk home with you, too." Kitty stopped walking. I stopped. She took my arm and turned me to her so we could face each other. "And you know what *else*?"

What could be better than the news I'd just heard? "No."

"She said I could go to your house some days and play with you if I want to. Can you beat that?"

I couldn't. "How come?"

Kitty shrugged. "I don't know but I think it's because you don't live on a colored street like Union Avenue."

"Sort of like Miss Fanny Murray don't want me playing on the white side of Maple Street."

"Grown-ups sure can be weird sometimes," said Kitty.

We continued walking to the top of the hill, then said good-bye, and I walked slowly home with muddled thoughts.

Apparently my father had kept his promise to speak to Joe Donovan and Joe Donovan had persuaded his wife to change her mind. He was certainly a man of contradictions. He *had* listened to me, gone out of his way to support me in this case, yet had been painfully inattentive when I tried to tell him about my progress in school, had criticized me for the way I kept my hair and lashed me with switches for minor transgressions.

For me so far, my father had been one-dimensional, had revealed only his strict side, but that day he had exposed a new dimension; his mean side had been muted by a softer, more thoughtful side.

I couldn't fathom his reason for that long talk with me then, but when he was sitting at my table talking about his childhood, I began to understand.

*"One time when I was real little I lived in Tyler's Row. Tyler was an old white man, mean as hell. He owned a lumberyard. Had this row of houses on stilts that he used to rent out to poor people. Two colored families, us and another family, I can't remember their name for the life of me, and some Italians and Irish lived there then. They were the worst people to come in contact with, those Irish. They brought a lot of hatred with them from Ireland. They hated Italians, and colored people even worse. They used to fight me all the time. Call me nigger and shine. Called the Italians names, too. Wops and guineas. Oh, we all had some fightin times down there. Many's the time Joe Donovan saved my behind. He lived down there, too. The Donovans weren't Catholic like the other Irish, and they hated his family. Anyway, them Catholic school kids would catch me on the way home—I was just a little fellow then, about six. Goin to first grade. Then we didn't live on Union Avenue like the rest of the colored folks, I didn't have any protection of a big group of kids. Those white kids traveled in swarms like bees and would get me on the ground and kick me like a dog. For nothin. Just for bein colored. Many's the day Joe would chase them or kick their behinds and they called him a nigger lover. His mother used to watch me sometimes on Saturday when Mama went to work. And the grandfather, he was this old white-headed man with false teeth. He used to push them out of his mouth and click them at me. Scared me half to death. He'd tell me all about Ireland and the trouble they had over there. Them people had some hard times. Eatin grass. Maybe that's why they were mean as dogs when they got over here. Who knows."*

BY THE END of the week Kitty was jumping double Dutch as well as Luetta, who was such a patient teacher, demonstrating how to jump in and out and turn around and touch the ground.

One evening my father was walking around to Aunt Leona's and saw us jumping. He stopped and watched us for a few seconds and in a rush of happiness I ran over to him and pointed at Kitty and said, "Hey, Daddy, there's Kitty!"

As if he couldn't see her. He smiled and said that was nice and for me to be good and that night as I said my prayers I swore I was going to be good and begged God to help me stay that way and not do anything else to make my mother or father angry.

Or Miss Minnie.

Or Miss Fanny Murray.

Or any other grown-ups who could give me trouble.

# SIXTEEN

After Kitty began playing in Union Avenue, every day after school I dashed up Beechwood Avenue, up the driveway, into the kitchen, and slammed my books on the table. "It's me!" Then up the steps into my room to throw off my school clothes and jump into my play clothes, bookety-book back down the steps. "I'm goin!" And *bang!* would go the screen door behind me.

Miss Minnie didn't stand for that too long.

One afternoon she stopped me at the steps. " 'Deed, I'm scared of children who throw their books around like you little Beales! You got to learn to put everything in its place! First Lonnie, then James, then you, running in and out and jumping in and out of your clothes. Running in here all heated up and sweating. You gonna fall out. Wait! I got to wipe that dirty sweat off your face. Lord, Lord, Lord. Where'd all this dirt come from? And stop that jittering! Those children ain't going nowhere."

I stopped with a sigh and stood like a rock while Miss Minnie wiped my face and brushed off my hair. I doubted that she had ever been young enough to play hopscotch, ever nimble enough to jump double Dutch.

But from then on I walked. Up the driveway. Into the kitchen. Softly closed the kitchen door, slowly climbed the steps. Laid my books on my bed and my shoes under it. Hung up my school clothes in the closet. Tipped back down the steps.

WITH THE HOUSE empty, Miss Minnie spent peaceful afternoons sitting in the yard with one of her hand-crocheted shawls over her thin shoulders, enjoying the warm autumn sun and darning socks with her little wicker mending basket resting on a table beside her. But by the end of November the trees had dropped most of their leaves. They were brown and crisp and it seemed as if a mischievous giant had scattered giant cornflakes over the streets and yards.

After Miss Quinlan dismissed us from our after-school lesson, Kitty and I usually walked home through Union Avenue. We would stop and chat with the kids on Union Avenue, then go home and come back to play. But now with the leaves on the ground, we liked to walk home the long way, crunching the leaves under our feet and kicking them into huge piles so we could roll in them, or toss handfuls of them at each other all the way up Hillcrest Avenue.

One afternoon Luetta waited for us and expressed her displeasure. "Kitty can walk through Union Avenue now. Why you all walkin up Hillcrest Avenue?"

"Ain't no fun walkin through Union Avenue," said James, who had been rolling in leaves with us for a few days. "Ain't no leaves."

She grimaced. "Fun." But she walked up Hillcrest Avenue with us that day, and other days, too, kicking leaves and screaming louder than anybody else.

Soon it started getting dark earlier, the sun weaker, the air colder. Lonnie still stayed outside, unless it rained, to play football, but the only time James and I were out in cold weather was when it snowed. And so far we had not been so lucky.

Miss Minnie, who had called us wild in warmer weather, found out just how much wilder we could be when confined to the house. We wrassled and romped in the living room, played hide and seek from the third floor to the first. Miss Minnie, asleep in the kitchen, would snap awake and leap up. "Lonnie! Amy! James! You all stop that romping around! You hear me! I'm going to tell your father on you!"

Only then would we stop. Then later that evening when my mother came home, she would complain and we would fuss.

Then the door would slam open, bringing my father with a gust of cold air and a roar. "What is goin on in here!" Miss Minnie would jump up like a jack-in-the-box and run upstairs. We would jump into our chairs and bend over our homework. After two full minutes of silence my father would growl and wave his hand and we would scuttle upstairs to bed.

And so the days wore on. And more and more often my father began going around to Aunt Leona's during the week to gamble. One night as he was leaving the kitchen (he had just begun this new routine) my mother questioned him about it in front of us. My father frowned. He didn't like her to question him about adult business in front of the children. And my mother must have been very upset if she did it.

But he answered her. "What am I supposed to do every night? Sit around here and stare at the walls?"

"What do other men do at home?" she snapped back. "Maybe you should ask some of them."

He looked at her hard. Then opened the door and left.

"Where does Daddy go, Mama?" said James.

"Out to gamble," said Lonnie.

Mama shot him a look and he ran upstairs.

It was at this time that I began to pay closer attention to my father. When the weather was warmer I had been outside playing and when I saw him during the week he was dressed and leaving for Aunt Leona's or coming in from Aunt Leona's. Up in Westville, he had not been away every night during the week, but whenever I saw him, he looked as if he were stepping out. But now with colder weather we were all in the house together and I was aware of his every move.

I noticed at first how clean he was. He lugged up his own water to the tub at least three times a week, four including Fridays. In Westville, even though we'd had no inside toilet, we had running hot water, and baths were easy to take. "That's the washinest man I ever seen," Lonnie said one night.

When he came home from work he had a set routine. First he would go up into the bathroom and put grease and water on his hair and pull on his stocking cap over his head. Then, being also one of the press-ingest men we had ever seen, he would set up the ironing board in the living room and press his pants and iron a shirt if Mama hadn't had time to iron one. Then he would hang his shirt up in the doorway to the bathroom and place his pants carefully across the back of the sofa. Then he would shine his shoes and place them on the floor by the sofa.

While he worked, he sang. He had a nice voice, a croon, and we would lie at the top of the third-floor steps and listen.

> *Nights are long since you went awaaaaaay,*
> *I think about you all through the day.*
> *My buddy . . . my hmmmm-hmmmm*
> *No buddy . . . quite so truuuuuue . . .*

He sang a lot of different songs, but they were all the same kind. Sad, lonely songs. " 'Mexicali Rose, stop cryyyyying, I'll come back to you some sunny day' " or " 'Remember the niiight, the night you said, "I love you," remember?' "

Then he would go take a bath.

Since the bathroom was also Miss Minnie's bedroom, he didn't delay there any more time than it took him to bathe, and he always took it while she was cooking dinner.

After his bath he would come downstairs and eat dinner with us. Mama would still be at work, so the other grown-up at the table was Miss Minnie, and conversation was limited to comments by Daddy or Miss Minnie.

After dinner dishes were done, he would take a cracked mirror from the number shelf and place it on the one over the kitchen sink and shave and afterwards rub his face with Noxzema, remove his stocking cap and smooth down his hair, then take the mirror down and put it away. Then, while we stayed in the kitchen, he'd go upstairs, leaving the kitchen reeking of Noxzema and men's cologne. He would dress upstairs and come back down again a totally different man from the trashman who had entered in baggy old work clothes two hours before. Oh, he was sharp. Sharp as a tack, as they said at that time.

Sometimes he would give us a nickel or a dime just before he went out.

My mother would come in from work not too long after he left; she would smell the cologne and the Noxzema, she would frown, but she never said anything. Not to us, and not to Miss Minnie, as far as we could determine. And soon his absences became as much a part of the family routine as breakfast, lunch, and dinner. But no arguments arose from those visits during the week, for he came home from Aunt Leona's sober as a judge. His drinking, Aunt Leona felt, was due to his early marriage to that ignorant country girl.

Weekends were different. He got paid on Fridays, and after getting dressed he'd reach in his pocket and give us a whole quarter apiece if he was feeling expansive. Otherwise a dime each. He would leave and return on Sunday nights. These were the absences that caused the arguments. When I heard him stumble into the house, I would pull the covers up and hope that he and my mother wouldn't start arguing. If they did, then I mashed a pillow over my head to block out the sounds. If she began crying, I got on my knees and prayed and jumped back into bed, trying to sleep, then I would have the falling dreams. Or the running dreams, and I'd wake up the next morning as tired as if I'd run a marathon.

Lonnie and James and I never talked about these disturbances. They were up on the third floor and probably didn't hear anything. Of course, Miss Minnie was gone every weekend. So I kept everything inside of me, and by the time I got through the day and saw my mother and father in the evenings, their arguments seemed to be part of my dreams.

※

I OFTEN WONDERED why my father couldn't be like the fathers of the kids we knew in Westville and on Union Avenue. When the weather was warmer I would see them coming home from work, quiet, work-worn men who put their arms around the children's shoulders as they ran to greet them. Later in the evening I would see them sitting outside on the sidewalks talking to their neighbors. Smoking. Laughing. Talking. Down in their backyards pitching horseshoes. Now that the weather was cold, they were inside listening to the radio. I learned that from listening to Bumpsy or Luetta complain because their fathers would never let them listen to the radio progams they wanted to hear. We were fortunate. Our mother read (she was an avid reader of *True Detective* magazine) and let us listen to anything we wanted. And so we were glad for that.

JACK BEALE needed more than prayers, my mother had told Miss Minnie. But I mentioned him every night in mine. "Please help me be good so I won't get any more beatins. Please help Mama and Daddy get along better so she can stop cryin. And please lead my father out of temptation and deliver him from evil." I thought that if I prayed, and Miss Minnie prayed, and my mother prayed, that the combined power of our prayers would work the miracle that had been wrought when I had asked God to help Mama hit the number. Of course Lonnie had told me since numbers were illegal God wouldn't help, but she had wanted the money for a good cause at the time, and I knew from Sunday school that God was a good and loving Father to His children and helped them when they were in trouble, and He had. But it seemed as if this time God didn't hear me.

As winter approached, with it came the depression that shorter days bring. And I was tired of living in a house with no running hot water. Oh, I was weary of lugging buckets of hot water up to the bathroom for a bath. My mother had been letting us bathe in a tin washtub in the kitchen, but my father had put an end to that one night when he came in and found Lonnie scrunched up in the tub and James and me pouring water on him. He could not have been more surprised if we had greeted him with loaded six-shooters.

It had been a long time since he had seen any of us taking a bath. James and I were fully clothed, but the sight of Lonnie naked in the tub made him realize that this boy was just about grown. My father remained calm. He sat at the table and with a solemn face he said, "How old are you now, Amy?" Eleven in February, I answered. "And you, Lonnie?" Thirteen in May, he replied. James he didn't question, and the thought entered my mind that this too had something to do with whatever he'd been trying to tell me in the kitchen when he'd told me about men. I guessed that he didn't want me around Lonnie now that he was bigger. But Mama had already taken care of that a while ago by barring me from the kitchen until he was in the tub. And we had been aware of the differences between girls and boys since we were born. Boys had teapots and girls had weewees.

From then on Lonnie and James took a bath together upstairs in the big tub and my mother merely added more water for me and I had to step into water they had used. But after a few times I balked. I was getting finicky; I was no longer satisfied to step into their scummy water. One evening we were in the bathroom arguing about bathing order and our father came in to see why we were fussing.

"I'm tired of gettin in water with your old scrubbed-off skin floatin on top!"

"You just think 'cause you're a girl you should take your bath first!"

"I always have to bring your water first and then have to add some in for me, and I always have to clean the tub!"

"Well, I think Amy can have her own bath after this," said my father. "If you and James want to take your bath first, then you bring up your own water. But you have to drain and clean the tub so Amy can take her bath."

CHRISTMAS WAS COMING, and with it an excitement in school that infected us all with the fever of the upcoming holiday. Miss Quinlan read *A Christmas Carol* to us every afternoon for a week. On the last day of school there was a Christmas assembly in the morning; the choir sang and the pageant took place and our class did the choral speaking. And the afternoon before we left we had a little party, and school was out for the holidays. Two whole weeks of vacation.

With Christmas Day came surprise and embarrassment. On our doorstep was a Christmas basket, which, according to a note, had been delivered by one of the many men's clubs of Hillsboro. It was a wonderful bushel basket, wrapped in red paper, filled with a turkey and all the trimmings. Up in Westville people were just as poor as we were, but no baskets had been left on doorsteps. The Negro and white churches had joined in their efforts to find those families among the poor who were the neediest and these people had applied to the church and received a turkey and trimmings. Since we had Aunt Leona and Aunt Louise, we had never been that much in need. Our table was always laden at Thanksgiving and Christmas and Easter with turkey and ham and greens and pumpkin or coconut custard pies and eggnog and there was plenty of whiskey for the neighbors who stopped by for a holiday drink.

But here in Hillsboro, through the intervention of the schools, the names of the children on welfare were passed on to the clubs of the businessmen, and this Christmas effort was supported by them. In addition to the food, toys that were broken or no longer wanted were donated by the more fortunate citizens of Hillsboro and these clubs volunteered time and money to help the firemen and policemen fix the toys for children who would otherwise find little or nothing under the Christmas tree.

So on Christmas morning we arose to a wonderful sight. A tree, tall and shimmering, which we had decorated the night before, now resting its lower branches on toys we never expected. A football for Lonnie, a clothesline for me to make a jump rope, a red wagon for James, and books and puzzles and games for all of us. Stockings filled with oranges, apples, nuts, candy.

And it was after we had screamed with delight and laughed until we were hoarse that we ran down to the kitchen to find Mama all smiles, taking food from the basket. We were poor, it was true, but it was not until that morning that I was embarrassed to be poor. Oh, I had known we were on welfare. After all, we got our clothes at the Goodwill, we went to rummage sales, and we used stamps to purchase our shoes, as did many other people we knew. But this basket seemed to send a message. You are so poor we need to give you food. I remember being so glad that we lived up a driveway and that our door was in a secluded yard, so glad that we didn't have a front door where our neighbors could have seen the basket.

However, the feeling of shame didn't remain with me long. For I knew that I was sure to get one gift that wasn't a hand-me-down. One from Aunt Louise. Each Christmas she gave us clothing, beautiful dresses for me, handsome sweaters or pants or suits for Lonnie and James, which we always grew out of by the next Christmas. She and Uncle Lee had no children and although she used rough language, she had excellent taste.

As soon as we got washed and dressed, we hurried around to her house. Before Lonnie could knock, Aunt Louise opened the door. "Well. You sound like a herd of billy goats on this porch. Come on in here before you let the heat out." In the hallway she took our coats. "And what brought you all around here?"

We giggled and looked at the floor.

"Well, go on in the living room and say hello to your Uncle Lee."

We walked in straight and stiff in our good clothes and sat on the edge of a leather settee with oak arms. Uncle Lee, sitting in his armchair with one leg crossed over the other, reading as usual, lowered his paper and looked up when we spoke. He was a slim man of medium height and fair skin, a dark pencil mustache, and dark hair. Between his teeth he held a cigar tipped with a gray ash. "Good afternoon." He took a puff on his cigar, studied us a second, then winked.

"Well, what wind blew you all around here?" Another puff.

We giggled. "None."

"None, heh?" He squinted at us through the smoke curling up from his cigar. He listened carefully as we told him everything we got for Christmas. Then he started reading his paper again.

We sat quietly until Aunt Louise came in carrying an armful of packages and sat down.

"How's your mother? Ain't seen her for a while."

"Fine," we said.

"And how's your pappy?"

Uncle Lee rattled his paper. I noticed he always did that when Aunt Louise was approaching a subject that might be too sensitive. I also noticed that Aunt Louise was not blunt and coarse when she was in his presence. She seemed almost meek.

James piped up, "Daddy ain't home," and Lonnie pinched his leg and James ooched and rubbed his leg.

"Up there in Westville—" Another rattle of the newspaper and Aunt

Louise changed the subject. "Well . . . let's see what we have for you today." The packages, next to her, were wrapped in red paper and tied with silver ribbon. She handed the two smaller packages to Lonnie and James. For me there was a very long box.

Aunt Louise sat back as we tried to open them without ripping the paper, but she ended up opening them and handing them to us. Lonnie and James opened theirs first. Blue sweaters, exactly alike, and shirts and ties to go under them. When she opened my present I gasped. She carefully unfolded the tissue paper and lifted out a navy blue coat with a white collar. And in that same box was a beautiful dress, pale blue with puffed sleeves and a white organza collar with lace around the edges. A dainty party dress. A Sunday dress. Aunt Louise held it up to me. "I bought it a little big so you'd have it to wear this spring at Easter, with your coat. You children grow like weeds."

I wanted to jump over and thank her with a hug, but I controlled that impulse and thanked her with a smile instead, as did Lonnie and James. We were so anxious to get back home we almost forgot to thank Uncle Lee, but James didn't. He ran up to him and gave him a hug as he lowered his paper, and Lonnie and I went over, but we didn't hug him. We stood back and grinned, and he gave us another wink and told us to come around before next Christmas.

Outside, we jumped off the porch steps three at a time and stood on the sidewalk. I looked toward Aunt Leona's house. "We should go down to Aunt Leona's."

James screwed up his nose. "Do we have to? She only gives us apples or oranges and a quarter."

"I don't want to go, but Daddy's gonna ask us why we didn't go if we don't," I said. "And he'll blame Mama if we don't go. Besides, Aunt Leona will probably give us more money this year since we're bigger. Maybe a dollar. Don't you want a dollar?"

James nodded. But Lonnie pointed out that if we went down to Aunt Leona's with the presents from Aunt Louise, "she might even want to look at our presents, and say somethin to Aunt Louise, and Aunt Louise would get on us for takin them down there."

In the end we agreed that going there with the presents from Aunt

Louise would create a family disturbance and we certainly didn't want that to happen. We would take the presents home and show them to Mama and then come back around to see Aunt Leona.

But in our effort not to create one problem we created another. As soon as we jumped into the kitchen and threw our packages on the table and opened the boxes for our mother, our father came home. He'd been drinking, we could tell by the smell of him, but he wasn't drunk. Probably not expecting to see us all gathered in the kitchen to witness his entrance, he spoke in a surly tone and came to look at the presents, and as soon as he learned who had given them to us, asked, "Did you stop in to see your Aunt Leona?" He was questioning us, but his eyes were on Mama. Accusing eyes.

We shook our heads, then James said quickly, "We was goin around there, but we had these big boxes, and I kept droppin mine."

I continued. "And so we thought we should bring them home first and then we could go back to see Aunt Leona after we left them here."

The scowl left my father's face, a smile came to my mother's, and the tension in the kitchen eased. We rebuttoned our coats and left for Aunt Leona's.

"You see Daddy lookin at Mama?" said Lonnie, shivering in the wind. "He *was* gonna blame her 'cause we didn't go see Aunt Leona. He'd probably be startin somethin with her right now if James didn't say what he did." He patted James on the shoulder. "You saved the day, boy."

James grinned all the way around to Aunt Leona's.

When we got inside she held out her arms for our coats and invited us to stay for some cocoa, but we hastily replied we had to help Mama cook and didn't take off our coats and hats; in fact, I pulled my hat down further onto my head so it covered my eyebrows. After we mumbled answers to a few mundane questions (how is your father, how is your mother, how are you doing in school) she reached up onto the mantel and handed us each an envelope. We thanked her and made a hasty retreat and as soon as we got out of sight we ripped our envelopes open. In each one was a crisp new dollar bill.

# SEVENTEEN

❧

$M$any of those days during our vacation were turbulent; a few were happy. The turbulence was due partly to the absence of Miss Minnie. She had left for Philadelphia on Christmas Eve to spend two weeks with her sister. Two weeks with us children at home all day in the dead of winter would probably have sent her to her grave, Mama said. But during those two weeks we began to appreciate the place she'd held in our daily lives.

My father now took it upon himself to act as overseer when he came home from work and reverted to the manner of supervision he had practiced up in Westville: restraint, reinforced with his old companions, the switch and the scowl. We didn't mind the switch so much; he applied it to our legs, lightly, if we hadn't completed our chores by the time he got home—dishwashing (from breakfast and lunch), bed making, bathroom cleaning, kitchen sweeping, dusting, table setting (since he was cooking dinner he liked it set before he got home). The scowl accompanied the switches or signified disapproval of the ways our chores were done. Silverware not arranged correctly, beds not made smoothly, toilet bowl not snow white, and so on. But our chief complaint was the restraint. We were so busy with chores we had no time to get outside during the day, and darkness came early and we didn't feel like going out then. Once in a while he'd let us go around to Union Avenue right after he came home, since there was still about an hour of daylight left. We would eat dinner about five-thirty and he would dress and go out just before Mama was expected from work. Seven, sometimes eight o'clock at night.

❧

ON THE FRIDAY evening after Christmas, Mr. Linwood and two other men drove up into the yard with a truck loaded with building material. They had passed by a house being torn down and thought my father could use some of the wood, since we had a coal furnace. As they threw the wood into the yard, Lonnie and James and I helped drag it into the shed. While we were working my father came home. He was overjoyed to see the men and all the backslapping and laughing and joking reminded me of the way he used to be up in Westville. Animated, lively, as if there was a light inside of him that could be lit only when he was with these friends.

They chopped the wood into kindling and afterwards came into the house for a holiday drink, which soon became several drinks. My father sent me around to Weiner's for two chickens which he fried while they sat around in the kitchen and talked and told stories. Lonnie, James, and I lay at the top of the stairs peeping down at them, but when the jokes and stories began to get risqué, my father closed the door. But we could still hear the noise.

At dinnertime they had still not gone home. We were playing Monopoly on the living room floor when we heard my mother, who had worked half a day, come home. The sounds of laughter stopped when she came in. We could hear the men greeting her, then she came upstairs scowling. She asked us if we'd had our dinner, and we said no, and she pressed her lips together and went around into the bathroom, where she often went when she wanted to be alone; she would go in there and lie on Miss Minnie's cot.

"What's wrong with Mama?" said James.

"Tired, I guess," said Lonnie. And we went back to playing Monopoly.

The noise downstairs subsided, and within a half hour there was silence in the kitchen. My mother got up and went downstairs. Apparently my father was alone, for we heard her say to him, "Who in the hell wants to come home tired from workin all day and run into a bunch of niggers sittin around in their kitchen swillin whiskey?"

A low answer from my father.

"And down here eatin and didn't even feed your children. What are they supposed to eat? Air?"

Another low answer.

"Sandwiches. You were gonna make your *children* sandwiches. And you and your good *friends* down here eatin chicken." A pot bangs. *"Chicken!"* Another pot. "I'm out here workin my fingers to the bone and you sittin at home gettin drunk!"

A door slamming. Then pots banging. Then, "Amy! Lonnie! James! Come on down here and get something to eat!"

"I wish Miss Minnie was here," said James.

And that night I prayed, "Dear God, please don't let Daddy come home until tomorrow night and don't let Mama and Daddy be mad anymore when he comes."

MY FATHER didn't come home until Monday night, the night before New Year's Eve. Lonnie and James and I were standing around the kitchen table playing jacks. My mother was upstairs listening to *Manhattan Merry-Go-Round*. He fell into the kitchen with a white man, both of them holding on to each other as if they were inseparable. Lonnie sprang for a chair and helped my father up on it, then got another one and helped the white man up. I ran and closed the door to the stairwell, thinking that if Mama couldn't hear them she wouldn't come running down the steps.

We stood and looked at the men, both of them resting their heads on their arms on the table.

"Ain't that Joe Donovan, the cop?" said Lonnie. He went closer and looked into his face. "Yuuuuup." He stood back, grimacing. "His breath stinks!"

"Shall I go get Mama?" said James.

"No!" Lonnie took him by the arm. "You go around there and sit down!"

We watched them a few moments. They sat as if dead. Then I had an inspiration. "Maybe I should make them some coffee. That's what Mama does. She makes Daddy coffee. Real strong and black, with lots of egg shells in it."

"She'll smell it and come down here," said Lonnie.

"Maybe we should throw some water on them," said James.

"So they'll wake up mad," said Lonnie. "Boy, you sure are simple."

"No I ain't, neither!"

"So you go throw some water on them and see if you don't get a whippin!"

I put in my two cents. "Why don't you all be quiet before Mama comes down here!"

She heard our voices and she did come down, and I sucked in my breath, expecting an explosion like the one on Saturday, but she just stood silently in the doorway and looked at my father and Joe Donovan in disgust, then made a pot of coffee and some sandwiches. An hour later we had them sitting up at the table eating and drinking coffee, mumbling and muttering about how no good they were and dribbling saliva into their food.

Two hours later they were sober. Lonnie and James and I sat on the other side of the table, watching them with wide eyes. My father was penitent. "Sorry, Leatha." He lowered his head. "I guess I'm just an outcast."

To my surprise, my mother didn't give him a snappy answer. She said calmly, "Well, it's almost New Year's Eve." And that was all. It seemed that sobering up a drunk at home was more amenable to her than coming home and finding a drunk getting drunker while she had been "workin her fingers to the bone." Then she went to the shed and came back with what I thought was a quart of milk, but she set it on the table and said, "I made some eggnog," and went to a corner beside the staircase and got a bottle. Rum.

Joe Donovan looked at my father and laughed. "Say, Jack, maybe you need to stay home! Who knows what Arleatha keeps stashed in these corners!" He had been very quiet since Mama had come into the kitchen as if he didn't want to be the spark to set her off.

Then Mama poured them eggnog, and gave a glass to us children, and a little rum into ours, too, and soon everybody was relaxed and laughing almost as if we were at one of my father's parties.

James leaned across the table and shyly thanked Joe Donovan for the red wagon. "I'm going to the A & P on Saturdays and carry groceries home for people."

"You're too little, boy," said Lonnie.

"No, I ain't!"

"Lonnie," said my father.

"I had a hard time keepin that wagon," said Joe. "Four or five people asked for it, but I told them it was reserved. You know, once I went down to the basement and somebody was on the way out of the door with it." He made his forefinger into a gun barrel and pointed it at James. "And I said, 'Halt, you're under arrest! That wagon is for James Beale!' "

Everybody laughed and laughed and then my father and Joe Donovan sat and drank eggnog and Daddy sang "Remember" and another old song, and Joe sang an Irish song, "I'll Take You Home Again, Kathleen," and Lonnie and I joined joined in because we had it in school and he got tears in his eyes when we sang. "That's my wife's name, you know. Kathleen." He started wiping his eyes and my father told him no blubbering in his kitchen, and I swear I think tears were in his eyes, too. Then he pushed the table back to do some dances, like the black bottom and the boogie woogie; then Joe Donovan got up to do an Irish jig. And they were surprised that we knew how to do that, too. And we jumped up to show him.

"We learned it in school in the gym!" We puffed as we danced. "We learned the minuet, we learned the polka, we learned the waltz, we learned the Virginia reel! A lot of dances!"

Then we were all surprised when Mama jumped up and did a jig with us, and her hair, which she kept twisted and pinned to her head, rolled down and fell around her face and she looked like a woodlands spirit from the illustrated book of fairy tales on Miss Quinlan's classroom bookshelf. All eyes were on her, especially my father's, who seemed more surprised than any of us.

Joe Donovan asked her where she learned to do the Irish jig and she said, "From an old white man named Tommy Scanlon."

Joe Donovan laughed. "In Virginia?"

"All the Irish didn't settle in the slums up North," said Mama. "Some of them came to Virginia, and one of the first things they did was find themselves a colored woman and get some colored children."

"Who can blame them for that if they were as pretty as you?" said Joe Donovan. And he jumped up. "Let's show them how the jig is done." And he jumped up and he and Mama did a wild dance in the kitchen that shook the walls and the floor. And then they fell into their chairs laughing, and my father's eyes glittered as he laughed along with them, and his smile was wide and stiff and his teeth shone pearl white and even. And we drank more eggnog, and sang, and finally my father sent us up to bed. And I knelt by my bed and thanked God for answering my prayers and then dove under the covers and fell into a deep, dreamless sleep.

❧

"AMY!" The whisper was urgent.

I mumbled and shook off the hand that was shaking me.

"Amy!" Lips were touching my ear.

I struggled awake. A dark form was bending over me. My heart leaped up. "Amy!"

I sat straight up. "What's the matter?"

It was Lonnie. "Mama's cryin."

"Why's she cryin?"

"I don't know."

We listened, hearing only our breathing. "I don't hear nothin." How could Mama be crying? Loud enough for Lonnie to hear but not me?

I listened intently. "She must've stopped."

Suddenly a moan. Loud then muffled. Lonnie grabbed my arm. "See, I told you."

I slipped out of the bed and we felt our way down the black hallway to the small narrow one that led to the living room. The floor gleamed from a weak light coming from the living room. We dropped to our knees and crawled to the curtained closet under the steps. Then, certain that we hadn't been heard, we eased out and stretched out on the floor and peeped in.

In the soft glow of the lamplight I saw my mother sitting on the side of the bed in a slip. My father was standing over her, in boxer shorts and a ribbed undershirt. One side of my mother's hair was loose, hanging down, hiding her hands, which were covering her face. My father had some of her hair in a fist and was mumbling in a low voice. He jerked her hair. She gave a muffled cry. He pulled her head back by the hair and slapped her face.

"So pretty . . ." Another slap. "So white."

"Please . . . Jack."

I covered my eyes.

"So fine . . . so white."

Water was leaking through my fingers, running down my chin, my neck. Then by some trick of the mind I fall back in time and I am a young child, and I am so small I have to rise on my tippy toes to peep through a keyhole that Lonnie is looking through . . . No, it's not a keyhole—a doorknob is missing. There is a hole. I hear moaning. I push at Lonnie so I can see through the hole. It is bright beyond the hole. I see part of Mama. Her shoulder. She is on the floor and I see her feet . . . and I see my father's knees. They are bent. Lonnie pushes me away. . . . He looks. I hear a sound, a dragging sound, and I hear Mama. *Oh, stop, Jack,* and Lonnie whispers he's draggin Mama by the hair, he's draggin Mama by the hair, and he starts kicking and screaming and beating the door with his fists. . . . Then I hear someone beating at another door. *Jack! Jack! Open this goddamn door! You hear me!* And Lonnie is crying and crying.

Now the soft sounds of crying were mine and Lonnie was moaning softly into his fist. "That black nigger. That black nigger . . ." He was wiping his face with his fist. "That black nigger . . . He wouldn't do that if Miss Minnie was here."

We heard a noise. A shuffling in the hallway, a bumping into the wall. It had to be James. Still on the floor we snaked backward into the closet under the steps. We parted the curtain to see James passing by. Missing us, probably, coming to find us. My heart fluttered like the wings of a captured butterfly.

"Mama." James, rubbing his eyes, went into the living room.

We slipped quickly to the doorway. James was standing in the living room rubbing his eyes. My father had let go of my mother's hair and was now standing away from her. My mother had thrown herself down in the bed and was drawing the covers up around her.

James walked over to her, still rubbing his eyes. "Mama . . ." He dropped his hands, looking at her, then Daddy, frowning. "Mama, I'm scared . . ." Oh, his voice was so little, so pitiful. "I heard somebody cryin."

Daddy went over and sat on the bed and pulled James onto his lap. "What are you havin, nightmares? Where's Lonnie and Amy?"

"They're not in their room."

Daddy stood up and reached for his hand. "Well, let's go find them, okay?"

But James, dissatisfied, stretched his hand up to Mama. "Mama . . . Mama . . . are you sick, Mama?"

Mama leaned over to him. "No, honey. I just have a headache." Her voice was normal. "You go with Daddy and find Lonnie and Amy."

James stood a moment, looking at her. Daddy took his hand. "Come on, James. Let's find them."

Lonnie and I eased backward and flew down the hall to my room. I jumped into my bed; Lonnie stretched out on the floor and pretended he was asleep. We lay there, scarcely breathing. My father came in, talking to James. He turned on the light. "I bet you Amy and Lonnie are right here. See? Here they are."

Lonnie kept still on the floor. I rolled over but did not sit up and mumbled, "What's the matter?"

My father was at my bed, speaking softly to James. "See. Here they are. Asleep. Here's Amy. And here's Lonnie. See?"

James laughed softly. "Yeah. I see them."

I felt the bed give as he climbed in and slipped down beside me. I heard my father's footsteps as he put out the light. Then I turned on my side and curled around James's body like a spoon. I threw my arms around him and hugged him tight. I didn't speak, just stared wide-eyed into the dark and listened for more sounds from the living room, but there was nothing.

I lay there staring at the wall.

Before that night if I had ever been called to testify about my father's mistreatment of my mother, I would have honestly had to answer that I heard her and my father arguing, that I heard her crying at night or saw her puffy faced some mornings after a night of crying, that sometimes she came and got in my bed, but I could not have said, "Yes, I saw my father hit my mother."

But that night I had seen him slap her, pull her hair. And while I was watching him, the memory of that earlier time had come back to me. I had been so young that it had receded into my subconscious, only to be recalled by the shock of seeing his actions that night. How much else had I seen and not remembered?

And what about Lonnie?

He was two years older than I. Who knew what he had seen, how much he had seen, how often he had cried, how often he'd been sick to his stomach as I was that night, staring into the dark? How much did he remember? And why did my father call my mother white? Mama wasn't white. She was our mother. From what I had seen in my father's eyes that night in the kitchen I suspected that he didn't like Mama dancing with Joe Donovan. The fact that he was white hadn't occurred to me. Wasn't he my father's friend? Wisps of memory drifted through my mind, words drawn out like a ribbon of smoke. *Don't know . . . do what I do. Whiskey . . . whiskey.*

I heard the open-mouthed sounds that Lonnie and James made when they were sleeping. Soothing sounds. Finally I dropped off to sleep and I dreamed of running up endless flights of collapsing stairs and falling into bottomless pits; several times I woke up with a thumping heart, wondering where I was. Each time I fell back into a restless sleep.

NEW YEAR'S DAY. My mother cooked a ham and Aunt Louise and Uncle Lee came around to dinner, the first time they had ever eaten at our house. Lonnie wasn't surprised. When he and Mama had gone to the store she had stopped by Aunt Louise's and he'd heard them talking about Daddy slapping her. I don't think Uncle Lee would've let

Aunt Louise say anything to my father, but their presence at our house would surely have sent him a signal: They knew about the other night and they were watching him.

My father never showed up to get the message, but when he came home from work the next day James excitedly reported their visit by offering him a Tootsie Roll from a large bag of candy that Uncle Lee had brought him. My father smiled and shook his head; the next few nights there were no arguments or other disturbances.

# EIGHTEEN

Miss Minnie returned on Sunday night and with her came the first snowfall of the season. Fine flakes began falling late Sunday night and tapered off just before dawn on Monday morning. And on the first school day of the new year we awakened to a scene from Currier and Ives.

Miss Minnie wrapped us up like mummies and we stepped from our house into a yard knee-deep in snow. Beechwood Avenue seemed covered with powdered sugar and ground-up glass; the trees, the streets, the hedges sparkled in the sunlight. We made our way to the street where the snow had been rutted by automobiles and James and I walked in the ruts behind Lonnie. Before we reached the corner we fell three times. Out of breath, we slogged up Maple Street, and as we drew near Weiner's Delicatessen Lonnie stopped and pointed. "Look."

Up ahead outside of the store two boys, stiff in layers of clothing, were pushing and shoving each other. We inched forward, then Lonnie yelled, "It's Asbury and Marvin!" We skittered to the corner and stood watching the slow-motion battle across the street. Asbury and Marvin were slugging the air, punching at each other and grunting, their breaths coming in little white puffs. Marvin made contact; they fell to the ground and Asbury rolled over and jumped on top of Marvin and punched him with one hand while he tried to straighten his glasses, which had become dislodged and were hanging from his nose, with the other. Marvin began sliding around under him on the icy sidewalk, and then suddenly he jerked his body up and Asbury fell off him onto the ground and his glasses fell from his face. Marvin slid away from him, still on his back, then he rolled over and, slipping and sliding around, got to his knees and then stood, arms rotating like the blades on a windmill as he tried to keep his balance. While Asbury was feeling around in the snow for his glasses, Marvin grabbed a bottle of frozen milk from the crate standing near the front door and raised the bottle like a club and swung at Asbury so hard he lost his balance just as the bottle smacked against Asbury's head and frozen milk and glass flew into the air. Now they were both on the ground.

We were jumping up and down, screaming and laughing loudly enough to arouse everyone in Hillsboro. Mr. Weiner came to his door and stuck his moon face out, then quickly shut the door. Miss Fanny Murray came onto her porch in a blue quilted housecoat and saw us rolling with laughter on her sidewalk and scolded us and ran back inside and stood at a window peeping out. The Maple Street women were looking out of their doors, their heads, big with curlers, bobbing as they called to each other. One of them waved for me to come over. I turned my head.

Then a siren wailed and the only police car in Hillsboro slid down Maple Street and skidded to a stop. Two policemen jumped out. Mr. Weiner came to his door and went over to them, arms waving and shouting what happened. The cops took in the scene, the broken glass and the blood mixed in with the frozen milk and snow and the two boys struggling on the icy pavement. The policemen pulled them apart and dragged them to the car and stuffed them in the back, jumped in the front, and after spinning and sliding around, with the siren blaring, proceeded cautiously down Maple Street.

We slid and scrambled and laughed our way up Union Avenue. "Did you see that fairy?" said Lonnie. "He sure knew how to use that bottle! Haaaaah! I bet Asbury won't bother anybody else for a while!"

That evening at dinner we discussed the event and howled with joy. James and I pounded our forks on the table. Lonnie gave a speech about how it was a good thing Marvin got Asbury; he would've been hurt worse if he'd got hold of him. As if he would have. Hunh. Not so long as he lived under our father's roof.

Miss Minnie was shocked by our glee. "How can you all rejoice at a child being hit over the head with a frozen milk bottle! Why, he might have been killed!"

Mama chimed in. "I know you all didn't get along with Asbury, but what did that boy do to you all to make you want to see him all bloody in the street?"

"We had to fight him almost every day!"

"He wouldn't let us go to school!" said James.

"And Miss Ruby Davis had to go after him one mornin for scarin Marvin, too!" I told her about Miss Ruby's run-in with Asbury. "And she told Marvin to fight him back if he kept botherin him!"

"Well," said Mama, "why in the world didn't you all tell me or your Daddy?"

"We did!" we chorused.

"When we told you all about him the second day we went to school, remember? And nobody even listened to us," added Lonnie. "Daddy just listened to what Miss Geneva told him and said he was gonna beat us if we bothered Asbury anymore. And you didn't say nothin except ask if he bothered us when we took the number money up."

Mama flushed. "Well, that didn't mean you was to let him pick on you whenever he felt like it. Especially when you was on your way to school. I sure never knew nothin about him botherin you all them times."

"Children, you should have told your mother about it," said Miss Minnie. "That's what your parents are here for. To help you."

"Even if we did tell Mama," countered Lonnie, "if she said somethin to Miss Geneva or somethin, then Daddy would get us anyway because he wants to keep on Miss Geneva's good side because he plays the number with her. Or else him and Mama would start fussin and stuff . . . so we just didn't say nothin."

"He fought me and Amy the most because Lonnie wasn't with us," said James.

"Poor children," said Miss Minnie.

My mother looked at Lonnie queerly, was quiet for a moment. "Well, you won't have to worry about Asbury anymore. I was around Geneva's this afternoon and she said she's sendin him to Virginia to stay." Then without any more talk, she shook her head and got up and she and Miss Minnie started clearing the table.

THAT SAME WEEK that our war with Asbury ended another war was brought to our attention. On our weekly trips to the movies, the March of Time and Paramount News were acquainting us with Herr Hitler and *sieg heil* and bombs and European refugees and the Japanese bayonetting of Chinese babies.

In school we were helping with the war effort by bringing in anything that could be recycled into war matériel. Tin cans, opened on both ends and flattened. I did not understand the relationship of grease left over from cooking to oil for machines, but I was one of the champion grease collectors in my class; the weekly supply of bacon fat from our house and Aunt Louise's was enough to make grease for a thousand ball bearings. And Kitty was the silver-foil queen. She and I did double duty chewing gum instead of eating candy, and each week she handed over huge silver balls to Miss Quinlan. Lonnie and James scavenged for pots and pans. And of course, there were the squares that we learned to knit in school so we could pile them up to make afghans for the poor soldiers wounded in battle. Some of the girls knitted mittens and socks and scarves but I liked to work on something I could finish quickly. Squares took only two afternoons. Sometimes one. And Miss Minnie always added to the piles that I took to school.

I SPENT A LOT of time on the war effort. One evening just before dinner I was in the kitchen knitting and James had come to me for help with making his. Everyone in his class was learning to knit squares for an afghan and James was excited because he was almost finished with his first square.

"Bobby Leeds, he's done three already. He said his mother helped him at home but Miss Edwards said she could help him but she couldn't do them for him." He held his up to me. "Does mine look all right, Amy?"

It was green and lumpy and more octagonal than square, but he was finally getting the hang of it so I nodded my approval.

"It was *hard* at first. The rest of the boys could knit better than me, but now I'm gonna catch up to them."

"You can have a couple of my squares if you want. Or Miss Minnie can knit a couple for you."

"Oh, no." His voice was solemn. "We have to make our own or it'll be cheatin. This is supposed to be our own afghan from our class." He bent over his work, frowning.

Then my father came home from work and I jumped up to set the table for dinner. James, head bent over his knitting, spoke but did not go to meet him as usual and he leaned across the table to investigate. "Hey, buddy, what you doing?"

James held up his square. "I'm knittin a square."

The look on my father's face meant trouble. "It's for the war effort in school," I said quickly.

"War effort!" He reached out and snatched the needles and the yarn. "Boys don't knit. That's something that girls do. If they want you to do something for the war effort, they'll have to find something else."

Tears sprang into James's eyes. "But Miss Edwards—"

"You tell Miss Edwards your father said you do not knit! If you want some squares, Miss Minnie and Amy can do some for you."

James looked at him with upside-down eyes. "But we have to do it ourself or we're cheatin!"

My father sat down at the table and took James's hand. "Now listen to Daddy, James. If other boys see you knitting, they'll laugh at you. You don't want them to laugh at you, do you?"

James shook his head. "No, but the other boys—"

"Do you see me or Lonnie knitting?"

Tears spilled over. "No." Softly.

"Tell him, Amy. Do any of the boys you know knit?"

"The boys in his class do."

"Do any of the boys *you* know knit?"

"No." Marvin might, but I didn't bring that up.

"There. See?" Daddy put the needles on the shelf. "Now if you want some squares to take to school, then the women in this house will knit them. All right?"

"But what if my teacher asks me about mine?"

My father cut off any further discussion. He patted James's head and told him that Mama would write a note to his teacher and explain. Then he went upstairs to dress for his nightly excursion around to Aunt Leona's to do what men do.

And when he went back through the kitchen, James watched him leave with the same upside-down eyes.

# NINETEEN

Throughout the winter I continued to dye my hair. I usually chose a Saturday morning so I would not have to worry about being discovered. My mother was usually working, Miss Minnie visiting her sister, and my father away on his weekend frolics. Lonnie had already told James why I smelled like coffee. They both thought I was silly, but they kept my secret.

Once I got bold and was almost caught. One afternoon I came home from school and Miss Minnie was out and there was leftover coffee in the pot. I poured it into a bowl and took it and a cup up to my room. I dyed my hair and washed it and wrapped it in a towel and fell across my bed to read. I fell asleep and awoke to find Miss Minnie straightening up my room.

She had come across the bowl I used for dipping my hair along with several cups under my bed. "I declare, child, if your mother finds her good cups up here under your bed she will raise the roof!"

There weren't any other kind of cups except those, I told Miss Minnie.

"Well, what in the world do you need cups up here for?"

"For my watercolors." The lie slipped from my tongue as if it had been oiled. The watercolor set and a book to go with it had been among the presents under the Christmas tree and had kept James and me quiet many afternoons, and Miss Minnie had no intention of jeopardizing her good fortune. She thought a moment. "Well," she said, "I'll bring you some old cups and saucers from my sister's house. She's got plenty of them. You shouldn't use your mother's cups for those paints, child." She screwed up her nose. "And this bowl, I don't know what you been doing with it, but it smells like coffee."

"I ran out of brown paint."

She threw up her hands and piled the cups into the bowl and took them downstairs. I went to the mirror and unwrapped the towel and inspected my hair. It looked the same. I leaned closer and held a strand up to the sunlight. Well, maybe it was a *teeny* bit darker. I looked at my face in the mirror, turning my head left, then right, lifting my eyebrows, smiling, whispering to myself. Looking for signs that I might be pretty someday, perhaps as pretty as my mother. I lifted my chin up and wrapped a plait under my chin and stuck my tongue out at myself, then I turned and looked over my shoulder and winked. "Hel-loooooow."

"Who you talkin to."

I jumped away from the mirror. Lonnie was leaning against the doorjamb, arms crossed, grinning. He eyed the comb in my hand. "You gonna comb your hair *again* today? You feel okay?"

Sometimes he made me so sick. "You shut up."

"Why you combin your hair?"

"You just get out of my room so I can comb it."

"You mean rake it. If you ever combed it good you'd have a headache for two days."

"You better leave me alone or I'll tell Daddy on you."

" 'Tell Daddy on you.' " He sniffed. "Mmmm-hmm. Dyein that stuff again. Ain't nothin gonna help that nappy head! And you better stop usin Mama's cups!" Laughing, he backed out of the room.

My silly mood disappeared. I sat on my bed and raised the comb to my head and wished I had done it while it was damp. Now it was dry; I would have hell combing it. I winced and tackled the kinks and knots until the comb went through my hair easily, and my head ached so much that I determined to ask my mother when she came from work that night if I could go to the hairdresser.

Oh, I remember that silly girl looking in the mirror. Pitiful child. She wanted to feel beautiful. She couldn't help it, for that desire is with us when we are born. Like the seed of a flower, it lies in a sheltered place under the breastbone a little to the left of the heart where it takes root, and soon, like a flower, it buds and blossoms in gentle rain and summer sun, or shrivels and dies if lacking either.

I felt the stirrings that day, but I saw only a girl with kinky red hair that was the bane of her existence. Hair was a woman's crowing glory, my mother used to say. And mine was not glorious, a fact pointed out to me whenever anyone was moved to do so, as Lonnie had just done. But it could be pretty, I was certain, if I could only get it straightened. Maybe as pretty as Kitty's.

But straightening wasn't part of her plans for my hair, my mother informed me that night. She was reading *True Detective* and soaking her corns. "Not until your body changes."

"When is my body going to change?"

Lonnie giggled into his geography book. "When you get titties."

"All right, Lonnie," said Mama, but she did not deny it. When my body changed, then my hair would change, too, she went on to say. Become stronger and able to withstand the heat of the straightening comb and the hot curler.

"Luetta's mother don't worry about her hair fallin out!" I said.

"Luetta don't have titties, neither," said James.

"How do you know, James?" said Lonnie. "You been lookin?"

"That's enough, you two," said Mama. "Amy," she said to me, "you was sick and your hair fell out and it took me all this time to get it to growin good." She licked her finger and turned the page of her magazine. "And besides, Luetta's hair is coarse. Yours is fine. Fine hair burns easier than coarse hair. Especially if you get somebody who don't know what they're doin."

"Luetta's gonna get it curled for when we get our Mother's Day pictures taken in school."

"Well, that's not until May. It's only February."

"But they take the pictures the last week in February so they can be back by May. That's what Miss Quinlan says."

"Well, you get your picture taken like you always look and I'll look at it years from now and smile and remember you like you are now."

"I don't *want* to look like I look now."

"*I* like the way you look now," said Mama, laughing. "And the picture's for me, isn't it?"

I didn't answer. Just clumped around to my room and sulked.

※

THE LAST WEEK in February was mild. Warm enough to play outside wearing a heavy sweater or a light jacket. On Sunday afternoon James and Lonnie went around to Union Avenue. My mother went to visit Aunt Louise. I went upstairs to read. I had read all the books Miss Quinlan recommended and had discovered what a pleasure reading was. Every weekend I came home with one or two books from her classroom library. I had just lain across the bed with a peanut butter sandwich and book in hand when I heard a knock at the door.

It was Kitty Donovan. In curls. Long red-gold curls dangling down her back, spilling over her shoulders, enlivened by the sun. Stunned, I held the door open.

"Hi, Ame." Kitty stepped into the kitchen. "Can you come out?" She spoke around a mouthful of bubble gum.

"Gee! You have curls!"

"Oh, yeah." She blew a big bubble. "My mom did it. She's always nice to me after she beats me. See?" She hitched up her skirt to expose angry red and blue welts.

At that moment I had no interest in welts, but I said politely, "Does it hurt?"

"Nah. I just bruise easy, that's all." She flopped into a chair and when I showed no curiosity about it, she continued. "Guess what she beat me for."

I lifted one of her curls. "Why?"

Kitty popped a bubble. "I caught her and my pop doin it."

"Doin it!"

"You know, screwin!"

I gasped.

"They had this big fight last night and then this morning I went into my mom's room to get the brush and they're goin like crazy."

"Ewwwww."

"So she jumps up and beats me with the hairbrush. And I screamed real loud and afterwards she said she was sorry and curled my hair."

"Look. Your hair curls right around my finger, just like a spring. And it's so *silky*." I sat down next to her. "I wish I could get my hair curled."

"Why don'tcha." Another pop. "Luetta's got hers curled. I just seen her goin in the Jew store."

"She *does*!"

"Yup. All over her head. I wish my hair would curl up like that. Mine just falls down. Especially if it's damp or rains."

"See." My voice wobbled. "Everybody's gonna have their hair curled for the Mother's Day pictures except me."

"Not me," said Kitty. "Mine will fall out overnight. Unless I roll up my hair like my sister. She's always rolling hers up to look nice for her husband. Not me. Jeez. They hurt like hell when you lay on them."

"At least your hair will be straight," I mumbled.

"Jeez. Who wants straight hair? Curly hair's better." She jumped up. "Let's play jacks."

We cleared the kitchen table and played jacks and I could hardly keep my attention on the game for watching Kitty's curls bounce and roll with every movement she made.

❦

THE END OF FEBRUARY. My birthday. My mother made a chocolate cake and Miss Minnie made banana ice cream. After dinner Mama put eleven candles on the cake and lit them and I blew them out and closed my eyes and made a secret wish. And then everybody sang happy birthday and we went upstairs and listened to Jack Benny.

James asked me later what I wished for and I swore him to secrecy. He crossed his heart and hoped to die and I whispered it to him. I wanted to go to the hairdresser.

"Aw, that ain't no wish," he said.

"Why?"

"A wish is for something *hard*. Like a hundred dollars . . . or like a trip to the World's Fair." Most of the children in James's class had been to New York two or three times and brought back a tiny replica of the "ball" and the "needle" and he wanted one very badly.

"Well, it's hard for me to get to the hairdresser."

"Well, you just wasted a wish," said the practical James. "Mama already said you could go when you get bigger."

*Why is it so hard for everybody to understand?* I later whispered to my reflection in the mirror. *I want to go to the hairdresser now. I want to look in the mirror and see curls like Kitty's now. I want everybody to stop making fun of my hair now.* I wanted it so much that my eyes filled with tears and I fell dramatically on my bed and sniffled but after a few minutes I stopped. No one was around to hear or pity me. But my wish was about to be granted.

Around on Union Avenue my Aunt Leona could not possibly hear me. And I'm sure she was unaware to what depths of despair I had sunk. From conversations with my father she was probably aware that Aunt Louise had given me a Sunday dress and a beautiful spring coat for Christmas. Easter was approaching, and what better time for Aunt Louise to take her niece to church and show off her Christmas present than on Easter Sunday? And in Aunt Leona's mind an idea was hatching. I'd like to think that she was thinking of me, how pretty I would look, how happy I would be, if I had pretty hair as well as pretty clothes when I went to church. *Her* church as well as Aunt Louise's. And I imagine she thought her neighbors might have the following conversation.

"Seen Louise Hyatt at church today. Had her niece with her."

"Oh, yeas. Arleatha's daughter. Had on a beautiful outfit."

"Yeas. I understand Louise bought it for her."

"She buys them children beautiful clothes."

Now she couldn't let her neighbors think that my mother's sister cared more about their niece than she did. So the only thing for her to do was to get my hair straightened. Then her neighbors could see what she did for her brother's daughter. This is what I think went on. However, regardless of the reason, I was soon to be the beneficiary of an offer from Aunt Leona that would have unexpected consequences.

# TWENTY

The mild weather continued throughout March. The month was unusually warm and the forsythia sprayed bright yellow flowers over lavender and red azaleas. In the first week of April the dogwood trees bloomed; their branches were covered with thousands of pink and white butterflies and the big old sycamore trees on Hillcrest Avenue unfurled their leaves and whispered in the winds. The sun was warmer, the days longer and brighter, drawing the children on Union Avenue to play outside until long past dinnertime.

In school things were brighter too. We had good grades on our report cards. James was reading up a storm. Lonnie was the best artist in the school and got an award in assembly. Miss Duckett gave it to him and shook his hand, pumping his hand and grinning as if she hadn't left him back or smacked him on the hand with a ruler. And I won a certificate for the best handwriting in the fifth grade. The Palmer Handwriting Award, it said, in beautiful Palmer cursive in gold and signed by Miss Duckett as well as Miss Quinlan.

JUST BEFORE EASTER we came down with the measles. James got it first. He had a headache and his nose was running and his eyes were red. My mother thought he'd caught a cold from running around outside without his winter jacket and was fussing at him about it, but when she looked in his mouth to see if he had a sore throat she said, "This child has the measles." The doctor came from the health center and confirmed her diagnosis. A few hours later another man came from the health center and nailed a big red sign with big black letters up on our kitchen door.

## QUARANTINED

Within a few days Lonnie and I were as sick as James. We had to stay in bed with the shades down. According to Miss Minnie and Mama bright light would blind you the first few days and we must stay in a dark room. We didn't mind. We slept most of the time.

After a week we were up. My father gave money to Miss Minnie, who saw to it that we were amply supplied with comic books. We whizzed through Metropolis with Superman, tracked down the Joker with Batman, and leaped through tropical undergrowth with Sheena, Queen of the Jungle. My mother brought home armfuls of *National Geographic* magazine from work, and my brothers' eyes popped with the strain of ogling the breasts of the native women. The pictures of Ubangi women with long lips had us rolling on the floor laughing so loudly that Miss Minnie came up and collected the magazines and muttered something about us laughing ourselves into a relapse and the human body being only a shell for the soul.

Easter vacation came. We stared longingly out of the window. But we couldn't go out, no matter how nice the weather. We would only get sick again, according to my mother. Then one day just after Easter, the doctor gave us permission to return to school. We leaped around the living room dancing and screaming and the only way Miss Minnie could get us quiet was to promise to get us some ice cream. She left us in the living room playing Parcheesi and hadn't been gone five minutes before we were arguing and throwing the pegs at each other and when we ran out of them, we threw checkers, dice, marbles, and all the other parts of every game we had.

I was on my knees behind an armchair screaming because Lonnie and James had ganged up on me when a voice called up the steps. "What's all this racket?"

It was Aunt Louise. We froze.

Now I could see the top of her head. "I thought somebody was supposed to be sick!" Now the top of her body. "Up here jumpin around like Barbary apes!"

I scooted over to the middle of the floor and sat down next to my brothers. Aunt Louise was holding on to the railing as she climbed the last step, puffing as if she'd just climbed Mount Everest. She crossed the dining room and sat in an armchair. "Where's Miss Minnie? Ain't she supposed to be here with you all?" She leaned over and picked up a few checkers. "Here." She handed them to Lonnie. "Pick up this mess on the floor."

As we scrambled around picking up the pieces Aunt Louise repeated her question. "I said where's Miss Minnie."

"She went to the store," I said.

"She oughta know she can't leave you all alone for a second, much less a few minutes. You fools'll be done shook the house down by the time she gets back."

I sat back on my heels. "It was mostly Lonnie and James jumpin around throwin all this stuff," I said.

"Stop tattlin," said Aunt Louise. "Come on down here to the kitchen. I got somethin for you." She stood up and talked as we made our way down. "Since you all was sick Easter Sunday we didn't see you, and your uncle Lee and me thought we should bring this around here before it gets stale."

"This" was a huge Easter basket almost as big as the basket left at Christmas. It sat on the kitchen table, glorious in its display of fruits, and cookies, and candy. On top of all this was a large overstuffed bunny.

Awed, we went over to the basket and inspected carefully.

"Ooooh," I said. "Black jelly beans!"

"Your uncle Lee thought maybe James would like the rabbit," Aunt Louise continued, "although maybe he thinks he's too big for a stuffed animal now that he's in school."

"Oh, I want it!" said James. Then a shadow crossed his face. He looked at me. "Would Daddy get mad?"

"Daddy!" Aunt Louise drew back. "What's your Daddy got to do with it?" She looked at me. "What is he talkin about?"

I hesitated. If James was recalling my father's admonition about what was proper for boys, I certainly didn't want to be the one to tell about it. "I don't know," I said to Aunt Louise.

"If he talkin about me or Lee bringin stuff around here for you all then he better say somethin to me, not to you children."

"He don't get mad at nothin like that," said Lonnie.

"Then what is the boy talkin about?"

Lonnie shrugged. "I don't know."

Aunt Louise took the rabbit and jammed it into James's arms. "You take this rabbit, honey. And if your daddy says anything to you about it you tell him Aunt Louise and Uncle Lee said it's all right for you to have it."

Miss Minnie came in and that ended the discussion about the rabbit. The sight of Aunt Louise agitated her. She was worried that we might have been misbehaving, but Aunt Louise calmed her down and before she left gave the other reason for her visit. "I was goin to take you to church on Easter Sunday in your new outfits, but since you was sick, I guess we'll have to wait for Mother's Day."

That night after dinner my mother asked James about the rabbit. Apparently she had stopped by Aunt Louise's and learned what James had said that afternoon. "Why would your daddy be mad about the rabbit, honey?"

"Oh, my my," said Miss Minnie. "I hope this don't mean you and Mr. Jack are going to start arguing. I get so nervous."

"Well, Miss Minnie," said Mama, "you go on upstairs and listen to the radio."

" 'Deed, Mrs. Beale, Lonnie claims that radio for his own. If his story is on you have to listen to what he wants to hear."

Mama jumped up and went over to the steps and called up. "Lonnie! Lonnie! Come down here!"

Her tone of voice brought Lonnie galloping down the stairs. "What's the matter?" he asked from the stairwell.

"Have you finished your homework?"

He looked over at me, puzzled. "Almost."

"Are you listening to the radio?"

"Yes." He frowned.

"Then turn it off and come down here. I want to talk about something."

"Awwww . . ."

My mother sent him her look; he turned and went back upstairs. She turned back to Miss Minnie and said gently, "Now go on upstairs. And ain't nobody gonna say nothin to Jack. But I have to find out what's disturbin my children."

Lonnie came back down and Miss Minnie went upstairs. He scowled over at my mother. "What you want to talk about anyway?"

Mama pressed her lips together. "You'll find out in a minute. First thing, though. I want to talk to you about the way you act toward people. I been puttin it off because I know you started off havin a hard time when we moved here. But we been here almost a year. And you gettin too fresh. The way you talk to Miss Minnie. And your sister. Yes, your sister. And no, she ain't been down here complainin about you."

Lonnie's eyes grew big. "But what did I do?"

"Nothin specific. But just now Miss Minnie wanted to go up and listen to the radio, and she was scared to ask you if she could listen to something she wanted to hear."

"I don't say nothin to that woman."

"That's just what I mean. She is not 'that woman.' She is an old lady who takes care of you and your brother and sister. And you don't need to say anything. It's the way you look. Scowlin. Mutterin under your breath." She paused. "You are gettin to be just like Jack Beale. If you can't do it your way, it won't get done at all."

Lonnie's eyes began to water. "I'm not like Daddy."

"The apple don't fall far from the tree. Now if you don't want to be like him, you better find a better way to act. Be polite." She leaned toward him. "I'll tell you what. You treat Miss Minnie to her face the way you treat your Aunt Louise or your Aunt Leona. You don't treat her like that now, do you?"

"No."

"Do you think you can?"

"Yes." Under his breath with a scowl.

"Oh, I expect you to get mad at me. I'm your mother. But when I come in this house and ask my children to come down and talk to me, I want them to remember one thing. I am your mother. I won't be mean to you because I'm not mean spirited. But I don't have to be as nice."

There was a silence. Then Lonnie leaned over and wiped his eyes and asked if he could go upstairs. Mama nodded and he left.

James, big-eyed, then told my mother about the squares he had been knitting for the war effort.

"Is that why your father asked me to write a note?" Mama said to me. "Because he thought James wouldn't be a man if he knitted squares?"

Afraid of her reaction, I winced and nodded.

But she said nothing for a moment. Then she told James to come to her and she hugged him. "Honey, a man is a human bein just like a woman. And knitting or sewing doesn't make you not be a man, just like drinkin and stayin out all night don't make you more of a man. Now, you think about Uncle Lee. Is he a man?"

James nodded.

"Do you think he would give you a stuffed animal if he thought it would make you a sissy?"

James shook his head.

"Then if you want that rabbit, you keep that rabbit. It's only a toy. And I can't help you now about the squares. I thought you just didn't want to knit them."

"Miss Evans lets me bring in tin cans now. And you know what? I bring in more tin cans than anybody. Don't I, Amy? And it's harder than knittin. I have to wash them out and open them at both ends, and make them flat. And I get a lot of them in my wagon." He went proudly on to tell Mama about his contribution to the war effort.

And later that night I told him that if he wanted to leave the rabbit in my room he could. If he wanted to. Then Daddy might think it was mine. But he shook his head and took it up to his room.

# TWENTY-ONE

"Lord, what in the world has happened to all my cups, I'd like to know." Mother's Day was coming, and before every holiday my mother would get a cleaning fit. Curtains must be washed and ironed. Rooms cleaned. Floors scrubbed and waxed. And every dish washed and counted. "I can only find one cup. Amy, go up to your room and see if you have any cups up there. I bet you been usin them for your watercolors again. Gettin all that dark stain in my good cups. Every one of them. Look at this." She held the cup under my nose. A china cup with a blue rim and little flowers. "My mother gave me those cups." During her cleaning fit she had run across a cup and a pot I had under my bed and now was of a mind that I was the cause of her disappearing cups. "Go see if any more are up there."

I was drying dishes and swore I had no cups upstairs.

Miss Minnie, cleaning the stove, came to my rescue. "I'm glad you mentioned cups, Mrs. Beale. Just the other day Ruby Davis asked me if you could use some mugs. Mr. Joe said the high school is getting new dishes and the principal told him he could have some of the old mugs and he got a cellar full. More than he can use, anyway. Ruby Davis asked me if you could use some and I told her I was sure you could. She said they're nice and heavy and ain't easy to break. And they must be good if they been used for years by rough children. And they ain't got a chip in them."

"Well, yes indeed," said Mama. "I'll take as many as she can give me. Amy and James can go around there tomorrow after school and get them in James's wagon." She handed me her only cup to dry.

The following afternoon James and I took his wagon around to Miss Ruby Davis's house to get the mugs. I knocked on her front door and told her why we were there, then we went around to her backyard and up to her cellar window and she handed the mugs out to us two at a time. Thick white mugs with thick white handles. Thick to keep in the heat of the liquid. Thick to survive a drop to a concrete floor. Finally we had enough to cover the bottom of the wagon, and Miss Ruby Davis came out with a heavy cloth and spread it over the mugs. "Nobody's business what you got in the wagon," she said.

We thanked her and started out of the yard and the mugs rattled and clinked against each other as the wagon bumped across the grass and onto the sidewalk. As we turned the corner onto Union Avenue I heard Aunt Leona's voice. "Aimeeeee!"

I stopped dead. "That lady don't ever leave her porch."

"I ain't stoppin," said James, and he kept walking, kept pulling the wagon.

"I gotta go see what she wants! I'll be right back!"

James huffed, turned his wagon wheels so the wagon wouldn't roll back, and plopped himself down on the curb. "Well, you better hurry up!"

I ran up on the steps and into the sunporch and stood by the door so I could see James through the blinds. Miss Minnie had brushed my hair before I left home so I knew it didn't look wild enough for Aunt Leona to fuss about. What could she want me for? With half an ear I listened as I watched Miss Ruby's door open. Marvin appeared in the doorway and began talking to James.

". . . talking to your father and wondering if you'd like to go to the hairdresser once in a while," Aunt Leona was saying.

Talking to my father, who had naturally informed her that I was going to church with Aunt Louise on Mother's Day. And, I suspected, being thwarted by my illness at Easter when I had been unable to go to church, she was determined to see that I didn't get to church in my new clothes without getting my hair done, thanks to her.

*Hairdresser.* I turned around. Aunt Leona was picking at a sick-looking pink geranium on a table near the window.

"Of course your mother has straight hair and doesn't understand about sending you to the hairdresser. Maybe I could send you once or twice a month. . . ." She stopped picking at the flower and went into her living room.

A thrill ran through me. Once a month! Then I thought of my mother. She wouldn't let me go even if Aunt Leona did pay for it. James was looking over at the house, now standing up. I opened the door and waved at him. "I'm comin!"

Aunt Leona was back on the porch. "I just called Miss Alma. She said she can take you right now. Here." She pressed a fifty-cent piece into my hand. "This is enough for washing and straightening." Without giving me a chance to say anything she stepped to the door and opened it. "Hurry up now. She's waiting for you."

I hurried outside and ran to the first step, hardly able to take in what had just happened. Then I stopped and turned. I was going to tell her I didn't think I'd better go. Then she would ask me why. And I couldn't tell her that my mother would be angry, could I? Then I would risk my father's anger. And I couldn't just keep straight on home without going to Miss Alma's. Her shop was across the street and up a little way from Aunt Leona's and she was going to stand on her porch and watch me until I went inside. Oh, what a dilemma! I stood in the bright sunlight squinting up at Aunt Leona frowning down at me, and suddenly Kitty's bright curls flashed across my mind, and I called up to Aunt Leona, to say "I forgot to say thank you," and she smiled and I turned and galloped down the steps and over to James.

James picked up the handle of the wagon and we started walking. "What did she want?"

"She wants me to go to Miss Alma and get my hair done."

James squinted up at me. "For what?"

I shrugged. "I don't know. To get used to it, I guess. All girls have to get their hair straightened. You know, like boys go to the barbershop."

"Oh," said James. "When you goin?"

We had reached Miss Alma's beauty shop. "Now."

"Now!" He tugged at the wagon. "Girl, I ain't waitin."

"You just tell Miss Minnie where I am, okay?"

He nodded. I turned and went up onto the porch. At last I was going to find out what went on in a beauty shop. From what Luetta had told me there would be ladies gossiping as they got their hair done or waited for their turn; ladies laughing, smoking, teasing as they chose hair styles from numerous magazines. "This one would look good on you, child. No, my face is too fat. It would look good on somebody with one of them heart-shape faces. Lord, Ann! I didn't know your hair was this nappy. I always thought you had halfway good hair. Did you see Melva Douglas in church last week? That hat! Her face was lost under it. Lookin like an orphan in the wind. I heard you workin for Mrs. Porter now. That woman is something. She don't even have a stool in the kitchen for me to sit on. I told you not to go work for her. But you wouldn't listen to me. When you need money you work for a dog if you have to. Child, listen. I heard—"

Miss Alma was waiting at the door. She opened it and I followed her inside. She was tall, pumpernickel brown, and wore her hair in a long pageboy. Over her dress she wore a green smock with large pockets. I knew her from seeing her at church and on my trips around to Marvin's house. She was a good friend of Miss Ruby Davis and she and Miss Ruby would sit on the back porch and smoke and talk over a drink. She always asked about my mother and sent her regards.

We had entered one large room that reminded me of Mr. Chauncey's barbershop, but it was wider. To one side was a swivel chair and against the wall were two floor-model hair dryers. And just as you entered was a line of chairs. Empty chairs, I noted with disgust. I was to hear no news today. There would be no gossip that I could repeat to Lonnie and James.

Miss Alma nodded toward a chair with wheels on it near the end of the room and I went and sat in it. "Well, you sure are growing, Amy. How old are you now?"

"Eleven."

"Well, you're tall for eleven." She was scrubbing a big black comb with a brush. "I'll be finished here in a minute."

I studied the room. On the opposite wall was a wide mirror and under it a long shelf that held several jars. On the end of this shelf was a cloth pad, and next to it was a pipe, like a water pipe, sticking out from the wall. On top of the pipe was a holder of some kind. And there was a smell in the air, the smell of burning feathers, like our kitchen smelled when my mother singed a chicken.

Miss Alma walked over to me and unplaited my hair and ran her fingers through it. "Your Aunt Leona said to give you a wash and a press."

I nodded and handed her the fifty-cent piece and she began. First she massaged my head and it felt so wonderful that I wanted to roll my head around under her fingers, but I didn't dare move. I just sat saying nothing.

Apparently Miss Alma didn't need me to talk; her talking seemed to be part of her therapy. "Well, your first time to a hairdresser. How's that little brother? He still got all those curls? Your hair's fine. Won't need pulling or much grease. Easy to straighten. Pretty color, too. Gettin darker, too. I remember when you were real little it was much redder. Are you tender headed?"

I nodded.

"Thought so. People with fine hair usually are. Well, I might hurt you a little, but if I do, just say so."

I hoped I wouldn't scream or cry.

She tied a large white cloth around my neck and rolled me over to the sink and fitted a drain board (Luetta had described one perfectly) over my shoulders and eased my head back and began to wash my hair. I looked up into her face. She looked so serious as she lathered my head, but once or twice she looked into my eyes and smiled.

"Not so bad, is it?"

"No."

A few minutes later I was sitting in the swivel chair and Miss Alma was parting my hair into little sections and rubbing my scalp with a towel. When she finished she reached over to the shelf and scooped grease from one of the jars, rubbed it onto the palms of her hands, placed her hands firmly on the sides of my head, drew them back over my hair, and rubbed the ends of my hair between her palms. Then with the wide-toothed comb she parted my hair in the middle and smoothed it down so it covered my face. And all that time I didn't feel one twinge.

For that she deserved praise. "You don't hurt my head when you comb my hair," I said. "When Mama combs it she really hurts."

"Well, your mother has good hair. She probably don't know how to comb kinky hair. You got to comb it when it's damp with grease on it right after you wash it. Otherwise you'll never get the kinks out without pulling all your hair out." She laughed. "Or your brains."

In a few seconds I was under the dryer with warm air blowing on my hair, looking at the pictures on the wall. I didn't like any of the hairstyles up there. I wanted loose curls. Not tight curls over my head. Then I remembered what she had said. A wash and a press. Did that include curls too? I drowsed. Soon Miss Alma lifted the hood and felt my hair. It was dry. She removed the hood and I went back to the swivel chair.

"You sure got a head full of hair," said Miss Alma.

She whirled me around so I could see myself in the mirror. I stared. I saw a small face under hair that stood up as if I was wearing a huge cinnamon-colored fur hat.

Now the straightening was to begin and Miss Alma gave me explicit instructions. The most important: Sit *perfectly still*. Especially when the hot comb (she held a metal comb in front of my eyes) was near my face or ears. Then she turned a knob on the pipe coming from the wall. I heard the hiss of gas. She struck a match over the metal grill on top of the pipe (I could see now that's what it was). *Pouf!* Flames leaped up. She turned the knob to adjust them, then laid the hot comb on the grill. Once in a while she picked the comb up and flicked water on it. After a few times it sizzled and smoked like a pan with hot grease in it. She laid it on the pad and wiped it and took a chunk of my hair. I felt a tug as she sank the teeth of the comb into my hair; then she pulled it through to the end, then through again.

"Well," she said. "This hair is easy to straighten. Here." She took my hand and placed it on the piece of straightened hair. "Feel it."

I ran my fingers down the piece of hair. It was warm and smooth. I shivered. I was going to have straight hair!

"Feel okay?" said Miss Alma.

I nodded.

And, humming and pulling, every once in a while answering the telephone and taking appointments, Miss Alma worked through my hair until finally she said, "Finished . . . Soon as I do the edges you can look in the mirror." She brushed the hair back from my face and cautioned me to be very still and brought the smoking comb so close to my face I almost wet myself. One eye closed, I winced the whole time she was at my temples and above my forehead. "Hold your ear," she said, and folded it down from my head and put my finger on it and tugged the hair behind it. After the ears, she bent my head forward. "Look at the floor. Got to get that kitchen."

I felt the heat of the comb at the nape of my neck. "Mama says if it wasn't for my kitchen and nappy edges my hair wouldn't look so bad. One time she cut it off."

"Your mama ain't never seen a nappy kitchen if she thinks yours is nappy. She stand here all day and look at the heads I look at she'd *see* some nappy kitchens and thank God yours is as easy to fix as it is . . . there. Done. Lift your head up." She laid the comb on the pad and brushed my hair back from my face and smoothed it down on my head.

I put my hand up and felt it. "That feels nice."

"You ready to look?" Miss Alma swung me around so I could look in the mirror.

I stared at this new Amy in the mirror. My hair was hanging straight down to my shoulders. I never knew it was *that* long. Miss Alma's face smiled at me and, embarrassed, I smiled back.

"Well, shall I plait it?"

No curls. I turned away from the mirror to hide my disappointment. But Miss Alma must have known how much a girl that age wants curls. "You've been such a good girl, I'm going to give you some curls. Ain't nobody in here now so we won't be takin anything away from anybody. Besides, I'd like to see what you look like with curls."

Within a half hour, the only sound in the room the click click click of the curlers, she had curled my hair all over my head. From the corner of my eye I could see them in the mirror, dangling and dancing with the slightest movement of my head. Then, before I could blink, Miss Alma took a stiff brush and brushed out every curl and plastered my hair against my scalp. Tears watered my eyes. I looked like a wet rat. My curls! She had changed her mind. She was going to plait my hair after all.

But Miss Alma was a professional. And professionals don't offer explanations. They let the results tell the story. She took the cold straightening comb and held it by the teeth and placed the round handle against my head and brushed a piece of hair around it, slid the handle out and a big fat curl dangled at the side of my head. She did this around my head, and in a few minutes she had finished. Then she stood back and smiled. "There." She swiveled me around to face the mirror. "Do you like it?"

"Oh, yes," I whispered. That girl in the mirror wasn't Amy. Not that pretty stranger. I couldn't take my eyes from her and all those curls.

"Prettier than Luetta's, too."

My eyes met hers in the mirror. How did she know about me and Luetta?

"And don't you worry, honey. Your hair is a pretty color. Don't let anybody tell you it ain't. Most colored folks don't know nothin about hair anyway." She gave me a hug. "Now I guess you better hurry on home. It's almost six o'clock."

I hopped down from the chair. "Thank you, Miss Alma!" I heard her laughing as I flew out of the door. I felt my curls bouncing and I stopped running. I didn't want them to fall out before I got home.

I WALKED UP Union Avenue in a dream, not moving my head lest a hair move out of place. No one was outside. I was disappointed. I wanted Luetta to be out on her porch so her mouth could drop open when I passed by. But it was dinnertime and everyone was inside.

Just as I reached the corner of Maple Street, I saw Kitty come onto her porch. I waved frantically. "Kitteee! Kitteee!"

Kitty stopped, crossed the street, and came over, listing to the left, squinting at the strange sight in front of her. "Hi." She cocked her head like a quizzical puppy. "Amy?"

Feeling shy and foolish I walked toward her. "Hi."

Kitty's mouth was open.

"I've been to the hairdresser." I laughed. I felt so silly.

For a full minute we stood looking at each other, Kitty's eyes like full moons, my grin like a new one.

Finally Kitty spoke. "Jeez. What did she do to it?"

I certainly wasn't going to tell her about nappy hair and straightening combs. It would have been too embarrassing. And Kitty would've asked a thousand questions. So I merely said, "She curled it with a curling iron."

"Jeez, Ame. It looks great. Really great." She reached out and touched a curl. "And it's red. Like mine."

"Yeah. I know."

"Jeez."

We started walking toward my street. Kitty kept looking over at me. "Whenever I get curls, they always fall out. Especially if the weather is damp or it rains."

"Yeah. You told me." I shook my head slightly so the curls would move. "I don't know what mine will do. I never had it curled before."

"Are you going to wear it like that all the time?"

"Oh, I don't think so."

"Yeah." Kitty sounded relieved. "It would be too much trouble."

We stood at my corner a few moments, not talking, almost like strangers. "Well, I gotta go," I said finally.

"See ya," Kitty said wistfully.

❦

WITH TREMBLING HANDS I opened the screen door and stepped into the kitchen. Everyone was sitting around the table. James, my mother, Miss Minnie, Lonnie. And my father. Apparently James had given them all the news and they were waiting to see the results. On every face was a look of astonishment. I stood at the door, paralyzed with stage fright.

"Lord, here this gal is at last," said my mother. Was she angry? I couldn't tell.

"Well, well, well," said my father with a smile like the Cheshire cat.

Lonnie and James stared, speechless.

Miss Minnie, hands folded against her chest, whispered, "The duckling has become a swan."

On shaky legs I walked over to a chair and sat down and blurted, "I went to the hairdresser." Then I giggled.

Lonnie came to life. "Look at Amy's hair."

And James. "It looks like a white girl's hair."

I looked over at my mother. She gave me a stiff little smile. "Your hair does look pretty, Amy. Just like I knew it would." But the look on her face did not match the words she spoke.

I looked at my father. He was biting his lip, a sure sign of annoyance. My mother got up from the table and started over to the steps. "Your dinner's still warm, Amy. Miss Minnie, give Amy her plate out of the warmer, please." So polite. So polite. She turned and went up the stairs.

Miss Minnie handed me the plate, but I didn't feel like eating. We all sat in silence, then my father got up and went upstairs. He and my mother started talking in low voices.

Miss Minnie stood up. "I think I'll go out in the yard and sit a while. Amy, when you finish eatin call me so we can do the dishes." She shook her head. "Lord, I do hope Mrs. Beale curbs her tongue. She does let the words fly sometimes."

I sat looking at my food. I wanted to cry, but I couldn't squeeze out a tear. I was too happy. I wanted to go upstairs and look in the mirror and admire my new hair, but I knew I couldn't until my mother or father came down.

James came around and stood near me. "Did it hurt, Amy?"

"No, boy. Don't be so dumb."

"Well, when Mama used to comb your hair it hurt."

"That's because she didn't know how," I said, armed with my recently acquired knowledge.

"That wasn't such a dumb question," said Lonnie. "Hairdressers use hot combs. She could burn you. Luetta Robey gets burned all the time."

I smugly dispensed more information. "That's because her hair is so short. Miss Alma probably has to grab at it and she can't keep from touchin her." I shook my head for effect.

"Can I feel your hair?" said James.

"Yes." I bent my head.

He reached out and touched a curl. "It's so soft," he whispered. "Just like Mama's."

Lonnie snorted. "Ain't gonna be like that long. She gonna get to jumpin and runnin and it'll snap right back to red naps. Then she'll be just plain old Amy again."

"So what." I stuck my tongue out at him. "At least my hair can be straight sometimes. You're always gonna have kinks."

"Boys don't need to straighten their hair. We get it cut."

"You shut up!"

"Make me!" He got up and started toward me, then stopped at the sound of my mother's voice.

"Yes, that's *just* what I said." Her voice was at a high pitch. As always, my father's answer was low, indistinct.

We hunched our shoulders in silence, eyed the stairway.

My mother again. "Then let her get up off her fat ass and get some girls of her own! Tell her I said *that,* hear me? Tell her I said *that,* Jack Beale!"

No answer from my father. We could hear his footsteps pounding toward the steps. Lonnie and James jumped for the kitchen door and ran out into the yard. I was pretending to eat when he got down to the kitchen. Not looking at him, I took up a fork of collard greens.

He stopped next to me. "Your hair looks nice, Amy." He put his hand on top of my head. "Real nice." Then he left.

I sat there leaking tears into my mashed potatoes and greens and I looked around and my eyes fell on the mugs on the counter waiting to be washed. The mugs that James and I got from Miss Ruby Davis. The mugs we needed because I broke Mama's cups pouring coffee over my hair. But I knew it wasn't just the mugs. I could have told Aunt Leona that I couldn't go to the hairdresser before I asked Mama. But I hadn't taken her into account. I did what I wanted. And I sat there crying because I did.

Right after I finished eating, I went up to my room and fell across my bed, being careful not to muss my curls. Crying had made me drowsy and I fell into a fitful sleep. I woke once when Mama came in to see if I was all right; I undressed and got into bed and this time slept soundly all night.

# TWENTY-TWO

The next morning I woke up feeling sluggish and tired, and lay a few moments remembering the night before. Then I realized it was late, and I listened for sounds, but the house was silent, empty, scary. I ran down to look at the clock in the kitchen. Eleven o'clock. I ate a bowl of cereal and waited for someone to appear, but no one did, so I dashed back upstairs, washed up and got dressed and ran a comb through my hair, taking no time to admire my curls. I ran around to Aunt Louise's house. If my mother hadn't gone to work, she would be around there.

Aunt Louise opened the door and stared. "Well, well." She ran her hand over my head. "Looks pretty. Hunh. So this is what the fuss is all about." She stepped back and let me in. "You all can't leave your mother alone for five minutes."

I heard my mother's voice. "Who is that, Louise . . . Amy?"

"You know it's one of yours. Don't matter which one, do it?"

I followed her into the kitchen. My mother was sitting at the table drinking coffee. Her eyes were swollen. "What's the matter?"

I took a deep breath. "Nobody's home."

"I'm comin home in a minute." She turned her head away.

"Your mama don't have no babies," said Aunt Louise. "I know you ain't scared to stay home by yourself as big as you is. Where's Lonnie and James?"

227

"I told them they could go down to the train station," said Mama. She opened her pocketbook and took out a nickel. "Here. Take this and go on outside and play until I come out."

"Ain't nobody out there to play with."

"Gal!" Aunt Louise turned from the sink and flapped a dishrag at me. "You hear your mother talkin to you! Pull in that mouth before I slap it in with this dishrag!"

Head on chest, I stood stubbornly at the door.

Aunt Louise started toward me. "Them curls must be goin to your head."

"Don't, Louise," said my mother. "Amy, go into the front room and read a magazine, then."

I sat on the leather settee in the living room wishing I had never come. I kicked the leg of the settee. I was never going to worry about Mama again. My eyes began to blur and burn and I couldn't see the page of the magazine in my lap. I sat back and let tears leak down my face, then I sat forward, listening to Mama and Aunt Louise. I had been aware of the rise and fall of their voices, but suddenly the words erupted from my mother like an avalanche.

"He said he was going to do better when we moved down here. Stop drinkin and gamblin. And what does he do. Around there at his sister's house doin the same thing. She gamblin and playin cards and sellin whiskey every night like a man and talkin about the way I raise my children. Makin Amy feel bad about her hair. What do she know about Amy's hair? My child was sick for a *month*. Did she put her foot in our house to see about her? She don't know how that child felt when we had to plait it in them teeny little plaits like a pickaninny. She don't know how that child came home cryin every day when them little children teased her at school. Callin her pickaninny and Topsy. Even Lonnie. Poor little girl. And all she could do was holler and scream when I tried to comb it. Her scalp was tender and her hair turned to little fine kinks and dried out like it was charred. And I do know what the doctor told me. To wash it and keep it clean with as little grease as possible and plaited so it would grow. And she needed it to grow so she'd feel better. And that didn't mean singeing it off tryin to get it straight to please some people who think hair don't look good unless it's straightened..." She choked, then, winding down. "And it did grow."

Neither she nor Aunt Louise spoke for a minute. Then my mother went on, calmer, more contained. "And if Jack wanted Amy to go to the hairdresser so bad, why didn't he give me the money to send her? He got money for Lonnie and James to get a haircut. I ask him for money, he ain't never got any. But his sister does. I guess she do. She only got herself and her men and her cards. She can afford to send every nappy-headed nigger in this town to the hairdresser five days a week..." Then she broke down again and began crying so hard and Aunt Louise kept telling her to hush, hush, hush, as if she was talking to a little child.

And I sat on that stiff settee crying too. I wanted to jump up and run into the kitchen and say I wouldn't ever go to the hairdresser again. That I was sorry I screamed when she combed my hair when she was trying her best to make it grow because she knew I was unhappy. That I would've knocked me in the head every time with the hairbrush if I'd been her. I sat until I stopped shuddering. Then I wiped my eyes with the hem of my dress and got up and sneaked out of the front door and ran home.

❧

ABOUT TWO HOURS LATER my mother came home. I had wrung all the water from my body and now sat dry-eyed on the sofa reading. She came and sat in an armchair across from me and slipped her shoes off and looked at me suspiciously. "You been cryin?"

I had a story ready in case she asked about my swollen eyes. "I hit my shin when I was comin up the steps."

She leaned her head back and sighed. "Lord, Amy, you always bumpin yourself on somethin. Let me see it." I limped over to her and she felt my shin and I ooched and ouched dramatically at her touch. "Did you run cold water over it?" Cold water was her answer for every bump, lump, or laceration. To carry out the deception I went to the bathroom and put my leg in the sink and ran cold water over it and looked in the mirror over the sink.

The new Amy still looked back at me. I had slept with my head hanging off the bed and the curls were still there, looser and more beautiful than the day before. Suddenly I got an idea. I dried my leg and went into my room and got a piece of blue ribbon and I took it with the hairbrush and the comb to the living room. My mother was leaning back in the chair, her eyes closed. I kneeled on the floor in front of her.

"Mama, will you brush my hair?"

Her legs moved against my back. "Brush your hair?"

I held the brush and comb up over my shoulder. "I want to fix my hair another way."

She said nothing for a moment. Then I felt her hand on my head. "Your hair's fine," she said softly. "Just like mine was when I was little. Only mine was redder. You wouldn't believe that lookin at it now."

"Yes, I would." I wanted to tell her that I was dyeing my hair, but my throat was tight and I couldn't talk.

She started brushing my hair, long strokes like she used to when I was little, before I was sick, when my hair was long and easy to comb. "I didn't realize it was so long. It's down to your shoulders."

"I know." I hesitated, then, "I don't think it would be this long if you hadn't greased it and plaited it and didn't let me get it straightened. It probably would have got burned and broke off just like you said."

My mother kept brushing. Then, "Did you like goin to Miss Alma?"

"I don't know. Miss Alma didn't hurt. But it takes a long time." I twisted around to look up at her. "Maybe you could learn to straighten my hair if we had a straightening comb. Or Miss Minnie could do it. Or me. I bet I could learn if Miss Minnie showed me how."

"Maybe." My mother smiled.

I held up the blue ribbon. "Can you fix my hair like yours when you were little?"

"When I was your age, I wore two plaits. And on Sundays I wore two long curls. Your hair ain't as long as mine was, but we can still make two curls on the side. Or else"—she pushed my hair back from my face—"we can put the ribbon around it and make a bow on top." She took the blue ribbon and fixed it quickly. "Tomorrow is Mother's

Day and your Aunt Louise wants to take you to church since you missed goin on Easter Sunday. You can wear your new coat."

I had worn my new dress to get my picture taken, but the coat was hanging in the closet in the same place where I'd hung it Christmas Day, and this opportunity to show it off dampened any aversion I had to attending church with Aunt Louise.

The next morning I was up with the sun and bathed, powdered, and perfumed by nine o'clock. Lonnie and James had declined Aunt Louise's invitation, so I was alone when I stepped out into the yard to receive her smile of approval.

Inside the church I looked around in surprise. It wasn't dull and brown like the rooms below where the Sunday school classes were held. Here the sun streamed through the high stained-glass windows of the apse and played on vaulted ceilings.

As Aunt Louise and I walked down the center aisle, there was a hssssst! And I looked over and saw Miss Ruby Davis waving at us. We went back and sat next to her and I had a chance to look around. Rows of pews, divided into two sections, were filled with the colored residents of Hillsboro and many from the surrounding communities, for I recognized many people from Woodlynne and Westville. Miss Fanny Murray came in and waved and nodded as she went down to a pew in the front. My heart stopped, then raced. A few pews behind Miss Fanny sat Miss Edie. I hadn't thought of her since that time in Aunt Leona's garden. I looked quickly away and stared at the backs of the flowered hats in front of me and a picture sneaked into my mind. Legs under the table and a hand moving . . . I took a hymnbook from the rack in front of me and looked through it. Then I heard the deep voices of the men in the choir and the memory disappeared.

*Oh Lord I want*

And the high soprano voices of the women.

*Two wings to fly away*

And all joined in harmony.

*To where the world won't do me no harm.*

Now time for Reverend Mickens. He was a tall fair-skinned man with a deep, resonant voice. I stared up at him and wondered if he really did stand on the corner watching young girls as they said in the barbershop. He began to speak about Mother's Day and the significance of it.

He started out low, soothingly. "Brethren, today we are here to honor the most valuable person in our lives, the most valuable person in the family—Mother. It is a small thing, I believe, to do this for her one day out of the year, when you and I know that Mother should be honored every day of the year. Mother is the *glue*. She is the *bond* that holds the family together. She toils, sweats, and sheds tears over her family—her husband, her children—yet many times she is nothing more than a shadow in their lives; they notice her as they would notice a shadow. Hardly ever."

His voice began to rise. "We don't *need* a shadow. But we need Mother. We seek her out in our need. Track her down. Where do we go to for comfort when we hurt? To Mother. For aid when we need help? To Mother. For a sympathetic ear when our hearts are troubled? To Mother. When we fail in our endeavors? To *Mother*. Mother never says Son, I would like to comfort you, but I'm weary. Daughter, I would like to listen, but I'm weary. Husband, I would like to encourage you, but I'm weary. No, Mother never denies us."

Then softly. "Yes. Mother is the source of comfort. Mother is the glue. The bond. The mortar. The grout."

By this time the congregation was worked up. Muttering. Mumbling. Nodding. Amen-ing.

And even more softly, "Honor thy mother as she honors her duty to you." He let those words sink in; then he opened his Bible. "Today I turn to the letter of Paul to the Ephesians, 4:32, where he speaks of kindness. 'Be ye kind one to another, tenderhearted, forgiving each other, even as God also in Christ forgave you.' Now in that statement are six words. Six little words that every mother whispers to the Lord every night and to herself every morning when she rises. Words that she would place in the hearts of the members of her family, from the young child to the grandparents. Six simple little words, words that Paul wrote for us right here in Ephesians. What are these words that this man said so many years ago that mothers would whisper them in their children's ears, shout them down the steps, even write them on the walls?"

Silence. He waited, then spoke as if measuring every word. " 'Be ye kind one to another.' Such simple words. And yet so strong. Each time we hear them we should be ashamed. For we have not been kind. To each other. To Mother. To Ourselves. *Be ye kind one to another!* "

(Amen!)

"We have forgotten our duties . . ."

(Yes!)

"Husbands to wives . . ."

(Amen!)

"Sons to mothers . . ."

(Lord!)

"Daughters to mothers . . ."

(Amen, amen!)

"Families to Christ!"

(Good God!)

"We are FRAIL!"

(Hallelujah!)

"WEAK!"

(Hallelujah!)

"Husbands! Sons! Daughters! Take these six words to your heart! Shout them every morning! Whisper them every night! *Be ye kind one to another!* The words that every mother carries in her heart. Cries in her sleep."

He stopped. The cries from the pews subsided. Hushed. He was finished.

The choir sang again. We passed the plate. Reverend Mickens said the benediction. We went outside. People stood around and shook hands with Reverend Mickens and remarked upon the sermon. I followed Aunt Louise from group to group. *My, my, don't she look pretty today. And look at that hair shining in the sun. . . . Don't she look like Arleatha? My, my.*

Aunt Leona was standing with a group watching us. She was wearing a big yellow hat that almost swallowed her face. I went over to her to show her my hair. She smiled and introduced me to the ladies, whom I didn't know, and made it known that she had supplied the money for the curls. And while I was there with her, I saw Miss Edie from the corner of my eye. She had been standing on the corner and I had been debating whether to go over and speak. As I watched she ran across the street to a black car sitting at the curb, and I could have sworn my father was sitting in the front seat. I strained to get a better look. But he wasn't there. Then Aunt Leona said good-bye and went over to the same car and got in the front seat. So my father couldn't have been there. Miss Edie was in the back. I think she waved to me, but I didn't wave back.

Aunt Louise came over to me. "Hmph. That Leona got a new car every time you turn around." She took my arm. "Come on. Let's cross this street. I got to get home and get these shoes off."

I hurried along beside her singing softly to myself. "Oh, Lord, I want two wings to fly away . . ."

That day happiness was inside me like bubbles from a pipe that grow bigger and bigger and float up and up in the air and twirl around and around shining in the sunlight. My soul was as light as a bird with wings spread wide, soaring, savoring the wind and tasting the freedom of a limitless sky. And it seemed to me then that living in Hillsboro wouldn't be so bad after all.

# TWENTY-THREE

My mother used to say that troubles come in three's. I often doubted the truth of the statement for it seemed to me that they came in clusters, like the purple grapes on the vine in Mr. Tivoli's backyard. Take death. If there was one, there were always at least three or four more to follow. My mother had a wide circle of friends, relatives, and acquaintances, near and far, ranging in age from nine minutes to ninety years, so somebody was always dying. She and Aunt Louise hit more numbers playing "Death" and the names of those who died than any others in the dream book. And we knew the numbers by heart. Death, 769. Dead, 712.

We were steeped in other kinds of trouble as well. There was always someone who was Sick (164) or a lot of Sickness (416) around. So it was only natural that 769, 712, 164, and 416 were popular numbers and were played every day by practically everyone in the area. In fact, some days they were played so heavily that the bankers were unable to pay off, or else the play on a particular number was so heavy that they conspired to change the number before it came out. People groused but there was nothing they could do. It happened rarely, and, after all, it *was* illegal.

Sickness was the trouble that took Miss Minnie from our house. The Monday after Mother's Day she told my mother that Eula, her sister, was so sick that she didn't think she'd last through the week. And Miss Minnie wanted to be with her those last moments. Of course Mama

gave Miss Minnie all the sympathy she could muster, told her to come
back as soon as she could, that she would always be welcome in our
house. Then she hugged her and we did, too, for I think that we realized by then that Miss Minnie was making a big difference in the
quality of our life.

Trouble came to me the very day after she left in the form of rain.
A sudden downpour. Kitty and Luetta and I were playing hopscotch
on the broad sidewalks at the end of Union Avenue when it started
falling. Three or four big splats, then boom! A clap of thunder sent us
skittering for home. The sky opened up and poured down rain like
water from a bucket. The lightning flashed and scratched the sky.
When I reached my yard another boom. I threw the door open and
jumped into the kitchen. The rain slashed through the screen, making
a puddle on the floor. My clothes were sticking to me and I ran upstairs
and changed them. And when I looked in the mirror I saw that it was
the end of my curls. When my hair dried I would be back to the old
Amy again. But I had learned something from Miss Alma. Comb it
while it was wet. So I combed my hair and made my three old plaits
and sat around morosely while Lonnie and James eyed me. Perhaps
Lonnie was remembering my mother's admonition of a few weeks earlier to stop teasing me. He didn't say a word. But I could see the
laughter in his eyes.

The following morning Luetta greeted me without a second glance,
not with a stare as I had expected her to do. For her it was natural to
flip between straight hair and kinky hair. But there was only amazement
in Kitty's eyes when she saw me.

"Jeez, Ame. What happened to your hair?" She reached out to touch
it but I held my head away from her hand.

"The curls came out yesterday in all that rain," I replied, hoping she
wouldn't be curious about the texture of my hair as well as the loss of
the curls. "So I plaited it."

"Oh, yeah," said Kitty. "Curls are hard to keep."

Even the girls in my class weren't overtly curious, considering their
amazed outbursts the day before when I had come back to school with
a halo of silken curls. Today a few of them sneaked glances at me, but

by morning recess they probably considered the reason for the disappearance of my curls no different from theirs. Damp weather.

THE NEXT BIT of trouble began on Saturday afternoon. Lonnie and James had gone out. I was in the living room reading.

"Whooee! Amy!"

I heard the screen door bang and closed my book and ran down to the kitchen. My mother was sitting at the table, smiling. She pushed a paper bag toward me. "Here's somethin somebody sent you."

I took the bag and pulled out a straightening comb. Elated, I held it up and turned it slowly around. "Thanks, Mama!" I gave her a hug and stepped back, embarrassed.

Mama seemed flustered by that hug, too. "Miss Alma sent it around. She said she had a couple of extra ones. Don't forget to go around there and thank her for it."

I immediately got to work. I got the cracked mirror from the shelf and set it up on the table, and unplaited my hair and combed it. Then under my mother's eye I turned on the gas stove, heated the comb and began to straighten my hair. Mama tried it once, but she laughed and said she was afraid she'd burn my scalp. When I finished, she braided it and put rubber bands on the plaits and then she and I went around to Union Avenue. She went to see Aunt Louise. I went to thank Miss Alma for the comb.

On our way we met Luetta, who walked along with us forlornly. She had no one to play hopscotch with. The old reliable Bumpsy Lewis was off somewhere playing with Marvin Davis. Bumpsy had been showing him a lot of respect ever since he'd bopped Asbury Tate with that bottle of frozen milk. James, who would play sometimes during the week, was around at the shoe shop playing with Alfred Tivoli. I told her I'd play with her and we walked my mother to Aunt Louise's house and I went to Miss Alma's. Luetta waited on the porch while I went in to thank her for the straightening comb.

The salon was crowded. More like what I'd expected the day I got my hair curled—filled with chatting ladies and reeking with the smell of singed hair. I thanked Miss Alma and quickly got back outside.

"Why'd you have to go in there?" said Luetta. "You goin to the hairdresser *again?*"

"Nah, Miss Alma gave me a straightenin comb and I had to thank her. And now I can get my hair straight when I want. See?" I bent my head toward her.

She inspected my straightened plaits. "Oh, yeah. Did your mother do it?"

"Nope. I did."

"*You* did." She snorted in disbelief. "And you didn't burn yourself?"

"Nope. And if you don't believe me you can come with me and my mother will tell you I did."

"I didn't say you didn't," said Luetta, peeved.

We stepped off the porch and went searching for Bumpsy and Marvin. We found them on Marvin's back porch playing checkers. Bumpsy leaped up, happy to see us. The activities that Marvin preferred were too confining for him; he was used to more physical exertion.

"Wanna go jump some rope?" said Luetta.

"Yeah!" Bumpsy jumped off the porch.

Marvin stood up. "Can I jump, too?"

I looked at Luetta with raised brows. She shrugged. Anybody could turn a rope. But we were soon to discover that Marvin could do more than turn. Marvin could *jump*.

Most of the boys we knew were unable to coordinate their feet with the rhythm of the rope. They bent their knees and went up in the air and came down on flat feet like kangaroos. But Marvin had our eyes bugging. At his insistence, Luetta and I turned double Dutch and the rope slapped against the pavement three times while that long, bony boy stood back, moved back and forth like a boxer, then jumped in between the ropes without missing a beat.

"Wow!" I said.

"Man!" said Bumpsy.

"Go on, Marvin!" said Luetta.

And Marvin went on, his legs lifted high as if he were jumping over spikes, chanting the words along with us.

*Teddy bear, teddy bear, turn around (around he went).*
*Teddy bear, teddy bear, touch the ground (down he went).*
*Teddy bear, teddy bear, tie your shoe (down he went).*
*Teddy bear, teddy bear, now you're through.*

As I turned I swayed and shook my head and flapped my plaits to the rhythm and Luetta was shooting looks at me but she said not a word. Just glared.

Marvin jumped out. Luetta and Bumpsy wanted to jump next. I got angry. Then Luetta gave the rope to Bumpsy so we could jump together and Marvin and Bumpsy turned single while Luetta and I jumped to "House for Rent."

I was to start first, then Luetta would jump in at the appropriate line. I jumped in and we started chanting.

*House for rent, inquire within,*
*A lady got arrested for drinkin gin.*
*I'll find out what it's all about*
*So I'll jump out and you jump in.*

My plaits were bouncing while I was jumping, and I was so busy looking at them and flinging them around that I tripped when it was time for me to jump out and the rope got fouled up and Luetta couldn't get her turn.

"If you would stop lookin at them old plaits you could jump right."

I flung my plaits back and went over and took the rope from Marvin. "Well, you can jump with Marvin. I'll turn."

But Marvin preferred jumping alone and said he was going home. So Bumpsy and I were left to turn, and I kept bouncing to make my plaits move and Luetta missed a jump. We stopped turning. Luetta was furious. "Why'n't you watch what you're doin! Floppin them old plaits around! I turned right for you!"

"You didn't turn for me! Marvin and Bumpsy did!"

"You still got your turn!"

I was tired of Luetta and Bumpsy. I didn't want to jump singles anyway which was all we could jump since Marvin had left. I shook my plaits. "Awww, you're just jealous!"

"No, I ain't, you nigger!"

"You're the nigger, nigger!"

Luetta came over and pushed me and I pushed her back, then Bumpsy pushed me. I couldn't fight both. I flew around to Beechwood Avenue with Luetta and Bumpsy hot on my tail. When I reached my driveway I picked up a handful of gravel and threw it back at them. They stopped. I dashed into my yard and ducked behind the corner of the house. After a few moments, I peeped around the corner.

Luetta and Bumpsy were on the sidewalk. When they saw my face they threw a stone.

I ducked behind the house and yelled out, "Come up here and throw that rock! I dee double dare you!"

No answer. I peeped out again; another stone whizzed by my head. I jumped out into plain sight and we had a rock throwing fit. I would jump out; they would throw rocks; I'd throw a few rocks, jump back behind the house, and yell. "You and Bumpsy better get off my sidewalk!"

Stones whizzed by like bullets and rattled on the hard ground of the yard. "Come on down here and make us, blackie!" yelled Bumpsy.

"I ain't as black as you, you ink spot!"

Luetta yelled up her favorite taunt. "Amy is a nappy head! Red, red, nappy head!"

I threw caution to the wind. I jumped into the middle of the driveway and shimmied and waggled my hips.

"If you light you all right! If you brown stick around! But if you black get back! Get back! Get back!"

Bumpsy and Luetta were so angry they couldn't throw straight. "You old nappy-headed red nigger!"

"Darkies!"

"The blacker the berry the sweeter the juice!"

I was in a frenzy now, waving and flapping my hands and ducking stones. "And when it's too black it ain't no use! It ain't no use! It ain't—!"

"*Amy!*" My father's voice roared through the yard.

The life went out of me. I slumped like a marionette whose strings had suddenly broken.

*"Come here!"*

I almost vomited. For one crazy moment I thought of running. Maybe I would have but I was frozen to the spot. My father must have thought I might run, for the door flew open and he stepped out. Bumpsy, seeing me still for those few seconds, threw a rock and hit me upside my head and sank to his knees laughing. Blood ran down the side of my face. I opened my mouth canyon wide and screamed. Bumpsy and Luetta disappeared in a cloud of sneakers. The blood kept coming and when I saw it dripping down the front of my dress I held my arms out and closed my eyes and screamed even more loudly.

My father rushed over to me. "Good God! Good God!" He scooped me up and ran into the kitchen and put me in a chair and slammed around and found a clean cloth which he ran under cold water.

I was still crying. But not from pain. From fear. Fear that my father would beat me. I blubbered softly, hoping my tears would delay the punishment that was sure to come.

My father knelt by my chair and wiped my face. "Now, now, Amy. Daddy's gonna fix it. Daddy's gonna fix it. Don't cry."

I didn't dare stop.

"Here . . . let me see . . . look at this gash. Right at the corner of your eye. They might've blinded you. Those little—I'm sure gonna tell Malcolm Lewis and Bill Robey about this. And if they don't tear their behinds up I will . . . darned kids ganging up on people's children and throwin rocks tryin to blind them. Hush, hush now."

At that moment I could say I was glad that Bumpsy hit me with a rock.

My father sat down and pulled me onto his lap and I laid my head against his shoulder. "Close your eyes, now. Rest."

I did as I was told, and an odd feeling came over me. He and my mother weren't the kind who held us in their arms and hugged us. The feeling was strange but comforting.

I heaved a sigh. I was more exhausted than I thought. I felt drowsy, and my father, probably thinking I was asleep, carried me upstairs to my bed and tiptoed away. I fell asleep and awakened a few hours later. My head was throbbing and felt heavy. And I was hungry. Just as I was ready to get up and go downstairs, my mother came in and sat down on the edge of my bed. I stared. Her hair had been cut in a bob. Like the woman in picture number one on the wall in Mr. Chauncey's barbershop. With the hair falling forward to curl on her cheek she looked prettier, younger than the woman I saw every day with the braids wrapped around her head.

She laughed at the look on my face. "I thought I'd like a different hairdo." She flushed. "Do you like it?"

"Yes."

She smiled and hugged me. And I wondered. All these hugs. Her. Daddy. What did it mean?

"I'm going to bring you some dinner. You stay in the bed and read."

I picked up a book but no sooner had she left than Lonnie and James stuck their heads in, then entered cautiously as if they were entering a hospital room and sat on the foot of the bed.

"Wow!" said James. "Look at that bandage!"

I wobbled over to the mirror. "Wow!" A large white patch was taped over the lump above my eye.

"That must've hurt," said Lonnie. "Who threw the rock? I bet it was Bumpsy."

"Him and Luetta were throwin them," I said. "But Bumpsy hit me in the head. And he was laughin about it, too."

"We saw them," said Lonnie. "Around on Union Avenue. They were scared. And they knew they were gonna get a beatin, too."

"And they was tryin to blame each other," said James.

"What were you fightin about?" said Lonnie.

I explained, leaving out the part about my plaits and a few other details. But he knew the whole story.

"You know Luetta was gonna get mad if you had your hair straightened and your plaits were bouncin. You probably made them bounce so you could make her jealous."

"She called me red nappy head."

"Well," said Lonnie, "Luetta said you called them black."

"You call them black."

"Yeah, but I'm black. And I can fight."

"Awww, that old Luetta's mad because you're cute and she ain't," said James.

Lonnie hushed him. "Don't tell her that, James. That'll just swell her head up some more. That's how she got it busted open today."

"Hmph." I snatched up my book and opened it.

Taking the hint, he and James went down to dinner and my mother brought mine up and when she bent over and pulled a card table toward me and put my plate there, her hair moved forward and the curl kept falling on her cheek. Fried fish, macaroni and cheese covered with stewed tomatoes, and a cornmeal muffin dripping with butter. I dipped my fork into the macaroni, but I wasn't as hungry as I thought. Frowning, I picked over my food, thinking about what Lonnie had just said. If he gave me a lecture, what was my father going to do? A few more moments thinking, then I giggled. Cute. James said I was cute.

THAT NIGHT I had a strange dream. I was in something. A room? A big box? It was pitch black. And velvety. But there was enough air. It just seemed close. Then through this pitch blackness a pinpoint of light appeared. I moved toward it. Slowly, awkwardly, as if I were moving through deep water. As I moved forward, the light grew bigger and bigger, then the room; I could see that it was a room now. And it had two doors. And the door where the light was was black. And the other door was yellow. Lemon yellow. And I started moving toward the door with the light. And as I moved toward it I started falling. It was as if I had dropped through a hole in the floor. And I was screaming. Screaming. And I woke up and my heart was racing.

It was morning and I smelled bacon and coffee.

I lay there a while, then I went down to breakfast. My mother and Lonnie and James were eating breakfast, and as usual she had her dream book out. I sat down and told her my dream.

"You probably had a weird dream because you got knocked in the head," said Lonnie.

My mother was more practical. "Well, we know fallin is seven-fifty-six. Now "—she thumbed through the book—"darkness . . . let me see . . . here it is . . . 'darkness,' four-sixteen."

"What about screamin, Mama? In my other dreams when I fall, I don't scream. I'm just scared."

"Well, screamin . . . screamin . . . 'screaming.' Nine-twenty-five."

"That sounds like a nightmare to me," said Lonnie. "You said the dream book don't tell about nightmares."

"Were you scared in the dream, Amy?" said Mama.

"No. Not until the end."

"Then it wasn't a nightmare."

She wrote her numbers down on a little piece of paper as usual. "Lonnie, remember to take these numbers now. Miss Minnie won't be here to remind you anymore."

"Aw, I didn't need her around to remind me," said Lonnie.

I could recall at least three times that Miss Minnie had reminded him, but I said nothing. Lonnie had been trying hard to be nice since my mother had chided him for his surly attitude, and my remark would only have irritated him.

When I finished eating my mother went back upstairs with me to my room. I was to stay in bed as much as I could the rest of the day. "Sometimes a knock in the head don't show any effects until a day or two later." She plumped two pillows behind my head. "I brought some new magazines for you to read. And here's a couple of comic books. I don't know if you already read them."

I hadn't. I began to read one but I was more tired than I thought and fell asleep with it in my hand. A few hours later my eyes flew open. Why, I didn't know. Something I'd heard? I lay a few moments looking up at the ceiling at a big water spot shaped like an old woman with a hooked nose and a long chin. I turned my head in several directions, but it still looked like an old woman with a hooked nose and a long chin. Maybe wearing a bonnet like pioneer women wore.

Then I heard a groan . . . a moan . . . I held my breath. Mama. Mama was moaning. My stomach lurched. Thoughts whirled around in my head. Was my father hitting her again? Had they been arguing again because of me calling Bumpsy and Luetta those names? Again I heard the sound and the memory returned. Of him pulling her hair. Her holding her face. Moaning. Trying to hold her cries so we wouldn't hear her.

Rage swelled into my chest. I slid out of my bed, dropped to my knees like a stalking animal. I didn't know what I was going to do, but I was going to do something. I crawled to the door, pushed it open wider, slid out into the hall. Slithered along on my belly. The sound again. But not from the living room where they slept. No . . . the bathroom. Miss Minnie's room. The door was closed but I could hear the sounds. Sounds of someone falling onto Miss Minnie's cot. I was at the door now. It was slightly ajar, opening inward. I lay flat, hardly breathing, put my finger against the door, pushed it slightly. Waited. No reaction from inside. Just moans.

The opening was only the width of a yardstick, but wide enough for me to see Miss Minnie's cot, and more, with my right eye. That one peep and I fell back, my hand over my mouth. My eye had snapped a picture that remains with me to this day. A picture of my mother and my father on that old cot, she underneath him, her legs around his waist, his behind raised in the air, and they were moving, moving . . . and groaning.

I flattened out on the floor and quickly pushed myself backward down the wooden floor of the hall like a lizard. If not for my pajamas my stomach would have looked like the back of a porcupine. I kept watching the door but I was certain that I had been undetected. When I got in my room I jumped up and eased my door shut and ran to the mirror. I put my hands on my cheeks and stared at my reflection. My eyes were big as quarters and my face felt as if I had a fever. "Did you see that?" I whispered to the girl in the mirror. "God, that was awful!" I stared a moment more, then I sniggered. *"Awful."*

I turned and jumped in my bed and put the pillow over my head. That was what Kitty had seen when she saw her mother and father "doin it." And that was why her mother had whipped her. I shut my eyes tight, trying to black that scene out. Finally I sat up and got a comic book, but I couldn't read it for thinking about what I'd just seen. Suddenly, tears began rolling down my face, but I wasn't crying. Not the way I usually cried. The water just came up and into my eyes and flowed out. After a few moments I stopped. My eyelids grew heavy and I flopped down and closed my eyes and dropped off to sleep.

I couldn't muster enough nerve to go downstairs and eat with the family that evening. Who knows what I might have done. I was so nervous I might have burst out laughing at the table. A bad habit I had, laughing to release tension. So I ate in my room and after dinner my father came up for a "little talk." He pulled a chair up to my bed, and sat facing me.

I put my hand up to my head and tears leaked out again.

"Now, Amy," my father said gently, "don't cry." He reached into his back pocket and pulled out his big white handkerchief and handed it to me.

I took it and blew my nose.

Then he spoke in the same gentle voice, asking how Luetta and I started fighting. I answered him in a trembling voice and told him all about it. Except the name calling.

My father frowned. "Mmm-hmm. Well, what was that you were saying in the yard?"

I almost passed out. I couldn't answer.

"You know. About them being black and to get back. Where did you hear that?"

"All the kids say it." My voice was faint. "Luetta and Bumpsy, too. All those kids on Union Avenue."

"They do."

"Yep. And they're always callin people niggers and blackies and stuff. And then if I call them the same thing back they get mad. They always call me red wench and red nigger . . ."

"Well, two wrongs don't make a right. You know that."

"Yes." I stared at a spot past his shoulder.

He looked down at the floor. After a moment he said, "Amy, look at me."

I swung my eyes to his, dark brown, serious. I was finding that hard to do because I was getting a terrible urge to giggle. I twisted my lip and bit it.

"Amy, I want you to listen to me for a minute. I don't know if you'll understand everything I'm going to tell you, but . . . well, I want you to remember what I say." I nodded and he looked away. "You're getting older now." He looked back at me again and said slowly, "Don't you nnnnnever . . . never call anybody black. Do you hear me?"

He held my eyes with his and I felt as if he were looking into my very soul. I shivered inside. It was as if he had said, *"Don't hate God."*

"You're a light brown girl, Amy. And Bumpsy and Luetta are dark brown. Right?"

I nodded.

"Well . . . it isn't the same when they call you black and then you call them black . . . because they're dark and you aren't."

I knew that. Lonnie had said the same thing. And I asked my father why. Why was it right for them to call me names and hurt my feelings and I couldn't do the same to them.

He cleared his throat. "Well, a lot of colored people around think it's better to be light or fair-skinned than it is to be dark-skinned. And . . . dark-skinned people know this. So when you call them . . . black . . . they think you mean you're better than they are."

"Aunt Louise ain't light and she says black all the time. And nigger, too."

His eyes darkened. "Your Aunt Louise . . . well, your Aunt Louise is ignorant. She says a lot of things she shouldn't. Especially around children. A lot of grown-ups do. But a lot of grown-ups, and you'll grow up some day, get mad when somebody calls them black. Mad enough to kill, sometimes."

I looked down and fixed my eyes on a spot in the linoleum where there was a hole the size of a quarter.

"Do you understand what I'm trying to tell you, Amy?"

I understood enough. Enough to know that *black* was not to be part of my vocabulary when I got mad at anybody. I nodded.

"And you promise not to do that anymore?"

I bent my head and whispered, "I promise."

Satisfied, he smiled and patted my shoulder. "How's your head? Good enough to go to school tomorrow?"

I nodded, but my mother made me stay home the next day and she stayed home with me. My father came home during that day, something he'd never done before, after Lonnie and James had gone back to school. And I heard him and my mother talking and laughing down in the kitchen. "Doing it" seemed to have made them happier.

And when he left she sang around the house the rest of the day.

# TWENTY-FOUR

The next morning Lonnie and James went off to school without me. I wanted to straighten my hair around the edges, I told them, but there was another reason I was delaying. All night I had worried about facing Luetta in the morning, and now that the time was here, my stomach was as tight as a board. I was even thinking of going back upstairs to bed and telling my mother I felt dizzy after I ate my breakfast.

Lonnie eyed me with disgust. "Look, girl, if you got to use that hot comb every morning, you better get up earlier, because me and James ain't waitin for you just because you want to iron them nappy edges." He opened the screen door and stepped out. "Come on, James. Let her walk by herself."

"I don't care. I know how to get to school by myself."

James had hesitated but now he ran outside to Lonnie. "If you late Miss Duckett's gonna get you with her rubber hose!"

I tried to do my edges in a hurry, but I soon found out that rushing caused me to make mistakes, and after two touches of the hot comb to my temples, I gave up. I looked at the clock. Eight-twenty-five. Maybe Luetta had already gone. She was usually in the schoolyard by this time.

I was running up Union Avenue when I saw Luetta sitting on her porch steps. When she saw me coming she stood up. I slowed down, wondering if I should pass by or stop if she spoke to me. In either case, I certainly wasn't going to speak to her unless she spoke to me first.

She spoke first. "You don't have to run, Amy. It's only eight-thirty." A signal that everything was all right again. "I got a beatin," she said, by way of apology.

"Well, I got a lump," I said, and pointed to my forehead. We giggled, then laughed, and stood there in the middle of Union Avenue laughing like crazy fools.

At morning recess I rushed to the swings. I had been wondering about something since Sunday and I was certain that Kitty could provide me with the answer. Of course, she was curious about my lump, and I had to explain that first. I didn't tell her that Luetta and I were calling each other niggers and blackies. I merely described the fight.

"Jeez," said Kitty, examining the fading bruise, "she could'a put your eye out."

"Luetta didn't throw the rock. Bumpsy did. And you should'a seen that blood."

"Ugh! I hate blood!"

We were quiet for a moment. Then I decided to dive in. "Can I ask you somethin and you won't laugh?"

Of course she laughed before I even told her, and I turned my head, embarrassed, and she stopped laughing and squinted at me, hand over her eyes. "What?"

"When married people are mad at each other, how do they make up?"

"Jeez. I dunno. When my mom and pop are mad and then make up they start kissin and huggin and stuff all around the house. And my sister and her husband are always fightin and then kissin in our kitchen. They're sickening."

"Well . . . are they mad at each other when they . . . do it?"

Kitty grinned. "You see your mom and pop screwin?"

That *awful* word. I shrugged.

"Yes, you did. Jeez!" She started twisting around on her swing. When she turned she must have noticed my discomfort. She lifted her feet and whirled around until the swing was straight.

"Well, don't they have to be happy when they're doin it?" I looked at her anxiously. "They don't do that if they're mad at each other, do they? Don't they have to be in love?"

Kitty frowned. "Well . . . maybe. But I don't think they have to be *happy*. I think it has somethin to do with the hots."

"What's 'the hots'? "

"Boy, you don't know anything. Jeez." Kitty got off her swing and came and stood in front of me and extended her left hand and touched each finger with her right forefinger as she ticked off her explanation. "You got brothers, right?"

I nodded.

"And they got dingalings, right?"

I nodded.

"Well, when they grow up and get married and they don't do it enough, their dingalings will swell up and bust. Like boilin over. And that's what the hots is. Like boilin over."

I was aghast. "Do women get it?"

Kitty shrugged. "I don't think so. Or if they do, it ain't the same way. I know that since my sister's married, she comes home cryin a lot. And my mother tells her that she must submit or somethin like that to her husband. That means when he gets the hots she got to let him screw her."

*Now* I understood. That's why my mother had been moaning. She was *submitting*. But she had seemed happy afterward. Oh, it was so confusing to think about. And embarrassing. I started swinging slowly.

Kitty sat down and swung along beside me. "What are you askin me all these questions for?"

I hesitated. Even though I had heard my mother accuse my father of infidelity, even though I knew my father was the one with his hands on Miss Edie's leg, I could not bring myself to believe that he and Miss Edie had done *that*. What he and my mother had been doing. And after all, hadn't Kitty just said boys did that when they grew up and got married? And my father wasn't *married* to Miss Edie. He was married to my mother. So I asked Kitty. "Can you do that—you know— screw—can you do that in an outhouse? You know—an outside toilet? I heard somebody say that once."

"Naaah." Kitty was adamant. "We use an outhouse in Jersey and you can't screw in there. You gotta lay down to screw. There's only room to stand up, or sit on the seat."

I let out a breath of relief. "That's what I say." I pushed back on my swing, then let go, and forward I went. Then up, and back, and up higher and back higher, and on and on until I was high, high in the air.

❧

WE MISSED Miss Minnie most at lunchtime. Our time was short, and we had to hurry and fix lunch ourselves. Every day when we got home she'd had our sandwiches ready, soup in the bowl, and some sort of cookies or a slice of cake after our meal. If we were late coming home, or delayed in the bathroom, or dawdled over our food she'd reminded us constantly of the time. "You're late and you have a half hour now to eat and get back to school. You gonna ruin your stomachs gulping down your food!" But she always had us out of the house in time for a leisurely walk back to school.

One Friday afternoon we had to stop in Weiner's on our way home to get baloney for our sandwiches. It was the beginning of June, two weeks before school was out, and unusually warm that day and we were taking our time in the heat. We got home later than usual. After we ate, Lonnie and James went outside. They said they had time for a game of marbles. I doubted it, but I didn't want to play so I went upstairs to comb my hair.

I can't remember how long I was there admiring myself in the mirror, for I had straightened my hair the night before. But I do remember trying my plaits different ways on my head. I do remember that when I got downstairs Lonnie and James had tricked me and left without calling me. And I do remember puffing into the schoolyard just as the bell rang for the lines to go in.

Lonnie's class was near mine and as I ran to my line he laughed and I stuck out my tongue at him. "See. I made it! It's just one o'clock!"

As I jumped in line, Lonnie ran over to me. "Did you take the money up to Miss Geneva?" When I shook my head his face turned gray and he turned and went back to his line. Even if he had run back home it would have been no use. Numbers had to be in by one o'clock, and the bell had signaled that the time was up.

All afternoon I thought about that number money. It wasn't the first time he'd forgotten it, but Miss Minnie had always been there to remind him if he went out of the door without it. Since she had been gone, I had remembered and caught up with him, even taking it up myself if he had gone on ahead. But today I was looking at myself in the mirror too long and I had to run out of the house and in my hurry I forgot to look on the shelf.

I was worried. That morning my father had played only one number, 656, and that for fifty cents. That meant he had a very strong hunch. Also for the past week he'd been more irritable than usual. My mother had been hitting regularly, only for a nickel each time, but it had been enough to keep her smiling and him scowling and chewing his lip. "I oughta stop playin these numbers. Then if I stop they'll come right out." But he didn't stop. Just came home scowling and chewing his lip.

After school Lonnie took off; I was close at his heels. I caught up with him at the gate outside of the athletic field. He slowed to a walk. "Maybe Daddy won't yell at me if he knows I didn't do it on purpose."

I nodded.

"You don't think it came out, do you?"

"How's that old number gonna come out? It didn't come out for two months, did it?" I said that, but I didn't believe it. The dumb thing about numbers was that you could never tell when they were coming out. There wasn't any system to them.

"And when I give him the money back, he'll know I really forgot and didn't mean to keep it, won't he."

"Sure. Everybody forgets something sometime. Everybody ain't perfect." But I was thinking of Westville and Andrew Gates and his whipping for the same mistake.

By the time we reached the steps leading up to Miss Geneva's we were dragging along, sick inside. Lonnie, looking like a kicked dog, touched my arm. "You go up and find out, Amy."

I couldn't have made it up all those steps by myself. "Unh-uhhhh. Let's both go."

We started up. My legs felt like sticks. It seemed we'd never reach the top. Just as we got to the landing, the screen door to Miss Geneva's kitchen opened, and out stepped Benjamin Otis Turner, looking like an oversized teddy bear. He swayed and blinked, then started down toward us. At the landing he stopped. "Hello, children." His breath smelled like whiskey and tobacco.

"Hello," we said. Then I was so nervous I popped the question that had been worrying me all afternoon. "What was the number, B.O.?" I clapped my hand over my mouth.

B. O. Turner didn't notice what I'd said. He'd only heard the word *number.* "Lord, you know, I almost hit that number today. I just missed it by *two*." He held up two shaky fingers. "Some old drunk give it to me the day before yestiddy. 'Benjamin'—and that's the truth, you know. A old drunk will give you the number every time. Or near it. 'Benjamin,' he said, 'you play six-fifty-two, that's what.' And then I came home and changed it some every day. Yestiddy I played six-fifty-one and today I played six-fifty and it come out six-fifty-two just like he told me to play. Lordy."

"Six-fifty-two!" screamed Lonnie. With a whoop he jumped down the steps three at a time. I jumped down two at a time and caught him down by the Jew store, dancing around and laughing. "Six-fifty-two! Six-fifty-two! Wheeeee!"

I huffed up to him. "Don't stop now. You better get home and get that money off the shelf and think up somethin to tell Daddy!"

Lonnie sobered up. As we turned into our driveway he stopped. "Daddy oughta be glad he's got an extra fifty cents. He ought not to whip us for forgettin just one time."

"Us!" I screeched. "He didn't tell *me* to take any numbers. He told *you*!" I looked over at him, and I felt ashamed. "Well, if I was him I'd just be glad it didn't come out and I might fuss and tell you not to forget again and I'd let you go."

Lonnie nodded. "I know I would, too."

We walked the rest of the way in silence. James was sitting in the yard looking like a lost lamb because we hadn't waited for him. When we told him about the numbers, he looked gloomier than ever. We went inside and did our chores, dragging through them instead of rushing as we usually did so we could get back into the yard. When we finished Lonnie got a pile of comic books and we went outside and sat against the fence and read.

But I couldn't read for thinking about my father. Since he was already in a bad mood, maybe Lonnie shouldn't tell him. "Don't say nothin, Lonnie."

Lonnie lowered his comic book. "Yeah. And get killed."

"No. I mean wait until Mama comes home and then tell her and she can tell him."

"Yeah!" said James. "Then when she tells him, you won't be around and when he sees you he might be mad, but not mad enough to beat you."

"Aw, who said he's gonna beat me? I didn't do nothin *bad*."

I said nothing else. Neither did James. We sat reading and waiting for my father to come through the back alley. Then we heard him coming.

We stood up.

My father came into the yard mopping his forehead with the big white handkerchief he always carried in his back pocket. And the first thing he asked us, even before greeting us: "What was it today?"

*What was it today?* How many times before and since have I heard those words, but never with the trepidation I did that afternoon.

"Six-fifty-two," said Lonnie.

"Darn! Missed that damn number by four. By four! Mmph, mmph. Well, I guess you can't hit them all. Fifty more cents down the drain."

Then Lonnie told him. I suppose seeing our father so calm about it and shaking his head over fifty more cents gone made Lonnie think he'd be happy not to have wasted his money. So he reached into his back pocket and pulled it out, still wrapped up in the white paper, and held it out.

"What's this?" My father took the wad of paper. But even as he unwrapped that white lump, I could tell he knew what it was, and his face began to change. His lips tightened, his eyes narrowed, and the muscles along his jaw started twitching. "What's this, I said?"

"Well . . . today . . . today . . ." Lonnie was stammering. "Today we were almost late for school and I forgot to—"

That's all he got to say. My father reached out to snatch him, but Lonnie stepped back. The cords in my father's neck began to swell and jump and he clenched his teeth and pointed to the kitchen door. "You forgot! You forgot! I'll teach you to forget!" He unbuckled his belt and jerked it once and it slithered from around his waist and it came alive in his hands like a long black snake and he stalked after Lonnie who was crying before he got to the door and James and I started crying, too.

And James and I are outside huddled on the steps of the kitchen door and I hear my father whipping Lonnie and he's screaming, Oh Daddy, oh Daddy I won't do it no more, and Daddy is saying, You right (*wham*), you right (*wham*), and James and I are crying and crying and we huddle there and I am leaking tears onto the top of James's head.

The whipping stopped.

Lonnie was moaning in a low voice. My father mumbled something and I heard Lonnie stumbling up the steps. James and I sat, not moving. My insides were churning and I wished I was brave enough to run into the house and say you're a mean old terrible black son of a bitch and you didn't have no business beatin Lonnie and you oughta put the numbers in yourself and it ain't right to play them anyway and someday God is gonna make you pay for all the times you beat us and Mama and I wish you were dead. And when I said that I shuddered, but I didn't take the wish back. It wouldn't happen anyway.

James and I sat there a long time. There was no sound from the kitchen. It was getting late. The sun was going down and there was an orange streak in the sky turning paler and paler.

Then the sound of footsteps on the gravel in the driveway and my mother appeared. James and I jumped up and ran over to her and James put his head against her and started crying softly so my father wouldn't hear him. My mother asked me what was wrong but I was afraid to speak.

Then James whispered into her stomach, "Daddy beat Lonnie."

Mama pushed him aside and went into the house, then we heard her voice, loud, high. "That's all you know! Beat! Beat! Beat!"

Then came the sound of clumping up the steps and the kitchen door banged open and my father came out scowling. He passed James and me as if we were not there. We ran into the house and up the stairs to Lonnie's room.

Lonnie was lying on his bed with his hands behind his head, staring at the ceiling. When James and I ran in he didn't look at us, just kept staring at the ceiling. We went over to him, said nothing. His face was streaked and hard, like stone.

I sat on the floor near his bed and my mother came in with a jar of Noxzema and sat on the bed and told Lonnie to turn over and she lifted up his shirt and looked at the welts and then she started rubbing the cream on his back. When I saw the tears in her eyes, mine filled up again, and I wiped them with a corner of the bedspread.

"That old nigger's just mad because he can't hit the number, that's all," I said.

"Hush, Amy," said my mother. And she kept rubbing Lonnie's back, rubbing and staring into space.

# T WENTY-FIVE

*There's* a ring around the moon," said James.

We were out on the roof over the shed lying on a blanket. It was a few days after Lonnie's beating and too hot to be in the house; my mother told us we could take a blanket out and lie on the shed roof if we were careful. The roof was flat and wide and there was a cool breeze blowing across it.

James and I were lying on our backs looking up at the sky. "It's got a orange ring around it," he said.

The moon was lopsided and pumpkin yellow in the purple-gray mist. "Mama says when there's a ring around the moon that means it's gonna rain the next day," I said.

Lonnie was lying on his stomach with his head resting on his arms. He hadn't lain on his back since that whipping. Now he looked over at me. "That's just a superstition. I've seen a ring around the moon plenty of times. One time I even waited to see if it would rain the next day, and it didn't. I waited a whole week and it didn't rain."

"I wish Miss Minnie was back," James said dreamily.

"Me, too," said Lonnie.

Who would ever have thought we would say anything like that when she first came.

James sat up. "We can't go nowhere. We can't do nothin."

"Mama said she's comin back," said Lonnie. "Her sister died, so she'll be back soon as she gets things straight."

Soon wouldn't be soon enough for me. Here school had been out for two days and our father kept us penned up. Even though he wasn't with us during the day, we were afraid someone would spot us on the street if we left the yard, and we didn't want to suffer the consequences, so we suffered in silence.

I didn't mind too much. Kitty had gone away the day after school closed. She and her little brothers and her sister Maureen. Off to some place called Down the Shore. She'd be back off and on during the summer, she told me. So I was left with Luetta. And even though we were getting along fine, I didn't want to spend every hour of every day with her. I decided to take Miss Quinlan's advice and read over the summer and she'd see that my sixth-grade teacher would give me extra credit for each book I read. But I didn't know how Lonnie and James were going to make it through the summer. They were wanderers at heart.

THE NEXT DAY it did rain, in such a steady downpour that it resembled a crystal bead curtain swaying in the wind. Before Mama went to work she warned us. "No rompin around. Play some quiet games and read some magazines. You got plenty of both of them."

For most of the morning we sat at the living room window and watched the rain and sang to it.

> *Rain, rain, go away,*
> *Come again another day.*

But the rain didn't go away. It hit against the window and made crackling sounds like radio static and formed little puddles on the roof and each drop of rain made little circles in the puddles like a pool when a pebble is thrown in it. It was chilly in the house, and watching it made us sleepy. We all ran to our rooms and hopped into bed to keep warm. I read and slept for a while.

Later we were back at the window, yawning, watching the rain. Suddenly Lonnie said, "Let's play a game."

"Hide 'n' seek!" said James.

"Big Black Daddy," said Lonnie.

I shook my head. "Nope. Mama said to play quiet games."

"We been quiet all day," said James.

"You want to get in trouble and get a beatin?" I said.

"We ain't gonna get in trouble," said Lonnie. "We ain't gonna wrassle, and we sure ain't gonna romp around, especially if we play Big Black Daddy. We can play it right here in the middle of the floor."

"Who's gonna be Daddy first?" I asked.

"Me," said Lonnie.

"Okay. But if you hit too hard, I'm stoppin."

"I ain't gonna hit you hard, girl."

"You better not hit me like he beat you the last time."

"Girl, I said I ain't gonna hit you hard! Now you gonna play or not? If you ain't, you can go back to your room and read. And me and James will play by ourself."

So I played. But this time the game was different. Lonnie went to a drawer in my mother's sewing machine and got out the hair she'd had cut off when she had it bobbed. Then he got one of my father's belts. And a pair of his shorts. And one of Mama's white damask dinner napkins.

He took my hand and sat me in a chair and he pinned the long hair to my head with tortoiseshell hairpins and it fell to my shoulders. Then he put my father's shorts on over his pants, and the napkin he pinned around James like a diaper.

And all this time we said not a word. And then we played the game. I can see us now, moving across my brain like a slow-motion dream.

I'm in a chair in the middle of the room and Lonnie has hold of my hair and he's jerking my head. The hair comes loose and Lonnie puts it back. And now James is on his knees begging Lonnie not to beat him ... Lonnie is snapping the belt around in the air like Zorro ... and James looks so strange in that diaper and now Lonnie is jerking my hair again and my hands are at my face and I say, Oh, please, Jack, and James says, Please don't beat me, Big Black Daddy ... and Lonnie snaps the belt at him. Then I'm tired of being Mama and I yank off the hair and I'm just Amy.

"I don't want to be Mama anymore," I told Lonnie. "And you said you were gonna let me be Daddy."

"Okay, after this time. You can act better than James."

And act I did. Lonnie stood above me with the belt doubled in his hand, whirring it over my head, and I was on my hands and knees swaying and moaning. "Oh, please don't beat me again, Big Black Daddy. I won't forget to take the numbers up no more. And James was the one that broke the couch, not me. He was the last one to jump on it and it cracked. Please, please don't beat me anymore, Big Black Daddy." I scrambled on the floor. I jumped up and wailed and screeched. But Lonnie and James didn't laugh as they usually did and I looked up at Lonnie.

He was standing in front of me, the belt hanging from his hand, staring past me. I turned my head and looked over my shoulder and saw my father. He stood bent slightly forward as if he'd been shot in the stomach, and his face was twisted as if he had a terrible pain. And he was slowly clenching and unclenching his fists.

I looked at the floor and wished I were dead.

Then my father said, his voice low, raspy, "I've told you children to stop this wrasslin a hundred times. Now go find something quiet to do." He turned and clumped down to the kitchen.

I picked Mama's hair up from the floor. Silently we went over to the couch and sat down and waited for my father to come back up. There was no sound from the kitchen. Yet, the door had not banged so he must still be down there. We waited. And waited, listening to the rain scratching at the windows, trickling down the gutters. We watched it run down the windows, dance on the roof. We sat, I holding Mama's hair, James wearing the napkin, Lonnie in the shorts. Still my father did not come upstairs.

Finally we heard the screen door bang. We sat forward and listened. Nothing. We got up and moved toward the steps, tipping, tipping. At the top of the stairs we listened. No sound. We crept down the steps. No sound. Lonnie eased the door open at the bottom. "There's nobody here," he whispered back to James and me. We came down and looked. The light over by the sink was lit and threw a big shadow on the wall and made the kitchen look dark and spooky.

We turned and went back upstairs and sat in the dark and fell asleep.

I woke up when the door banged. Then I heard my mother's voice. "Whoooeeee!"

"We're up here!" called Lonnie.

Any other time we would've fallen over each other getting down the steps to meet her. But that night we didn't move. My mother came hurrying up the steps.

"What are you all doin sittin up here in the dark?"

"We didn't turn on the light," said Lonnie.

"Well . . . why . . ." She stopped. "Why ain't you fixed no dinner? Amy, I told you to open that can of beans." She was feeling around for the lamp. "And there's hot dogs and you could'a warmed up the greens from yesterday!" On went the light and her hands went up to her mouth. "Jesus wept!"

James began to cry. "Daddy's gonna beat us."

"Why are you all dressed like that?"

We all started talking, then we stopped and let Lonnie tell her. Before he finished we all started crying again. "I can't understand a thing you all are sayin. Now tell me again."

This time I told her in one sentence. "We were playin Big Black Daddy and Lonnie was beatin me and James and Daddy came in and saw us and heard me sayin, don't beat me, Big Black Daddy." I finished with a whoop and a hiccup and stuffed my dress into my mouth.

And Lonnie and James were heaving and crying and my mother kept telling us to hush. Finally we wound down to a sniffle. My mother sat, shoulders slumped.

Why were we dressed the way we were? she asked. And "What are you doin with my hair, Amy?"

I burst into tears. "That night when Daddy was hittin you, me and Lonnie heard him and we sneaked into the closet and we saw him pullin—"

We all cried. My mother along with us and Lonnie got up and hugged her around the shoulders. "Don't cry, Mama. We're sorry. Don't cry."

I got on my knees and laid my head on her lap and James got into her lap and we cried again. "Don't cry, Mama. We're sorry."

We must've said it a hundred times. We must have shed a thousand tears.

At last the crying was over and my mother said she'd be all right and she took the napkin from around James and blew her nose and heaved a sigh and said, "Well, what's done is done." Then she got up and said she was going to fix dinner and for us to stay upstairs and listen to the radio until she called us.

But I went into my room and fell on my bed. I couldn't stop thinking of the look on my father's face. I imagined the conversation he would have with me before he whipped me. Why did you say those words, Amy? Haven't I told you about that word *black*? Didn't you promise not to say it again? And I would look at the floor and cry.

# T W E N T Y - S I X

*All my uncles and cousins were railroad men so they wasn't home all the time. They were hot-tempered, violent men. Once when I was about eight years old I was down in Virginia and I saw my Aunt Jenny beat Grandmom. Grandmom didn't like something Jenny cooked for lunch and threw it on the floor and Jenny beat her with switches from the hedge. Tied her up so she couldn't get away and beat her till she hollered loud enough to wake up the dead. When my uncle came home two days later I got scared when I saw him coming up the steps. Grandmom told him, James, your wife beat me. She couldn't remember names. Your wife beat me. The little boy can tell you the same thing. The wife was in their bedroom getting dressed and he goes in there and says, Jenny, my mother says you beat her, and she says, no, James! Don't you tell me no lie! No, James! I was on the steps and I could see her looking at me. I could see from the way she was looking she was afraid I would tell on her. And then he asked me. Did you see her beat Grandmom? And I knew he would've beat her so I said no, she didn't do it. And when my mother came home she told me it was the best thing I could've done. That James would've killed his wife and buried her right out in the front yard, she said. My uncle James was a nice man, but he had a terrible temper. A terrible temper."*

⚘

LATER THAT NIGHT my father came home drunk. Lord have mercy. Lonnie and James and I were at the kitchen table playing jacks. My mother was humming and cleaning the gas stove. Then my father burst through the door smelling as if he'd drunk up all the whiskey in West-ville. We stopped playing jacks. My mother gave him a look, pressed her lips together and bent over and wrung out her cloth and kept washing the stove. My father stood at the door, wavering. "Time for you all to be in bed, ain't it?"

We left the jacks in the middle of the table and flew up the steps and went around to my room and closed the door. "I hope Mama don't say nothin to him," said Lonnie in a low voice. "Then maybe he won't say nothin to her. Maybe he'll just go to bed." He was quiet a moment. Then he added, "You and your big mouth."

"What do you mean?"

"Aw, shut up, girl. You can't even speak in a low voice."

I lowered my voice. "Why is it my fault? I didn't even want to play that game. You did. You and James. It ain't my fault Daddy came home and caught us."

"Wait—listen." Lonnie touched my arm.

We listened a moment.

"They're down there arguin," said James.

"He better not hit her," said Lonnie. "If he does, when I grow up I'm'a kill him."

I opened the door and stuck my head out. We could hear my mother's voice, high and nervous.

Lonnie pushed past me. "Let's go listen." We went to the steps and sat our way down. The door was closed, but since there was no latch it wouldn't stay completely shut and Lonnie eased it open a bit. He put his eye to the crack and I stooped under his arm and looked.

My mother and father were sitting at the table. His back was toward the door and she was directly across from him. At his left hand was a white mug, one of the mugs that Miss Ruby Davis had given us from the school cafeteria. My mother had one in front of her, too. I supposed they were drinking coffee.

It hurt my heart to look at my mother. Tears were streaming down her face and her mouth was twisted from an effort to stop crying. She kept wiping her face with a balled-up handkerchief but it wasn't helping.

"You always use that word 'black' around them," my father was saying. "You and that sister of yours filling their heads with black, black, black."

My mother's voice quivered. "Ain't nobody fillin their heads—"

"Why do they say it then? Are the words hanging in the air for them to breathe in and breathe out? Where do they get this from, calling their own father black?"

"That's your name, ain't it? Blackjack Beale? That's what your friends call you . . . and this ain't the only place they hear that word. Children in the street all day callin each other black and nigger and everything else they can think of."

"That ain't the same as hearing their mother and that damned sister of yours say it. That's one reason I didn't want to come to live in Hillsboro. That's all that comes out of her mouth. Everybody she knows is either black or yallah. Like being black is somethin dirty or nasty. If you're black, you're no good. If you beat your children, you're mean. And if you're mean, you're black. You're a big black daddy."

"I ain't the one who beats them so bad they can't stand up. They don't play Big Black Mama, or Big Yallah Mama either. If your children mock you it's because they want to, not because they're told to . . . Yes, it's the worst thing in the world to call somebody black, but it ain't nothin wrong with gettin drunk and fallin out on the floor in front of them, is it?"

"Ain't nobody said a word about drunk, but now that you brought it up you know what you can do if you don't like it." My father stood up and slammed his fist on the table so hard that his mug rattled. "You can pack your rags and take your yallah ass right out of here and around to that yallah sister of yours!"

My mother looked at him and said calmly, "I tried that once, remember. But you came after me with a gun . . . in one of your brave drunk moods . . . yes, you brave when you drunk."

My father sat down. "Keep it up, Leatha. Keep it up . . . we won't worry about that, hear. But I'm tellin you now, if I hear 'black' in this house—"

Mama stood up this time and leaned toward him, her voice rising. "Who says 'black' any more than you do? Who? You can call anybody you want a black son of a bitch or a black bastard or a black anything you want, yes, and a yallah one, too, when *you* want to, but it don't mean nothin because *you* said it. But when somebody calls Jack Beale black he wants to beat up everybody in sight because he can't *stand* bein *black*!"

My father half stood and put his fist at her face. I squeezed my eyes shut as tight as I could.

"Leatha, if you keep on filling these kids' heads with nonsense, I'll kill you."

I began to cry softly. "He's gonna hit her, Lonnie. Don't let him hit her." I squeezed his arm.

"What can I do?" he whispered.

"Maybe we can run around and get Aunt Louise."

"Who's goin through there, you?"

"We can go upstairs and jump off the roof on the shed."

Suddenly my father stood up and yelled, "They don't go to see my sister, only yours! Mine's too black for them to visit! The only time they go to my black sister's house is when I make them go!"

Then everything happened so fast I could hardly follow. My mother screamed, "What do I care if my children visit your damned black sister!"

*The words are barely out when my father picks up his mug from the table and throws it at her and it hits her on the side of the head and falls to the floor with a clunk and rolls under the table. My mother grabs the side of her head and slips to the floor, and lies there moaning, and Lonnie and I fall out from behind the door and Lonnie jumps at my father, swinging his fists and screaming, "You killed my mother! You killed my mother!"*

*Lonnie is like a wild animal. My father stands motionless, dumb, his hands hanging at his sides while Lonnie flails at him, beating him with his fists. Lonnie screams at me to run for the police and I leap across the kitchen and then I am outside, and when my feet hit the pebbles on the cold ground I remember my shoes. But it's too late. I run to the alley; then I hear James screaming behind me. "Amy! Don't leave me! Don't leave me!" I stop, grab his hand, and we fly through the pitch-black alley and head for the police station around the corner.*

SOME MEMORIES of things that happen to us when we are young fade and disappear, while others, when we recall them, are like looking back at faded photographs; some memories are fragments of a distant past, and like broken pieces of stained glass, are part of a whole. Some we can dismiss with a rueful smile, some seem to be part of another life, perhaps memories from the life of someone else that were mixed in with ours, like old stories we have heard so often they become part of us.

The memory of that night has never faded for me. I remember it in every detail, and whenever I remember, as I often do, I feel the anger, the sorrow, the rage that I felt that night so long ago. Those feelings have been muted, perhaps, by the passage of time and the knowledge that comes with experience, but they have not been forgotten. No, not forgotten.

"BE GOOD until I . . ." said Mama from the stretcher. She raised her arm and tried to continue, but she was so weak it fell to her side and James began to wail and she tried to sit up and hug him but the police moved to the door with her.

"He'll be all right, Mama," I said, putting my arm around him. And I wasn't crying. I remember that. I wasn't crying.

Lonnie followed them out. He was going around to Union Avenue to tell Aunt Louise what happened. I pulled James over to the stairs and we huddled together there and watched my father who was sitting at the table with his head in his hands. Joe Donovan was standing next to him. He heard James sniffling and turned and asked me to take him up to bed. "Poor little tyke looks worn out."

I nodded and we climbed the steps like an old man and an old woman. James didn't want to go to bed until Lonnie came back, so he rested on the living room sofa and I crept back to the steps and eased down halfway so I could see into the kitchen.

Joe Donovan was talking to my father. "Well, Jack, you know you've done it now."

My father mumbled something that I couldn't understand.

"Listen, Jack, this is no good. I know you got problems. Everybody's got problems. You. Me. God, do I have problems. My problems ain't your problems, but I still got problems. And you can't solve your problems by drinkin like you do. I grew up with you, for God's sake. You're a decent guy. But when you drink you can't control yourself. You just shouldn't drink. I've told you before."

My father twisted his head in his hands. "I know . . . I know."

"Well, that bottle ain't worth spendin your life in jail. You didn't kill anybody tonight, but you could've. And I've seen it happen. A drink too many, an argument, time in jail . . . the answers to your problem aren't in that bottle. Nobody's are."

Then my father began to cry. My father was *crying*.

Joe Donovan laid his hand on his shoulder. "How do you think your kids feel? Beatin on their mother. And she's a good woman, Jack. There ain't many like her, let me tell you."

My father moaned. "I know . . ."

"And if you keep it up, I might be takin that son of yours in for manslaughter . . . You don't know what that boy might do someday. Maybe it would be best if you leave."

"I can't leave my children . . . I can't leave them."

"You have to do somethin, then, Jack. Stop drinkin. And if you can't, then leave. Somethin. They'll only grow to hate you in the end."

Then my father began sobbing. Awful, gut-wrenching sobs, and I began crying too, not understanding how I could feel sorry for him and hate him at the same time. I wiped the tears from my face and neck and leaned forward, straining to hear over his cries.

"Well, you'll have time tonight to think about it. You know you gotta come with me."

To jail, he meant. Up to that cell in the town hall with that little cot and the striped pillow. I eased up the steps and went to my room and lay across my bed and stared into the dark thinking about my mother and father until I wanted to scream and scream and scream.

Sometime during that night I remember Aunt Louise helping me get my clothes off so I could get into the bed and I remember her saying something about me coming around to her house the next day to get some food. I wasn't really awake when all that took place. All that crying had exhausted me.

❦

THE NEXT DAY, Aunt Louise had a lot to say about the fight. I got to her house just before noon and after she got me in the kitchen she gave me a cookie and an apple. "Well," she said, "did you see Jack hit Leatha?"

Now hadn't Lonnie told her everything that happened when he came to get her last night? But I suppose she had to hear it again so when she repeated it she could tell it from all angles like Paramount News: the Eyes and Ears of the World.

I stuffed the cookie in my mouth and nodded.

"Hmph." She went over to the sink and started to wash the two or three dishes on the counter. "What did he hit her for?"

I sighed and said, "Well . . ." I said around the cookie. Suddenly I felt faint. I put my hand up to my mouth and stopped chewing.

Aunt Louise turned. "Well, what? I said what did he hit her for this time?"

My cookie finally went down and I said, "Daddy caught us playin a game about him, and him and Mama started arguin and he got mad because Mama called Aunt Leona black." Then a big lump came up from my chest to my throat and I began blinking rapidly. I knew if I said anything else my voice would shake, so I stuffed another cookie into my mouth.

"Hmph. What else is she." Aunt Louise was now polishing the stove with Bon Ami.

"Mmmmmmmm." The cookie was gooey.

"What kind of game?"

I hesitated. Aunt Louise turned again, so I said, "Big Black Daddy." The goo was sticking to my mouth like a blob of peanut butter.

"Hunh! Big Black Daddy! If you children ain't the—where'd you think up a game like that?"

I opened my mouth to answer, but intead I burst out crying so hard I thought I'd heave up my stomach.

"Lord, child." Aunt Louise came over to me and pushed my head against her stomach and tears were running down into my mouth mixing in with the cookie. It loosened the goo and I swallowed the lump and then I was blubbering and talking and explaining the game and how my father caught us and told my mother that she was teaching us to look down on him. I left out what he said about her.

"Look down on him!" said Aunt Louise, rubbing my back. "It takes more than just gettin babies to be a father. I can't understand how these men go on to plant the seeds and then expect the gardens to grow with no weeds in them. Hmph. Look down on him. And how does he expect you to look up? Gamblin every night, drinkin every weekend. Beatin your mother. Hmph. Big Black Daddy. Wouldn't make no difference if he was blue, green, grizzled or gray. He acts like a big black daddy." She pressed my face closer to her and told me to hush crying, but I told her I couldn't help it.

Finally I did quiet down, and she put a tea kettle on the stove and got a wet paper towel over my eyes. When the kettle whistled she poured us both a cup of tea and sat down across from me. Occasionally I sniffled as I looked at the floor and out the window, at the ceiling, everywhere but at Aunt Louise, who was stirring her tea around and around helping it to cool.

Then, as if all that stirring wound her up, she began to talk. "Black-jack Beale. Marry a yallah woman so he can look good. Take more than that to make that man look good. Nigger acts like a fool, and there ain't nothin worse than a black fool . . . Leatha should've knowed it. She had one for a father. Beatin our mother like a dog when he got in them drunk rages, then sneakin around like a damn black shadow for two or three weeks. And she marries a nigger who could be his twin."

"Like being black is something dirty or nasty." As I listened to Aunt Louise, I remembered the words my father had said the night before. And suddenly I was ashamed and the tears came to my eyes again, and I wanted to run out, but I knew I wasn't going anywhere until I drank that tea, so I took up the cup and drank it straight down and stood up.

"Well, you feel better?" said Aunt Louise.

I nodded.

"After I come from the hospital I'll be around to see if you all are all right." She got up and went to the stove and picked up a long dish covered with wax paper and put it in a bag. "I was going to bring this when I came, but you take it now. I guess Lonnie and James must be hungry. Hold it flat, now."

I walked to the door with my arms in front of me and the dish resting on my arms.

Aunt Louise opened the door. "You all stay home till I get there."

I nodded and went down the steps and headed for home.

# TWENTY-SEVEN

W hen I stepped into the kitchen my heart jumped up. Miss Minnie was standing at the stove, apron tied around her waist, getting ready to make herself some tea. When I saw her I knew everything would be all right and I stood at the door with the dish still in my arms and burst into tears again.

Miss Minnie took the package and told me to sit down. She put two mugs on the table, one for herself, one in front of me. She was going to make me a cup of tea in one of those mugs Daddy had thrown at Mama last night. I didn't think it would be polite if I told her I would throw up if I had to drink tea from that mug and I supposed she would feel very bad about using it, too, so I told her I just had a cup at Aunt Louise's and I sat with her at the table while she drank hers.

"How did you know about Mama?" I asked. She had come so quickly. And I didn't think Aunt Louise had called her. She would've told me. "Oh, child, I didn't know. Lonnie and James told me when I came home."

Home. Oh, that sounded so nice.

"I had packed last night and as soon as I could this morning I got the subway and the trolley and here I came back to this terrible news."

Lonnie and James heard me talking and came galloping down the steps. Lonnie's eyes were swollen and James's eyes were upside down with sorrow.

"My sister's dead and buried," Miss Minnie continued, "And I've rented out her house. And I don't have to go to Philadelphia again. But to come back to this . . . Poor little children."

"It's my fault Mama's in the hospital," whispered Lonnie.

"No, it ain't," I said. "It's mine."

Miss Minnie began unwrapping the dish that Aunt Louise had sent around. "Listen to me, children. Of course, I know you think I'm an old lady and don't know much."

"No, we don't," we whispered.

But first Miss Minnie set the food on the table. Aunt Louise had made a pan of fried chicken. On top of it were two bowls covered with waxed paper: string beans in one and potato salad in the other. Rolls were wrapped up and placed at the side. "Now look at this nice meal Miss Louise made for you all. I'll make some iced tea and we can have a little picnic outside this afternoon."

We said we'd like that, but we sat sadly at the table.

Then Miss Minnie sat down with us and spoke to us in her shaky voice. "You think it's your fault, what happened. Playing that game Lonnie told me about. Well, I am an old lady. And I've seen a lot of things. And I know a lot of things, too. I know things don't always look like they seem. But there are things between your mother and father that don't have a thing to do with your game. I can tell you that the trouble started before that. Way before that. Yes, indeedy."

"But Daddy heard us callin him Big Black Daddy," I said.

"Mr. Jack ain't no angel. He call people black when he wants to." Miss Minnie raised her mug. "Now I told your mother about the mugs, didn't I? So you could say it was my fault. If the mugs weren't here, Mr. Jack couldn't have thrown it, could he."

We shook our heads.

"And if I thought the mugs had anything to do with what happened, well, I guess I wouldn't be drinking out of it now. But I know Mr. Jack threw one of these mugs because it was the first thing he could lay his hands on. He'd probably have thrown a knife if there was one on the table. That's what people do when they get enraged. Foolish things. Then afterwards they're sorry. Always sorry.

"And your game was just a silly game. Everybody plays silly games when they're children. That's how you learn. Now when I was little we didn't play any beating games because my mother and father talked to us. My sister and me were always in trouble. My mother said we were like jumping beans." She laughed, almost a giggle. "But they sat us down and talked to us. 'Why did you do that, Minnie?' That's what they'd say. And then they'd make me see how I was wrong. So we played 'preacher' games. Eula and I took turns preaching."

"Daddy don't ever talk to us like that," said Lonnie. "All he does is tell us what he heard about us or what we better not do."

"Well, that's necessary. That's necessary. I know my mother and father *preached*. Lord! I used to get so tired of them preaching. Talking and preaching. Preaching and talking."

"Daddy does that," said James.

"Well, my father always made me see a point to my actions. A point."

"Sometimes Daddy talks to me like that," I whispered.

"When?" said Lonnie.

"A couple times."

"Probably because you're a girl. He don't talk to me and James like that, does he, James?"

"No." James shook his head.

"Well, sometimes fathers treat their sons different from their daughters," said Miss Minnie. "And that's all right sometimes and wrong sometimes."

"He beats me when he beats them!" I said.

"Well, if you were my children, I know what I'd say. Do you know?"

We shrugged.

"Well, maybe I'd say something about being careful about the words coming out of our mouths. Maybe I'd say something about being careful about what you say and do."

My eyes stung. My father had said that to me. Watch out for that word *black,* Amy. *It'll make some people mad enough to kill.*

Miss Minnie noticed my tears. "Now see that. That's why lots of times parents don't like to talk to their children. They love them and they don't like to see them cry."

Lonnie wiped his eyes. "They beat them and make them cry."

"Yes," said Miss Minnie, "yes they do. Some of them. But at least they know why you're crying. They're hurting you for something you did that they didn't want you to do. Something harmful to yourself or somebody else."

"When they get mad and it ain't your fault they could just talk to you then," whispered Lonnie.

"That's true," said Miss Minnie. "But grown-ups aren't perfect. Only God is perfect. Half the time grown-ups don't look before they leap. They realize that later and then apologize. Sometimes. But sometimes, like yesterday, when words hurt them bad, they stop thinking and go into a rage and just start swinging. Then sometimes words stay inside for a long time and fester."

"What's fester?" said James.

"Well, it's when things don't heal. And when they're inside you they start out like little tumors . . . and then they grow and get bigger and bigger until they bust open."

"Ewww," I said.

"Does it hurt?" said James.

"I guess it does," said Miss Minnie. "But my father told me once that sometimes it takes hurting inside to help you remember things you shouldn't do."

Miss Minnie talked so much that morning she probably surprised herself and had to be more amazed that we sat quietly and listened to her. But we did, the way children give attention to a respected teacher.

Later in the day Miss Minnie went to the hospital and returned with Aunt Louise and they gave us the news about our mother.

Miss Minnie began with a gentle explanation. "Children, your mother's ear was damaged, but she's getting better every hour. She said she'll be home the day after tomorrow and you all be good and she sends you her love."

Aunt Louise took over and gave her unvarnished version of the facts. "That nigger masqueradin as a father like to broke your mother's head open. The doctor said the blood was hemorrhagin like a waterfall but thank God they managed to stop the bleedin and sew up the gash in her head. They had to cut the hair off her head on that side and of course, she'll probably have trouble hearin in that ear the rest of her life."

Then after determining that we were in good hands and that she would be like a second left hand if she stayed, she went home, promising to return when the hospital released my mother.

We couldn't have our mother coming home to an untidy house, Miss Minnie told us, and we went upstairs and began to clean. Lonnie and James went to their room to pick up their things while Miss Minnie started with mine. She was poking under my bed with the broom when she hit the pot I used to bring coffee up to my room. She pulled it out with the broom and held it up. "Child, what is this? This pot smells like coffee. Lord, you're going to have rats and roaches and ants and all kinds of insects up here."

I took a deep breath. "I been dyein my hair with coffee."

"What in the world for?"

"The other kids keep teasin me. Lonnie, too. They always call me red nappy head."

Miss Minnie was flabbergasted. "Well, I do." She shook her head. "Child, you can't pay attention to children who keep teasing you about your hair. Having red hair don't mean it's bad to have red hair. After you went to the hairdresser, didn't you think it looked beautiful?"

"Yes. But it's not always straight."

"Oh, child. Child. The things that bother us when we are children." She got busy sweeping. "Now when I was your age, my mother didn't believe in straightening hair. Hair wasn't meant to be ironed, she used to say. And there weren't any hairdressers as such. If you could get hold of a straightening comb your friends did it. But the children teased me about my hair. And that hurt my feelings. When I grew old enough to make my own decisions, I straightened it a couple of times, but it wouldn't hold a curl and I looked like a wet rat. So I just washed it and made a few twists. And now I just keep it short and wear my hairnet. I had to learn to fix my hair the way it suited me. And knowing what's right for you is a hard lesson to learn."

I listened but I didn't say anything. I could think of nothing to say. I just hung my head. But I thought about what she said and made my decision and later on when I came down to the yard to set the table for our picnic dinner I said, "Miss Minnie, I ain't gonna dye my hair anymore. I don't care if it turns red as fire. And those kids can call me names all they want to."

"Well," said Miss Minnie, "that's a good start."

"But I'm gonna keep straightenin it though. I don't like it when it's nappy. It's too hard to comb."

Miss Minnie laughed so hard. I'd never seen her laugh like that before. "Well, child, that's still a good start." She began serving the plates. "Call your brothers down to dinner."

We had almost finished eating when my father came into the yard. He mumbled a greeting and went straight upstairs. I remember being surprised that he was home so soon. It seemed he should have stayed in jail for at least three days if my mother had to stay in the hospital for three days. We heard rumbling upstairs and I thought he was getting ready to move away or something but after dinner when we went upstairs he was nowhere in sight.

"He must be on the third floor," said Lonnie. "I hope he ain't in my bed."

"Mine either," said James.

We sneaked up to take a look. My father was in neither bed. He had removed the junk from the little room across from the big room and set it in the hall. The door to the room was open and we could see his feet at the bottom of a cot.

We went downstairs and sat on my bed, wondering what was going to happen. "It looks to me like he's gonna sleep up there," I said.

"Maybe he's goin to sleep there because Mama's head is sore," said James.

"Hmph," said Lonnie. "He ain't gonna sleep here long because Mama's gonna put him out. You wait and see."

They left and went to listen to the radio, and I lay across my bed and stared at the ceiling and sighed. Everything was going to be different now. Just when my mother and father seemed to be getting along I had to play Big Black Daddy. Say that word after I promised him not to. I turned on my stomach and seemed to roll onto a lump. Maybe it was a tumor like Miss Minnie said. Maybe it would rot inside of me and swell up and burst. I pulled the pillow over my head and started crying and I held the pillow tightly so no one could hear me. And it seemed as if something rotten was breaking loose, like the seeds in a cantaloupe when you shake it then cut it open and see them caught up in the mush.

Then I stopped crying and sat up and went to the mirror. I looked at the new Amy with the straight plaits. I don't know how long I looked. I don't know what I was thinking, but I went into the bathroom and got the scissors from Miss Minnie's sewing basket and came back to my room and I held up my plaits one by one and cut them off. All three of them.

❧

THE NEXT MORNING I awakened with my eyes so swollen I felt as if I were looking through slits. Then I smelled all those Sunday breakfast smells—frying potatoes and coffee and bacon and for a moment I was confused. It was Monday but it smelled like Sunday. Then I remembered Miss Minnie. I got up and went into the bathroom and splashed cold water on my face. I didn't look in the mirror. Then I went downstairs to face Miss Minnie and my brothers.

"Child!" Aghast, poor Miss Minnie dropped the spatula onto the floor.

"Ooooooh," said James.

Lonnie said nothing. Just shook his head. "Mmph, mmph, mmph."

And nothing else was said and I slid around the table and sat down and ate my breakfast.

When Aunt Louise came by that afternoon and saw my hair she was shocked into silence. Said not a word about it. Just shook her head. "Your mother's comin home tomorrow. I stopped by to see if you all need anything." And she sat down with a whoosh.

"Well, thank God she only cut off her plaits," said Miss Minnie, who had said nothing about my hair until that moment. "I can curl it for her until it grows out when she wants to go someplace special. Otherwise she'll just have to wear short plaits."

Like Luetta.

MY MOTHER came home from the hospital the next day. Aunt Louise and Miss Minnie installed her on the sofa bed in the living room and Lonnie and James and I sat on the floor next to her. Her head was bandaged over the ear; her eye was swollen on that side, too. When she saw my hair she didn't notice I'd cut it at first because Miss Minnie had curled it all over my head in a mass of curls. Mama ran her hand over my head and said they looked pretty. Then when she realized how short it was, she gasped. "Who cut your hair off?" When I told her I did, she said, "Why did you do that, Amy? What got into you?"

"I don't know." My eyes filled up. "I'm sorry."

"The children were all feeling upset, Mrs. Beale," said Miss Minnie. "Feeling like what happened was their fault."

"Lord, Lord, Lord," said Mama. Tears came into her eyes. She laid back against the arm of the sofa. There was a short silence.

Then Lonnie tried to inject some humor into the atmosphere. "She wanted to look like Luetta."

Nobody laughed. Again, sniffling, I said I was sorry.

"No need to cry over spilled milk," said Aunt Louise. "You need to walk around looking like a pickaninny for a while. Then you won't be so quick to take the scissors to them naps."

"The child has fast-growing hair," said Miss Minnie. "By next year it'll be almost as long as it was before she cut it."

Mama sighed and hugged me. Aunt Louise let us all talk to her for about ten minutes then made us leave so we wouldn't tire her out.

LONNIE AND I wondered what was going to happen about Daddy. He was like a shadow around the house. We knew he was there because we heard him get up in the morning and go out to work. And we saw him come in at night and go upstairs to the little room. If we saw him, we spoke. We didn't hear any conversation between him and Mama.

"Do you think Daddy's goin to live here again?" I said.

"Hmph," said Lonnie. "I don't care where he lives. He oughta be gone by now. But if he stays with us, I know he just better not hit my mother anymore, that's all."

I found out the answer to my question a few days later in my usual way. Miss Minnie had been sitting with Mama, but she had taken a break and gone to visit Miss Ruby Davis. I was sitting with Mama instead. Then Aunt Louise came and sent me from the room. So I couldn't hear their conversation, I knew. But I went into the bathroom and lay on Miss Minnie's cot and heard every word they said.

"Well," said Aunt Louise, "you made up your mind about Jack?" Mama didn't answer, then Aunt Louise again. "Well, that judge oughta be shot. Keepin him overnight and lettin him go because he's the breadwinner. I guess he never heard of female breadwinners."

"That ain't exactly what the judge said," said Mama. "He told him that since I pressed charges against him he could go to jail for a few months or go to the army and make out his insurance and a allotment to me."

"And when's he goin to the army?"

"I haven't asked him."

"Suppose he ask to come back? His type always do, you know."

"He asked me the other day to come back. I may be a fool, but I ain't crazy. When I pressed those charges he knew he wasn't stayin here anymore. And if he don't leave, I'm gonna take him back to the court."

"I guess that mug knocked some sense into your head."

Mama didn't seem to like that too well. There was a long silence. Since the conversation seemed to be over, I went back into the living room. Aunt Louise had gone. Mama was reading a magazine. Her water pitcher was empty so I took it and went down to the shed to chip some ice and fill it again. While I was there I heard someone go into the kitchen and upstairs. Miss Minnie or one of my brothers, I thought. I went back into the kitchen and stopped to get the water, then I heard my father's voice.

I tipped up the steps far enough to see over the landing and peer across the room to the couch where Mama was sitting. Daddy was sitting in an armchair he had pulled up to the sofa. I could see her face, but not his.

"I told you the other day, Jack. No."

"Arleatha, please . . ."

"Louise was just here and I got mad when she told me that mug must've knocked some sense into me. But it wasn't the mug. It was those three days in the hospital. I don't know the last time when I've had three whole days to myself to think. And you know what I thought about? All them promises you been makin. The promise you made before we left Westville . . . how you was gonna stop drinkin . . . how you was gonna come home at nights . . . but I swear . . . it seems when we got down here, you got worse . . . not better."

"I know . . . I know . . ." Daddy put his hand out to touch Mama's arm, but she pulled it away.

"When I was a little girl my mama told me every week that I was hardheaded . . ." Her voice was starting to quiver. "I guess she was right. Sure wasn't nobody could get it into my head that I shouldn't marry a man who had a drinkin habit. Oh, they tried . . . they tried. You know that old sayin about love bein blind? Well, it took a lot of slappin and cheatin for me to see . . . That old song 'Amazing Grace' was written for me . . . me . . . I was 'lost and now I'm found, was blind and now I see.' " She was crying now.

My father was crying, too. "I'm sorry, Leatha. I'm sorry."

"I believe you're sorry. I believe it. You're sorry today. Then you'll take a drink tomorrow and forget all about today. I know. I know. I've had fourteen years. But it wasn't just the mug, Jack. I want you to know that. If there wasn't any children, I'd probably be a fool again and take another chance. But you are drivin your children crazy. Got poor little James wonderin what it is to be a man."

"James?" Daddy was bewildered. "What about James?"

"Tellin him men don't knit. And him askin us if it was all right to have a toy bunny rabbit at Easter. 'Will Daddy be mad if I have it?' That's what he said. 'Will Daddy be mad?'"

Daddy lowered his head to his hands. "Oh, God . . ."

"That's what I said. Oh, God. And what kind of man is his daddy with the example he sets for him? Drinkin and comin in drunk. Beatin his mother . . . What kind of man is that? And Amy, she cuttin off her hair because she think that's what made you and me argue all the time. Oh, she didn't say so, she probably don't even realize it herself. But why else would she do it? Leona round there on Union Avenue tellin you every time the child passes by her house with a loose plait. And if you stayed you wouldn't stop drinkin and if you drink you're gonna go back to your old habit of slappin me when you get mad at the world, and Lonnie would have to kill you some day. He has a temper just like yours. And that's just what would happen. Or you'd end up killin him." She paused for a moment, then added "No, I don't need you or any man so much that I'm willin to put up with *anything*. Even a dog leads a better life than the one I have with you. You need to start prayin for some help, Jack."

She stopped. After a moment Daddy got up and went upstairs.

My father stayed with us another week, then went into the army. I saw him about a year later. I was on my knees in the kitchen scrubbing the floor. Miss Minnie and Mama had gone to the store for groceries and James had gone with them to pull them home in his wagon. Lonnie was out somewhere cutting grass so he could make some money of his own.

I had the table pushed back and I came to the part of the floor that had the hole worn in it. That hole I had kept my eye fixed on when Daddy told me not to ever call anyone black. The spot had worn through to the floor and Mama had tacked another piece of linoleum over it. I was scrubbing it, thinking of that time, when I realized that someone was in the room with me. I turned on my knees and saw a pair of black shoes in front of me. I looked up. A chill ran through me. My father was standing there, as if my very thoughts had materialized.

He was in his uniform, lean, dark, and handsome. I felt the blood come up to my face. I wanted to jump up, run to him, like children do after a long absence of a father, but I was too embarrassed. Holding the scrub brush, I sat back on my heels.

"Hello, Amy," he said.

"Hi, Daddy."

We didn't say anything else, just looked at each other, then away. Finally I stood up and brushed off my knees.

"You should put a pad under your knees."

"I know."

"Where's everybody at?"

"Lonnie is out cuttin grass. Mama and Miss Minnie went to the American Store and James went with them to bring the food home." I put the brush in the bucket. "Want me to go see if I can find them?"

"No. No." He turned to the door. "I'll go." As he went out he said, "Don't forget about those knees."

I nodded. I stood for a moment, then took some newspaper and folded it and kneeled down and began scrubbing again.

When Mama got home she was surprised that Daddy had stopped by. She'd heard he was around at Leona's, but no, she hadn't run into him today. Miss Minnie was sorry she hadn't seen him in his uniform, and James asked Mama if he could run around to Aunt Leona's to see if he could find him. She said yes; James came back later, looking sad. Aunt Leona said he'd gone back to camp. So I was the only one who'd seen him that day, and his last words to me were about getting my knees dirty.

WHEN THE WAR began some changes went on at our house besides that of having to use ration books. The first thing was that Mama got a new job. Lonnie and I helped her get it. One day we were at the kitchen table doing our homework when she came home and asked us to help her with arithmetic. How could she not know how to do arithmetic? She always helped us with ours when we were little.

"If I can learn to do fractions and dividing decimals, I can pass a test to get a job in a war plant. Then I can make a lot more money than I do now. I used to know how to do them, but I forgot."

I was still weak at dividing with decimals. Lonnie helped her to do that. I helped her with fractions. Every night we'd sit around the table and she'd pick out what she wanted to learn from our arithmetic books. She learned very quickly and within a month after we started she came home and told us she had the job making at least fifty dollars a week. Fifty whole dollars! As much as she earned in a month! And more if she worked overtime.

So every morning at three A.M. she got up and turned on the radio and I'd lie in the bed and listen to Jan Peerce sing "The Bluebird of Happiness" and Eddy Arnold sing "Cattle Call" as Mama cooked her breakfast and packed her lunch. At first I'd get up and watch her and we'd talk a little about nothing—maybe about a dream and a number, or how I was doing in school. She wore overalls then, a bandanna around her head, and carried a large lunch pail with a rounded top for her thermos bottle. She caught the bus at four o'clock every morning (they were running all night then because of the war) to a canning factory that had been converted to a war factory. After a while I wouldn't get up because I'd get lonely after she left, so I'd stay in the bed and listen to the music from my room.

Since food was rationed and farmers provided crops for the troops, citizens were encouraged to grow victory gardens, and Mama delved in with gusto. She and Aunt Louise and Uncle Lee dug up that old yard and we all went out into the country and got bags of horse and cow manure to enrich the ground, and they planted all kinds of vegetables: tomatoes and lettuce and carrots and potatoes and more. And Aunt Louise planted marigolds among the vegetables to keep out the pests and hollyhocks against the rickety fence to give the garden a beautiful background. Around the borders she planted sweet alyssum, which gave off a wonderful odor at night when we sat talking softly in the yard.

Calm and peaceful were those days after my father left. The clouds had passed over the sun and the days were bright again. It was as if the dream I'd had of being in a dark room had to do with Mama, too. We had both been in the darkness and I had fallen through a hole, but she had reached the bottom and had no way to go but up. She had made it to that distant light and gathered her children around her to keep us together on her own. She was the bond that kept our family together, just as Reverend Mickens had deftly pointed out in his sermon, "Mother is the glue."

MY FATHER was in the army for three more years. And when he got out he came back to Hillsboro and lived with Aunt Leona for a while. Then he disappeared into Philadelphia. He never came home again, but he did return to Hillsboro again to live with Aunt Leona after he retired.

※

ON MY PORCH that day enough years had passed for me to ask him about his version of what had happened when he was with my mother. But he'd never talk about what happened during his marriage. Only up until the time he met her. At the time we talked I thought I was old enough then to ask him a question that had always bothered me. "Daddy, did you love Mama?" I said.

He looked away for a while; then he said, "Yes, I loved your mother, Amy, but sometimes, love isn't enough."

I wanted to tell him that love is enough, that married love requires sacrifice, that he was incapable of the selflessness that is necessary to sustain a marriage. But he was an old man. I would have hurt his feelings, and it wouldn't have set anything right. "Jack Beale loves himself, do you hear me? His *self*." My mother spoke the truth all those years ago. I'm convinced that he did not know how to do otherwise.

※

A FEW WEEKS AGO I started to read again the story I'd written down when he told me about his early life, and as I read, tears came to my eyes for the kind of man that little boy was to become, and I wondered what he'd have been like if his father had lived.

He missed having a father. He never told me that, but I surmised it from a song he used to sing when I was a child, a plaintive little song he sang every Christmas. He'd be a little high and his eyes would grow watery. The song was about a child who was asking Santa Claus for a present:

> Don't want no toys, like other girls and boys.
> Please, Santa, bring back my daddy to me.

Often I've thought of the years I had with my father, and I always try to end my thoughts with a happy memory. And one memory always returns as clear as a Technicolor dream. I see a green and yellow world, sunny and bright. I see Mama holding James in her arms. She's smiling at Daddy and Lonnie and me. We're standing by some hedges, so tall they look like green trees. And I'm holding my arms out to Daddy, who has a white rabbit in his arms. He's showing it to Lonnie and me and now he's kneeling and holding it out so we can pet it. And he's smiling and he's telling us we can pet it but we can't pet it too hard, it's so little and we might hurt it, and the little rabbit's nose is so pink and he's trembling in Daddy's arms.

I was three years old then, and to me he was God.